Steve is 30 and lives in Leeds. He is the author of one previous novel, *The Third Person*, which is also available in Orion paperback. Visit his website at www.theleftroom.co.uk.

THE CUTTING CREW

STEVE MOSBY

An Orion paperback

First published in Great Britain in 2005
by Orion
This paperback edition published in 2006
by Orion Books Ltd,
Orion House, 5 Upper St Martin's Lane,
London WC2H 9EA

A CIP catalogue record for this book is available
from the British Library.

Typeset by Deltatype Limited, Birkenhead, Merseyside
Printed and bound in Great Britain by
Clays Ltd, St Ives plc

The Orion Publishing Group's policy is to use papers that
are natural, renewable and recyclable products and
made from wood grown in sustainable forests. The logging
and manufacturing processes are expected to conform to
the environmental regulations of the country of origin.

www.orionbooks.co.uk

For Angela Mark

Thanks, in no particular order, are due to: Jon Wood, Genevieve Pegg, Gaby Young, Nicola Jeanes, and everyone else at Orion who helped with this book and the first; my agent, Carolyn Whitaker; an anonymous graffiti artist whose work in Leeds helped to inspire a part of what follows; the writers John Connor and Simon Logan; Marie, Debbie, Carolyn, Nicola, Sarah, Emma, Jodie, Nic and everyone here in Sociology; Keleigh, Rich, Neil, Helen, Jonny, Cassie, Yoav and Ben; Becki and Rainy; Katrina; Emma Lindley; and Lynn, for putting up with me in the torturous final stages and being wonderful. As always, thanks to Mum, Dad, John and Roy.

Most of all, thanks to Angela, without whom I couldn't have done any of it. And so this book is dedicated to you, with gratitude and love.

PROLOGUE

I undid the clasps on the box – one click, two – and flipped open the lid. Then, I sat back on my haunches, rubbing the skin around my mouth and inspecting the contents. The rifle was in three pieces. It looked like a musical instrument that somebody had really loved: as expensive and well-kept as a flute.

Beautiful too, in its own way. It had been oiled recently, and I was willing to bet it was calibrated and fine. As accurate as when Sean and I had last gone shooting together, which meant he'd taken care of it and probably intended to use it. It was only right in an odd way, because a gun as well-designed as this probably deserved to be fired.

If you were going to be killed by something – if you absolutely had no choice – then you might as well be killed by a weapon like this.

I took the barrel out of the velvet case – and then turned suddenly, distracted by a cheer from the crowd outside.

There was an arched window at the far end of the room. Outside, the sky was so bright that the edges of the windowframe seemed to be dissolving into the light. The sun was visible in wedges, illuminating motes of dust hanging in the air. They were undisturbed for the moment but – a full storey above amongst the open beams – there were birds nesting, and every so often one would flutter down and out, and it would set this still world in motion.

Another huge cheer – a rumbling, contagious thing boiling steadily up from far below. I checked my watch and figured that the first of the boxers must have been coming out. It was about the right time, which meant it was time for me to start doing what I did best. Although given what I generally fucked up, that wasn't saying much.

I put the gun together methodically and carefully, but it didn't take long – one piece slotted naturally and inevitably into the next. There was no mystery or difficulty to it. Sean had kept bullets in the case. I loaded it without thinking too much about what I was going to do – with premeditated murder, I've found that you need to think very clearly about nothing at all. When you're killing bad men, there's always emotion that will carry you through if you let it. But if you think too much then your reason gets hold of that emotion and keeps your hand in check. So you learn not to think. You let the anger fill you up, and then it's done before you know it: an immense act that's actually surprisingly ordinary.

Most of the time anyway.

I headed over to the window. The spread of the city appeared, stretching away into the distance. It was a sandy, fractured tapestry of jagged roofs. As I walked closer, the buildings opposite came into view, and, as I stopped, the main square itself, eight storeys below. Not so much a square as an octagon, really. It was about five hundred metres across, bordered on all sides by three- and four-storey buildings that gave it a sense of dusty enclosure. I peered down carefully.

There were thousands of people here. They were crammed onto the balconies, waving scarves and flags and arms. Hanging out of the windows. All of the buildings looked papered with them. The main square was tight with thousands more: packed all the way from the streets that led off into the city's districts to the very centre of the square, with people crowding as close to the boxing ring as the barriers and stewards would let them. There were occasional breaks in the crowd for official tents and food vans, steam spiralling up from them, but other than that the square was simply full of people. Some had even climbed up the streetlights and were now balancing precariously down their length. A patchwork of men and women. It was only really possible to separate them into individuals when they moved, but, even then, so many of them moved at once that it was pointless trying.

And here I was: far above it all. This clocktower was visible from the furthest districts of the city, sticking up on the edge of the square. Not so much like a needle as a stack of odd, dirty blocks piled roughly in line. The top held a bell tower, but that hadn't worked for longer than I'd been alive. The enormous iron bells above me appeared to be rusted in place by damp and cobwebs, and on the outside, the white, circular clockface was stuck at a perpetual three-thirty.

Nobody came here – certainly not this high up – but there were ways in. Admittedly, you had to trust your luck a bit in climbing the maze of broken staircases to reach the top, but I'd stopped feeling as though luck had any part to play in what had been happening to me, and so I'd been quietly confident on my way up here. Now, here I was, with a clear view of the city's annual inter-district spectacle. The best seat in the house.

If you were going to shoot someone, you might as well choose a vantage point like this.

3

Historically, our city is divided into sixteen different districts, all of them named after animals. Every year in late Spring, we hold a competition. Eight districts compete one year, with the remaining eight competing the next. It involves weeks of build-up, training and publicity. Fighters are chosen via a series of internal bouts, amidst a great deal of fervour and marching and shit-talking, and then the final eight boxers come together for an overall tournament. Hundreds of thousands of people from across the city cram themselves into the main square, or as close as they can get, to watch and cheer; and more people travel from all corners of the country. We're a tourist attraction. For this single day each year, if you want a hotel anywhere in the city you'd better book early.

I checked out the ring. There were three fighters around the edge already. I stepped back from the window and, keeping both eyes open, took aim through the scope. As I centred on the topless, blocky men at the weigh-in, my vision doubled; I closed my left eye and one of the fighters came into focus. Whirls of hair on his chest, all the way down to the red and blue sash of Snail tied around his thick waist. Solid and old. He looked confident but more than a little stupid, and I didn't think he was going to win much here today beyond a trip to St Harven's.

Another rumbling cheer. I swung the aim of the rifle around across the craning necks and arms of the crowd and caught sight of the fourth fighter making his way along a path that had been cleared by the stewards. People from his district – he was wearing the purple and white sash of Horse – were slapping hands with him as he went. Through the rifle scope, I could see them shouting advice and encouragement, but the man

4

was ignoring them and looked full of concentration. I'd have bet more money on him than the Snail fighter. He looked like a man who had something difficult to do, and I felt a certain kinship with him on that one. Plus, although I was brought up in Turtle, I lived in Horse now, so there was that allegiance to think about too.

I put the rifle down and moved away from the window.

Nearly time.

Nothing as complicated and intricate as our city ever comes about by chance, but there are lots of different stories and histories about the how and the why of it.

In many ways, it's just like a person. People you meet have their reasons for being the way they are: the down and dirty reasons they won't acknowledge even to themselves; the boring 'this happened' stuff that everybody already knows; and the legends – the stories, half-truths and wish-fulfilments in their heads about triumphs and failures, loves and fears. Generally, most of the real stuff falls into the middle category, but people can be difficult to disentangle and the truth is sometimes a complicated amalgam of all three. Our city is no different. Here is one story of how we got where we are.

A long time ago, there were eight brothers who owned all of this. Back then, it was just farmland and woods, but the brothers lived here with their servants and they cultivated the ground and made a living for themselves. There was a stream where they could get water, and there were animals to hunt or farm; there were plentiful natural resources – although that didn't mean much to the brothers as they had no real contact with the outside world.

Everything was fine for a while, but one year all

eight of them left the estate and travelled in different directions to seek out a wife. Two years later, they all returned and brought their new families with them, and a small community began to take shape. But as well as coming back with wives and children, each brother returned with skills and experience from the different areas they'd visited. One came back and took over the estate's finances, for example; another returned with knowledge of science and power. A third brought back music and literature, while a fourth had received medical training and could tend to everybody's health. One had become a teacher; another took responsibility for law and order. And so on. Each brother represented a specific element of society, and together they complemented each other and thrived. Often in opposition but, deep down, working as a team.

When our teacher had told us this story, she'd told us to picture all eight brothers in a circle, holding hands and leaning as far backwards as they could. They were all pulling in their own directions: all straining against one another. And, bizarrely, that was what kept each of them from falling over.

But the thing was, legend had it that one of the brothers had visited darker areas while he'd been away, and he'd returned to the estate representing crime. What happened was, he ended up pulling too hard – or too cleverly. He betrayed them all. His hands slipped and the circle collapsed and fell. The estate was over-run by his associates and burned to the ground; all eight brothers and their families were killed (Ms Roberts had embellished this part with a few gory details to keep us hooked); and our fair city grew up and out of the ashes.

It's not a bad story. I remember hearing it as a child and being captivated for about a day. It was the idea

6

that everything was working and fine: not perfect, but as good as it was going to get. Then one of the brothers had to try to make it that little bit better for himself, and in the process he ruined it for everyone. How fucked up is that? Although obviously my child's mind didn't frame it in quite those words.

But you grow older and you forget. It's just a story after all – a fable intended to illustrate a point. It falls into the third category I mentioned, when everyone knows that the real, grown-up history of the city can be found in the second one: the dull tale of bricks and dust and sweat that occupies the history books. But I believe now that the legend really is the city's idea of where it came from: something it has repeated in its sleep, until the idea of it has become written into the stones and the glass and the streetlights. And, just like a person, I believe our city is difficult to disentangle. The truth – if there is such a thing – can be found in those hard facts accepted by historians, but it's also present in dreams that are so dark and old and inescapable that they make the buildings shudder each night to bear them.

Another roar from the crowd as the next fighter arrived. I snapped my eyes open, not realising where I was for a moment. Then, I remembered: sitting on my heels with my back against the dusty wall, waiting. When the first bout started – that was when I would do it. In the meantime, I thought about all of the reasons why this man deserved what was coming to him. He'd been responsible for murder and rape and torture, and he would be again. They were the usual reasons to take justice into your own hands, but on this occasion things were different. This time, the people who'd been hurt included people I cared very deeply about. They had included me.

If you were going to kill someone, and you were me, then it would very definitely be this man.

This time, the anger was easy to find. I felt it churning inside me: an intense hatred for him and what he'd done. I didn't need to think about pictures or witness statements. I just concentrated on thinking of nothing, allowing the rage to seep in and fill my head. Over the noise of the crowd, I could hear that ringing in the air – the ominous sound of loneliness and space that I now knew was also something else. It was the sensation of my heartbeat coming into time with the city's own. I just sat there, watching the opposite wall, with my vision slowly starring over. When all the fighters had arrived the first match would begin, and then I could let this feeling out of me. For now, it was folding back on itself, growing larger and larger.

Another roar. I didn't even blink.

CHAPTER ONE

Let's start with my flat.

The rent cost me a little under half my monthly payslip, which would certainly have been too much for me to afford if I hadn't had alternative sources of funding. By the time that Sean got in touch with me, the police had stopped paying me anyway – but the money for the flat had always come out of my savings. It was four months after I left Rachel and moved in that I finally heard from Sean, and I hadn't been to work for at least three of those. Everything seemed to go downhill when I moved here. But we'll get to that.

The flat itself was small, but not as bad as I'd expected. I'd looked around three different places – all of them pokey little holes where you needed to turn sideways just to get from one end to the other. I was beginning to despair, and then I found this. It had three rooms – a living area with a double bed, a kitchen, a bathroom – all connected by a single corridor. Space-wise, you could swing a dead cat if you aimed right, but you didn't feel as though the previous tenant might have left one somewhere so you could try. On the downside, the ceiling was riddled with damp, there was no shower and I would discover that the boiler didn't work. But I could live with these things.

'Recently painted,' the estate agent pointed out, ignoring the deformities in the brickwork as he tapped the wall with his pen. 'Nice and clean. Close to all the local amenities and handy for the centre. All in all, it's a good property.'

All in all, it was a shit property and we both knew it, but the rent was fair and I was desperate. The day before, Rachel had said that she wanted me out. In truth, I'd probably been waiting for her to say it to save me the extra guilt of leaving of my own accord, but it meant that I needed somewhere to go and that I didn't have the luxury to pick and choose. This place, I decided, would do.

'I'll take it,' I said.

The contract would be six months to begin with, and then a month at a time, depending on how much the estate agent and I pissed each other off. I signed for it, and then went home and told Rachel that night. She just nodded. We'd agreed that our separation was temporary, but the decision to separate in the first place had been mine, and it had whacked a lot out of her. For me, it was over between us, but it had felt okay to soften the blow a little by agreeing to that word: *temporary*. A six-month contract was a big thing, but you could pretend that it wasn't permanent if you squinted at it and looked away quickly.

Anyway, there wasn't much to say after that. She nodded, looking pale and hollow, as though I'd killed her. When I began packing some basic stuff, I think she started crying and went out. I don't know where she went.

I didn't take much, due to the lack of space – just my favourite books, some music, most of my clothes. I took my laptop, knowing that I'd need the internet to maintain some perfunctory contact with the outside world. My guitar was broken, so I figured I'd just buy a new one. I used a wedge of the money I'd stored away to kit the flat out a little better: new covers and cloths, plates and cups and cutlery. If I was going to be living there, then I needed it to feel like some kind of home. Of course, it wasn't really living as such; it was more like existing, hand to mouth. In my head, searching for some way to occupy myself from hour to hour was like leaping between stepping stones, and I would find myself hoping that the far bank came into view before those stones ran out.

'Any problems, just give us a ring,' the estate agent said. He had a false smile, and his tone of voice suggested that he didn't expect to hear from me.

'I'm sure I'll be very happy here,' I said.

But I wouldn't and I knew it. At that point, it was like one of my engines had been shot out and I was spiralling down to earth. The flat was just more of the same. Full of my things, it still seemed empty; when I put music on, it still felt quiet. Perhaps it was just me.

Four months later, Sean got in touch. That night, I'd been out.

Most of the time in the flat I just spent watching television, reading, surfing the internet: just generally passing the time. But after a while – like anyone – I'd get bored and lonely, and so sometimes I'd go out on an evening and get drunk in company that, if not exactly better than my own, was at least plural and so better in theory.

The estate agent had told me that the flat was convenient for the centre, but what he'd meant was that I was close to the western wing of Wasp. I lived on the edge of Horse, which houses the city's university and much of its student population. On the eastern side of Horse, you have Wasp, which is where most of the city's red-light activities took place. Five minutes and I'm there.

That night, I started in Whitelocks, which is about as close to Wasp as you could get while still keeping in Horse.

Whitelocks is the oldest pub in the city. You walk in and straight away you can imagine it years back – full of navvies and engineers, all sooty and smelling of earth and smoke and steam. Most of the fittings haven't changed in the meantime. The windows are stained-glass, ancient and misty, and the building itself is painted black to about chest-height, and then white from there on up. There are benches outside, and brass rails running along the walls. Inside, more brass separates you from a raised bar, and everything else is divided into dark alcoves and occasional mirrors.

I was planning to go to a club afterwards and, since I was on my own, I wanted to be reasonably drunk when I arrived. I bought two pints of strong beer, downed one at the bar and then went and sat outside on a bench to drink the other.

It was nice – a cool night, but pleasant and fresh. The sky was clear; the stars, bright and defined. On the bench next to me, an older woman was sitting drinking wine. She was dressed in a blue suit and was smoking a cigarette – although it seemed more like the cigarette was smoking her: wrinkling up her skin; sucking something out of her and turning it into greasy air. She was staring straight in front, almost motionless, except that her hands had a bar-fly shudder. A swift sex change, I thought, and here was my future.

I checked my mobile. No messages.

I finished the beer and headed out, but stopped at the bottom of the red-brick alleyway that led on to the main street, where someone had taped an A4 sheet of paper to the wall. There was a photograph of an eye in the centre of it, and it had obviously been digitally altered because the retina was violet. It seemed to watch me as I moved past, and I wondered why it was there. Local bands often put up flyers, but it seemed too unusual for that. There was no writing on it for one thing.

I forgot it quickly.

The club I was going to was called Spooks, but I hit three other bars on the way there. By the time I walked into the club, a good kilometre into Wasp, I was light on my feet and feeling relaxed and natural.

Let me tell you about Spooks. Every city has one: clubs that aren't exactly rough so much as cheap and nasty. They have a reputation for being full of older, slightly desperate women: housewives out for a fling; hard divorcees that have been aerobicised and tanned until they resemble fruit. The men all sport barrel chests that have spilled out at the bottom, and shirts a decade too young for them. Basically, it's a meat market – except that everything is offal. You would very possibly kill a minor relative before admitting to going there.

Why was I here? Like I said, I spent a lot of the time in the flat feeling lonely, and sometimes I just wanted some company. Not necessarily anything serious, but if that happened then I could live with it. And it did happen every now and then. I was younger than most of the men in here by quite some distance, and although I wasn't particularly good-looking I didn't break the mirrors either. But it didn't happen often: I never actually made a move on anyone, because sly lounge lizard wasn't really my style, and so I tended to just stand there, watching the dancefloor, drinking beer after beer and killing time.

Once I'd relaxed about it, there was something quite therapeutic about pretending to be above it all. I'd always been a people-watcher for one thing. Even though at some vague point in the last four months I'd stopped being a cop, it was partly a leftover from that, and partly just the way I was. And in Spooks you had people in all their dull glory to watch to your heart's content.

That was what I was doing, perfectly happily, until about half-eleven when the trouble flared up.

There were some guys over on the far side of the dancefloor that were a hell of a lot younger even than me, and probably too young to be in here. Some part of me – and this *was* mostly cop leftovers – had clocked them the first time I saw them, and I'd subconsciously kept tabs on them ever since. There were five of them – three skinny guys, one wiry athlete and a chunky amateur weight-trainer – but basic shape aside, they all looked the same: neat shirts and smart-casual trousers, short hair, sweaty faces. Each was holding a bottle of designer lager against his solar-plexus.

I knew their sort, and it was trouble. It wasn't because they were evil or anything; they were just too young to have figured out the way to behave. If you caught my eye by accident, for example, I might smile at you; if you caught theirs, there might be a fight. You just needed to avoid them until they grew up enough to be at ease with themselves. At that age, it's all image. Too many films; too many magazines. Being anywhere near them was like being in a Mexican stand-off where nerves might cause someone to open fire at any moment.

They were standing in a rough circle. Occasionally one of them would turn to look at somebody – checking out a girl – head twisting around. Nodding and laughing.

I saw the poor guy bump into them before he got anywhere near; it was a *Titanic*-iceberg situation. I tracked him across the floor as he headed back from the toilets towards the bar: early thirties, neat haircut, glasses. He was wearing a jumper and smart trousers. One look and you knew that there was nothing physical about him: you could beat three of him up on half a cup of coffee. In a place like this, he might as well have had 'victim' tattooed on his forehead.

One of the skinny kids laughed at something and stepped back, but the neat guy was heading to the bar and wasn't watching; two seconds later, he smacked into the kid. Just a slight jostle; nothing much. But beer slopped out of the kid's bottle, and immediately all of them turned. Faces hard as stone. They knew how they had to act.

I moved a little closer, leaning against a pillar.

The neat guy held his hands up to say sorry, and paused there, looking at them and waiting for his apology to be accepted. But the skinny kid was pissed off; he shook his head and gestured at his shirt, which seemed to have caught some of his beer.

I couldn't hear what he was saying, and I didn't need to. *My shirt's ruined; look what you've fucking done.*

The neat guy just seemed helpless and unsure. It was there on his face: what was he going to do – reverse the flow of time? As nervous as he was, he certainly wasn't going to buy the kid another beer to replace the mouthful he'd just lost. So there was an awkward couple of seconds, and then the guy said sorry again and walked away.

The kids conferred amongst themselves. Their heads kept craning just like before – except that now they were all hunting out this disrespectful bastard. Where had he gone? Who was he with? How many of them were there?

I saw what they did: the guy arrived at the bar and met who I imagined must be his girlfriend. She looked a little alarmed as he leaned in and spoke to her; and then she glanced up, saw the boys watching and looked away quickly. She said something to the guy and he nodded, and instead of buying a drink they headed off around the other side of the club. The exit was round that way.

I checked my mobile.

Still no messages.

When I looked back up, the boys had started moving: swigging their beers back and walking in the same direction as the couple. Three of them were just following – ambling along – but the two in front were actively stalking, watching the undergrowth for signs of attack as they went. I noted those two for future reference. The three behind were buoyed by them: consequently, they would be deflated along with them.

I let them get past me, downed the last of my beer and headed off. I was pretty drunk at that point and didn't know what exactly I was going to do. A small, sober part of me was telling me to leave it alone and not bother. After all, my brain knew full well that I invariably let myself down in any situation that demanded heroism, moral gravity or much in the way of considered, rational thought. This, it told me now, would turn out badly.

You're not a cop anymore, it said. And that was true, but I kept walking anyway.

The crowds were sparse near the double doors at the exit. The bouncers there were bulked up in long, punch-proof black coats, watching what was unfolding outside with professional interest, the way a security expert might examine a lock-pick he'd found on the street. It was obvious, even before I walked out into the sharp night air, that they were going to do precisely fuck all about what was happening. Why would they? Outside is outside. There were a fair few other people, as well – couples and groups – all standing and watching. I saw a girl wince, just as I started to hear the sounds of the fight: grunts and blows, and someone calling for help, sounding frightened and angry and upset. Other people were walking past, looking back, pausing to see. Some of the guys were smiling. Others looked nervous, disgusted. A whole range of human response, but no real action.

I got out, turned right and there it was.

The man was on the floor, rolling, trying to cover his head but not really succeeding. The last thirty seconds had taken any fight out of him. The skinny guy with the ruined shirt was viciously kicking out and stamping at him, catching him wherever he could, while the wiry kid was leaning down, hooking punches in at his face. The other three were just watching. Two were forming a barrier to keep the girlfriend back. The third – the weight-trainer – was holding his drink and watching the beating carefully, as though he might step in if he found it lacking.

The skinny kid kicked the man in the head and he went limp. Perhaps they didn't realise, or maybe they did, but whatever – the pair of them got him onto his back and the wiry kid held his hair and started punching him in the face. The other boy was putting his foot into the guy's ribs, over and over.

'Stop it,' I said loudly.

Amazingly, they did. I walked over, staggering slightly, unsteady on my feet. I hadn't realised how drunk I was, but it wasn't going to be a problem. In fact, it would probably make everything a whole lot easier.

I said, 'You're going to kill him.'

They were, as well. People watch too many movies, and too many movies have no real conception of the effects of proper violence. In a film, someone'll get punched and just look pissed off; you punch people like you're saying hello. In real life, the guy on the pavement was already in hospital for a long time. You don't get kicked in the head and then go get a burger. We're all pretty flimsy. It can take a lot to beat someone to death, or it can take a little. You just never know.

The weight-trainer gestured with his bottle and said, 'What the fuck is it to you?'

He probably thought he was quite tough. Certainly, he didn't look unduly bothered by the idea of fighting me. He was probably more concerned with the fact that I was spoiling their evening.

'You've done enough to him,' I said.

The wiry kid stood up.

'Mind your own fucking business.'

He had blood on his knuckles. I remember that. And the skinny kid, glaring at me, had blood all over his shirt.

I looked around. Nobody was going to back me up at all. A few people even looked pissed with me for stopping the show. I looked back at the guy, who was bleeding on the tarmac and something clicked inside me. Some stupid kids were going to kill a guy because of a slop of spilled beer, and nobody here actually gave a shit. Crowds of people standing around thinking: *he's going to get what he gets and there's nothing I can do.*

And suddenly, I was very annoyed about all of that.

'Right, you motherfuckers,' I said.

I pulled out my gun and started firing.

All this came back to me later, piecemeal.

I woke up, dimly aware that something wasn't right but physically unwilling to do much investigation into what it might be. Opening half an eye was enough to confirm that I'd fallen asleep with the light on; and, as I became more conscious of my body, I realised I was also fully dressed, curled in a vaguely foetal position on the floor by my bed. Not grand. I'd had enough self-awareness to stick a cushion beneath my head before passing out, but that had surely taken more effort than simply clambering upright and just falling onto the bed. Drunken logic is a curious thing.

I sat up slowly, beginning to shiver.

What had happened? Fragments came back to me slowly and disjointedly: the old woman in Whitelocks; the dancefloor at Spooks. I remembered the text from Rachel, which had arrived as I unlocked the front door on my way back in.

miss u so much :-(please ring me. need to talk. xx

Drunk last night, my first reaction had been disappointment that the message had been from her and not Lucy. Now, I felt upset and sad, but the underlying sentiment remained.

I remembered the fight about the same time I realised that my shoulder was aching. I rubbed it absently, wondering why.

Then went cold.

Oh shit.

Had I shot somebody last night? Surely I hadn't, but I knew that I'd fired the gun – I could dimly remember the shots, and then screams and people running. Sirens in the distance. A hazy memory of the world wobbling around me as I ran, drunk and desperate.

Fuck.

I scrambled to my feet too quickly and had to fight back the urge to be sick. Then I scrabbled around and found the gun. The clip was empty.

Fuck.

Carefully, I tried to put the events of the evening together. It was like threading beads onto a thin wire – but I only had about four beads to work with and I kept dropping those, so any necklace was going to be patchy at best.

I was trying to decide whether I'd shot *at* someone, or just up in the air to frighten everybody away, when I noticed the envelope on the table.

It wasn't mine, and it hadn't been there the last time I'd looked at the table and paid it any attention. Where had it come from? I thought about it, and finally remembered that it had been lying on the doormat waiting for me when I'd got back inside. I'd received the text at the same time and I'd only had enough mental cohesion to handle one at once. The text had won out; the envelope – I'd just carried it upstairs, put it down and forgotten about it. Now, I picked it up.

Martin

Just my first name and no address, so it must have been delivered by hand. But I recognised Sean's writing from the stacks of police paperwork we'd shared and sent between us. My ex-partner.

How did you find me? I wondered, ripping the envelope open and emptying the contents on the bed, sitting down beside them. There wasn't much inside – just two sheets of paper – but the first thing I saw brought back a hundred unwelcome memories. It was a photograph of a dead girl. *The* dead girl, in fact – despite our best efforts she'd never had a name or an identity beyond that sad title. We'd never discovered who she was.

I'd seen the picture itself many times, and I didn't need to study it again now. I knew it off by heart. That was where it hit you, and that was where it stayed.

The second sheet was a photocopy of a driver's licence. The ink was faint, but I could make out a name – *Alison Sheldon* – and an address out of town. The photograph in the top corner showed a pretty girl, smiling sweetly for the camera.

And Sean's handwriting again, underneath it.

It said:

I found her.

CHAPTER TWO

I had been a cop in the city for nearly six years, and I left because it felt like it was slowly killing me. Maybe it sounds stupid, but I got into law enforcement because I wanted to enforce laws; more than that – I wanted to save people, help them, serve them. As I was growing up, police officers were pointed out as men and women to look up to. The ones I saw always wore smart blue suits that gave them an air of authority, wisdom and judgement – they were good characters who were on my side and would help me when I needed them, and as I got older that was who I wanted myself to be. It was a job that seemed good, in the way that shuffling paper or firing people for a living didn't. More useful, more rewarding. That's why I joined and that's why I left.

Here is the reality of how crime works in the city, and where we as police fit into that.

Let's start with the big stuff.

First of all, you have gangland crimes, pretty much all of which occur or at least originate in the east wing of Wasp. Most of these, you let go. You have to. The vast majority are committed by hardened criminals against other equally hardened criminals, and so you're faced with the triple difficulty of establishing any evidence, risking your life to bring the bad guy to book and actually giving much of a shit one way or the other. Add in the fact that half the force are taking kickbacks to look the other way (which means that if you get involved you might end up shot in the back by one of your own) and what you have is a genuine loser of a situation. *Fuck them*, you tend to think. *Let them sort their own out*. Which they do, of course. This is the way in which the dark merry-go-round of criminal society keeps itself turning.

At the other end of the spectrum you have corporate crimes. These are the activities that originate in Elephant: the district of commerce and big business. In the northern parts of that district, the buildings are all made of shining steel and sparkling glass, and most of the people are sharp-suited and serious-looking – the movers and shakers, although it's difficult to imagine them putting their briefcases and phones down long enough to shake anything properly. The buildings look clean and respectable, and all the hairstyles are very neat, but Elephant is just as dirty as Wasp. Money flows into and out of this district from each and every part of the city: some of it good and right, some of it legal but immoral, and some of it downright criminal.

And, just like Wasp, a lot of that money goes to the police, so you have to tread carefully. Crimes *between* these people? Forget them. Crimes *by* these people? Work around them. It's the crimes committed *against* these people – they're the crimes that need to be treated seriously and solved, because these are the *decent people*, and most of them contribute in some way to your salary. These are the people that you signed up to protect and serve, even if at the time you thought your aspirations were a little higher and the scope of your care was cast a little wider.

As a cop, these are the two main parameters you work within; and most of your life consists of checking that the clockwork keeps ticking, making sure no gears or cogs click out of place, and then writing up reports to let the more important people know that things are okay. At best, you solve one crime in ten. The rest go nowhere or somewhere, and either way you probably have to leave it. Every now and then, there'll be a shake-up and a few people will go down, but those instances are rare. Generally, what you have is the same people doing the same things to the same people, over and over, while you tick boxes, take whatever extras on the side you feel comfortable with and hang on for dear life.

In the meantime, you make headway where you can – solving the crimes that fall between these two poles. It's just a sad fact that, as a mostly privatised institution, the police aren't ultimately responsible to people who don't own shares, and so they don't often care that much about ordinary, everyday crimes. That's an exaggeration, because some cops *do* care – I was one, Sean was one – but the majority don't, and even the ones that would do something if they could often don't have the time. You do what you can, but you're expected to prioritise and you have to earn your keep. Muggings, beatings, the rape and murder of poor people, street people, whores, whatever – these crimes are low on the list simply because there's little money in it. A lot of these people don't even vote, never mind buy stuff. You have to focus on the middle classes and above, only dipping down lower when it's clear-cut, easy and you have a few spare hours to handle the paperwork.

That's the reality. I got into the job because I was idealistic but I quickly learned to hide my ideals away. Ideals in our city are like the stupid new kid at school. If people notice them then the pointing and laughing begins, the bullying follows quickly and, before you know it, entire years of your life will be filled with misery. So I kept my head down.

I resisted a lot of the traditional corruption – just creamed a bit where I could, and where it felt like it wouldn't matter – and concentrated on solving the crimes I could bring to some kind of completion. I took down minor burglars, minor dealers, rapists; solved a few murders of homeless people. You develop a nose for what can be done within the constraints. Sean was the same – although he'd done it a few years before me and made detective five years ahead, and so he was slightly wiser. When I made it to detective, I was recognised for what I was: someone who would look away when it was required of him, but who would disapprove while he did. And so they partnered me with Sean, because he'd been the same.

Sean was a small, neat guy – very self-contained, very dogged and determined. He threw himself into investigations, and you could tell it always hurt him a little when he was made to let them go. But he let go anyway. That was another reason why they put me with him: they figured he would keep me under control, and they were right. What he did was show me the ropes at detective level and teach me what I needed to know in order not to get clipped.

More than that, we became friends. When Rachel and I bought the house that I'd eventually leave, Sean was there to help us clean, decorate and move our things. He didn't have much in the way of family himself, and so he became a regular instalment in our home: coming round for dinner, or crashing on our settee after a long night's drunken philosophising. After a while, I figured out why I liked him so much: there was nothing objectionable about him. He cared about people and it haunted him, but it seemed like a worthy quest that you admired him for and instinctively wanted to help with. My career – if you can call it that – wouldn't have lasted half as long without Sean. Leaving aside the fact that I would have been dead five times over, I would have lost the enthusiasm and the desire. Without him to show me how ideals and reality could be reconciled, it would all have finished a lot sooner.

And I have something else to thank or blame him for. He showed me that you could play the game the way they wanted and *still* make some kind of difference, by presenting me with an alternative to more official methods of justice. Because when he trusted me enough, he introduced me to Rosh and Lucy.

The first time I went along with them, it was to see a mechanic named Timothy Hartley. At the time, he was running a chop shop out of western Wasp. A young girl had disappeared, and we had good reason to believe that Hartley was involved. He had form, but we also had a witness that placed him near the scene and less reliable sources that pinned him as the guy, and so we brought him in and leaned on him. The whole time, he laughed and joked and basically told us to go fuck ourselves.

Twenty-four hours into the questioning, I went to a firing range with Sean. We did that a lot: we were both good long-range shots, and we'd often compete a little, but it was mainly so that we could let off steam and talk the shit over the details of whatever case we were working on – see if there was anything we'd missed. In Hartley's case, there was nothing. We both knew that the case was going to fall.

'We know he did it,' I said.

Sean was loading his rifle. 'That's not enough, though, is it?'

'Yeah, well. It fucking should be.'

I was pissed off at myself, and doing a bad job of keeping it in check. It felt like there was something I should have been able to do to stop Hartley from walking. Of course, it was a familiar feeling and I was used to it by now – but it smarted all the same. I knew from Sean's hooded expression that he felt the same.

He held the button down, moving his target right the way to the back of the range. It quivered slightly as it went, then jerked to a stop. He raised his rifle, aimed and let loose a single shot. Then, he adjusted his grip slightly and fired two more.

When he lowered the weapon, he looked at me thoughtfully.

'What time are you off duty tonight?'

I shrugged. We both knew it didn't work like that.

'I don't know,' I said. 'Why?'

'Come out to Carpe Diem,' he said. 'I've got a couple of friends who want to meet you.'

Carpe Diem is a cop bar in Owl, close to the department. We often went for a drink there after work, and that's what we did that night as well. And that's where I met Lucy and Rosh properly for the first time.

Technically, I'd met Lucy before, but only in a professional capacity: she was in forensics and she handled major crime scenes. Even more so than me, her work was steeped in death – but you'd never know it, not to look at her anyway. She had long blond hair, a pretty face; she was small and slim and curvy. Physically, everything was right, but with that extra twist you can't describe and just know when you see it – that slight side-step that takes pretty and makes it sexy. The first time I'd seen her, I was almost intimidated by how attractive and alive she was. She'd induced a kind of awe in me.

But looks are only half the story. One of the other cops had told me to watch her. He said she was cold and distant, and – I thought he was joking – borderline psychopathic. Certainly, she was very professional, aloof even, but I'd caught a flash of humour in something she'd said to me, and I'd figured that a lot of the gossip and comments came down to resentment or jealousy: shit like that. She played her cards close to her chest. I thought that was fine.

That night at Carpe Diem, I discovered it was Lucy who'd introduced Sean to what we were about to do. Before that, she'd been recruited into it by Rosh.

Rosh had ten, maybe fifteen years on all of us, and he carried a lot of respect in the department. Partly it was because, on the surface, he was astute and good at playing the game and being accepted by the rest of the force. The other part was that he was frightening and dangerous, and so people didn't mess with him. Not only was he two metres tall and extremely well-built, he was also bald and probably one of the ugliest men you're ever likely to see. It was like his face had been mangled by something, then stretched back out in all the wrong directions. He never threw his weight around because he never seemed like he needed to. Despite his appearance, Rosh was one of the gentlest, most polite and demure men you would ever meet, and that made people even more careful. When you find that dichotomy in a person, you always get the feeling that it's better not to push and overbalance it. When it topples, you know instinctively that it'll take half the room with it.

Lucy and Rosh arrived and we chatted; they both

liked me and I liked them. We had a few drinks, sounded each other out, felt around each other a bit. I knew what they were suggesting without them saying it, and at that point I was fine with it.

So that was it. That was our crew.

As expected, Timothy Hartley was released. He clearly knew some people, and the legitimate witness withdrew his statement.

The next evening we paid Hartley a visit at his garage.

Like I said, Lucy was only small, but she had what my grandmother would call the life force in her, and when she wanted to she could let it go. Hartley was a sizeable guy, but he never knew what hit him. She tore him apart in about ten seconds, and then did some stuff to him that I wouldn't wish on anyone. Pretty quickly, he told us where the girl was.

Sean went off to check while we held Hartley there at gunpoint. After a few minutes he started to get his balls back. He told us that we'd never get away with this, that he'd see us all in prison, fucked and dead for what we'd done. None of it made any difference to Rosh or Lucy, but it was my first time out and I was beginning to get frightened. Eventually, Sean phoned to say he'd found the girl and that she was still alive. Ten seconds later, Lucy shot Hartley in the head, and then there wasn't enough time for me to be frightened about anything.

We planted enough false evidence in the garage to point any investigating officers to a rival gang, and nobody was ever any the wiser. The girl? We left her near the hospital and made an anonymous call.

That was the first time, and it fucked me up as much as you'd imagine. I thought my life was over – that I'd damned myself and I'd go to a hell I didn't believe in but was still afraid of. Or I'd be caught. All the thoughts you'd imagine. But I wasn't caught – we were too careful for that – and the more I thought about it, the less I felt, and then finally I started to feel okay. Hartley was a piece of shit, and we'd saved someone's life. I tried to rationalise it, playing devil's advocate with my conscience. What exactly, I asked myself, was wrong with what I'd done? I really wasn't sure. You couldn't argue with the results. In every way possible, we'd made the situation better.

I didn't go with the crew the next time they went out, but I did the time after that, and it went on from there.

All in all, I was involved in killing seven men in cold blood. With each one the feelings lessened; I'd make myself feel angry and then I'd make myself feel nothing at all. As we went on, it got to seem like the only way of getting any real justice in our city at all. By the time we killed Carl Halloran – the last person we ever visited as a team – I was almost fine about it. That was a couple of weeks before we found Alison, though, and I had no idea how everything was about to fall apart.

One thing about being a cop: it's surprising how abstracted it makes you feel. You start off with a desire to help people and serve their interests, but that soon fades into the background. What you do marks you out as different – there's a real sense of community among police officers, and at its most intense it creates an 'us against them' mentality. You realise quickly that a lot of the people you're protecting don't care about you. In fact, a good proportion of them fucking hate you. Sometimes we earn that, sometimes we don't.

As a result, you begin to see people differently. It

happened to me, and after a while I began looking sideways at the city itself. Sean felt the same, and that's partly what brought us together and cemented our friendship.

There were nights when he'd drive me out of the city and up into the hills nearby. We'd park and both look out over the buildings and the lights and the people below us, and it would seem to me that in some awful way the city was alive: that there was a dark heart flexing and thumping underneath the skin of concrete and soil. Everybody thinks that way sometimes, I guess, but Sean thought it most of the time, and his belief was infectious. He'd tell me his theories, and the feeling would bloom inside me. The more we talked and worked, the more I could sense the city's heart-beat. It made me feel powerless and awful and weak.

I was supposed to be in control of this city – this enormous creature that was bad from top to bottom – and it wanted none of it. Maybe it would let us get away with the little stuff, but the evil was too ingrained: any concerted attempt to dig it out would bring the buildings crashing down. That's what Sean said: it was like the human body if you removed all the water – all you'd be left with is a pile of sand.

That was how he saw the city, and after a while that's how I began to see it too. Partly it was because of the way things worked: everything was so orchestrated and coordinated that it was often difficult *not* to see a design under it all. But sometimes you only had to walk down the streets to start imagining them as veins and arteries, and on those occasions I often wondered if I could kneel down, press my hand to the pavement and feel the slow thud of the city's pulse.

Stupid, maybe, but that was how I started to see things.

Alison Sheldon's murder offered a kind of proof of it.

We didn't know her name then, of course. We didn't know who she was, only what she was.

Some kids found her, deep inside an old, abandoned building in Bull. Bull is a strange, eerie district in the top eastern corner of the city, expanding out far beyond the walls. To the far north-east, towards the hills, you have the power stations and towers, with smoke gusting out day and night. At the tops, you can see it unfolding ever so slowly, churning up and merging into the still grey of the sky. Closer to the city, the district is quiet, but there are always echoes and clangs in the distance. It's the industrial heart of the city, and probably one of the oldest parts, historically. Inside the city walls, the houses are all old millworkers' back-to-backs. They're where the navvies lived; where wool was spun; where the air was filled with smoke and soot and cholera. These buildings are mostly abandoned, dirty and dangerous, and because the district borders Wasp to the south, a lot of things go missing in them, including people.

Like I said, some kids found her. Bodies generally rest unattended in Bull for quite some time before they're stumbled on. These kids were exploring and got unlucky. It was pretty dark inside, and she was just a shape to them: a shape and a smell. They spilled out of the building and called us – probably the first time in their lives, and probably the last. Sean and I took the call.

It was an old house. With a lot of the back-to-backs round there, it wasn't always clear where one place stopped and another one started. The walls were often thin; some of them would be missing entirely. Boards were nailed across properties, dividing homes into smaller sections, many of which had been knocked through into their neighbours. The front doors were only ever a guide to the internal spread of properties. Where there were back doors, you couldn't get to them because the alleys were all filled with squat bin-bags and splintered timber.

The kids, and a few adults, waited outside while we went in with torches, wary of our footing.

I could sense death the second we entered the house. There was a *presence* to the place. It was very quiet, but it felt like someone was in there with us and keeping still so as to not make any noise. Like even though the girl we would find upstairs was dead, she was still aware and watching us: flickering in the corner behind a sound-proof screen that prevented her from screaming to us. Perhaps it was just the house itself: its mouldy walls broken down, paper peeling, everything reeking of damp and decay. The floor was covered with dust, old bricks, wood. Our flashlights carved across it, and wherever they weren't shining immediately seemed blacker as a result. We both had our guns drawn. Even though there was nothing alive in here to shoot, it felt like you might need to defend your soul against something.

We found her upstairs, exactly where the kids told us. Sean holstered his gun and got out a handkerchief to cover his face, while I toughed it out, shining the torch around the room to check what else was here. The walls were covered in shreds of paper, with strips of it hanging off, and the plaster beneath was mottled with damp and rot. A lot of old, stained graffiti. There didn't seem to be any furniture. The only real thing to note was a window opposite us, which was slatted, coated over with grey paper and thick with flies.

She was in the centre of the room, staining broken floorboards we could hardly see. Forensics would later determine that her body had been left balanced in a kneeling position. Her hands and feet had been bound behind her, and the cord around her neck had been tied tightly back to join the one at her ankles. When we arrived, however, decomposition had toppled her. She had lost most semblance of form, swollen from the slim girl she had once been into something awful and tight and black: something you'd have nightmares about. Her head looked like an odd pile of pebbles; you couldn't even tell where her eyes had been. A thin line of fungus trailed away across the floor, reaching for the window.

'Do you think she's dead?' Sean asked.

I gave him a look. Then we quickly checked around and went outside to call it in. Confirmed dead body; forensics required. They'd go in first and do whatever they needed to do before the scene became even more contaminated, and then we'd get a chance to examine the area and get a feel for what might have happened there. We took details from the children who'd found her, and I tipped one of the other kids some money to get us both a coffee, and then we waited out in the open air for people with scientific qualifications to arrive and start measuring shit.

'This is going to be a bad one,' Sean said.

I nodded. But really – back then – I had no idea.

We worked that investigation hard: all of us. Each person that touched the file on the dead girl in Bull felt it burn their fingertips a little and not want to leave them.

This wasn't a business hit; it had none of that cool efficiency. As a cop, you have a certain understanding of professional hits: you might not like them, but you know why it's been done and a lot of the time it ends up making your life a bit easier. It's about greed, and everybody feels greedy once in a while. You can relate. But this kind of crime stemmed from something darker and more unpleasant. And the worst part is that you can still relate. It's all the same building, but some crimes happen in the nice, clean offices upstairs, whereas others take place in the basement, beneath the rust and cobwebs, in rooms that you're scared to go into. You recognise the roots of everything you investigate, but you learn quickly that some are more uncomfortably damp than others.

The other reason we worked so tirelessly was Sean. As the case progressed – or didn't – he grew ever more distant and haunted. I saw less and less of him, and I started to realise that he wasn't sleeping much. There were days when he didn't turn up at all – he'd just be out on his own, running his own lines and walking grids that might not even have existed outside his own head. Everybody could see that he was unravelling. Bits of him were fading and becoming as indistinct as the girl – we didn't know her name, where she was from, who killed her and why. For some reason, it seemed like traces of Sean's mind were blowing away on these breezes of dead air, and, even if we didn't discuss the subject openly, I think we all figured that solving the case might save him.

Maybe it would have done, but we'll never know. However hard we looked and however many people we asked, we learned nothing. She had no name or identity, no family, no past, no future. And in the end, Sean literally went to pieces.

When I thought about the dead girl, I thought of it like this. People die in swamps or quicksand and they get sucked under for a long time – maybe even for ever.

But sometimes the ground shifts and the body is brought to the surface. It's not evil and there's no thought behind it; it's just what happens. The girl's corpse felt like that. It was as though our city had shifted awkwardly in a nightmare and one of its dead had rolled up into the light. Nameless and forgotten, she might have never been anyone at all. This was just what our city did. What went on underneath.

Eventually, as stupid as it might seem, you start thinking. Perhaps nobody killed her at all. Perhaps she was just dead there in the same way that the paint was peeling and the walls were crumbling. It sounds ridiculous, but on the nights when you can almost hear the city breathing it doesn't always feel it. Sean and I talked about it once, drunk as fuckers, and, although it was left unspoken, we both knew that it scared us how similarly we were starting to see the world. So I understood a little how and why it was haunting him so much, but I didn't appreciate it properly back then. Now I realise the feeling took him over and he simply couldn't cope anymore. People die in our city every day, and you learn to deal with it, but Alison's death was always different. We didn't know it then, of course, but it was tied into our city and its history, vibrating on a wavelength that Sean had begun to hear increasingly clearly. I could only vaguely sense the echoes, but even that was enough to frighten me.

And what happened was, Sean left.

One day he did his usual not-turning-in routine, but this time his absence stretched to two days, and then to three, and then he just never came back. I didn't hear from him, and after a week of no word it seemed pretty clear that he was gone, one way or another. The exact circumstances were unclear, but we learned a little, here and there. Sean had rented his flat and lived alone, and it turned out that he'd left instructions with his estate agents to say that he wouldn't be renewing his tenancy. On the last day, the landlord turned up, expecting an empty house and instead finding that all of Sean's things were still there. This was a few days before we went looking, and when we did we found the landlord, slightly aggravated, in the process of bagging and binning most of Sean's possessions. There was no forwarding address, no contact details. It was as though Sean had simply not come home one night.

We looked for him, of course. We tried all the obvious places and people, and then we moved on to the less obvious. Some of them, we leaned on pretty hard – but there was no trace of him. And in the months that had passed since – on those dark nights – I didn't find it impossible to believe that it had been a trade-off: that the city had accidentally let go of the girl's body in its sleep, realised its mistake and then lazily reached out and taken Sean instead.

The rest of us packed up and moved on. Photographs tacked to walls were taken down; papers were filed; people moved to different desks and started giving a shit about other things. But none of us – especially me – forgot about that girl properly. Like I said, she was different. A little more awful, a little more inexplicable. Without understanding why, she haunted us all in our own ways, whoever she was.

That was about five months ago, and those five months had been a blur: an emotional downhill roll in which I'd gathered speed until I couldn't even make out the scenery. Looking back now, it was tempting to see everything as starting with that dead girl. She got Sean first. It just took a bit more time for her to get me too.

A month after Sean vanished, the affair I'd had with

Lucy was over and I'd split with Rachel and moved into my new flat. A month after that and I wasn't going into work. I didn't officially quit, in that I never handed in my badge or gun, but Rosh and Lucy were aware I wasn't coming back and informed the necessary people. Nobody knew exactly where I was, but I don't think anyone looked that hard. I could live with it.

I lied when I said I left because the job wasn't good enough. That was certainly a factor – and after Sean disappeared there were no more night-time excursions to take the edge off the monotony. But it's not the whole story. The real truth is that I left because I couldn't work with Lucy anymore. We were good friends, and I hoped we always would be, but she didn't want our relationship to go on any longer and I'd realised too late that, despite everything, she was all I wanted. I was hurt and upset and sad, and it was breaking her heart to see me every day and know that it was her fault. So I left. I emailed her and said goodbye and that I'd always be her friend but I needed some time alone to get over these dumb feelings I had. I didn't know how long it would take, but I never guessed that four months on they'd be as strong as ever, with a bad case of cabin fever on top of it all.

Money? I had savings, and it's probably best not to enquire too much about that. Let's just say that you don't whack that many criminals without picking up some financial compensation along the way, and that last guy, Halloran, set the four of us up quite nicely. Most of my share was squirrelled away in bank accounts held in fake names. For example, the rent on my flat was paid by someone else on behalf of someone else. I paid for my shopping with a third person's credit card.

In the circumstances, how Sean had found me was something of a mystery: a neat trick I wished I could manage myself.

When I saw him again, I'd have to ask him the secret.

CHAPTER THREE

By the middle of the morning, I was fairly sure that I hadn't shot anyone the previous night – or not deliberately anyway. Technically, if you fire a bullet straight up in the air it will reach its zenith, fall down and, wind resistance aside, by the time it hits the earth again it'll be travelling as fast as when it left the barrel. So I might have killed someone by accident or possibly clipped an innocent bird, but these were outside chances and I figured I shouldn't worry. Instead, I drank consecutive cups of coffee, felt sorry for myself and tried to put it out of my head. We all do stupid things when we're drunk and the important thing is to learn.

I opened the blinds in the kitchen and watched the outside world. It was approaching Summer but today was a miserable day: shitty, rainy and overcast. My concentration drifted for a while, unfocused, but after I'd had enough caffeine to feel properly alive I went back through to the bedroom and turned my attention to the papers that Sean had sent to me.

First, the envelope. The only mark on it was my name, scrawled on the front in blue biro. No return address on the back, and no indication of where it had come from. The envelope itself was generic. Next, I looked at the papers that had been inside. The all-too-familiar picture of the girl's corpse had been printed on the station's colour laserjet, and since it was old and battered I presumed that it had once been part of Sean's original case file. Its horrors were old: the photocopy of the driver's licence was actually more shocking, because here was the girl – alive and smiling. She still didn't have a future, but the licence gave her a past of sorts and the contrast was telling.

I put the papers to one side.

Five months without a fucking word, Sean. And this is what you do?

There were a number of questions I wanted answered, many of them connected with who this girl was and why she'd been killed, but the ones that preyed on my mind most were to do with Sean. How he was and what he'd been doing. And why he hadn't delivered this envelope in person. The truth was, I really missed him.

My first instinct was to contact him, but there was no obvious way to do that. Someone else lived in his flat now, and after two months his mobile number had started coming up dead. Now, a quick and casual phone call to the police confirmed that he wasn't working in the department anymore – did I want to leave a message? I said no, and hung up. I'd thought that maybe he'd returned to work and nobody had been able to find me to tell me, but apparently not.

I went into the kitchen to make another coffee – the final straw, surely: the one that would send me into the street tap-dancing like a fool – and wondered what to do about Sean's delivery while the kettle slowly boiled. It was doubtful that he had sent me the information out of courtesy – he clearly expected me to act on it in some way. I thought it over. There was no point in me taking it to the police, as he could have done that himself, so more off-the-record enquiries seemed to be in order. As to why he hadn't established contact properly, I'd just have to trust that he had a good reason. I was his friend, after all, and I owed him that much. Perhaps it would become obvious.

I poured the coffee and took it through to the front room.

A couple of simple calls, then. And to be fair, it wasn't like I had anything else to do with my day.

Like most of the students in our city, Alison had travelled a long way to be with us. The address on her driver's licence was her parents' house, and they lived on the other side of the country in Bracken, where I guessed that she'd grown up. It took a little searching on the internet to get a phone number for them, and then ten minutes of planning before I decided what I was going to say. Then, I made the call.

A man answered after five rings:

'Hello?'

'Mr Sheldon?' I said.

'Uh-huh.' The line crackled a little. 'Who am I speaking to?'

'My name is Martin Weaver,' I told him. 'I'm a detective. I'd like to talk to you about your daughter.'

'Right. Go on then.'

His lack of concern took me aback a little, but I tried not to let it register. Instead, I took my first risk, figuring that Sean must have been in touch with this man at some point.

'I believe you spoke to one of my colleagues recently?'

'No, not me.'

'Oh,' I said. First risk taken and fucked up. 'In that case I must have been misinformed.'

'It was my wife who spoke to him.'

'Ah, right.'

Her parents were a logical place to start, I supposed. Of course, living so far away, it was unlikely that they'd have much insight into Alison's life in the city; they probably wouldn't know that much about what she did and who she did it with, or even – given the realities of teenage alienation – much about who she was. But Sean had given me their address for a reason, and so there must be something here.

Sheldon said, 'He rang up about a month ago. Sean something, I think. I don't know – my wife wrote it down. Said he was a policeman.'

'That's right,' I said, and it occurred to me how strange it was. Their daughter had been murdered and the only people who had contacted them about it were men claiming to be policemen who actually weren't.

I said, 'Could you tell me what he discussed with your wife?'

It was an awkward question anyway – as by all rights I should already know – but I knew that Sheldon's irritation and indifference could make it even worse. Fortunately, he wasn't paying attention.

'Yeah,' he told me. 'Said there had been a possible sighting that he was looking into. But since then we haven't heard anything. He asked us to get in touch if we heard from her.'

Okay, I thought. *They don't know she's dead.*

'Did he ask about anything else?'

'He asked about Alison,' Sheldon said. 'Wanted to know about her friends. Her work. Stuff like that.'

'And what did your wife tell him?'

'She told him she didn't know much about it. To be honest, Alison hardly ever contacts us. Wasn't much my wife could say. Anything he wanted to know would have been in the Missing Persons Report anyway.'

Missing Persons Report?

I almost said it out loud, but managed to stop myself just in time. We'd gone through every one of those reports for the months before and after we found the body, and Alison's name had never turned up. Right age, right physical characteristics – if she'd been there we would have seized on her file and run with it. When had it been made?

I spoke to Alison's father for a few more minutes, trying to find out if he knew anything else, but there was nothing. He was obviously uninterested by my enquiries, and it became apparent that Alison had been distanced from her parents for quite a while before her disappearance. Her father's attitude was that this was the kind of thing she did – no doubt she'd turn up eventually, and she shouldn't expect much of a welcoming committee when she did. It was very sad, but he didn't know what had happened and I tried hard – but unsuccessfully – not to hold it against him.

'Thanks for your time,' I said at the end of the conversation. 'We'll be in touch if we hear anything.'

The nearest Missing Persons Bureau is based a little out of town: around three hundred kilometres north, and then west a bit. It is notoriously efficient, mostly because it was founded twenty years ago by an everyday couple who had started off searching for their own missing son. It had expanded since then, of course, but it's still run on a voluntary basis by dedicated staff. The police force had trouble keeping track of things that happened ten minutes ago, but Missing Persons maintains files on every runaway and absentee reported to them since the operation began. Even better – the files are hard-copy and the staff know where to find them.

Missing Persons isn't a public operation, in that if you rang up anonymously and asked for information you wouldn't get it, but they work closely with the police. They keep the files but they certainly don't want them, and if the police find someone then they can throw a case away. We all cooperate and maintain a useful two-way exchange.

Of course, I was a normal member of the public now – I still had a badge, but the number was probably void. Fortunately, I'd worked with Missing Persons enough times to know a couple of the staff by name, and so I could call and ask for one of them personally. The sad fact is that missing people ended up in our city all the time, in various states of mental and physical cohesion, and I was one of the few cops who had conspicuously cared about putting names to some of them and maybe sending them home. As currency went in Missing Persons, I was a rich man until proven otherwise.

An hour after speaking to Mr Sheldon, I was sitting in an internet café, drinking yet another coffee and running through the details that had been faxed through to me on the colour machine at the other side of the room.

I'd lied on the phone, but only by omission. Yes, I might have some news for them soon – that was true. No, I wasn't in the office; I was out, so could they fax the details to this number, please? Also true. But they hadn't asked if I was still a cop and so I hadn't mentioned that I wasn't.

I had six pages. The first had a picture of Alison Sheldon in the top right-hand corner. It was a relaxed shot: someone had snapped her from one side, just as she turned, and she was squinting against a sun that lit

45

up her face. In this photograph she looked much prettier than she did on the driver's licence, and it was sad.

Sean always said that when people died all the photographs of them shifted into an emotional minor key. If you put ten prints in front of him, he could pick out the victims. In a way, people in pictures are always dead – because time passes and that particular person gets left behind – but there are still tendrils that attach images of the you in the past to the you in the present, and when people die the tendrils stop humming. Sean really thought he could sense that, and who was I to tell him he was wrong? Looking at the picture of Alison that had been faxed to me, I didn't understand how someone wouldn't know that she was dead.

The rest of that page was a brief bio, typed in Courier with headings underlined. I scanned it quickly, taking in the pertinent details. Alison was twenty when she disappeared, studying for a degree in Fine Art. There were details of her previous schools, and it said that she'd been arrested for a minor drugs offence in her mid-teens and cautioned, but apart from that her record was clean. Just bad luck getting caught, that one. When she disappeared, she didn't even have points on her driver's licence.

The other pages gave information about the circumstances of her disappearance, but not as much as I'd hoped. From the scant details, I got the impression that Alison had lived a very independent life. She had an address in Turtle, but it seemed that she often stayed over with friends, sleeping on floors and in spare rooms. Her boyfriend situation was generally fluid, but there was some indication – from comments made by friends – that it had settled somewhat in the weeks prior to her disappearance. Some people thought she was seeing another student; some, a lecturer. Others said they couldn't be sure that she was seeing anyone, only that she wasn't seeing them as much as she used to. In my experience of murder investigations, girls rarely benefit from having mysterious boyfriends. Despite the confusion, there was enough mention of a boyfriend for it to seem worth pursuing.

On to her actual disappearance, then. She hadn't been seen for a week and a half by the time she was reported missing. The last person to see her alive was her friend, Keleigh Groves. Alison had left for the library that morning, presumably after an evening of some kind of social debauchery, and she hadn't returned.

That wasn't unusual, Keleigh was quoted as saying. *She'd do that all the time. She had loads of friends she used to stay with. If she turned up, I let her stay and maybe other people would be there and we'd have a party. But I didn't worry if I didn't see her.*

Other people must have felt the same, because nobody had been particularly worried not to hear from Alison for that length of time, and the boyfriend – if there was one – seemed to have disappeared along with her. Nobody heard from her again. Not until some kids were fucking around in Bull and ended up running screaming out of that old, abandoned house. Then, she started speaking to Sean and me in our nightmares with a voice that – until yesterday – had no name. The Missing Persons Report was filed, a few relevant people were interviewed and that was that. People vanish all the time. Many of them because they want to.

And yet she hadn't vanished. We'd found her.

I checked through the dates on the sheet and put the chronology together in my head. We found her body around two weeks after she disappeared, and that was a good half week after this report had been filed. We would have picked it up. So why didn't we?

Certainly not incompetence – a large number of us worked this case very hard, and checking Missing Persons would have been one of the obvious avenues to pursue. The only real answer I could come up with was that someone *had* picked up the report: picked it up and buried it. Not me. Not Sean. Someone else in the department.

I rubbed my face a little and started to feel bad.

It occurred to me that Sean had sent a very small amount of information about Alison, which meant that he must have had a reason not to tell me a lot more. Maybe he didn't want to get me properly involved unless it was necessary. Which would mean that he'd sent me what he had as some kind of insurance.

I put it together in my head.

Sean investigates. Sean finds out something bad and realises that his life might be in danger. Sean sends me enough to get going so that if something bad does happen to him I can follow it up. Then I can get killed too. *Thanks a fucking bunch, Sean*, I would say to him, in whatever twisted version of heaven we ended up in.

It made a certain amount of sense.

He'd delivered it last night, so he'd been alive and fine yesterday. Perhaps something had been about to change. A deal or a meeting. Some kind of showdown.

I finished off my coffee and wondered where I was going next.

There was no question of putting this to one side. Sean was my friend and I needed to know that he was okay. That was the deal; since he'd always looked out for me, it was time to repay the favour. But even without that there was no question. I turned to the front of the file and looked again at the picture of

Alison. It was strange, but I still dreamed about her sometimes; and when that happened, I always woke up feeling that her murder had injected poison into my life. Everything after finding her had gone rotten. Discovering her killer wouldn't fix any of that, of course, but I felt compelled to try anyway, regardless of any danger that Sean might be in.

So: the first priority was probably a visit to the university. I'd see what her department could tell me. Maybe have a look at her emails too. Then, there was the boyfriend to check out – whether he had been a student, a lecturer or someone else altogether. I could look up a few of her friends; there were contact details for most of the ones who had given statements. And at some point I'd have to speak to Rosh or Lucy about who in the department might have hidden the report and why. But that was uncomfortable and it could wait.

Okay then, I thought, gathering up my papers.

As I paid up, I realised I was experiencing something I hadn't felt since I'd left the police: a kind of vague thrill. It was a buzzing feeling that wasn't quite excitement. You never enjoy the job, but sometimes you get the sensation of *rightness* – of things falling naturally into place. You shake the facts and drop them, and they begin to form a line that leads to the truth; and when that happens it can feel like you're coming into alignment with the world and doing exactly what you should.

I went outside, and was heading towards the university campus – which was a long walk away – when my mobile rang. The investigation vanished from my mind, and I thought *Lucy* as I took the phone out of my pocket. But then the display said *rachel home calling* and I looked at it for a good five seconds, debating whether to answer it or not, before finally pressing green.

'Hi,' I said.

'Didn't you get my text?'

'No.' But that was too much of a lie for it to live. 'Well, yes. But not until a few minutes ago. I've been busy.'

'Well, it's nice to know you're keeping yourself busy.'

'Right.'

Since I'd moved out, Rachel had two ways of dealing with me. The first was the tone of the text message last night: vulnerable and hurt, and not afraid to show it. The other way was the flipside of that: cold, detached, professionally annoyed – mainly at me, but also at herself for the times when she was more open. I wasn't sure which was the hardest to deal with, but it was clear I had the pared-down half-hatred to deal with today.

She said, 'I need to see you.'

'What do you need to see me about?'

'I need to talk. I know you're busy – apparently – but I need to.'

'Yeah,' I said. 'I am busy.'

'Well, I need to. I think you owe me that much at least.'

I checked my watch; the afternoon was passing quickly, and I wasn't going to have time to meet Rachel and then check out the university. It was one or the other. I closed my eyes.

Half of me thought that she was being unfair – that I didn't owe her anything, because life doesn't work like that. Relationships die, and usually one of you hurts a lot more than the other. I'd felt enough guilt to sink my entire life, and so I'd tried to convince myself over time that you can hurt someone very badly without it necessarily being wrong. But it never quite worked. For a start, there was my affair with Lucy; in reality, I had such a lot to be guilty about. If Rachel thought that meeting up and talking to me might numb the pain a little, then I could do that. Whatever she asked, in fact, I could probably do. It didn't balance against the one huge thing I couldn't do for her, but at least it was something.

I opened my eyes and said:

'Okay. Where do you want to meet?'

CHAPTER FOUR

At the western edge of Horse, where it borders Elephant, there is a place called the Clock Café. It's on the cusp of both studentland and the bohemian market end of the business district, and therefore it's needlessly trendy: nestled in between a fake authentic pizzeria and a shop filled with old clothes that had come back into fashion by virtue of simply being so revolting. The café itself is a mixture of glass-fronted utility and old-world décor that doesn't really work. On the front, above the window, somebody had painted an enormous white clockface – Roman numerals, and all – onto the brick, and obviously that doesn't work. And yet it's always full, presumably because students don't work either.

The drizzly rain had stopped now, and a fair few people were sitting outside at tables on the cramped pavement. There were too many couples and they seemed too happy. Whenever I saw people who were blatantly in love with each other, I was always torn between thinking that either they were very stupid or I was. Today, it was edging towards the latter.

I crossed the street heading for the café, but I stopped a little way down from the entrance as something caught my eye. A friend of society had spray-painted graffiti onto the flagstones in the middle of the pavement. It said:

I stared at it for a few seconds, feeling confused and intrigued by it, and then I shook my head. It was just graffiti.

I headed inside the café and ordered a cappuccino. The waiter – slick, tanned and ponytailed – was drying the inside of a cup with a tassel-edged tea towel, using an action that suggested a previous customer must have been drinking some kind of glue. He took my order imperiously and then set about taking as long as physically possible to make it. I sat down at a table not far from the counter, and decided that if he didn't bring my drink over within five minutes then I was very probably going to shoot him. It seemed reasonable.

He just made it and I almost scowled. Instead, I sipped the froth off the coffee, waited and remembered.

There's this strange thing. Whenever I travelled by train, I couldn't help looking for bodies out of the window. Macabre perhaps, but the side of railway tracks always seemed such a likely disposal site for corpses: all those wastelands and embankments and litter-strewn sidings. Looking out of the window, all you ever saw were fields and gravel, desiccated buildings and rubbish.

There were no bodies that day, as far as I could tell.

We were on a train, side by side, with me beside the aisle and Rachel by the window. She had been sleeping for most of the journey. I would have quite liked her to rest her head on my shoulder but instead she was facing forwards, her head tilted back slightly, with the four-four rattle of the tracks moving her gently.

Sitting opposite, there were two indifferent strangers, arms folded, bored and lolling. We were all doing our best not to touch knees or look at each other.

The tannoy system kept performing strange grammatical loops:

'The next station is Lindley. Lindley is the next station.'

I alternated between looking at the dirty, rubbery floor of the aisle and the landscape outside. In the distance, the bare trees turned slowly on the spot as we passed. Closer, the world accelerated: the yellow fields trotted backwards, the hedge was running, and then the gravel of the track was a blur of speeding complexity. In the carriage itself, there was peace: only the shudder of the tracks; the occasional shuffle.

I was thinking about how to break up with Rachel. A couple of weeks in and I was unhappy with the way things were going – or weren't going – and splitting up with her seemed like the best solution out of a bad bunch.

The main problem, as I saw it, was that we seemed to have nothing to say to each other. In my limited experience, the beginning of a new relationship should be full of passion and talk. There's too much to discover about the other person – in bed and in conversation – but you're compelled to try anyway and it feels great. You want to know what they think about everything, and then you're amazed by what they say. You want to take them to places that mean a lot to you, both to share them and also so that you can see those places in new ways.

With Rachel, there was none of that. Obviously, we had conversations, but there was an awkwardness to them, as though at any moment one of us might give a one-word answer and mess everything up and neither of us was willing to take the risk. And we did have sex, but most of the time it was this perfunctory, passion-less fucking. The one-word-answer nerves haunted that too; we just weren't relaxed. Even kissing felt difficult: every kiss felt like the first, like we still weren't sure that the other one actually wanted to.

Next to me, Rachel stirred slightly. I looked at her and she gave me a sleepy smile, then closed her eyes again and shuffled slightly. But she still didn't lean against me.

'The next station is Saltaire. Saltaire is the next station.'

Only two more stops to go but the journey felt interminable. The train shushed slowly to a halt against the platform, and the doors juddered open. A few people moved on and off, but Saltaire was a dead village and hardly anyone travelled to or from here. Soon, the doors closed, and then the train jerked once and whispered off towards the city. The whisper built up to a rush; the loud clatter of the tracks returned.

So: why hadn't I broken up with her already? I really wasn't sure. Perhaps the niggling doubt I was enter-taining was born out of fear. I'd never broken up with anyone in my life; it had always been the other way around. There were all kinds of things to consider. What would she say if I told her? What would her family think? I'd met them the previous night and they seemed nice; I didn't want her or them to hate me. What could I even say? There was nothing I could pin down exactly, beyond 'we don't get on', and that wasn't true because a lot of the time we did. It would be a mystery to Rachel. Give it time, she would say; we do get on; we do have things in common.

And a lot of me wasn't sure it would be right: why would I want to give up on this – someone who was prepared to take that chance on me? Perhaps it wasn't perfect, but what did I want from a relationship? Nothing was ever perfect, and it was stupid to expect that or even look for it. I should just be grateful I had someone who wanted me. That was a huge bonus. The rest, I could work on.

'The next station is Shipley. Shipley is the next station.'

Deep down I knew that I would stay with her, and my thoughts were circling that uncomfortable truth like an animal caught in a trap. Was it sensible? Was I selling myself short? I wanted to get up and run.

It's not right. It's not—

But what *wasn't* it, exactly? What I'd been promised in fairytales?

The train rattled out of Shipley and bore down on the edge of the city and I knew, as we approached the final station, that I was going to continue to see Rachel even though I didn't want to. And then, as we slowed, I decided the opposite. We were going to break up. And that was how it went: a circling of decision, with my mind changing and shifting with each clack of the tracks. As we came to a halt it ticked back and forth increasingly slowly. Split up. Stay together.

Split up.

Stay together.

'The train terminates at this stop.'

Everybody started to get up, to get their things together. The carriage was full of the sound of bags scraping off the luggage racks; the aisle, with bodies stretching and shifting. The politely tense commotion of a journey coming to its end. It was almost a competition, and I always avoided it.

Split up.

I stayed sitting down while everyone around me rummaged and shuffled, side-stepped and squeezed out in between people who would quite clearly love to kill everyone in their way.

But not Rachel. She was just sitting there. She'd woken up, but she still looked sleepy as she gave me a bleary-eyed smile. I got the impression that right now the borderline between the train and her bed was a little blurry, and suddenly there was something quite sweet about that. I smiled back.

'Hey,' she said.

'Hey.'

And then – without warning – she did what I'd wanted her to do all along: she rested her head on my shoulder and her loosely curled hand on my thigh. All around us, people were fighting to get off, and it was at this point that she'd finally decided to touch me, lean on me. She wasn't getting up and pressing me to move into the throng, but doing the exact opposite and keeping me seated. Maybe another day she would have got up. But that day it hadn't even entered her head; she'd just leaned against me because she wanted to.

Stay together.

So we sat like that for a bit. I put my hand on hers and gave it a squeeze. When the aisle was half-empty, Rachel turned her hand round and squeezed mine in return, and then she started to gather herself upright.

'Come on, then.'

'Yeah,' I said.

That was how it all started with Rachel. Not when I met her (that had been in a bar, where she'd been both startlingly and refreshingly indifferent to everyone, including me when I started speaking to her) but when I made the decision that the relationship was worth sticking with. Not because she lit up my life or because I was inspired by her, and not because it was perfect.

But simply because . . . she wanted me. And she clearly had something about her that was worth a lot. It felt like it should be enough to work with.

And as the months passed, I realised with some relief that it had been the right choice. Everything relaxed. We both let down those everyday guards that we hadn't been aware we'd had, and we accepted our mutual baggage: kicked it around a bit, got an idea of the shape and heft. Within a year, I couldn't imagine a life without her, and I know that she felt the same because even now, four months after we'd split up, she was finding it difficult.

The problem was the different feelings inside me at the time that led me to make that choice. I was telling myself that I needed to accept what I had, when I should have been appreciating the plain truth that there *was* nothing better. There are always problems. Nothing is perfect; every relationship requires effort and compromise. By not understanding that, I was setting myself up for a fall when someone came along who seemed to fulfil an ideal that only existed in my own head.

It's the same as a wound. Unless you get the bullet out, the skin might heal over the metal but the bullet's always there. You get these people sometimes: they live with shrapnel close to their spine or in their head, and there's always the danger that something might shift slightly and then suddenly everything's in jeopardy. My self-doubt was a little like that. I should have got rid of it somehow, and then perhaps everything would have been fine. I would have known that what I had with Rachel was as good as it gets, rather than having the dumb idea that it was just as good as it gets for me. But I didn't. And so when Lucy came along she shifted me, moved me, and everything that was sealed away inside began to rip.

About twenty minutes later, I was considering ordering another drink – weighing the caffeine jolt against the time and irritation necessary to obtain it – when Rachel walked in through the door and made the decision for me.

I gave her an awkward smile, looked away quickly, and then stood up and made my way over to the counter simply to give my body something to do.

'Another cappuccino.'

She joined me.

'Make it two,' she said. 'Hi.'

'Hi.'

In preparation for the meeting, she was wearing war clothes: things I hadn't seen before, very obviously bought in the time since I'd left. A smart black coat, down to her thighs. A dark blue crop-top. Short black skirt. Boots. I'd never seen her wearing anything like it. Change and experimentation are good, of course – but there are subtle gestures that reveal quiet confidence, and then there are gestures so dripping with overt meaning that they flip over and become the opposite. This seemed in danger of being one of those.

'You look nice,' I said.

'Thanks.'

I didn't know exactly what she meant by her response, but that was nothing new: everything we'd said to each other since the split had been subject to intense coding, both real and imagined. Conversations could suddenly veer off on dangerous tangents that neither of us had seen coming. Thanks, I know. Thanks for noticing. Thanks a lot.

I took my seat and she sat down opposite me.

'I didn't know you liked cappuccino,' I said, when the waiter finally brought our coffees.

She shook a packet of sugar, tore it and poured a hiss of it into her drink. It rested on the surface, and then began to sink into the foam.

'There's a lot about me you don't know.'

'Probably.'

She stirred the coffee and then took a sip.

'Thanks for taking time out from your busy schedule,' she said. 'I appreciate it.'

'No problem.'

'I want to talk about things.'

'What things?'

'The house, I suppose. Us.'

And then her resolve went – just like that. That one word kicked the legs out from under her, and her face crumpled like tissue. Without thinking, I reached out to touch her arm.

'Don't.' She almost flinched away. 'Don't fucking touch me, please.'

'Okay.' I drew back. 'I'm sorry.'

'You should be.'

She took a handkerchief from her bag and blew her nose. Then she swallowed back all the questions and accusations that were swarming to come out and returned to the script.

'I want the rest of your things out.'

'Okay.'

'I need you to get rid of them. Everywhere I look I see you. It's driving me insane.'

'Okay. I understand.'

'No you don't. You have no idea.'

The rest of the coffee shop receded from my consciousness – faded out to white as I concentrated on her. My skin was crawling at being the focus of so much awful emotion.

I'd been back to the house once since I'd left, when I was sure that she wouldn't be there. I'd needed a couple of disks that I'd forgotten the first time. Walking into the kitchen, I'd been shocked – I literally stopped in my tracks. Nothing was clean. There were empty packets everywhere. Empty bottles. The front room was a real mess: papers all over the floor, plates and old cups resting in piles and short towers, more bottles and glasses. The air had been grey and the house had seemed unwell, as though it was dying of some wasting disease. I'd wanted to do something to clean it up, but knew that there was nowhere to start and no point anyway. I got the disks and left, and I went home and cried for hours.

The hatred in her voice disappeared slightly.

'I love you so much.'

I just sat there and looked at the table. That was the way it had to be: just put my head down and get through it. One word in front of another.

'I just want you to love me,' she said quietly, 'and I don't understand why you don't.'

I touched the lip of my mug.

'That's all.' Her voice had reduced itself to a pained, embarrassed whisper. 'I'm sorry. I didn't want to be like this. I just love you.'

Closed my eyes.

'Rachel – '

'I know. I know.'

'I wish there was something I could say.'

'There is. You're just not going to.'

So I let her compose herself instead. After a moment, she said, 'I just don't understand.'

'I know.'

'But anyway. That's life, isn't it.' She shook herself a little, suddenly under control again. She'd always been good at that. 'I've said that I want your stuff out.'

'Yes.'

'But that doesn't mean I don't still want you.'

I looked at her. The hard ferocity in her face was totally at odds with what she'd just said. And she didn't still want me – how could she? If anything, she wanted things as they used to be – she wanted to be able to unwind the last four months, take them back and play everything differently. She wanted the me that had existed in the years up until that moment I'd told her I wasn't in love with her anymore. This me, she hated.

There are some things you do that you can't take back – like killing a man, or telling someone you don't love them anymore. A relationship is like a branch that's grown thick and strong over time. You can't have your partner snap that in half, and then just lay the two pieces next to each other and expect them to be whole again. However much glue you use, the original thing is always gone for ever.

She said, 'Will you do me a favour?'

'If I can.'

'It's not difficult.'

I didn't say anything.

'If you change your mind, you've got to let me know.'

I didn't say anything.

'Even if I'm married with kids. Well, no, maybe not if I have kids. But if I'm married, or with someone else, then you have to let me know.'

'Okay.'

'Because you're the love of my life. I want to make you happy.'

I closed my eyes again.

The worst thing was that I could imagine her planning this. That's what you do when you're hurt and want to change something. I would have bet money that she'd lain awake and run this scenario through her head, thinking very carefully about what she needed to say to convince me. And in her mind it would have worked. She would have settled on a script of exactly the right words.

I could imagine this, because I'd done it myself for Lucy.

Rachel said, 'And I always want to be with you. And I always will want to.'

With Lucy, when the hurt got too much, I'd write her an email. And I'd work on this fucking thing for hours. When I'd finished, it would say everything I wanted to say. It would, in fact, be as eloquent and convincing a piece of personal propaganda as had ever been committed to paper. But even as I was writing, I'd know that it wasn't really about persuading her to be with me. It was more about the fantasy of it: putting reality out of my head for an evening and imagining that things might be different. I'd let myself believe that she would read it, realise how deeply I loved her and want to be with me. Stupid, because if that was ever going to happen then it wouldn't matter what I wrote, but stupidity wasn't the point – it was always the solitary writing that was important: the act of imagination that twisted a few painful hours and made me feel less lonely. Then I'd press *send mail* and wish that I hadn't. The letter was gone then, and I'd realise how imperfect it had been. Days without a reply would follow, and I'd feel ashamed of myself and vow never to do it again.

'Okay,' I said to Rachel. 'I promise.'

I imagined her going home from the coffee shop and wondering which words she should have used instead — what the real magic ones had been. And then she'd come up with new ones, definitely magic this time, and want to see me again. She'd done this before. And I still wrote emails to Lucy.

'I'm sorry.' Rachel's chair scraped, and I opened my eyes. 'I've got to go.'

'Rachel—'

'No. I don't want to see you again.'

And she was gone, starting to hide her face and then deciding why the fuck should she bother. I watched her go, forcing myself to feel blank. When the door to the café closed, I turned back to the table and slowly drank my coffee: it had been expensive, after all. Not to mention so bastard time-consuming to come by.

I finished and left. The grey sky was beginning to darken: shadows deepening within shadows in clouds of damp pollution that you could taste at ground level. It was going to rain again soon. Maybe I had time to get to the university and start digging, but I thought: *fuck it*. I'd done enough for today, and it wasn't as if anybody gave a shit anyway.

I bought a bottle of vodka from an unfamiliar liquor store, and then stood in line for a late tram, getting slowly soaked by the first few stinging sheets of rain, but not really noticing or caring.

I left the brief file I was building on Alison on the table, and spent most of the evening on the computer, getting steadily drunk while I checked out a few removal agencies and storage companies. Apparently, my stuff was driving Rachel insane, and so it would have to be put somewhere. But I couldn't actually think what else I owned back at the house — never mind

64

whether I wanted it badly enough to care about what happened to it. The somewhere it was going to be put could be the rubbish tip for all I cared right now.

To be honest, the search was more just to give myself something to do while I was drinking. Just an excuse. An empty, pointless thing that would make the hours go by until I could go to sleep.

But when I'd searched as much as I could, I did something even more stupid than drinking – I got out the letters that Rachel had written me. I'd sent Lucy text messages and emails, but Rachel had never done that with me. It had always been face-to-face meetings and eloquent, handwritten letters that she'd give to me as she was leaving. I read through one of them now, finding the passage that my drunken mind had convinced me I wanted to read.

I don't think I know much, but I know that you always told me how much you loved me, and I always believed you. It made me feel happy and secure. I'm sorry if I did something wrong. If I did, I don't know what it was but I'd do anything to change it. I just can't believe that the love you had for me has gone. I think love changes because it has to. I don't feel the same about you as I did when we met, but my love for you has grown deeper as it's altered, and it's become something more wonderful. I think that if you look in your heart you'll realise that though a lot of that initial burst has disappeared you do still love me and you've given up everything in search of something else that's not really important. I understand and it's okay. But please come home.

Most of the vodka went, which is bad. But I didn't leave the flat and spend a vast amount of money in an overpriced club, and I didn't shoot at anyone, so I don't think it's fair to see the evening as a complete failure of character.

CHAPTER FIVE

The next day, a vague sense of impending and possibly even present hangover kept me in bed until nearly midday. I hadn't been sure whether the storm was approaching or retreating; hopefully I'd been asleep for the worst of it and could have safely come out from beneath the covers, but I erred on the side of caution. By one o'clock I was fed, washed and watered. Two coffees down and I was ready to face the world. Whether I was ready to face the university was more open to question.

Horse is the university district. The main campus takes up most of the centre: a sprawl of departmental buildings and walkways mixed in with subsidised shops and cheap accommodation. It is constantly evolving as new structures are added, and so the architecture is diverse and odd, with glistening new blocks nestling in between archaic stone buildings, next to abandoned churches that had been converted into cafés and bars. Directly surrounding the campus, there is a pedestrian precinct of charity shops, cafés, take-aways, chemists and bars; and then this deteriorates slowly as you reach the outskirts of the district – except to the west, where you find the markets and ethnic stores that segue slowly into the classier commerce of Elephant. At the other three edges of Horse, the shops give way to small estates: thin streets filled with back-to-backs and terraces; occasional patches of more middle-class semis. That was where I lived: close to the district's eastern border with Wasp.

There is a real cultural mix in these streets, which I liked, but because the student-to-local ratio is split roughly fifty-fifty there can often be trouble. The locals tend to be quite poor – and of course the students are too, but they're also generally young, loud and prone to partying like fuckers. The adult delights of Wasp are, after all, only a brief tram ride away. So people who have lived in the area all their lives have seen house prices driven up and their streets scattered with litter and vomit, and have been woken up in the early hours of the morning by people pissing against their hedges. Factor in a few posh accents and a general lack of self-awareness, and you can understand why the uneasy truce between the two populations was sometimes broken.

I took a deep breath and set off.

Ten minutes later, I could see Parkinson Tower and I knew I was getting close to the main campus. I was already beginning to feel the frustration build. At other times of year, students moved very slowly, but at least you knew where you were: you could trundle along on the same treadmill of lethargy, or else you could plot a course and dodge and weave along at the approximate pace of a normal human being. But this was exam time and so all bets were off. Some clusters of people were walking quickly, determined to arrive at their departments on time, while others were meandering, staring at bits of paper in last-ditch attempts to learn things; and yet more sections of the stream had clotted into groups that were smiling and hugging each other and generally unaware of anyone they might be in the way of. A few people were sitting on the edges of pavements, crying. Bars were full, and I found that I wanted to be in one.

Instead – as I reached the campus – I consulted a series of enormous but largely uninformative wall-mounted maps, relied a little on blind chance and eventually located the Fine Art department. It was based in one of the newest buildings on campus: a bright, shining block of glass and brick that was almost intimidating in its cleanliness. The automatic doors seemed to pause for a second before deciding to let me in; and while that might have been my imagination, the frostiness at reception certainly wasn't.

'No,' she said.

'No?'

The three secretaries working behind a glass screen in the main office were bathed in poor light from a slatted window somewhere behind them. It was a strange atmosphere: everything looked slightly off-colour and the only real sound was that of fingers tapping on keyboards. Two of the secretaries were studiously ignoring me, working away. They were deferring to the third, who was young and pretty in an icy sort of way – or might have been, if her smile had gone anywhere near her eyes. When I'd rung the bell, her name had been Marie and how could she help? Presumably her name hadn't changed, but her attitude had certainly shifted a few miles.

'We can't give out information about students,' she told me.

I gave her my most charming smile. As my badge had already been produced and had failed to impress, the smile was all I had left, although I supposed there was still the gun.

'Could you at least tell me who her personal tutor was?'

'Not even that.'

'Not even that,' I said, leaning away from the counter and tapping it gently. 'Thank you. You've been very helpful.'

'And you're very welcome.'

To be fair, I hadn't expected any different, what with data protection laws being what they were. I could be a mad parent or a vengeful ex-lover or even – god forbid – not a cop at all. And there would be legal hell to pay if the secretary had said, 'Yes, she's in room six,' and then I went off and killed her. No – I'd expected that I would need a warrant to get information out of them, and I wasn't likely to get one. Fortunately, I knew from previous investigations that there were easier – if slightly less ethical – options available to me.

A little over twenty minutes later, I was sitting in one of the university's computer rooms. Despite the fact that exams were underway, it was relatively busy, with rows of students typing, the noise undercut by the low, constant hum of the network. A few people were talking quietly, and there was an occasional sniff from someone waiting by the printer, but that was about it. I didn't like it in here: it was lit to clinical levels by artificial strip-bulbs in the mirrored ceiling, as though an operation was about to be performed. The air smelled of electricity, plastic and body odour.

I tapped a few keys quickly and logged in to the system.

The way computer accounts work at university is this: everybody gets one – staff and students – and because every single computer on campus is connected to a central server, you can log in on any of them and still have access to your own files – essays, spread-sheets, databases, internet bookmarks, emails – the

70

works. Anything that Alison Sheldon had been working on – and anyone she had been writing to or receiving email from – should still be available. Ten minutes logged into her account would tell me more than Marie-how-can-I-help-you could in two hours.

Breaking into a student's account is pretty simple. People forget their passwords all the time and so there needs to be some system in place for confirming your identity and then giving out the information you need to get into your mail. Fortunately, it's automated. All you need is your student identification number and your date of birth – you have those, and any computer you sit down at will happily remind you of your password. I had this information for Alison from her Missing Persons Report. Her password, if you're interested, was *gtwxkt*.

Once logged in, I began my search in her essay folder, but then realised quickly that there was no hope of reviewing all the material now: there was simply too much, and most of it looked irrelevant. But I'd brought a few blank disks with me, and so I copied everything just to be on the safe side. If there was nothing on television one night, at least I'd never be lost for something to read.

Next, I opened up her email account. Hopefully it would give me some kind of contact details for any friends not mentioned in the report, and also – if I was very lucky – there might be messages from the man she'd been seeing in the weeks leading up to her murder. But when the mail program loaded, I was met by an empty inbox: *No new messages* it told me, in a panel down the left-hand side, and underneath that: *No read messages*. Which was unusual, to say the least, because free email was one of the perks of university life, and usually the easiest way to keep in touch with absent friends. It wasn't just that she'd kept her inbox tidy, either – there weren't even any old-message folders. It was as though she'd never used it.

I frowned mentally. Okay – so perhaps she'd used an internet-based account for some reason. I had one myself; they were handy because it meant you could access your mail from anywhere in the world. But it was still odd that she hadn't used the university one at all. It was so nice and easy – right there on the desktop.

I double-clicked the internet browser icon to see if I could check what sites she'd been logging into. But, just like the email, it was empty.

No bookmarks; no drop-down URLs; no history.

My mental frown deepened. A student who hadn't surfed the internet? I looked around the room. At least half of the people in here were casual surfers, with a steady queue waiting to replace them. But apparently Alison never had. It felt like bullshit.

I thought it through, tapping my finger absently on the mouse. Perhaps Alison had cleared it all out before she was killed, because she was frightened of something or somebody. But that didn't sit well or make much sense – why would she bother? If you're in danger, you don't waste time clearing your email: you just get the fuck away from wherever you are. The net would probably be the last thing on your mind. But it was still possible.

If not Alison, Sean might have erased the data. It was a reasonably safe assumption that he'd been here before me and so I couldn't rule it out, but I also couldn't think why he would. Like the other explanations, it didn't seem right.

The third possibility was that someone else had logged in as Alison and methodically removed any evidence that had been there.

I had no way of knowing, but that idea felt more right than the others.

So, how thorough would they have been? It was a long-shot, but I found the email folder on the computer's hard drive and copied every non-program file I found there onto a second disk. Sometimes deleted mail could still be read, assuming you had a little technical knowledge. I didn't have that knowledge personally, but life can throw all sorts of odd people into your path.

I shut down the internet and was about to log out and leave when a pop-up window appeared and caught my eye for a moment. Pop-ups aren't unusual: there are loads of web pages where, when you close them down, they automatically open a new page. When I'd shut down the window, a page advertising a tiny camera had appeared, proclaiming that you could take pictures without anybody realising. The page was mostly taken up by a picture of a half-naked woman, posing seductively. I shook my head and closed it down, half-expecting another, but that was it. An empty desktop.

I paused.

Junk web pages.

So where was the junk email?

I opened up the mail program again, irritating the nearby queue of students, who had obviously pegged me as being about to leave and got their hopes up. Bags shifted and I heard a few sighs of annoyance.

Alison Sheldon had no junk email.

Everybody with an email account gets junk mail: it's called spam. Like cheap gold envelopes through your front door, it arrives in your inbox on a daily basis. I got maybe twenty spam mails a day, and yet Alison didn't seem to have received a single one since she'd died. Even if someone had cleared out her account very recently, there would still have been some.

I looked to see whether the account kept a record of earlier log-ins but there was nothing obvious, and so I stared at the screen for half a minute. Then, I felt a thrill of recognition, quickly opened up the *options* menu and saw it. All of Alison's mail was being forwarded to a different account. Anything that arrived in her inbox was sent to that and then immediately deleted from her university account. I'd known I was right even before I'd opened the menu. Once upon a time, I thought, I must have been a really fucking good detective.

The name of the destination account was **histmjh**, which meant it was someone in the History department with the initials mjh. Possibly another student, but I opened up the internet again anyway, heading to the History department's website. I clicked on the *Staff* tab and scrolled down the list to see if anyone there matched the initials.

Nearly halfway down: Dr Mark Harris.

There was a photograph of him too. He looked maybe thirty years old, with a smart, slightly smug face, jet black hair that had been gelled into wet tumbles hanging down as far as his eyebrows, and a smile that curled slightly – half arrogance, half seduction. I imagined his smile could shift very quickly, and that it would generally mean something very different to the girls than it did to the boys.

There was no middle initial in his profile, but his email address was *m.j.harris* and so I knew that I'd found my man. The profile was the usual mix of boring research and publication lists, but I read it through anyway. Harris had links with the Geography and Sociology departments, and his main research seemed to be based around city histories and legends. I made a few brief notes and then logged out and stood up. The students nearby breathed a sigh of relief, and my seat was taken almost instantly. Vultures. But I was too busy thinking to care.

Alison had been Fine Art – it wasn't a million miles away from History, and I figured there might even be some crossover, but it was hard to imagine a professional connection between Alison and Harris, and much easier to think about that boyfriend from the report. Harris was young and smarmily good-looking enough to have been on the radar for a girl her age, and so he seemed like a good candidate for her mystery man. *Best to keep an open mind*, I thought, as I walked out into the corridor, but the fact was that Alison's mail was all currently being forwarded to Dr Mark Harris. It was time to find out why.

I should have known better. It was the middle of a normal working day and so any self-respecting academic would be at home doing nothing. It took a little bit of time to discover this. First, I tried his office. It was just one green door on a corridor lined with them, although he had stuck a photocopy of an unfunny newspaper cartoon beneath his nameplate, and his open-door times were listed on the wall beside the door. I checked my watch. This wasn't one of them. But I knocked anyway. There was no answer, and his office sounded very quiet. So, the man was elsewhere.

The next step was to consult the timetables on the common-room noticeboard, but there was no joy to be had there either. It was exam time, so none of his lectures were running. Finally, I built myself up and went to the History department main office, and asked a rather more helpful woman than Marie where I might find Dr Mark Harris.

'Mark's working from home today,' she said. 'Can I take a message for him?'

'No, it's okay,' I said. 'Thanks.'

'Are you sure? It's no problem.'

'No – but thanks anyway.'

'Well, you might try getting in touch with him by email? That's probably best.'

'I might well do that,' I said, backing away from the counter. 'Thank you for your time.'

'You're welcome.'

She gave me a big smile, and I thought that Marie in Fine Art could take some lessons from her. But despite her friendliness, there was no way she'd have given me Harris's home address and so I hadn't risked killing the mood by asking. I'd have to find that one out on my own.

It was slightly galling to have to queue up in the computer room again but I did it anyway – and then got bored and pushed in when a terminal near me became free and allowed me to get there first. It was frowned upon, and there were a few tuts, but everybody was too polite to actually say anything. I logged in as Alison and opened up the internet.

There were a few sites I could try, and I worked my way through them – phone listings, address listings, a few of the more clandestine webpages – but Harris was ex-directory or unavailable on all of them. The police department's intranet would list him, but unfortunately my username and password had been revoked.

If I couldn't do it any other way, I thought, perhaps I could go to Rosh or Lucy.

In the thick of things, I hadn't really thought about Lucy all day, and so I got my phone out now to check for messages. I would have felt the vibration if I'd been sent anything, but I was still hoping for a *1 message received* notice and still disappointed to see just the time and date. No new messages. I put the phone back in my pocket, felt suddenly melancholy and turned back to the computer.

There was a website address I knew off by heart, and I typed it now and hit *go*. The screen was blank and thoughtful for a moment as the page loaded slowly. About a minute later there he was, staring out at me.

His name was Rich. He was a little older than I was. Not particularly good-looking. Average build. This was his company's website, and Rich's professional appearance gave away none of the wonderful sense of humour he undoubtedly possessed. I visited this page quite often, always as a form of mild self-torture. Four months ago, I'd left Rachel because I felt I wanted to be with Lucy instead. But Lucy ended our affair and picked this man, Rich, over me.

I would have hated him but I couldn't quite bring myself to do it. Despite the things I'd done to people in my life, hate had always been a difficult emotion for me; I could generate it, but it dissipated quickly. For a lot of people, hate is a flowchart emotion: somebody hurts them – fuck the reason – and they hate them for it; but I could never work like that. Some of the time I hated Rich, but then my mind kept taking steps back and forcing me to see the whole situation: to turn it around and feel the different angles. Most of them glinted with tragedy, but not all of that was mine.

Hatred is something very personal that you only ever feel in close-up, when you don't take other people's feelings into account. Whenever you see things from a distance, it's not possible to sustain it. Not for me, anyway. For example, the kids who beat that guy up the night before last – at the time, I hated them for what they'd done. But if you move back a bit and watch them growing up, and listen to their hopes and dreams, try to understand everything that blocks and hurts them, then it all changes. The sad contradiction behind every single crime is that hardly anybody thinks they're a bad person. We're all products of this fucking city, acting as best we can with what we've been given; and whatever we do, there's everything we've done and everything we've had done to us pushing it along from behind.

Rich and Lucy were just trying to make themselves happy, stumbling along like the rest of us.

Fuck it.

I logged out and left.

The walk back through Horse was easier: it was later on in the afternoon now and there were fewer students, less overall hassle. The pubs and bars were getting fuller and noisier, but that was okay and I didn't resent it so much now. And it was colder too, so people weren't just hanging around. I phased it all out and tried to think about what, if anything, I'd learned. I still knew very little, although I now had some ideas to kick around and see if they squealed. There was Harris to follow up, and there were Alison's friends to visit. But first, I would go home, get washed and changed, and top up my lagging caffeine reserves.

By the time I reached the edge of Horse, the melancholy seemed to have lifted slightly. There were things to do, and after months of inactivity it felt good to have some kind of purpose again.

But when I got home, there was another package waiting for me.

CHAPTER SIX

It was a different type of envelope, and it had my name written in neat letters across the front in handwriting I didn't recognise. I opened it downstairs and found a video inside, with no label and no letter of explanation. Perhaps what was on it would be explanation enough. I took it upstairs, slotted it into my old deck and pressed play.

There were a few seconds of blank screen, and then the clip started running. My first impression was that the picture was fuzzy and unprofessional, but the quality was good enough for me to see what was happening. My second thought was that I didn't like it.

It was a static shot of a room, although as the seconds crept by the camera wobbled a little, as though it was on a cheap tripod resting on uneven floorboards and people were moving about nearby. But there was nobody in shot. The room itself was bare, derelict and full of sick-looking air. Most of the paper had been stripped from the mouldy walls, and the plaster beneath was pitted and stained and scratched and scarred – covered in more graffiti than the room knew what to do with. The walls were shouting a thousand scrawled arguments to each other, whispering and muttering a thousand more.

The quality of the picture dipped. A saturation of colour occurred, disrupted by flickering lines of blurry black and white. Then it returned to normal.

Maybe it was the quality, or perhaps it was that I'd only ever seen the place spot-lit before now, but it took me a few moments to recognise where it was. When I did, I hit pause and sat back on the bed, feeling the air hum a little. It was the room where Sean and I had found Alison's body.

The pause was unsteady. A wave of incoherence rolled steadily up the screen.

Fuck. Even though it was just an empty room – lit by a bulb hanging down from above – it was a haunted place for me. Anyone looking at it would have known that it was a killing room: a place full of dead moths and flies and lice; a place where everything was rotting.

I looked at the envelope again but I didn't touch it. There were prints to be considered, although whoever had sent this had no doubt been very careful. There were no visible marks apart from the name. No address. Like the letter from Sean, it had been hand-delivered. I looked up again. The video was fluttering, making a noise like a dog shaking water from itself.

I pressed play. The screen fuzzed up for a second as the video pulled itself together, and then it cleared. The empty room. I knew that I was going to see something awful. Alison's murder, perhaps. Or something else altogether.

There was no sound – the tape had been made without a microphone. Also, I thought, the light. My mind was picking the scene apart, turning it around. There was a bulb hanging from the ceiling. But when we'd found Alison, there had been an empty socket.

Three figures moved into view, startling me. There were two big men, both dressed in black, on either side of another man, who was naked and who seemed barely able to stand by himself. Quickly, they shoved him towards the opposite corner and moved back out of view.

Not Alison, then.

The naked man stumbled a little but kept his footing. He was shivering; hugging himself. He was well-muscled, but the light from above made him look pale as milk: weak and vulnerable. After a moment, he turned around to face the camera, almost directly in the centre of the frame. It was Sean. Staring at me and looking as terrified as I'd ever seen a person look.

I made some kind of noise, sat forward on the bed. Reached out towards the screen to take something that wasn't there, and then withdrew my hand. It was shaking as I brought it to my mouth.

Before Sean had time to react, the two other men moved back into view. They were wearing balaclavas and carrying what looked like baseball bats. The man on the left side of the screen took a good, two-handed grip and swung as hard as he could. Sean saw it coming of course – he held his arms up in front of his face, and they took the full force. I saw him scream, even though I couldn't hear it. The other man came in quickly, swinging the bat into Sean's side. His defensive huddle collapsed, and then the first man hit again, catching him on the top of the shoulder and taking him down to the floor.

My whole body was shaking. I had the controller in my hand, my thumb hovering over *pause*, and I wanted so badly to press it. But that would only stop the video.

The men took it in turns: bang, bang, bang. I felt each one. They had to keep stepping back and taking better grips on the bats. Sean maintained a feeble defence for as long as he could, with his body stubbornly refusing to stop fighting for life, but then a blow to the head put him flat on his back, semi-conscious. With his arms down by his side, fingers broken, there was nothing to stop them. They took massive, overhead swings that made the camera shake, and me along with it.

The video went on for another minute. By the end of it, his head was ruined, his eyes were gone, his jaw was half off. But even then, he was still moving slightly: his fingers tapping on the floorboards. Watching him, I couldn't imagine what was going on in his mind. Perhaps nothing; perhaps just electrical impulses still running half-heartedly through ruined circuitry. One of the men aimed more carefully and really hit him hard: a killing shot. Sean's body went slack and lifeless. The clawing stopped.

The two men stood in shot for a second, breathing heavily, and then exchanged a few words. After a moment, one of them moved out of view. The camera shook a little more aggressively and then the scene cut to white noise. I knew that something inside me was going to snap, but I also knew I had to keep it together for a little longer. There might be more. So I visual-searched the remaining hour of videotape, but it was all blank. That was the end.

Then, I lost it entirely.

Frustration. The feeling of needing to run as fast as you can but being forced to walk very slowly; when there's simply too much space and not enough time between you and where you urgently need to be. I had frustration now in spades.

The tram was so slow that I had to resist the urge to stick the barrel of my gun in the driver's ear and tell him to fucking step on it. But running was out of the question, even if the mindless exercise of it would have helped, so I was stuck on public transport: bottled up in an oppressive, bright cannister that was trundling painfully slowly through the city.

Early evening had thickened into night. The sky was blue-black, and the windows of the tram gave back pale reflections of the interior: people nodding asleep; people hanging on to overhead bars. And me – staring blankly out at dark buildings I could hardly see, feeling frustration and hiding it behind a face full of hate. There was no difficulty generating it now. It must have been coming off me in waves.

We skirted the main square at one point, and everyone craned their necks a little to check out the boxing ring. It was only a few days away, I supposed. The square would be crammed with people, all watching fighters representing the city's districts hammering the crap out of each other all day. The ring had actually been there for over a week now, but they were still working on the scaffolding for the speaker system and the big screen. The ring itself was spot-lit at night and everybody on the tram seemed fascinated by it. I looked away. Gritted my teeth. Thought: *come on.*

I got out on the edge of Bull, into air that was cold and vivid: a slap in the face. The doors shushed closed behind me and the tram chugged away into the night. After a moment, I was left with the distant clanking of machinery. It was the sound of enormous steam hammers pounding the ground, but the faraway noise of it was strangely muffled by the blocky spread of abandoned factories, foundries and mills. The district bulges off the edge of the city like a tumour. The businesses build up the ground, burn it down again and move ever outwards.

Now I could run.

I had the gun out of my pocket, and the safety off,

and when I started running it was like a switch had been thrown inside me. It was lucky that there was nobody around. Sections of the video clip kept looping and repeating in my head, with fragments of scenes flashing up. Now that I was running, frustration had turned to panic.

It took five minutes to get to the house, and I didn't see a single person the whole time. By the time I arrived, the night sky had blackened, spread and opened; rain had started to fall. Not a heavy shower, but persistent, and it smelled slightly of chemicals: bleach and ethanol. The street looked like dark rubber. At the house itself, the wood of the boards and timber was soaked. I flicked on the torch I'd brought with me and clambered carefully through the ruins of the front door.

The walls on the ground floor were shiny with rain, rolling down from the levels above, and in the few places where the paper remained it was raised up in boils of damp. I padded along the corridor, and the floorboards felt soft beneath my feet. The building was in an advanced state of decay – far more deteriorated than my first visit. And again, I had the impression that somebody was here with me, except this time it was more likely. The person who sent me the clip would have expected me to come. So I made my way up the weak stairs slowly, ready and eager to unload a full clip into anything stupid enough to move.

I stopped on the landing. The door at the far end of the corridor was closed, but outlined with soft yellow light. Somebody had left the bulb switched on for me. Either that, or someone was in there right now.

Someone other than Sean anyway.

Three other doors on the corridor. One was boarded up tight, but the other two were slightly ajar and the insides of the rooms were dark. Real problems. I hesitated for about a second, and then decided to head straight on: deep down, it didn't really feel like there was anybody waiting for me in here. It was just the house, with its heavy memories. You walk into a place like that, you can't help but feel them.

A deep breath, and then I moved.

Straight for the end room, kicking the door open – but not so hard that it bounced off the wall and shut again – my gun up in front, trigger already half pulled. But the room was empty. No body on the floor. I swept it and then moved in, turning on my heels to cover the area behind the door. Still nothing. Nobody waiting here. Nothing.

I closed the door behind me, shutting myself off from the other rooms in the house.

No body. But there was a lot of dried blood on the floorboards, and spatters all over the walls, too. Remnants of mould, as well. After all, this was an abandoned house; Alison's body had been taken away for burial but nobody had come in to clean up afterwards. And now Sean. This room was death upon death, like some kind of trap people wandered into. Unlike Alison, however, the people who had beaten Sean to death had taken his body away with them. He might never be found or receive a proper burial. Insult to injury.

The reality of what I'd seen hit me again, and I felt like sliding down the wall and collapsing. Suddenly, it felt as though there was nobody within a hundred miles of me: nothing but a spread of empty houses and rusting factories; pistons moving through pointless, automated arcs and machines turning this way and that in the distance. I imagined that the noise of it was echoing away, diminishing from the hard, anvil sound of metal upon metal until it became as quiet as falling snow by the time it reached the city or the night sky or the hills in the distance. I could have walked outside the house and screamed, and no one would have heard.

But instead of sitting down, I forced myself to take in the room: to see all the details and try to make sense of it all. There wasn't much, and I knew my mind was a little too strained for anything like a careful analysis: that would come later. But at least one thing caught my eye. I walked over to the far corner of the room, stepping over the section where Sean had been killed, and crouched down carefully to examine the wall, tilting my head a little to match the slight incline of the writing there. There was some newer graffiti, written in what looked like blood.

Eli is rising.

I didn't know what it meant, but there was something familiar about it.

I stood up, just as I felt the vibration in my pocket. A text message, now of all times. I took out the phone, expecting to see my wife's name there, but instead it was Lucy. I frowned and pressed the *read message* option.

i hope ur ok. pls stp hurting. im sorry about rich. hope u undrstnd. didn't mean to hurt u. :(

She certainly picked her moments. I didn't know how long it had been since she'd last been in touch, or how many plaintive messages I'd sent to her in the meantime, and this was when she'd finally replied. If she hadn't, then things might have panned out differently.

I typed a reply: *no am not ok. need u n rosh. its sean.*

I gave her the address and a few more details. Then – finally – I found a clean patch of floor and sat down to wait.

CHAPTER SEVEN

The relationship I had with Lucy was founded on sex and murder. Put like that, I know it sounds bad. And it was bad, too, not least because I was married to Rachel the whole time.

The most that can be said in my defence is that at least Rachel never knew, as it would have hurt her even more. As 'most's go, I appreciate that's really not much, but she didn't deserve to feel any pain at all, let alone the extra dose that knowing would have given her. My wife never did anything wrong. When I told her it was over between us it came as a complete shock; it literally knocked the air out of her the way a punch would. It's awful to fall out of love with someone; it's the kind of thing you don't want to talk about when it's happening, and then one day you realise that it's simply too late. It's hard for the other person to understand, as well. But as hard and confusing as it must have been for Rachel, knowing the real reason would have been far worse.

It was after work. We were on a night out, a group of us, drinking in cop places where we could cut loose a little. One of us was escaping – retiring – and we were seeing him off in fine style: drinking, singing and dancing, laughing like lunatics. The air was thick with smoke and the music was loud enough to set it moving. We were all drunk, and – thinking back – it was the last time Sean ever came out with us before he disappeared.

Late on, someone decided we should all head out to a nearby restaurant for a curry and so we did, but for some reason Lucy and I walked a little more slowly than everyone else and ended up lagging behind. We were chatting and didn't really notice. That was when she told me she liked me, and later on that night I kissed her. A couple of weeks later, it happened again. It built up from there. Pretty soon we were sleeping together.

The guilt I felt about sex with Lucy was exactly the same as the guilt I felt about the murders we'd committed together. I was sure deep down that it was wrong, because it *felt* wrong. My gut told me that there was no grey area here; no doubt. But I managed to overcome that feeling with cool logic. I was like someone trying to give up smoking and telling himself that just one won't hurt. I found excuses because I wanted to. If nobody knew about it, I figured, then nobody could get hurt. That kind of shit. I'd try to imagine the sum of happiness in the world and I'd argue that – as things stood – my actions had actually increased that sum. It made a kind of sense. But of course, in the long term, I was ruining everybody's happiness, and pretty soon things wouldn't be standing at all.

Why did I do it? Because I was stupid.

Here's one thing, though. During the day, Lucy was as hard as they come: cool, detached, confident, cynical. Loads of cops wanted her, but each of them knew in their gut that they didn't stand a chance of getting anywhere near her. So it made me feel strange inside that she chose me – out of everyone that she could have. It made me feel special, happy. And even more so, because when we were together she let her guard down. Being with her was like watching something thaw. You could see the tentative steps she took towards affection, towards openness. When you see someone cut most people dead – and if we're honest, scare the living shit out of them – it's quite amazing when they behave so differently with you: opening up, giving you access, handing you these sharp emotional weapons that you could use to hurt them and trusting that you won't.

So to begin with, perhaps because she made me feel special, I was too weak and stupid to say no. And then, as time went on, that weakness began to be coupled with a desire not to hurt her. And all of it was tinged through with fear: I felt out of control and started to quietly panic about everything, as though my life was a balancing act that was going to topple. One time, I told Lucy that I would never leave Rachel and she got mad with me – not because of what I'd said, but because I'd felt the need to say it at all. Over and over again, she told me: *I'm not an idiot and I know it's not going anywhere. I just like you and want you.*

And so it carried on for a while. I was worried that I was taking advantage of her. When she thawed enough, it was clear that she was unhappy and sad. But it was stupid of me to imagine she didn't know exactly what she was doing. Even more dumb was this: I was scared that she'd fall in love with me and get hurt. I was assuming that would be the way it worked: her falling for me; me remaining ambivalent; me wondering why these pesky women couldn't separate sex from love, as I so obviously could. And of course, my assumption turned out to be more than a little back-to-front.

To explain what happened, I need to break a promise.

*

'Have you ever loved anyone?' I asked Lucy one day.

It was two weeks after Sean had vanished and the investigation into Alison's murder had stalled, and Lucy and I were in a cheap hotel room at the edge of the city, lying in a bed that was approaching double in size without quite getting there. We were naked, with sweat drying on us, and Lucy was smoking a cigarette. It was dark outside, but still early enough for me to be out for a drink after work with colleagues, or working late ... or whatever, really. If I needed an excuse, I'd think of one later. Right then, I wasn't thinking of much.

Cars were rushing past the window: their tyres crackled on the wet tarmac outside; their headlights came through the cheap, pale curtains and went quickly around the room in a sinister circle.

'Yes,' she said.

I knew it wasn't me, but I was stupid enough to think it might be.

I said, 'Who?'

'No, it's weird. You'll think I'm strange.'

'I already think you're strange,' I said. 'That's why we get on so well.'

'Well, you might be right there.'

'Go on.'

'No. I don't know if I should tell you.'

'Don't if you don't want to.'

She smoked the cigarette until it was nearly down to the filter, and there were a few seconds of silence while she did. Two cars went past, and then she said:

'It's someone I've never slept with.'

'Okay.'

'I've never even kissed him.'

'Wow.'

'Someone I don't even see anymore.'

She stubbed the cigarette out then. Twisted it methodically into the glass base of the ashtray by the bed.

'Who?' I said.

'Can you keep a secret?'

'Sure.'

'Seriously, I mean. None of my family even know.'

'I am serious,' I said. 'I didn't even know you had any family. But I can keep a secret, I promise.'

'Okay.' But then she thought about it and shook her head. 'It's something you need to see. I can't explain it very well. I'll let you know later.'

'Wow,' I said again.

It had seemed like a simple enough question, and now I was really curious – something I would actually need to *see*. I wondered what it could be, and also whether I'd regret finding out. When you're getting to know someone, questions can open trapdoors. You fall into them – unsuspecting – and suddenly you're in a world you never knew existed. Often without a ladder.

The next day, a mid-shift break found me in an internet café, sitting in front of an old, battered monitor. I was just one person in a sea of plastic that was dotted with the tops of heads. There was no way I was risking logging in to this at home, because Rachel used the internet and she wasn't stupid. I straightened out a piece of paper in front of my mouse. There were two lines of text written on it in shitty biro, which was all she'd had in her handbag last night.

The first line was an email address: richjohnson@the-leftroom.com.

The second was the password: *truelove*.

I logged on to the account and then clicked on the inbox.

There were actually more like forty, but Lucy had
logged in and read a few over the years – reminding
herself of what she'd written. The night before, she'd
said: 'You pour your heart out to someone, taking the
time to make every word right, and then ten minutes
later you start doubting yourself and you need to go
back to check.' I'd said I understood, but back then I
didn't really. Sitting in the café, I scrolled down the list
of emails and read the headers. The messages had all
been sent from Lucy's own email account. She told me
it would be okay for me to read any of the ones that
had already been opened. The rest were just for him.

I clicked on one.

My dearest Rich, it began. *I was thinking about you
today. I know I promised not to last time, but I
couldn't stop myself. I think about you every day, every
second. Even if you're not there, you're still there.*

So – she thought about him every second. I didn't
recognise it then, but I think those first few sentences
broke my heart – like one of those mythical kung fu
strikes that you don't actually feel until a little time
after the blow lands. 'He's the only person I've ever
loved,' she'd told me the night before. 'There was never
anything physical between us, but I know that what I
felt for him was real, true love. And I've never felt
anything like it since.'

This was their history: they'd been childhood friends
– members of a mixed group that had played together
as little kids and hung out together as bigger kids.
They'd been held in place by the tight geography of
Goat's terraced streets and the glue of parental friend-
ships. Thick as thieves but much more loyal, Rich and
Lucy were always close, and there was something

between them that they both knew was special. Despite that, they never got together as a couple.

'I don't know why we didn't,' she told me, in that hotel bedroom. She was smoking again. 'I wish we had; everything would have been different then. God knows how it didn't happen. Maybe it was just bad timing – just that one of us would always be with someone else when the other was free.'

So they drifted around – never having an actual relationship, never quite landing – but they got on so well that their friendship survived intact.

'Nobody has ever made me laugh like he did. Nobody has ever made me feel so totally at ease about just being myself,' she told me. 'It's like we were designed for each other or something.'

'Nobody's designed for anybody.'

I was watching her smoke, and I was bothered despite myself. Suddenly I didn't feel so special anymore. I was just ordinary. Second place. She was making do with me when there was someone else out there she wanted more. I was married, of course, so I couldn't really complain. But even so – I realised that the flippancy of our relationship hurt a lot more now that I was on the receiving end. As she told me the story, the both of us lying there, I felt something twisting inside me. Something that was not good.

When they were seventeen, Rich's girlfriend had fallen pregnant. He was devastated; but he was a responsible kid and he listened carefully to other people, and since her parents were adamant that the couple get married he decided that they would. It was all planned quickly; the pregnancy was an undertone that was rarely mentioned. The night before the ceremony, Lucy met with Rich in their local and they sank a few beers together. Lucy hardly ever drank when she was younger, but that night she'd wanted to. She'd never felt so miserable, and had only recently begun to understand why. Over the course of the conversation, it became clear that Rich was as miserable as she was, and that they were both feeling that way for the same reason.

'If you want to run away,' he told her towards the end of the night, 'then I'll come with you.'

She didn't tell him not to be so stupid, because she wanted to say yes.

'But I couldn't,' she told me. 'His girlfriend was five months pregnant, and I just couldn't do that to her. I wish I had done now, as bad as that is, but I told him no. And I genuinely watched his heart fucking break.'

Rich married his girlfriend the next day, and he was still married to her now. They had two sons; the oldest was fifteen years old and the spitting image of his father. Lucy had been haunted by her non-relationship with Rich ever since. She had never struck me as being the kind of person who believed in souls, but she said more than once that he had been her soul-mate. *Had been*, she said; *always will be*, she meant. So I had nothing to worry about. She was never going to fall in love with me.

Because of the situation we were in and because of everything I'd said, as we were lying in the hotel room she had no idea how much this was hurting me.

'I set up that email account in his name,' she said. 'And every now and then I write to him. I know that he'll never see them, and it's stupid. But sometimes I think about sending him the address and password and letting him read what I've put there. I wonder if he's been thinking about me the whole time like I have about him.'

'Maybe he has,' I said, although I doubted it.

The last thing she said about it was, 'I know that I'll never have him, but I also know I'll never get over him.'

So, the next day I read a few of the messages, and then I logged out and went back to work. Lucy and I spoke that evening, and then after that we didn't talk about it much. On the surface, we were as close as ever, but below the surface there was something wrong, and it was all with me. I knew I should be grateful she thought enough of me to tell me what she had, but for some reason it didn't offer much consolation. From that point, the rot set in.

Over the next two weeks, I did bad things. Because she had given me the log-in details, I convinced myself that it was okay to use them. I opened the account every now and then, and each time she sent him a new message it hurt me more and more. I had nobody to blame apart from myself, of course, but the relationship started to be all I could think about. I wanted her to want me. Rachel was there the whole time, never suspecting, but she wasn't in my thoughts at all. Like I said, it was a shock to her when it finally happened. She never expected I'd be so stupid.

I hadn't seen Lucy for a couple of days, and I was feeling shit about the whole thing – more out of control than ever. It was obviously falling apart, and part of me knew that I should allow it to, return to Rachel in my head and count my blessings that she hadn't found out. But I was on a break, and I found myself sitting in a net café once again, logging in to Rich's account.

This time, it was different:

No new messages

I looked at the screen for a while, feeling the kind of

sheer, sudden panic you'd get if you were sitting there happily and a tiger walked into the room. I was very still, not wanting to move in case I made anything worse.

She's read them all, I thought after a moment, attempting to convince myself. And failing.

I clicked *Inbox* to make sure the mailbox homepage wasn't lying to me out of spite, but it wasn't. All the messages were in plain text, while unread messages were always highlighted in bold.

So either she'd read them all, or else she'd finally done what she'd always wanted and sent Rich the account details.

I clicked the *Sent Items* icon and saw that somebody had sent Lucy an email the night before. I clicked on it, read it. And of course, it was from Rich. They had arranged to meet each other on a respective break. I checked my watch and realised that they would be with each other now. Talking things over.

'I hope you'll be very happy,' I said. I logged out and left.

That night, I told Rachel that I didn't love her anymore. It was a combination of everything. I'd thought about it all day, and the conclusion I'd come to – the realisation, I suppose – was that I was in love with Lucy and I needed to tell her. I hadn't thought about Rachel all day, beyond how hard it was going to be to do this and how much I was risking. But I wanted Lucy now. If I didn't move quickly then I'd lose her for ever, and that meant I had to convince her that I was serious. I really don't know what the fuck I was thinking.

I went home and saw Rachel, and she was smiling and happy; she said hi, and came over and tried to kiss me. I hated myself at that moment more than ever, and it made me realise that – regardless of what happened with Lucy – Rachel deserved better than me and always had. And in some ways, because I kept that thought in mind, it was easier to do than I'd expected.

So Lucy and I both had news for each other the next time we met. Except that I didn't tell her, because she was so clearly happy and I didn't have the heart to do it – to her or to myself. Even though Rich was married, she found that everything she'd felt about him was still there, and she thought that he felt the same. As bad as it was, she was going to see him again that week. They would just be friends, she said. But I didn't believe her.

I'd had grand ideas about telling her I'd left Rachel, but it felt empty and pointless in light of the glow she had. It would achieve nothing. I'd known all along that she didn't love me – not like that – but I'd done it anyway. Now, all I had to cling to was that it was the right thing. If Rachel had known then she would have wanted it like this; and because she didn't it was harder for her – but that didn't change the fact that it was right. Rachel was better off without me. And when I saw that glow of happiness in Lucy, I realised that she was better off without me too.

And it's only a matter of time before you start generalising out from ideas like that and figure that everyone is. I moved out into my flat, and it took a month before I'd moved out of everything else as well.

CHAPTER EIGHT

Half an hour passed before I heard the car pull up. The noise made the walls hum slightly, and then the humming died, and then I heard two voices: a man and a woman making their way into the house. My first thought was that she'd brought Rich along with her. It was stupid, but he'd been on my mind and – despite the fact that he was still with his wife – it was possible that the two of them had been together when Lucy had got my message. But as the voices got closer, I recognised Rosh's voice, and shook my head. I'd asked her to phone him. This was all of our business, after all.

'In here,' I shouted.

'Martin?'

'In here.'

They walked in. As always, Lucy led the way – just that little bit more impatient and impetuous – with Rosh following behind: a little calmer, a little more careful. She looked exactly the same as I remembered, and there was something quite startling about that. Because her image had occupied my thoughts so totally, it was a surprise to find she actually looked like that; like if you saw a celebrity on the street. Behind her, Rosh was still Rosh. He looked like a monster out of a horror film: something that had calmed down, given up on attacking unsuspecting campers and undergone a little grooming.

They were both visibly tense as they entered, but

they relaxed a little when they saw it was only me in the room, sitting against the wall. Rosh holstered his gun. Lucy squatted down beside me, placed her stripped-down forensics kit on the floor, and touched my shoulder – gave it a squeeze.

'Martin. Are you okay?'

'Yes.'

'You don't look okay.'

I looked at her. 'Did you call this in?'

'No.' She stood up. 'We didn't know exactly what there was to call.'

'Good.'

Leaving aside the problem of who'd buried the Missing Persons Report, I still didn't want the department involved. Sean had passed this to me, and now I was sharing it with Rosh and Lucy. It wasn't police business: we'd taken care of things by ourselves in the past, and there was no reason why it should be any different now. Especially when it was one of our own.

'Good,' I said again, getting to my feet. 'We need to keep this away from the department at the moment. It's a big thing to ask, but I think it's necessary.'

If it really was a big thing to ask, neither of them seemed particularly perturbed. For a second, I experienced that flush of rightness again – the same as when the investigation had felt like it was coming together – and it seemed like no time had passed and nothing had changed. But that flush vanished quickly as Lucy opened up the kit and reminded me why we were here.

Rosh said:

'Start from the beginning then.'

Start from the beginning.

Later, as everything went to hell, I would begin to understand how difficult it was to start from the beginning. But right then, it was easy. Even if everything was mysterious and confusing, at least it all still seemed linear.

So I began with the delivery of Sean's note and the identification of Alison Sheldon; then I ran through my brief investigations with her parents and the Missing Persons Bureau. I mentioned the boyfriend, and then explained about the email forwarding to Dr Mark Harris I'd discovered when I visited the university. Finally, the delivery of the video, which led here: to me, slumped against the wall in a killing room.

As I told my story, Lucy processed the scene around us as best she could. Lucy handled evidence on a day-to-day basis. She was good: there were maybe two or three people in the department who could work a scene as well as she could. On the few occasions when our unofficial investigations had demanded it, she had used a stripped-down version of proper procedure, and that's what she did now: beginning by walking around carefully, getting a feel in her head for what had gone on here, and then taking photographs with a small digital camera. Click after click. Images of everything: the walls, the floor, the ceiling. Rosh and I moved out of the way so that she could get a picture of the wall where I'd been sitting.

'Where was the video camera?' she asked.

'Over here.' I pointed behind me and then gestured across the room. 'Filming in that direction.'

Lucy aimed the camera.

'About here?'

'Yeah.'

She took the picture. Later, we would be able to compare it to a still from the video and see what, if anything, had taken place in the room since the film was shot.

'Make sure you get that graffiti,' I said. 'Over there in the corner.'

Click.

' "Eli is rising",' she read out. 'What's that supposed to mean?'

'It might not mean anything,' I said. 'The name sounds familiar, but I don't know why.'

'Let's get it anyway.'

She took another picture and then put the camera away in the box. Now, she would work the room for prints. In a perfect world, the graffiti might be good for it, because it had been written by fingertip. The men in the video had been wearing gloves and so I wasn't holding out much hope, but you never knew. Maybe they had made a mistake somewhere, or else perhaps the graffiti was nothing to do with them. In either event, we'd see. After the prints, Lucy would take samples of blood, in the hope of identifying Sean and anyone else who might have been injured in here.

'We'll need to see the video,' Rosh told me. 'Where is it?'

'It's at home.'

'At home?'

The realisation hit me as he said it, and I closed my eyes.

'I was so upset that I didn't even think.'

The video was the best evidence we had. I'd watched it once and tried to look closely, but with the shock I was likely to have missed important details. However unpleasant, repeat viewings would be necessary. And what had I done? I'd left the tape at my house. Whoever had delivered it knew where I lived, and so if it was still there then we would all be very lucky. If not, we would have a break-in scene to process, and I would punch myself repeatedly in the face. Rosh was more charitable.

'If it's not there, I'm going to slap you,' he said. 'And you're getting out of shape so it won't be hard. We'll worry about it later.'

Lucy was dusting the wall around the graffiti with black powder.

'You said the men were wearing gloves?'

'Yes,' I told her. 'Gloves and masks. All black.'

'Well, there are some prints here. Did Sean touch the wall?'

I tried to think, but I couldn't be sure. I was still privately kicking myself about the video.

'I can't remember,' I said. 'Maybe.'

'Okay.'

One by one, she lifted prints from the wall onto tape and from there onto evidence cards. She labelled each one but moved quickly, giving an appearance of carelessness.

Rosh said, 'Did you see anyone on the way over here?'

'Nobody.'

'You took the tram?'

'Yes.'

'Did anyone get on at your stop?'

'No. Nobody got off at the same time, either.'

'And the video was delivered ... when? What was the window?'

I'd already thought this through while I was waiting for them to arrive.

'I left the house about one. It was about six by the time I got home. Maybe a little after, but I didn't check my watch.'

'Where do you live?'

I gave him the address. 'You know it?'

Rosh nodded. 'Vaguely, yeah. I'm not sure about coverage, but we do have cameras in that area. If we're lucky, we might have the delivery boy on film. That's something we'll need to check.'

Across the room, Lucy was now collecting samples of blood. She was scraping the wall very gently with the edge of a scalpel and catching the crumbling blood on a sheet of white paper. She transferred it to a small envelope, labelled it, and then started to take samples from the floorboards.

'Yeah,' I said. 'We'll need to check that.'

My mind had started whirling and I couldn't think properly. Rosh rested his hand on my shoulder.

'It's going to be okay,' he said. 'We'll find the bastards that did this.'

But I recognised the tone of voice: it was the one you used when you were talking to a witness or a victim or a relative – not a fellow officer. He was talking to one of *them*, not one of *us*. It was an awful sensation, and I felt myself unravelling even further inside. Had I become so incapable after just a few months? Had things disintegrated for me that much?

Rosh repeated it gently: 'We'll find them.'

Pull yourself together.

'Yes,' I said. 'We will.'

I don't remember much about leaving or about the drive back. We checked around outside carefully but there was nobody to see and so we headed off. Lucy had her car and Rosh had brought the van; without thinking too deeply about it, I went with him. We drove in relative silence, and a thought occurred to me: if I had brought the video with me, I could have been taken down and we would have lost it that way too. Even though I should have called Lucy the moment I'd seen it, leaving it at my flat hadn't been the worst error in the world. Perhaps I was being sensitive. I watched takeaways flash past, and flood-lit shopfronts, and bright amber porches; and it was hypnotic. Rosh kept the speed even and the ride fluid and smooth. By the time we pulled up outside my flat, Lucy's car idling by the kerb in front of us, I had been lulled into a dozy, nodding half-trance.

'Looks secure,' Rosh said as we got out.

'Looks it,' I agreed, getting my gun out but keeping it beneath my jacket. 'But there are back ways in.'

I unlocked the front door and we went inside. Off the shared entrance hall was a door into the hairdressing salon that I lived two storeys above. One floor up was my neighbour – a surly Spanish guy who played loud, thudding music day and night – and then the top floor was mine.

The corridor on the ground floor was dark but it looked safe enough. The door at the back, at least, was still shut tight and bolted from the inside.

'Looks okay.'

The three of us made our way upstairs.

My door was still locked, and so unless someone had scaled the outside of the house and broken in through a window, the flat was secure. I unlocked the door and led the way up the short series of steps to my hallway. Even after four months, the smell of must and paint from the redecoration was still present in the air – along with a slightly more underhand odour that I was immediately embarrassed by. My flat wasn't exactly a mansion at the best of times, and I hadn't been expecting company today. A couple of one-night stands aside, Lucy and Rosh were my first real guests.

'Sorry about the mess,' I said, switching on the front room light.

It wasn't as bad as I'd thought but, seeing it through their eyes, I cringed on my own behalf. The bed was half-made. The television was still on, flashing over at the far corner of the room, resting on a table covered with discarded bus tickets, receipts and creased flyers for clubs I'd never been to. Across from that was my computer, with a few empty, misty glasses beside it. There were also two empty bottles of vodka on the floor next to the chair, which I realised didn't look good. I saw Lucy eyeing them with a blank expression on her face and I wanted to tell her that it was okay – I hadn't drunk them both in one go, or anything. But then I realised that didn't really sound much better.

'Is the video still there?' Rosh said.

I checked.

'Yes.'

'We need to watch it.'

'Do you want a drink?' I said. 'A coffee, I mean.'

'Please.'

'Me too,' Lucy said.

'Okay.'

I went off to put the kettle on, and consoled myself with the fact that at least they hadn't seen the kitchen. While the water boiled, I washed out three mugs and thought to myself that decadence and living in hedonistic squalor were only romantic when there was nobody around to disapprove. I made the coffee with a clean spoon and took it back through.

'Thanks.'

Then we watched the video. This time I knew what to expect, and so I made a point of abstracting myself as much as possible from what I was seeing. Lucy and Rosh weren't so lucky; my description of it certainly hadn't prepared them, but then I imagined that nothing could. As police officers, we had often seen the after-effects of violence, but we'd never seen anything as extreme and upsetting as what was playing out on my television screen. At the end, Lucy was crying. Rosh was pale and his hands were trembling.

He said it again: 'We're going to find these bastards.'

Lucy nodded. 'And we're going to fucking kill them.'

That didn't leave me much room to make a suggestion and, once again, I felt a little removed from their world. Instead, I repeated what I'd discovered that day, finishing with the forwarding that had been set up on Alison's email account.

Rosh looked thoughtful.

'Do you really think Sean was killed because he was looking into that girl's murder?'

'Yes,' I said immediately. 'And I think he sent me the information because he was scared of something. He knew that he was in danger. There's the Missing Persons Report, for one thing. I think that someone in the department maybe knew something about Alison's death and kept her ID hidden from the investigation deliberately.'

Lucy was glaring at the television. 'We need to know who.'

'We can find out who,' Rosh told her. 'And when we find out who, we can find out why.'

'Right now,' Lucy said, 'I'd settle for the who.'

Neither of us disagreed with her.

'We have Harris to work with,' I said. 'I've seen his picture, and he looks like a sleazeball but not a killer. It feels to me as though maybe he's covering something up. But he'll be able to tell us that.'

'He's the first stop,' Rosh said, standing up. 'Can I use your computer?'

'Knock yourself out.' I gestured over towards my desk. 'Just don't look at the bookmarks.'

He gave me a wry, if somewhat reluctant, grin and then went over and booted up the laptop. While he had his back to us, I caught Lucy's eye and smiled. She smiled back, but her expression was complicated. Yes, I'm pleased to see you, it said; yes, I'm pleased you're okay; but no, I'm not convinced that you're *really* okay.

Across the room, Rosh accessed the net and logged on to the police system. In less than a minute, he had Mark Harris's address on screen, and – moving towards the computer with Lucy and standing a little apart from her – I was reminded of the ease with which they could get information I had to scrabble for, and aware again of the gulf that had grown between us. It didn't matter, I told myself. Because this wasn't police business: this was our business, and what was important was that we had the address. Harris had a flat in Turtle, of all places. In fact, I knew the street.

That was what mattered.

CHAPTER NINE

In terms of the city's annual competition, my allegiance on paper was to the green and red flag of Turtle. I grew up there, soaking up its atmosphere and imbibing a sense of its civic pride. But I was never sporty and never particularly interested when, every year, the flags and tapestries were hung out, and the lanterns lit, and the older boys began their marches through the streets, decked out in the district's colours. Perhaps it was just because I knew most of them, and had been beaten up or robbed by a few, and so I figured that the apparent pride and discipline on display were somewhat at odds with the fact that a good percentage of them were bastards who I knew would end up in prison. Of course, at the time, I didn't realise that it would be me that put some of them there.

But Turtle is that kind of place. In many ways, it's a good, solid district to grow up in. You might end up getting a few knocks, but that's not necessarily the worst thing in the world – depending, of course. I met people there now, and I'd notice that a lot of the parents had the same look on their face: one that says they're always watching who their kids are hanging around with and always aware that things can go either way for them, and sometimes very quickly. Characterising the district as a cop, it's the sort of place that needs a clip round the ear every so often. It's not serious or nasty, and it's mostly good humoured. But nevertheless, it's still in occasional need of a firm hand and a watchful eye.

I'd always liked it, and I'd never wished I'd been born anywhere else. You could live in Rabbit and be rich, but that was more of a nice place to aspire to: maybe you missed out on something if you grew up there and got it for free. Or there was Snail or Mouse – maybe even Bull – with their shabby back-to-backs, but unless you were very lucky then you were starting off too low. Once you get to a certain depth, fighting your way to the surface can be difficult, no matter what the movies might tell you. Where else? You can have a condo in Elephant, but that kind of shit is transitory at best. Those places are filing cabinets for very important bits of paper that won't matter much inside two years. Horse? It's all students – nobody lives there for long. In every sense, it's almost all takeaways.

But Turtle? Like Goat and Bear, it's not too rich, not too poor. You can generalise a little by playing district zodiac: if you're born in Turtle then you have little truck with airs and graces. You work hard. You swear too much – you may even *burp* while you're swearing – and you never take anything good you get for granted.

Turtle is where I grew up, and it's also where I lived with Rachel; and where she still lived, in fact – only two streets away from Harris. As Lucy headed off to the department to work the evidence she'd taken from Bull, Rosh and I drove away from my flat and went to pay him a visit. I felt slightly awkward. I hadn't been that close since I'd moved out, and in some ways it felt like my old district wasn't mine anymore. But I wasn't thinking specifically about Harris's flat being close to Rachel's, because that was just a coincidence. And of course, that's all it was. Later, I would begin to understand exactly what that meant.

Ten o'clock at night found the streets of Turtle quiet, the houses curtained and secure, and the late-night shops amber-bright and busy. Rosh drove us slowly and evenly: only ever turning the wheel enough to take the gentle corners. Although I'd worked with him and knew him quite well, I'd never partnered him officially, but on the times we'd been out on private business he'd always been like this: never wasting movement, as though he knew instinctively what was needed and what wasn't. He was all minimum effort, whether he was walking around, beating on someone or driving somewhere – just plain efficient, cutting directly to whatever chase he was on and taking it slow. His conversation was the same. No unnecessary introductions.

'There was a shooting in Wasp the other night,' he said.

'Oh?'

'Yeah. Nobody got hurt – just some guy firing shots up in the air to break up a fight.'

I shook my head. 'These have-a-go heroes.'

'Yeah,' Rosh said. 'You know anything about it? It's just that if you don't then somebody's stolen your gun. We matched the bullets to it.'

I'd considered that the morning after without really thinking about it. The department kept a record of all our firearms. Whenever we'd gone out as a group, we'd used unlicensed, unmarked weapons and disposed of them afterwards. Sensible and careful. And then outside Spooks I'd just happily discharged my own gun. I didn't say anything, figuring that Rosh wasn't about to drag me in over it.

Instead, he said: 'So do you miss being a cop?'

'No.'

The streetlights in Turtle were like whalebones: thin, looping up from the pavements on either side, almost meeting above the centre of the street. There was little other traffic tonight, and most of the houses were keeping to themselves. This part of Turtle was filled with people you couldn't see; it was as though they knew something you didn't, like villagers locking themselves away on the night of the full moon, pretending they couldn't hear the stranger in town knocking on the doors in panic.

Rosh corrected himself.

'Well – maybe "miss" is the wrong word.'

I watched the houses go past: short, black blocks, randomly illuminated from within. Being with Rosh could sometimes feel like being with my parents – I knew he meant well, so I couldn't quite bring myself to tell him to fuck off and mind his own business. Rosh had started all of this for Sean, Lucy and me, but his approach had always been a little different, and I didn't think he understood exactly what was going on in our heads. Lucy could be borderline psychotic; Sean had been delusional; and I was just a mess. I had no doubt that Rosh, who had always been so exact and grounded, felt responsible, concerned, worried. It was only natural that he would intrude a little, and I tried not to take it too badly.

'It's not a case of missing anything,' I said. 'It just wasn't working for me anymore.'

'Holy shit. Did it ever work for you?'

'Once upon a time.' I shrugged. 'I guess it wasn't just that. There were lots of things.'

I thought about Lucy. Nothing in particular about

her – a jumble of images and memories that were more like the mental scent of her than an actual thought.

He turned the wheel slightly.

'You mean your wife?'

This time I didn't even shrug. Rosh had a cop's instinct for hunting out thoughts through conversation. That's what you get like: you use words to rustle people's undergrowth and then watch what bolts out. At the moment, I didn't particularly feel like being prey.

'Lots of things,' I said. 'You want to go left here.'

He followed my direction and was quiet for a moment.

'I grew up round here,' I said.

'I know. Harris's address is just up ahead, isn't it?'

I looked up the road, saw the block of shops. 'Yes.'

Rosh pulled the car over to the kerb and put on the handbrake. He left the engine running and tapped the wheel a couple of times, staring out front and thinking.

'That's the post office, isn't it?' he said.

I looked out. The furthest building to the left had red shutters all the way to the ground and a postbox flush with the brick wall beside it. I used to go in there all the time with my mother; I had memories of her unclasping her handbag and searching for change, while I looked at the cards and the rack of small, cheap toys, and the tray of assorted sweets that the owners kept near the window. The last man we'd killed together as a group – Carl Halloran – had robbed this post office, tying up and eventually shooting the people who owned it. For no real reason; just because he could. That was why we found him and killed him.

I stared at the shutters out of the van window, remembering him a little. Another insignificant man. To see him die, you'd never have thought he could have had such a terrible impact on the world, but I guess it doesn't take much.

'That's the one,' I said.

'Hmm.'

After a moment, Rosh clicked off the engine and opened the door.

'Well, there's no time like the present.'

'Yeah,' I said. 'Come on.'

We approached the line of shops. After the post office, there was an estate agent's with an illuminated display in the window of properties that surely nobody around here could afford. Next door, there was a fat, low liquor store: bright and open and full of treasure, although the counter guy was reading a paper and didn't seem to be doing much business. Then, a small driveway leading down. Then, a shuttered-up café and a blacked-out newsagent's. And last of all, more rusty, grey shutters, this time down over a pharmacy. After that, there were houses. Harris was renting the flat above the café. I looked up and saw that the lights were on. I looked back down. There were no residential doors on the main street.

'Round back, I guess.'

We headed down the driveway onto a spread of wasteland that was probably supposed to be a car park. The security light here was already on so there wasn't much we could do to avoid being seen. Two cars were parked – quiet, still and full of shadow. We both noted the licence plate on the nearest.

'The good doctor is home,' Rosh said.

'Seems that way.'

The buildings were humming slightly in the way that backs of shops always do. There was a set of wooden steps leading up to a slight extension on the rear of the café, and I figured that it must be the entrance to

Harris's flat. We headed up and found a half-glass back door that a strong wind would have blown down.

And then, we both took out our guns.

'Do you want to knock?' Rosh asked. 'Or shall I?'

'The pleasure's all yours,' I said. 'Especially since you're the investigating officer here.'

He gave me a smile and then kicked the door off its hinges. Only one smash, but a loud one – Harris was going to know he had visitors. We moved quickly into a dark kitchen. Rosh shouted out:

'Police!'

No answer.

We moved through the kitchen and up a flight of stairs that led onto a narrow hallway. Two doors – one left, one right – and one at the far end. We each took one of the side doors. I kicked my way into what turned out to be a small, empty bathroom. Rosh emerged from across the corridor at the same time as I did, and we took the far door together, into the lounge above the café, where the light was on.

The front room was empty. Maybe Harris had left the light on to deter burglars. I began to say something to that effect, but Rosh interrupted me.

'You hear what I hear?'

I listened. The sound of an engine. Tyres on gravel.

'Fuck.'

I started to run back down the corridor.

'You'll never make it,' Rosh said, and he was right. So I turned halfway and joined him again at the front room window. He pulled the curtains aside and we watched Harris's car disappear down the main street. I couldn't make out who was inside, beyond the fact that it was just one man, hunched over the wheel.

'Sneaky fucker,' Rosh said, glaring at the vehicle as it rounded a corner and went out of sight.

I was annoyed as well. Maybe my time out from the job was catching: the security light out back should have told us that someone had been moving around there very recently, and we hadn't even bothered to check if there had been anyone crouching down out of sight.

Rosh stopped glaring and sighed. 'I'll call it in.'

'Do we want this official?'

He shook his head. 'We'll do a cut-up.'

'Fine.'

We did that every now and then, like everyone else in the department. Off duty and out on the road, if a guy pissed us off – say by cutting us up and flipping us off – we'd report the car in question and teach him a lesson. Perk of the job. Another cop would pull him over and give us a call, and any resulting carnage would be off the record. Carnage sounds bad, I know, but it was only ever a case of scaring people a little bit.

I said, 'Let's clear this place first.'

We looked around the living room, but there actually wasn't much to see: for a man who lived alone, Harris seemed to be remarkably house-proud, although perhaps that was only in comparison to me. Where I'd done nothing to my flat since I'd moved in beyond sit in it and rot, Harris had made his own place feel like home. The carpet was new; he had a matching suite in good condition, with the settee and chairs clustered like friends around a coffee table; there was a natural fire. The man had even indulged in three modern art prints that formed a neatly arranged triptych on the wall behind the settee. I made do with patches of damp.

I walked across and looked at the artwork. It was two eyes, spread over the three canvases, and they were spaced out correctly to give the illusion of a face. I frowned. The irises were purple. I'd seen this somewhere before, and after a second or two I placed it. It reminded me of the picture taped to the wall in the alley by Whitelocks. But I couldn't remember that well enough to say whether it was the same artist.

'Computer,' Rosh said, and I turned around.

There were alcoves to either side of the fireplace, filled from about halfway up with crammed bookshelves. Underneath the bottom shelf in the left-hand alcove, there was a television and video set-up; in the right – sure enough – a computer desk. The monitor was on stand-by and the hard drive, pushed back underneath the table, was humming gently to itself. We'd obviously interrupted him. Although I did wonder how he had known that we were on our way.

I walked over and gave the mouse a nudge.

'You got something?' Rosh said.

'Hopefully. Let's see.'

Rosh might have had a few advantages over me – still officially being a cop; still sharp from the life – but he was nowhere near as good with computers as I was. He watched as I clicked carefully around Harris's desktop, locating his email account and opening it up.

'Here we go.'

Harris was using a personal email address, but he had it set up to download messages from his university account – presumably so that he could spend as little time at work as physically possible. There were about three hundred messages in his inbox and no other folders. I hit the tab at the top of the window that sorted the mail by subject matter and then scrolled down until I found the messages beginning *fwd*. These were the ones that had been automatically forwarded from Alison Sheldon's account to Harris, and then downloaded from work to his computer here. There were about twenty of them in all. On first glance, they mostly looked like circulars, but after all this effort I hoped that there'd be something here worth looking at.

'This is what we want,' I said.

'Let's just take the hard drive,' he said. 'Be easier.'

'I hope that you have an authority for seizure?'

'I'm sure I can rustle something up.'

'I trust you. Hang on for a second.'

I sorted the emails by date, so that the program showed me the most recent ones first. The last one he'd received had been about an hour ago, and there was a little tick next to it, which indicated that it had been read. The address caught my attention. It wasn't a *fwd*. It was more interesting than that.

'Look at this.'

Rosh peered over my shoulder and frowned, probably mostly because he didn't understand what he was looking at.

'Did that come from Alison's email account?' he asked.

I shook my head.

'No, there's a couple from her further down. But this one's different.'

The address was just a load of random numbers, followed by an inoffensive-looking server address. I might have even mistaken it for spam if not for the unusual size of the message – over two megabytes – and the subject line, which read *urgent, doctor*. So the message had a large attachment, and it had been sent for Harris's specific attention.

I double-clicked the envelope icon to open it up.

Doctor,

You have been shirking your duties and they grow pressing. We will not tolerate further delays. There

117

is growing interest in our activities and you have
been less than careful. The other girl knows too
much. You will bring her to us as you brought the
detective.

If at this late stage your conscience is bothering you
may we direct your attention to the video attached?
Copies can easily be sent to the authorities in
addition to members of your family. And perhaps
even to members of the family of the young man in
question. That is how we will begin with you.

Delete this email immediately. Arrange to meet the
girl as soon as possible and we will be in touch.

'This is from the people who killed Sean,' Rosh said.

'Yes,' I told him quietly.

I was thinking. I'd been wondering why Sean had
sent me the information when he did – what had been
about to go down that made him feel he needed
insurance. Now, we knew. Some kind of meeting with
Harris.

'Harris helped them get him,' Rosh said.

'It looks like that.'

'Why?'

I said, 'We'll find that out when we get our fucking
hands on him.'

'Too right. Who sent it?' Rosh nodded at the screen.
'The address is . . . what the fuck is that?'

'An anonymity server,' I said. 'There are these sites
on the internet. You set up an account and they let you
send messages through that, and all of the detail gets
wiped clean off. Gives you a false address, basically. It's
a way of sending faceless mail.'

I double-clicked on the attachment. The computer
whirred a little, thinking carefully about whether it

could handle a file this large. Then it grumbled to itself and got on with it.

Rosh said, 'A site like that must keep records.'

'Probably not,' I said. 'And if it did, we'd never get our hands on them. It's probably not based in this country, and even if it was the people who run these things don't tend to cooperate with the authorities.'

In fact, they were generally the equivalent of those separatists that live in the woods, shooting at trees and wearing camouflage combat pants twenty-four-seven. Just a bit nerdier.

'They'd cooperate with us,' he said, but I was hardly listening.

Harris.

I repeated the name in my head and made it sound hard and angry and full of hate, so that my memory of Sean's murder could finally have a soundtrack. From the email message, it looked as though Harris had been blackmailed and forced to lure Sean into some kind of trap; and we were about to find out what these bastards had on him.

Harris.

For a few seconds the computer had been carefully circling the attachment. Now, a video package opened up, filling the screen, and a grainy movie clip started playing. Like the film of Sean, it was amateur in quality – dark, probably filmed on a hidden camera – but good enough to make out what was happening. It was a stationary shot of a bedroom, with the camera elevated and placed far enough away to fit the whole bed into the shot. Harris was on it, naked, moving on top of a very young boy. You could tell it was Harris because he was looking into the camera; the boy could have been anyone. The clip lasted maybe twenty seconds.

Rosh and I watched it without talking. When it had finished, he said:

'We need to find the girl they're talking about in the message. Before Harris does.'

I agreed completely. 'Let's take the hard drive and get out of here.'

As I started to turn things off and remove wires, Rosh prompted:

'With one problem being that we don't know who the girl is?'

'Not for sure, no,' I said, unclipping the screwdriver on my penknife. 'But I have an idea where we can start.'

CHAPTER TEN

Remember I told you that Rabbit was a nice district? Well, that's not strictly true; it's more of a handy generalisation. The districts in our city are a lot like the people that live in them: parts of them are good and parts of them are bad. Rabbit is just rich, and that's not the same thing as nice.

Properties in the areas in west Rabbit are expensive and sought-after. That's because Rabbit sits directly north of Elephant, which is the district of commerce. If you walk around the west of Elephant without a suit on then you feel seriously under-dressed. It's where you find the big businesses. The buildings are all sleek steel and shining windows, and they house insurance companies, brokers, traders, wheelers and fucking dealers. The geographical divides between districts are rigid – set to the street – but socially it's a different story. So, in the west of Rabbit, the big-business side of Elephant gives way to yuppie condos, spreading away north, shrinking a little in height and melting into the plushest suburbs the city has to offer: fine houses, occasional gated communities, the sound of water sprinklers in well-tended gardens.

But as you move east through Elephant, you find youself moving into the city's main shopping centres and the markets. And the further east you go, the closer you get to Horse, the student district. To the north, Rabbit follows the same pattern: the further east you go, the more the accommodation goes downhill. Slightly less plush; slightly more affordable. Price-wise, the area degenerates. On the far eastern edge of Rabbit, just before it becomes Bull, it's just like anywhere else. There's a strip of estate where the houses are tightly packed: thin and tall, as though a barely comfortable number had shuffled together to let a few more in: the red-brick buildings had all sucked in their guts and then not been able to breathe out again. There was litter in the street, gangs of kids playing football against the walls. The usual estate stuff.

Because it was reasonably cheap and relatively close to Horse, it had a large student population. The majority were third years or postgrads, and so it was quieter than Horse and there wasn't much trouble. This is where we were driving to. According to the Missing Persons Report, Alison's friend Keleigh lived here.

'What makes you sure the email was meaning her?' Rosh asked.

'I'm not sure,' I told him. 'But she was the last person we know of to see Alison alive. Maybe she knows more than she said at the time.'

As we were approaching the estate, I glanced out of the van's window. The night was properly black now. It was the kind of serious dark that really means business, coming before midnight and not really drifting away until the mist arrives at dawn. Witching hours. The city slept through them, but always with an eye half-open. A lot of the time, you could feel the city breathing slowly: waiting for you to put a foot down wrong and irritate it too much.

Rosh took the van over a slight rise and the land dipped in front. In the distance ahead, Bull spread away downhill. At first, it was a random mess of amber streetlights – some in clusters, some more regular – and a sprinkle of pale house windows with blue and yellow lantern lights glinting amongst them. And then, further away, it was just factories and workshops. Most of that area was in darkness until the horizon, where you could see that something was burning. We slowed a little as we neared the border.

'Here,' I said.

Rosh turned left off the main road onto a smaller street that snaked into the estate. There were speed bumps every twenty metres. The road signs – all proclaiming a slow limit – were decorated with crayon drawings by children from the local school, reprinted endlessly by a council that could afford to spend money on the little things. There were a lot of streetlights, staining the old, red brick of the buildings closer to orange, and the green and blue lanterns and banners were all pretty much intact. The general impression was of an area that didn't welcome crime, wouldn't tolerate it and held regular civic meetings to discuss what to do about it. Official statistics told a different story.

'Quiet tonight,' I said.

'Too quiet,' Rosh deadpanned.

'Don't knock it. Keleigh's street is coming up soon. It's one of these on the right.'

The back streets betrayed the area's true nature. They were tight and narrow: the kind where on maps they give up putting the names and just pencil in a few abbreviations. Autumn Lane, Autumn Street, Autumn Mount, apparently leading to Autumn Court and Autumn Corner. There were endless versions of the same street, all of them identical: houses with windows like big black eyes, security grilles and gardens filled with old appliances and bagged rubbish that had been torn open during the night by foxes and dogs. Keleigh lived at the far end, on Autumn Grove.

'Here.'

Rosh pulled up by a house with no lights on and we got out and approached the gate. It was a dead-looking building if ever I'd seen one. The outside was chipped and pitted and damp; the guttering was cracked; the pipes were flaky with rust. It was badly in need of repair and unlikely ever to receive it. Someone had made an effort with the front garden, at least. The grass was overgrown but there were a few potted plants here and there, and a series of trays that appeared to contain budding vegetables of some kind. And, at first glance, there were no rusting white-goods or scorch marks on the lawn from bonfires.

'Let's knock nicely,' I said as we walked up the path. 'You got your ID handy?'

'I certainly have.'

Rosh pulled out his wallet and I leaned on the doorbell. Like I said, there wasn't much trouble around here, but as it got late it wasn't necessarily advisable to open your door to just anyone. A quick buzz on the bell was probably easier to ignore and pretend to sleep through – especially as the likelihood was that it was just some drunk hitting on the wrong address. Like anywhere else in the world, if there's a genuine emergency that's any of your business then people tend to phone you. So, to make sure we got an answer, I left my finger on the buzzer for a while – listening to the sound vibrate loudly behind the front door – before finally letting go.

A minute later, when there had been no response of any kind, I did it again – only this time I just left it there. I'd give it a bit longer, I thought, and then Rosh could kick the door in. It would be our duty as concerned citizens.

It wasn't necessary. Thirty seconds later, I heard the telltale screech of a window being pulled open on the floor above, and we looked up to see a guy peering out at us. His hair was hanging down a good half-metre below him, and he managed to sound thoroughly pissed off when he said simply:

'*What?*'

'Police,' Rosh said, holding up his wallet. The guy couldn't possibly see it from that height, but it wouldn't matter. 'Open the door, please.'

'Fucking hell. Just a second.'

The head withdrew and the window closed.

'I guess I must look like a cop,' Rosh said.

'If he opens the door to us based on that display, part of me thinks we should burgle his house on principle.'

'Don't be nasty. And you're meant to say, "You *are* a cop."'

'Of course, you're a cop,' I said. 'You just don't look like one.'

A minute later, the door opened – but only a few centimetres. The guy had kept the chain on.

'Can I see that badge, please?' he asked.

Rosh handed his wallet through, and after a second or two the kid handed it back, undid the chain and opened the door. It amazed me how trusting people were sometimes. We could have passed him a sheriff's star out of a cereal packet and he probably wouldn't have known the difference. There's not much point asking to see a badge if you don't know what you're looking for. A truth of life: you show somebody an ID with a watermark on it and they automatically assume you're on the level.

'What can I do for you?' He had both the smell and the slightly worried expression of a guy who'd been smoking weed all evening. Perhaps he imagined we might care.

'Keleigh Groves,' I said. 'We need to speak to her.'

'Oh. Right. Well, she's not here.'

'She lives here?'

'Yeah,' he said. 'She lives here. But she's not here, if you see what I mean.'

'Well, you got any idea where we can find her?'

'No, I don't know.' The kid wasn't meeting our eyes. He rubbed his face a little, and then seemed to remember something. 'Wait. She said she was going to her boyfriend's.'

'When was this?' Rosh said.

'Hours ago. I don't know when. Maybe about nine?'

'You asking us or telling us?' I said.

'It was nine. Maybe even before nine, but I wasn't paying much attention to be honest. Think he came in, picked her up. So is this about Jamie?'

'Jamie's her boyfriend, right?'

'Yeah.'

'Well, it might be about Jamie,' I said. 'What's Jamie look like?'

'He's got purple hair. I don't know what else apart from that. He turns up and that's all I see.'

The kid was annoying me. For one thing, he wouldn't look at us. Sometimes that can be a dead giveaway – it's a popular myth that people won't meet your eye when they're feeding you shit – but in reality that's not always the case. Some of the guilty ones look you in the eye all the time, and there are a good number who could tell you that two plus two was two and have you reaching for a calculator. It wasn't that this guy was lying to us; it was just that he was

126

intimidated, which was making him nervous and making him struggle with what he was saying.

I tried to break it down a little for him.

'How old is he? Is he your age?'

'I guess so. He looks it. He's at uni.'

'He's a student?'

'Yeah, yeah. He's on her course.'

'Okay,' I said, trying to think back through the Missing Persons Report for a Jamie. I couldn't remember one. But at least Keleigh hadn't gone off with Harris. 'Do you know where he lives? Or where they went?'

'She'll have gone to his, but I don't know where he lives. Horse somewhere, but I don't know what street.'

'You got his phone number?'

The kid shook his head.

'Keleigh's just a flatmate, you know. I don't even know her that well.'

I started to ask him something else, but we were interrupted by Rosh's phone ringing. He picked it out of his pocket and answered it, moving a little way down the path. It was probably Lucy; I hoped that she'd managed to find something at the lab. Regardless, it was time to pack things up here and leave.

'What's your name, kid?' I asked.

'Simon.'

'Okay, Simon. Listen to me. You're not in trouble, and neither is Keleigh or Jamie. We just need to talk to them real bad and make sure that they're okay.'

'Right.'

I pulled an old card out of my wallet that had my mobile number written on it and handed it to him.

'Soon as you hear from either of them, tell them to ring that number there. Okay? Tell them it's all right, but it's really important they get in touch. We just want to talk to them about Alison.'

'Okay.'

'You sure you got that, yeah?'

'Yeah, yeah. I'm sure.'

Rosh called out: 'Martin, we need to hustle.'

'I'm coming.'

'No – we really need to hustle.'

'Thanks for your help,' I told Simon, giving him what I hoped was a friendly smile, and then ran back down the path. Rosh was already clambering into the driver's seat. As he started the van's engine, I climbed in beside him.

'What news?' I said.

'It's Lucy.' I jerked back in my seat as he set off too quickly and then started to get faster. We left smoke, rubber and a screech behind us.

He said, 'She's in trouble.'

CHAPTER ELEVEN

Not everybody within our city walls was born here, and not everyone who was born here stays. Our population is as transitory as in any other big city. But we have the illusion of confinement, because most of the outer districts are walled up at their furthest borders, so that in many ways our city is more like an enormous, sprawling castle than a normal city or town. Obviously, though, there are hundreds of gateways in and out, and they're never manned: this isn't a prison. And there are places where the walls have been broken down. Bull expands out to the north-east, for example, like a spill of acid, burning at the cusp; and Fish in the north-west is largely flooded, so you can get out of there easily enough if you're a good swimmer with a bad nose. But heavy traffic like trucks and cars and coaches have only four main roads by which to enter or leave the city. Basically, we have a criss-cross of motorways at the heart of the city, slightly east of the central square, and if you want to drive in then you have to enter by one of these, and then peel off onto smaller roads. Leaving is the same in reverse. From the back streets, you push your way onto the main arteries and then get pumped out with everything else.

Rosh and I were heading north. It was after midnight now, but the motorway was still busy: mainly with articulated lorries that had brought in produce for the shops and markets. Rosh was weaving between them dangerously, slowing down for no-one.

'We'll get there,' I said.

He didn't answer – just gunned the accelerator a little and shot past a bleached-yellow van. The driver blared his horn, but the sound faded away quickly as we left him behind.

'We'll get there.'

Lucy was heading north as well, some way ahead of us. She was in her unmarked car, pushing the speed limit without quite breaking it. Behind her, there was a black van. It had tried to run her off the road as she left the police station, failed, and then been behind her ever since. She could see at least three men in the front, and I expected that there would be more in the back. Even if there weren't, three were too many for her to deal with. So she was leading them out of the city as slowly as she could risk, and Rosh and I were racing to catch up.

He said, 'Phone her.'

I did. It took a couple of seconds for her to answer. She said, 'Hey, Martin. How are you?'

'Hey,' I replied. 'I'm fine. But I hope for the sake of other drivers that you're on the hands-free.'

'Very funny.'

'Where are you?'

'Just out of the gates,' she said. 'Passed them about a minute ago. You guys?'

I looked out of the window. Yellow streetlights curled up from either side of the road. Beyond them, there wasn't much to differentiate the landscape: just a lot of wasteground and trees as the city thinned out.

'Close,' I said.

'Two minutes from the gate,' Rosh told me.

'Two minutes and closing,' I relayed.

'Okay,' she said. 'I'm taking them down the woods.'

'Our woods?'

'Yeah. A bit of quiet to deal with them in. Plenty of cover.'

Typical Lucy. I had no idea whether she was even remotely scared; she often reacted strangely and it was a bit difficult to predict. Generally, the more intense a situation got, the calmer she appeared. I'd only ever seen her vulnerable in the kind of intimate moments that other people weren't around to see. But whatever she was feeling, I was frightened for her even if she wasn't. As fast as Rosh was driving, I wanted him to accelerate.

'We'll be there by then,' I told her.

'Plenty of cover for all of us, then. These guys mean business.'

'We'll take them.'

She paused, and then said:

'Okay. I'm sorry about everything, Martin.'

'Don't talk like that. There's never been anything to be sorry about.'

'I just wanted you to know. It was bad, the way things turned out.'

'It's okay. We'll see you soon.'

'City gates,' Rosh called out. He accelerated under them and, finding his way blocked by a taxi, blared his horn a couple of times. The taxi driver swerved out of the way and gave us the finger as we passed him.

'Hear that?' I said. 'City gates.'

'Good.' Another pause, then: 'I'm at the turn-off now. Got to go.'

'Good luck,' I said. 'And don't get killed. Okay?'

'Remember who you're talking to here and don't be so fucking stupid.'

I hung up, feeling that it was the last time I'd ever

speak to her. But I didn't believe in fate – never had – and I reminded myself of that now. Whatever was going to happen would be decided when it did. I turned to Rosh.

'She's at the turn-off.'

'Two minutes away,' he said. 'But we'll make it in one.'

I nodded. Of course we would.

When the police arrested people, those people went to jail and then court and then – if we were lucky – jail again. But when the four of us arrested people out of hours – if we couldn't fake the scene well enough – those people disappeared. These weren't pleasant people we were dealing with after all; they had connections, and they would be missed. A corpse in a room is a question that needs an answer. But a missing person is more of a vague puzzle, and the even more unpleasant people who would want to know what had happened are left with nothing to go on. They would assume that a rival was responsible, but they'd have little to work with beyond their own back catalogues. And who knew – maybe the guy in question had just run.

Rosh had some land outside the city that he'd inherited from his parents when they died. It had once been used for farming, but now it wasn't used for much of anything: the main house was still standing, but Rosh had emptied it of any valuables, and the wooded acres of land around it were untended and overgrown. Old farm equipment rested wherever it had stopped, rusted now, wrapped in grass. The land itself was fenced off at the extremities and only really accessible by a series of half-roads that nobody would ever take by accident. So it was private and perfect for what we needed. Deep in the woods, there was an old skip and that was where we disposed of any evidence. Afterwards, we'd drive away from the house – down its dusty driveway and then onto the tangle of awkward trails – and we'd see the pinprick of fire behind us, burning in the woods. But nothing would ever be visible from the motorway, or anywhere else where unsuspecting drivers might see it and grow suspicious.

'Here we go,' Rosh said, peeling the van off to the left.

All that sounds bad, and it was. But we're talking about murderers, here. We're talking about serial rapists and abusers and major-league players whose absence in the world inarguably made it a better place. Who were we to make that decision, you might ask. We were just us.

Regardless, this was where Lucy was now leading the men who wanted to kill her. A bit of cover. A bit of privacy.

We bumped along. Within a minute, the road was barely wide enough for the van and the ground was churned up: all tractored muck and soil, frozen into a fractured wave. There was a little open space over a fence to the right – a field that might once have housed cattle or crops, or who knew what. Thick woods to the left.

'Get ready,' Rosh said.

He switched off the lights, slowing down only slightly, and drove blind. The van rolled up and down, from side to side, tracking the rough ground. I already had my gun in my hand. I checked it once and then forgot about it. It was fine.

And then, up ahead, I heard the noise of gunshots. They were hard sounds that hammered the air. Lots of them – more than one gun, maybe three or four. I was shaking – frightened of reaching them, frustrated that we weren't there already.

Lucy.

I said, 'Go faster.'

Rosh accelerated slightly around a corner we both knew was coming up – and then suddenly the world shattered, jerked, blew apart. My eyes were shut and all I could feel was pain from my shoulder to my hip, an enormous strain in my neck.

'Fuck.'

The van careered and stopped. There was another van ten metres away from us, half off the road now, its doors hanging open. We'd slammed it off the road, coming to rest a little way behind and to one side. The beam from its headlights illuminated the undergrowth. Silhouettes flashed across. I undid my seatbelt, beginning to feel panic rising and fighting it down.

There was a sudden spray of gunfire and our windscreen exploded.

'Out.'

We kicked open the doors and dived out to either side of the van. I crouched down, using the door as cover. More bullets thudded into it, coining the metal. One, two, three.

'Two of them by the van,' Rosh shouted.

The side window above shattered, covering me in glass.

'Shit!'

'One out in the fields this way.'

I caught the flash of a muzzle in the woods beside me, but the shots came nowhere near. Two of them by the van, and they must have sent a man out to either side to flank Lucy.

More flashes amongst the trees, and the air reverberated around me. As if things weren't bad enough, the guy in the woods had a fully automatic rifle.

I said, 'I've got one this side too. I'm on it.'

Optimism. Obviously I'd killed people before, but I'd never been involved in any kind of shootout or gun battle. Trained for it a little. Never in woodland.

I'm on it.

I took three deep breaths then stood and ran out from behind the door, hammering shots in the direction of the van we'd hit. A few came back, missing me. Just single shots, fired on instinct rather than aimed. Half of the first tree I passed blew apart in a hard, wet spray. Then more, tearing apart the undergrowth. I stopped firing and concentrated on running. The trees were dense here and I had to dodge between them, but the dark was on my side: the shots coming after me were wide of the mark and the shooters gave up quickly, deciding to concentrate on Rosh and Lucy. She must have been holed up by her car somewhere ahead. Not wanting to think about that, I slowed down and watched for the muzzle flashes amongst the trees. There – not far now. I crept carefully towards them. With a bit of luck, I'd get him before he knew I was here.

Then, a voice I didn't know shouted out: 'One in the woods, one on the field.'

The shooter in the woods went quiet. No more muzzle flashes.

Shit.

I stopped moving and crouched down. My hands were shaking.

There was another spatter of gunfire from the road. Then quiet held for a second. Then three solid shots, and someone started screaming. My heart flipped for a moment, but I didn't recognise the voice. Lucy or Rosh had clipped one of the men by the van. Probably Lucy – Rosh would be after the man in the field.

Immediately, more shots rang out at the road: flat and hard and sustained. A few people, exchanging fire. I heard glass shatter, angry shouting.

Keep moving.

But the woods in front of me were pitch black and dangerous, and without the muzzle flashes amongst the trees I was blind. I had an idea of where he'd been – not far ahead – but surely he would have moved by now. I kept low and worked my way quietly between the trees. The fucker knew I was here somewhere.

Automatic gunfire – like a hammer smacking an iron girder twenty times a second. I made it to the ground just as the noise and light exploded beside me, then above me, then past and over to one side. Pain jarred my arm and face, and the undergrowth was tangled and sharp, but I ignored it and concentrated on the man. Where was he? Then I caught a glimpse of him – slightly ahead of me, raking shots out through the woods, aiming a little high. The trees were flashing into life, and smoke was billowing between them. I edged to my left and fired once, twice, hitting nothing. My third shot caught him somewhere. The gunfire swirled upwards as he went back and down, bullets fluttering up like startled birds, shredding leaves, and I could hear him screaming over the sounds of the shots before they cut out. And then just screaming.

I got to my feet and moved quickly, circling him as quietly as I could. My heart was racing but my mind was strangely calm; it had slowed down completely and was talking to me in a small, confident voice.

You've got him, it's okay, just take it easy.

The man kept screaming, and then called out:

'Man down! Man down! Fuck!'

I was moving round to the left – *come on, it's okay, just relax* – when he started firing again, like an animal caught in a trap and lashing out. The shock made me dive down, but he was firing away from me, tearing apart the woodland where I'd been when I'd clipped him the first time. The shots laced back and forth, the flash from the muzzle illuminating the wood in staccato bursts of fire. And there he was at the centre, a shadow twisting on the ground, not much more than a series of lit contortions. I took aim and fired into the heart of them three times. Immediately, the shots stopped. This time, there was no screaming.

I paused, gathering myself together. My arm hurt where I'd hit the ground, and my cheek was stinging. I touched it carefully, and my hand came away wet. Had I been caught? I decided I wasn't in nearly enough pain; I'd probably just been cut by a thorn or nicked by a splinter of bark. The woods stank of smoke and sap.

The fight was continuing at the road, and the sound of shots turned me around and drew me back towards it, moving through the undergrowth as quickly as I dared, heading straight for the beacon of light spilling from the men's van. It was criss-crossed with the black lines of the trees. I heard more shots, interspersed with screams of pain. The sound of bullets pranging metal.

I kept to the treeline, heading alongside the road until I got near enough to work out what was going on. There was a dead man by the van, but the second was still alive, using the door to shield him from shots coming from up ahead. Lucy was still alive; still returning fire. Something inside me lurched with relief, and I felt a savage twist of desire to kill this man as quickly as possible and make sure she was safe. I couldn't see Rosh, but there was gunfire slamming the far side of the van from the dark field, and so he must have been out there somewhere. But the man was still firing off shots. He emptied his clip out front of the van and then fumbled in his belt for another, backing off slightly along the vehicle. I wanted to kill him. Instead, I stepped out and drew down on him and said:

'Drop it.'

He looked up at me – startled, terrified – and my aim faltered slightly as I caught sight of his face. It was Michael Kemp, an officer in our department. Sean and I had worked with him a couple of times, and although I didn't know him well I'd always liked him. I liked him a lot fucking less now, but at least I had him caught square with nowhere to go.

Regardless – panicking – he was still working at the gun. He got the clip in just as I said:

'Mike, for fuck's sake, drop the gun.'

But then he was aiming for me and I had no choice. His gun came up quick and I fired twice, catching him in the chest and throat. He went back into the van so hard that he left a dent in the side, but still managed to get a wild shot off. And then he was down, sprawled out and motionless. His gun clattered away from him.

I kept my aim on him as I moved over, shouting out to Lucy and Rosh:

'Hold your fire!'

I kicked the gun, sending it skidding off towards the field, and kept aiming, but Kemp wasn't moving and he never would. There was blood pooling out all around him and my second shot had removed most of his neck. Officer Michael Kemp was very fucking dead.

Rosh and Lucy held their fire as ordered, and the sudden hush was shocking after minutes of constant gunfire. My ears were ringing gently. It felt like an intrusion to shout in this new, bruised silence, but I did it anyway.

'We're clear.'

Then I put my back to the van and slid slowly down, finishing up crouched on my haunches. The adrenaline was running all the way through me, finding nowhere to go, and as I watched Lucy approaching cautiously from up ahead I realised that I was shivering badly.

'Martin?'

'Here.'

'You in one piece?'

'I'm fine,' I said. 'They're all dead.'

The shivering would become uncontrollable soon; it would be as though my thermostat had broken. Adrenaline would turn into what it always did – a cold, crawling poison that only time could take away.

Lucy collapsed next to me. She looked ragged and wild, but basically unscathed. I leaned against her, and she did me, and together – slumped there in support – we waited for Rosh.

'You get your man?' he asked when he arrived.

I nodded.

'I clipped mine,' he said, shaking his head and frowning. 'I know I did, because the fucker screamed and stopped shooting at me. I caught him dead centre, ten metres away – three, four hits – and I saw him go down. He wasn't getting back up.'

I said, 'And? You don't sound so sure.'

'I got closer, and he wasn't there. No body. Nothing.'

'You think he crawled off?'

Rosh just shook his head again.

'No. Even with body armour on, he wasn't going anywhere. I was on him in two, maybe three seconds.

No way he moved. It's like he fell down and turned to mist. His fucking gun was just sitting there.'

I looked around at the dark fields and woods. The breeze was rustling them slightly, and it was very cold. I started shivering even more. If Rosh said that he'd tagged his man, then I was sure he had. Perhaps he'd just misjudged where he'd fallen down. It was the middle of the night, after all. But whatever had happened, we needed to get out of here quickly.

'Let's just move,' I said.

This road was private, but not as private as the farm itself. Nobody from any main road would have seen or heard anything and it was unlikely that anyone would ever come this way by accident. Nevertheless, we still needed to clean the scene up a little.

It took all three of us to get the damaged van further off the road, a task made all the more unpleasant by the fact that when we first rammed it we'd pushed it over another one of the men – so that was five in total. He was dead by now, but still trapped under the back wheel. We placed what was left of him beside Kemp at the back of the van and then dragged the third man off the road by his heels. Lucy had caught him in the stomach, and then twice in the chest. Man down, indeed.

All three of them were dressed exactly the same. Black clothes. Gloves. Boots. Flak jacket. These guys had come meaning business.

'Serious,' I said.

Rosh nodded. 'You recognise any of the others?'

'No.'

Lucy shook her head as well.

'Me neither,' Rosh said. 'I've worked with Kemp a few times. I always thought he was a decent guy.'

'Me too.'

Lucy said, 'He tried to hit on me once, but he took it well when I told him to fuck himself. He seemed stand-up the other times I met him.'

'Obviously, that wasn't true.'

'He was on the take?' she said.

'Maybe.' I shrugged.

I was reluctant to go any further down that line of thinking for the moment, if only because what had happened here was so extreme that I couldn't understand *why*. What was so important about Alison Sheldon that a police officer would cover up her identity, blackmail a lecturer, kill Sean and then try to kill Lucy too? She was just a student. I shook my head.

'Let's finish up,' I said.

It was starting to rain. We loaded all three bodies into the back of the van and then closed the doors. We would leave Rosh's van at the farmhouse, where nobody else would go. If anybody drove past here they would imagine that Kemp's van had run off the road – presumably taking the corner too quickly – and then been abandoned. That was all. The two bodies we'd left off-road could stay there for now. Nobody was likely to stumble on them at the moment, and if they did then good luck to them. We could clean up properly when we had more time.

When we were done, Rosh and I brushed the glass away as best we could and got back in the van. Lucy took her car, and we drove the rest of the way down the road, taking the overgrown turning that led to Rosh's farmhouse. We wouldn't stay long, but we could clean up our minor wounds, regroup and work out what our next move should be. Rosh and I drove in silence, the rain pattering in on us. There was lots to talk about, but we needed the quiet time to digest what had happened. The keenest question was how many others there were out there. I had no doubt at all that we'd just killed at least some of the people who murdered Sean – but I didn't know why we'd been forced into that position or if what we'd done here tonight had ended all this for good. We needed to find Harris. We needed to find Keleigh.

I checked my phone to see if she had called or texted.

No Messages

It was raining properly when we arrived at the farm: great slices of water coming down at an incline, saturating us. You could see it flashing in the headlights and hear it on the roof of the van. It was quietly hypnotic. And I put it down to the rain that, as Rosh pulled the van to a halt at the front of the house, I didn't notice straight away that there was something terribly wrong.

Lucy backed her car up and swerved round slightly, drawing level beside us.

Rosh rested his forearms on the steering wheel, his chin on them, and stared out thoughtfully.

I said: 'It's all gone, isn't it?'

He nodded but didn't say anything. I supposed that it wasn't exactly true: the farmhouse wasn't gone. I could still see it straight ahead, illuminated at its base by our headlights. But the windows were empty and the familiar wooden door was missing. The white walls, where they hadn't tumbled down, were now stained black with soot. Through the gaps, you could see that the roof had fallen in, and the rain was streaking down into the shell of the building, soaking all of the ash and timber and ruin. I half expected to see smoke rising from the debris, but there was nothing. The building had been burned and the fire had gone out, leaving parts of the walls standing but nothing left of the inside. It was a husk. So in every real sense, it was all gone.

We got out of the van, guns in hand, and Lucy joined us. The only sound was the static hush of the rain, which made it seem as though something peaceful and secret was being told to us. I scanned the land around carefully. The fire had been set some time ago, but that didn't mean whoever had set it wasn't still around.

Rosh walked towards the remains of his home.

'Could be an accident,' Lucy said bitterly.

I shook my head, even though she hadn't meant it.

'I don't think so.'

Rosh stopped before we reached the door, stood still and looked at something on the ground by his feet. Burned rubbish, strewn around. It was as though the house had exploded as it died, scattering unwanted belongings around the yard. Lucy and I moved towards him.

'No,' Rosh said as we reached him. 'I don't think so either.'

And I realised that it wasn't rubbish by his feet. Burned, yes, and almost beyond recognition, but still very obviously a body. Something that had once been human and was now just black and hard and lifeless, like old wood. You could make out the broken head; the curled, melted shape of the rest of it. The rain was tapping on a single exposed tooth.

Lucy knelt down in the mud beside it, tilting her head slightly as she put together what was what. And then, gently, she rested her hand on it and closed her eyes. After a second, I placed my own hand on her shoulder. It was the first time I'd touched her in months, and I felt a slight jolt: a shiver of an earthquake deep inside me. Rosh stood still, but after a second he moved closer, bending over to pick up the object that had been left on top of the body. But we all knew what it was.

Officially, it would take forensics a long time to identify these remains. That wasn't going to happen; he would stay here. But there was no need anyway. Whoever had done this to Rosh's property – our property in important ways – had saved us the trouble. Out in the middle of nowhere, they'd burned the farmhouse almost to its foundations, and they'd burned this body beyond even that. But when it was done they'd returned and left us another message. On top of his body, they'd carefully placed Sean's wallet and badge.

CHAPTER TWELVE

Like I said before, I grew up in Turtle. My parents were good people by any standard you care to name. My father was hard-working and capable. He never found himself fitting into any traditional niche of employment, but he eventually founded his own business and did well. One of my clearest memories from when I was young is of my father, glasses on, peering over a sheet of finances that he didn't entirely understand but was determined to master regardless: sheer tenacity, and it paid off. It never seemed to bother him too much that my mother earned more than him – she had worked in the same store since she was a kid, and ended up being the manager – and it didn't seem to bother her either. My parents' marriage was a partnership in the truest sense, and I always got the impression that the work stuff and the money it brought in was just a means to an end. That end was being happy together, living a good life, and raising me well. They were the best.

And they still are. They don't live in the city anymore. There was a place two hours' drive away on the east coast that we used to go to every summer on holiday, and when my mother and father hit retirement age they studied their accounts and figured out they had enough to afford a down payment on a cottage there. That's where they live now. Despite the care and love with which they'd raised me, it was one of those strange, inexplicable tricks of life that I hadn't grown up all that close to them. In return, they know enough about my life to be proud of me, which obviously couldn't be much.

I remember those holidays, though. And the thing is, I was never that keen on where we ended up. I guess it was always fun – my parents made sure of that – but in lots of ways I was just kicking my heels: killing time until we were heading home again. It was the journeys I enjoyed the most: the trips in the car, listening to music and staring out of the windows; counting down the miles; wondering if when we passed over the next brow we'd be able to see the sea. And the service stations that we occasionally stopped at – I liked them more than anything else, and was always on at my father to take the turnings and let us call into one for a while. There was something magical about them: a sense of shifting home or of refuge. Of course, they were always disappointing, in that nobody really did anything there beyond buying a few snacks and scanning the magazine rack, but, even so, the second we were back on the road again I wanted to stop at the next one.

There was one time we stopped at a service station when I was quite young: maybe thirteen, surely not much older. I remember that we were on the way back from our holiday rather than on the way out, and that the holiday had been a good one. We were nearly back at the city by that point, but it was a hot day and my father had been driving for a long time, so he took the turning without any prompting from his son.

We pulled in; we all got out. The car park was enormous – space for a few hundred cars – with the main services at one end and a crappy little motel on one side. Trees everywhere else. That day, there was a gentle breeze but no cloud cover, and the summer sun was really punishing the tarmac. There was a surprisingly large number of holiday-makers: all glistening skin, bad outfits and red tan lines. We walked through them: up the slight ramp and into the main building, past the ice-cream van by the entrance. My mother and I waited by the phones while my father went to the toilet.

After a minute, my mother asked if I wanted anything from the shop, and I said no. She wanted a paper – my father had insisted that she didn't buy one all week, or else it wouldn't have been a proper holiday, and she was desperate to catch up with the news. I asked if I could wait for them both outside in the sun, and she thought about it and then said yes. After all, I was a sensible kid: she knew I wasn't going to head off anywhere I shouldn't, and that it would take handcuffs and chloroform for a stranger to take me away. So I went back down the walkway, squinting against the sun, and I'd swear to God that I knew something was wrong even before I heard it – before I turned my head to the right and saw it. But of course, I don't believe in God. Perhaps I should just swear.

When you see something out of the ordinary, you don't take everything in at once. Because most things that happen to you, you're used to them – they're everyday sorts of things that don't take much in the way of processing, and that means that you're very rarely startled or surprised by what occurs in front of you. It all just washes over, and it's only once in a while that you're forced to take a second look and *think* before you can understand exactly what's going on. Your brain, fooled into laziness by how normal things usually are, rubs its eyes, realises it might actually have to *work* for a living for once, and then immediately scrabbles desperately for reference points – something that it can at least start from in order to make sense of what you're seeing. That day, my first thought was: *fight*. A playground fight, where two kids go at it and everyone else rushes around, circling them, crowding in until they couldn't stop fighting if they wanted to.

The commotion to my right was a little like that, but different enough to chill me at a subconscious level. Looking back now, I can break it down. We weren't in a playground; this was an adult place where things like fights didn't happen, because adults were the ones who stopped them – that was their job. But the people moving over were grown-ups, and although there was nothing voyeuristic or eager about the way they approached there was also a sense of powerlessness to it. The steps they took were faltering. Latent civic duty was moving them over while their better judgement was telling them to stay still; and many were doing just that, perhaps pretending there was nothing to move over for. The ones who were paying attention clearly wanted to do something, but they knew that they couldn't: they were all twitching fingers, unsure expressions. A few people – afraid – were simply walking away as quickly as they could, looking as though they wanted to hide. I would understand later that what I was seeing here was group denial. The inability of any single person to take action resulting in nobody doing anything at all.

I walked over mindlessly, on auto-pilot and in slow motion, edging past the people who were moving away. When I got close enough, I stood and watched what was happening.

There were about ten rough-looking men in a circle, all facing outwards. Perhaps they were some kind of biker outfit, because they were all dressed in the same old black leather and a few of them were wearing matching bandannas. The majority of them were keeping the crowd at bay, utterly implacable, palms out and pushing, warning away anyone who came too close. It was the flip-side of group denial: nobody was going to fuck with these guys and they knew it. There were simply too many of them, and this was business as usual.

Inside the circle, a man on the ground was being beaten by another two. He was around my father's age and he was wearing dark-blue jeans and a pale-brown shirt. He had his eyes shut: screwed up against the pain from the kicks and punches he was receiving. There was something terribly foetal about him, curled up like that for protection, and I shivered as I realised that he was preparing himself for the end of his life. After that, I felt every blow he took, and experienced the same innate feeling of powerlessness that kept everyone else from doing anything either.

'Keep back.'

A member of the audience had gotten too close and had been pushed backwards. He staggered a little, and the biker who'd shoved him raised a finger to warn him off.

'Keep the fuck back,' he said, over the sound of blows landing thick and hard and constant behind him. 'He's going to die anyway. Just let him die.'

Suddenly, something happened and people began to move away.

'Shit! Get out of the way.'

They scattered: first a few, panicked into motion, and then everyone – everyone apart from me. A woman grabbed my arm and tried to pull me back, but I shook her off. Something was telling me that I needed to see what was going to happen. That it was important.

With the crowd thinning, I saw that the beating had stopped. Now, the man was resting on his forearms and knees, and he was looking up. His face was a bloody mess and his long hair was hanging down almost to the tarmac, matted and red. As I stared at him, a bead of blood fell from his ruined eyebrow and made a small, spidery circle on the ground underneath his chin.

I glanced at that, and then at his face, and I took a step back. Because the man was staring straight at me. His eyes were bright white and clear, in stark contrast to his red cheeks and forehead, and the black, glistening clot of his nose. He kept staring at me and I couldn't look away. I didn't see what happened – not properly – but one second he was looking at me and then suddenly his face had smashed forward into the ground, and a puff of red mist hung in the air. He didn't move, but after the briefest of pauses a solid rope of blood flung itself out from the top of his head, nearly reaching my shoes. And then another rope, slightly shorter. Painting the ground. Another, shorter still.

I looked up and saw that one of the men was holding a gun with a silencer on it. And he was staring at me.

I felt a hand clamp down on my shoulder.

'Martin.'

I turned to see my father standing behind me. My mother was beside him. They both looked frightened but determined.

'Dad—'

I was big for my age, but he picked me up almost effortlessly, turned me around and headed quickly away from the men. He held me firmly, confidently, but I could feel a strange electricity in his hands and I knew that he was terrified. My mother was walking beside us, watching the tarmac as though every step was a test she needed her full concentration to complete. There was a crackle in the air. Later – again – I would understand that they were expecting a bullet in their backs at any moment, and also that we were all genuinely lucky not to receive one. At the time, I wasn't scared. That would come later.

As we got closer to the car, my father put me down, but he left a strong, guiding hand on my shoulder. I remember that suddenly everything looked surprisingly normal. There were people walking between the cars, smiling at each other. There were the sounds of lorries, cars, trucks in the distance. Trees leaning slightly in the breeze with their leaves fluttering, seeming to catch the light in that fractured way that the sea does.

Here was the process in reverse, then. Walking back to the car, everything looked normal and everyday, but a part of my mind was now screaming that it wasn't, and I simply couldn't square the two. What was wrong? Why wasn't the sky blackening? Why weren't people's faces melting away? It was wrong – a trick was being played on me here. I was suspicious of this pretend calm and felt like narrowing my eyes and glaring. This was how nightmares were: everything right apart from one sinister thing you just couldn't put your finger on.

As we reached the car, my father rounded on my mother.

'For God's sake, Ann. What the hell were you thinking?'

'I just ... I didn't ...'

I stared at them both, because I'd never seen either of

them like this. Never seen my mother this flustered: this stuck for something to say. And my father's big hands were flexing slightly, as though he was in danger of losing it completely and hurting someone. But the expression on his face held more fear than genuine rage, with flickers of relief around the edges. Seeing your father scared is a bad thing. I don't think you're a child again after you do.

'I just thought he'd be fine.'

My father shook his head and unlocked the car. We were back through the city gates before anybody spoke again. There was never a question of reporting it to the police; someone else could do that. Even though the car was silent, I understood that a kind of peace was settling between my parents. My father's hands were shaking slightly and he took the remains of the journey slowly. My mother just stared out of the window, resting an elbow on the rim and hooding her face; she was crying but trying to hide it. Even so, ebbs of relief were thickening in the air, and I allowed myself to feel them. This was something that wouldn't be spoken of properly again. There would just be a sweet and desperate undercurrent in our lives, which would tell us quietly but clearly how precious and wonderful life really was.

'Martin?'

'Huh?'

I looked up to see that Lucy was watching me. She was leaning against the side of her car, smoking. Rosh was still inside the motel, booking us a room. In the rainbow light cast by the humming neon sign above us it was difficult to read Lucy's expression. I would have taken it for her standard issue nonchalance except that she sounded genuinely concerned when she asked:

'Are you okay?'

I looked back down at the stretch of ground in front of me. This was the exact spot where it had happened – as a child, I'd watched a man die here. It used to be services, but now it was just a car park, a motel and not much of anything else: dull floodlights at the end of a spread of darkening tarmac; cars rushing past on the road beyond. Exactly the kind of place that three people like us should end up for the night. I hadn't realised – even as Lucy had taken the turning – but now the memory couldn't have been clearer.

'I'm fine,' I said.

'You don't look fine. You're worried about—'

I shook my head, perhaps too quickly.

'No.'

I'm not worried about Rachel.

I wanted to shout that at her until it echoed – until it pranged back and forth between the handful of parked cars.

You see, there had been a time when Lucy would never have spoken Rachel's name out loud. It's no surprise, I guess – when you're fucking a guy you don't want to talk too much about his wife, even if you're pretending that it's all very casual and easy. But after she started seeing Rich again – when it was officially over between us – Rachel's name began to crop up more frequently, as though she was now suddenly welcome as a guest in our conversations.

'I'm not worried about Rachel,' I said.

'Yes, you are.'

I kicked the ground a little, not wanting to talk about this now and already slightly irritated by it. This was something else that Lucy did. She always seemed to think she had some kind of direct line into my head – that she could see straight through what I was thinking on the surface, all the way down to what was being whispered underneath – and she was always correcting me about stuff she couldn't possibly know. Despite the fact that I'd left my wife for her, she just *knew* that I didn't love her: that I was being silly, and that I'd go back to Rachel in the end. The force of her appraisals always made me go to extremes. *Yes, I do. I love you.* I'd insist it and feel even more stupid.

'If you must know,' I said, 'I was just thinking. I've been here before.'

She looked at the motel. 'Stayed here?'

'No. When I was young. It used to be services.'

'Right.'

I said, 'I was just thinking it was weird, that was all.'

It felt more than weird, though, and I kept staring at the ground and feeling shivers of recognition. It was like bumping into an old friend at a random party: just coincidence, but you're compelled to try and work out how the fuck you both ended up there. It's random but meaningful and, for no real reason I could identify, it seemed slightly ominous. Every time I moved my head, I could hear a whining in the air. We were miles out of the city – couldn't even see the swell of it, the pinprick spread of its lights – and yet I felt trapped by the crawling familiarity of being here. It seemed to soak everything that had happened in the last few days with a black inevitability.

Lucy ground out the cigarette under her heel. Obviously, she wasn't feeling anything like that.

'If you're worried, you should ring her,' she said.

I walked away from where I'd been standing and leaned against the car beside her.

'Bad idea,' I said. 'Anyway, she'll be fine.'

'You don't want to keep trying? She's your wife.'

'No,' I said. 'She's not. And she'll be fine. What the fuck would I tell her anyway?'

She inclined her head slightly, conceding the point. I said, 'Well, maybe you should ring Rich.'

The air between us stiffened, tensed, and suddenly I wished I wasn't standing quite so close to her anymore. That had been unfair and unnecessary, and we both knew it.

'He's at home,' she told me quietly.

She'd told me the same thing earlier on, as well, when the three of us had been debating what to do. The most worrying thing about the damage to Rosh's farmhouse wasn't the loss of the building: it was that someone had known enough about us to find it in the first place. If they knew that then what else did they know, and what else might they be prepared to do? Perhaps we'd killed all of them tonight, but until we spoke to Keleigh or found Harris we couldn't assume anything, and so going home was out of the question. Hence the motel. We'd also discussed whether anyone we cared about might be in danger, and after some deliberation I'd tried to phone Rachel. She hadn't answered. But it was late, and phonecalls from me weren't exactly welcome at the best of times.

'Okay,' Rosh said, the front doors of the motel closing behind him. He was swinging a key. 'We've got one family room between us.'

A family room? I could only imagine what the guy on the desk must have thought, what with Rosh coming in at this hour. On first glance, it was difficult to imagine Rosh having a family at all, or, if he did, what it might look like. And I guess Lucy and I must have looked pretty shit even to Rosh, because he frowned and said:

'You two okay?'

'Fine,' I said. Lucy didn't say anything.

He kept looking at me, concerned, for a couple of seconds, and then he seemed to shrug to himself. I wasn't sure how much Rosh knew about what had happened between me and Lucy, but whatever that might be he obviously figured that now wasn't the best time to bring it up or offer advice. Far smarter than either of us had been.

'Whatever,' he said. 'Come on – it's over this way.'

We followed him, Lucy heading off first and leaving me trailing behind. I glanced back as I went, taking one last look at the patch of tarmac where, as a child, I'd seen a man murdered. I hadn't been back here since and it still seemed odd that I'd ended up here now. If there really was one single event that had made me want to be a cop then I thought that one was as good a candidate as any. Strange. I turned around and hurried to catch up.

The motel was constructed around a rectangle, with all the rooms facing inwards on what had once – and presumably quite some time ago – been a swimming pool. Now it was just a dirty hole that would never be used again. I casually watched the closed, white doors as we passed, but there was nobody to see and not much to hear. Just the night-time rush of air, like a faraway river, and the muffled sound of someone's television. Apart from that, the motel felt silent and abandoned. Above us, the rain clouds had relaxed and untensed, and the sky was mostly clear now. Looking up, it was like I was wandering into a child's model – as though someone had taken the roof off a doll's house and was peering down at me.

Our room was on the second floor. We climbed slatted, wooden steps up onto the walkway there and then found our door, which was about halfway along one of the longer sides. Rosh opened up and we went in.

'This is a *family* room?' Lucy said.

'Apparently so.'

Rosh locked the door behind us.

About the only time you'd bring a family here, I thought, was if you'd kidnapped them. The wallpaper was piss-yellow, peeling in a few choice spots and speckled with damp in others. You could smell it in the air, like someone had left a rack of wet clothes to dry. There was one double bed and two singles, all of them sporting white bedsheets that looked more like cheap paper than anything else. There were no pillow-cases: just pillows the colour of old teabags. In an otherwise unprecedented nod towards convenience and comfort, there was a sink unit in the far corner, but the silver of it was tarnished by those brown stains that metal acquires steadily over time, and it looked as unhygienic as the rest of the room.

There was a single door leading off, which opened into a small bathroom. Lucy flicked the light switch, slapping everything with stunningly harsh white: the kind of light that would probably appear behind God if you received a visitation. There wasn't much to light up, though – surprisingly clean tiles and toilet, another sink and a thin metal radiator mounted high up by the tiny window. The radiator was humming to itself, sounding potentially dangerous.

'Not great,' Rosh said. 'But it'll do. I suggest we all get some sleep and talk in the morning.'

Part of me wanted to talk about everything now, but I was so tired that my mind probably wouldn't have been able to hold it all together anyway. Better perhaps to rest and then come at it vaguely refreshed in a few hours. We'd had a long night.

'Fine by me,' Lucy said.

Rosh and I took the single beds, allowing Lucy to spread out a little. They settled down first, and I went through to the bathroom to clean my face. The cut wasn't deep and it had already stopped bleeding, so there wasn't much to do but wash away the blood and clean whatever parts of the wound were still open to water.

Despite myself, I found I was thinking. We'd been forced to kill five men and at least one of them had been a cop. All because of Alison Sheldon. But who had she been? Just a student. Except that a number of men with automatic weaponry had a lot invested in making sure her murder went unsolved.

I ticked off the light and went back through into the pitch-black bedroom.

Lucy was already snoring gently. I recognised the sound. It stirred an uncertain pain inside me and I forced myself to ignore it. It was easier than it should have been, perhaps because I was still hurt and angry from the conversation we'd had outside. Rosh was making no noise at all, and I considered trying to talk to him but then discounted the idea. I just took off a few of my clothes and slipped into bed, leaving my gun within easy reach at the side. I was asleep before I could feel angry or sad or frightened, and I dreamed of nothing.

Later on, I remember sitting up in my bed. The room was growing lighter as dawn broke outside, but Lucy and Rosh were still asleep, both facing away from me. The covers over them were calmly rising and falling, and I felt very much alone, as though despite the slight movement I was trapped in a pocket of paused time. I picked up my mobile, knowing even as I did so that it was a bad idea. Rachel's number was programmed into the '1' key; I pressed it now, holding the phone up to my ear.

Straight to voicemail. She hadn't answered my last call, and sometime since she had switched off her phone.

CHAPTER THIRTEEN

Eight-thirty the next morning and the main crossroads at the centre of Elephant was saturated with commerce. You could breathe it in – a kind of sparkly damp in the air – and the black tiles on the walkways were soaked with the dew of it. Everyone walking around seemed full of purpose and direction, whereas I felt as though I'd got up very early after not enough sleep and was simply too slow to exist here for very long. Which was true.

There was all manner of shops here, lining the four pedestrian walkways that met in the centre. The traditional colours of Elephant were gold and white, but you couldn't see many lanterns or banners among the shopfronts, which all had awnings and blocky signs stretching out above multicoloured windows and doors. Cameras were recording everything from inside glass bulbs on top of tall, black poles. The crossroads itself was cornered by a chemist, a mobile phone shop, a coffee bar and a clothes store, and variations on these themes extended away as far as the eye could see. They were interspersed with expensive sandwich shops that had the pre-work masses queueing out of the doors, and there was a baked-potato shack outside the chemist, complete with rising steam and the sound of ovens being scraped and trays rattled into place. Everybody apart from Rosh, Lucy and me appeared to be wearing suits and marching in neat lines, with the occasional businessman weaving through at high speed. A fair few men and women were having intense conversations on very small phones. It was actually quite astonishing to see the dexterity with which the city handled its people: even in this place – this hub of activity – there were no collisions, no jostling, no shouting. It appeared to be a well-rehearsed perform- ance where everybody knew their spots.

'How many people live in this city?' Rosh asked.

'Close to ten million,' I told him. 'Last time I counted.'

Lucy nodded. 'And they're all here.'

She ground out her cigarette on the pavement. Her mood didn't seem to have improved much since last night, which was strange. She usually didn't stay pissed off with me for this long, but she'd hardly said a word to me all morning, despite my casual attempts at bridging the gap.

'You want to watch that,' I said, trying again. 'Littering.'

'There'll be a dirt trolley along any second.' She sniffed and looked bored. 'I'm sure all these pricks will survive in the meantime. God, I hate this fucking district.'

We were standing on the corner outside the clothes store. In the window behind us beige dummies model- ling expensive garments were staring out into the distance, imperious and stern. From here, if we headed west we'd end up among the shining, glass-fronted office blocks, while east would take us towards the markets and the university. That was where we'd parked this morning. North took us upmarket to the edge of Rabbit, while down the hill behind us the shops got gradually cheaper and more beaten down.

That way led to Owl, where you'd find the police department and law courts.

At the moment, we weren't going anywhere. We were waiting.

'What did he say he looked like?' Rosh asked me.

'He didn't.'

'He didn't say what he looked like?'

I shook my head.

The call had come through on my mobile a little after seven, waking us all up. My first thought, culled from the half-memory of trying to phone her, was that it would be Rachel. When I picked it up and looked at the display with bleary eyes I saw that the number wasn't recognised, and so instead I thought: *Keleigh*. But then, when I pressed green and said hello, it was a man's voice that answered me. And he hadn't told me what he looked like.

'He just said to meet him here.'

'Well, that's handy,' Lucy said quietly.

'Absolutely. I asked him, but he just said that we were cops. Said he was sure we'd spot him.'

Lucy didn't say anything at all to that – she just frowned and looked away down the street. Rosh was more thoughtful. I felt somewhere between the two of them: tired and irritable; expectant; cautiously interested. The adrenaline from yesterday was resting in me like vinegar, and perhaps this would be something to sweeten it with. I was nervous, though. There are good breaks and bad breaks, and after last night none of us was taking any chances. I had my gun within easy reach, and I was sure that Rosh and Lucy did too.

Lucy finished looking around and said, 'He's late.'

It was twenty to nine. He was only ten minutes late, but it still made me nervous. Nobody seemed to be paying us much attention, and yet I felt watched. In fact, I'd been feeling watched in some way or other for the last few days. Although the sheer impersonal *business* of the crossroads was the opposite of the solitude of the motel last night, the effect was very much the same: we were painfully visible; glaringly obvious. We stood out in the rush of people like rocks in a stream.

I looked to my left and started to say something, but I found that a man was standing there, directly next to me, and I immediately stopped talking and stepped quickly away. He seemed to have come from nowhere. My hand was inside my jacket and on my gun even as I realised that he wasn't paying us any attention. And on face value he wouldn't have been much of a threat if he was. Rosh and Lucy moved around next to me. The man was ignoring us and just staring down at the ground – although it was difficult to tell because he was wearing big, black goggles that wrapped around his face all the way from his nose to his ears.

He was about twenty years old, tall and almost painfully thin, dressed in an old white T-shirt and grey-green combats. His arms didn't seem to taper whatsoever between his wrist and his elbow and, as he crouched down beside me, I noticed that there was no contour to his thighs: no real muscle there beneath the paint-stained material. The kid – not a man at all – was like a set of straws placed at hard angles to each other. Now he was squatting the goggles enhanced the naturally insectile appearance of his skinny body and made him look almost alien. It probably didn't help much that he had long, bright purple hair, tied back in a pony-tail.

Purple hair, I thought. *So this must be Keleigh's boyfriend.*

A few people were looking at him as they walked

past, their eyes glancing from him to us and then away again: back to business. The boy didn't seem interested, either in the three of us or the throng passing behind him. Instead, he was studying the black-tiled pavement, where he had rested a sheet of card that had once been white and was now stained with a trampled rainbow. Before any of us could say anything, I heard a solid metallic rattle and then a hiss as he sprayed paint onto the card. His knuckles jutted out white, full of careful intent, moving the can he was holding steadily and efficiently back and forth across the card, covering it in yellow mist.

'Hey, Picasso,' Lucy said. 'What the fuck do you think you're doing?'

The boy ignored her. He sprayed the paint for another couple of seconds, and then Lucy started to move around me. At the same time, the hissing stopped and the can disappeared into the boy's knapsack. He moved the card away to reveal a stark yellow tattoo on the black tiles:

FONDLY

I THINK

OF YOU

I was so startled that I took a step back. Where had I seen this before? I thought back. It had been on the university campus, perhaps. Not the same words, but the style had been the same and I was in no doubt that the author was too.

'An old one,' the thin boy said. 'But it's my favourite.'

'Did you know graffiti is a crime?' Rosh asked.

The kid stood up and turned to face us, holding the card down by his side. Now, I could vaguely see the empty letters he'd carved out of it. With the goggles hiding the kid's eyes it was impossible to tell whether he was actually looking at us or just had his head pointing our way.

'It's art,' he said.

'It doesn't look like art to me,' Lucy said.

'And obviously she's a connoisseur,' I added.

'Well,' the kid said, breathing out and sounding entirely unbothered by the criticism. 'Maybe not. But you don't look like cops. It's a weird fucking world.'

'You're the guy that rang me this morning, then.'

His head didn't move, but his perception seemed to shift slightly towards me.

'Yeah, I rang you. You left your card with my friend.'

'That would make you Jamie, right?' I said.

'Yeah.'

'And you're Keleigh Groves's boyfriend.'

He shook his head, although not in denial, and said: 'I don't want to talk about it here.'

'Where, then?'

'Whitelocks,' he said. 'It's at the edge of Horse, over by—'

'I know where it is.'

As soon as he'd said it, I'd felt another jolt of recognition. First it had been the graffiti and now this. I'd started off in Whitelocks the night that Sean had sent me the letter. I remembered it well: the older woman smoking the cigarette; the picture of the eye taped to the wall at the bottom of the alleyway. And—

– and then suddenly, without warning, the people moving through the crossroads resolved themselves into a pattern I could see clearly. It was mathematical, predictable and obvious. I saw it for a full second, had chance to question what I was seeing and confirm it, and—

– and then it was gone again. And they were just people going about their random business.

I shook my head.

The boy had tilted his head and seemed to be staring at me from behind the goggles.

'That okay?'

'That's fine,' I said. 'When?'

'Half hour,' he said. 'I'll meet you there.'

Before any of us could do anything to stop him he was gone: moving off up the street, his head looking this way and that, goggles still in place. He swung the knapsack up onto a shoulder that looked too thin to support it, and then he disappeared among the people.

'What do you think?' I said.

Lucy stepped past me, stuffed her hands in her pockets and then turned back around.

'This is the guy that Keleigh was off with last night, when you went round?'

I nodded.

'Well then, I think we go to Whitelocks.'

'Good,' I said. 'It's not even nine yet, but I could do with a drink.'

We started walking and Lucy lit a cigarette.

Rosh said, 'God bless the twenty-four-hour city.'

Whitelocks: this time early morning and therefore a very different proposition. It was pretty much dead inside – just a handful of old guys, all sitting or leaning by themselves. The jangle of fruit machines had been replaced by the sizzle of breakfasts cooking and the clank of washed glasses being lined up overhead. People's attentions were all held by the television in the corner, which was showing news: the build-up to the annual boxing, mostly. What little conversation there was appeared to be coming entirely from behind the bar. In the broad alleyway outside, hanging baskets of flowers were leaking water and the slabs underneath were soaked. Further down, there was a scraping *swish*, as someone moved an old broom across the wet ground with a steady, authoritative rhythm.

The picture of the eye had been taken down, I noticed. Even so, I felt that odd sensation of being watched and yet not watched. I had a strange feeling that whatever the boy was going to tell us would be something so obvious that we'd known it already without realising.

He had bought himself a Coke and was waiting for us at one of the old brown benches outside. The goggles rested on the table in front of him, but you could still see the imprint of where they'd been on his forehead.

'Two minutes,' Rosh told us, heading inside to fetch some drinks.

Lucy and I sat down across from Jamie and waited for Rosh to come back. The kid didn't acknowledge us in any way, but when Rosh brought out three beers, he looked up and the sun caught his eyes. He was wearing purple contact lenses.

'So what can I do for you?' he said when we'd settled.

I took a sip of my beer and told him:

'We're here because of Alison.'

Jamie didn't seem unduly fazed by this.

'Yeah, we figured you would be.'

' "We" being you and Keleigh?' Rosh said.

' "We" being me and Keleigh. That's right.'

I asked, 'Where's Keleigh now?'

'She's safe.'

'Yeah,' I pressed. 'But where is she safe?'

'Safe somewhere.' He shook his head. 'Look, she doesn't want to be involved in this at the moment. Even if she did, I want to keep her out.'

'You're her boyfriend?' Lucy prompted.

He nodded.

That would have to do for now, I thought. We could give him a little rope, trust him slightly, hear him out. For one thing, he might be able to tell us just as much as Keleigh could, but it would also give us the chance to form an opinion. If he was on the level then we could tell him a little more, and maybe we could persuade him to take us to her then.

'Okay,' I said. 'And both of you knew Alison. How was that? It was through uni, right?'

'Yeah.'

He took another sip of Coke. Ice was clinking in the glass.

Rosh said, 'Can you tell us anything about her disappearance?'

Jamie considered this quietly, and I watched him while he did. I got the impression that there was probably a great deal he could tell us, but that he didn't know where to begin. Or maybe just how.

After a few moments, he settled on it.

'I can tell you I know she's dead.'

'How do you know that?' Lucy asked.

Jamie just looked at her. Even for Lucy, who could eyeball with the best of them, purple contacts were clearly a new experience. She actually looked away.

He said, 'Because I'm not an *idiot*?'

I decided to change tack a little.

'Right. Do you know a lecturer named Dr Mark Harris?'

Jamie frowned at that, putting the glass back down

on the table. Then, he slid it around slightly, blurring the circular water stain it had left on the wood.

'Harris worked with us a while on our art project,' he said, studying the glass. Then, he tilted it a little. 'He was sort of an advisor, I'd guess you'd say. Like a consultant.'

'He was in the History department, though?'

'Yeah,' Jamie said. 'Our project was based on the history of the city.'

Rosh said, 'And have you heard from him recently?'

'Why?'

The kid was frowning again – and because it was the second time it really caught my attention. The mention of Harris's name seemed to have genuinely confused him, as though he hadn't been expecting it to come up. I hoped that Keleigh really was safe, and not just safe somewhere with Harris.

Rosh said, 'Well, we have reason to believe he was involved in Alison's disappearance.'

Jamie shook his head immediately.

'No. He didn't have anything to do with that.'

'What makes you so sure?' I said.

'Trust me.' This time those purple eyes looked at me. He shook his head again. 'Harris really had nothing to do with it.'

I thought back to the email and the video attachment. We knew that Harris had been involved in luring Sean to his death and we strongly suspected he was after Keleigh now, so it wasn't a wild leap to imagine that he'd helped abduct Alison too. The question was why. He'd obviously done a good job of convincing Jamie he was on the level, and so I changed tack a little to work on the motive.

'Okay,' I said. 'Was Harris ever involved with Alison?'

Jamie moved the glass again.

'No. He was just an advisor.'

Rosh said, 'Has he been in touch with you recently?'

'No. I've not heard from him in a while. What's the big thing with Harris?'

'Has he been in touch with Keleigh?'

'I don't know.' Jamie put his glass down and leaned forwards. 'Why are you asking?'

I wasn't sure how much to reveal at this stage, but Rosh took charge.

'We have reason to believe he may be involved with some people who want to hurt Keleigh.'

'Oh.' Jamie leaned back. He didn't look surprised by the idea that someone might want to hurt his girlfriend so much as the idea that it might be Harris.

'So, that's why we're asking,' I added.

'Well, she's safe,' Jamie said. 'We've not heard from Harris in a while.'

'Okay,' Rosh said. 'If you do hear from him, whatever you might think of him right now, you should be careful.'

'All right.'

'So he was an advisor,' I said. 'And you mentioned something about an art project. Was Alison involved in that?'

Jamie nodded.

'It was four of us. Me and Kel. Alison. This guy Damian. We just met with Harris a few times for some background.'

'Background on what?'

'Our art was to do with the city,' he said. 'It was to do with personifying the city, yeah? Making the city seem human. That's what my graffiti is all about. It's giving a voice to the actual architecture of the city, so that you're looking around and it's like the buildings or the pavements are talking to you. Like they have something to say.'

'Doesn't sound like my kind of thing,' Rosh said, giving him a smile. 'I always preferred plain old paintings. Kind of boring, I guess.'

It was an attempt to relax him, but Jamie wasn't biting.

'Very boring.'

'So your more interesting version is these street logos?' I said.

'Well, it's not just the graffiti.' He gestured with his hands a little. 'The writing's only an initial object. The actual artwork is people's *experiences* as they walk past and see it. Everybody participates and makes it what it is. In theory, anyway. Like, if somebody wrote a letter to the paper complaining about it, then that would have been part of the final piece.'

Lucy was clearly unimpressed by this. Since I wasn't working anymore, my taxes weren't directly support- ing it and so I could afford to be a little more open- minded.

'And this is what Alison did, too? And Keleigh?'

'No.' Jamie shook his head. 'We all did different things. Keleigh did this thing with photographs. She had photos of eyes that she'd stick up on walls, giving the city a kind of sight. She took pictures, too, and left them places. Pictures of people taped to walls. Pictures of dogs and homeless people and things—'

I was fazing out, I realised: hardly taking in the rest of it. Pictures of eyes. Despite the noises around us, and the sound of Jamie talking, the main sound I could hear was ringing silence: this ominous, curling buzz in the air. I shuddered slightly.

Keep it together, I thought. But I wasn't sure why. Jamie was still talking.

'– and it's all to do with that, really. That was what Harris was advising us on – the city's history, the myth of the brothers – and we were working around that, some of us closer than others.'

Rosh said, 'Okay. So what happened?'

I noticed the expression on Jamie's face, and it reminded me of nothing so much as the hooded, thoughtful looks that Sean had given me from time to time.

'We were trying to present the city as a living thing,' he said. 'You see? We were looking at the city so closely. And so we really shouldn't have been surprised when it started looking back.'

Lucy had lit another cigarette and was now smoking quietly, studying the grain of the wooden table. I didn't know what she was thinking, but she still looked deeply unimpressed. She'd always been immune to the kind of thoughts that Sean often voiced, and I thought she was probably figuring that this whole conversation was a waste of time. Someone had killed Alison, but it wasn't anything to do with some stupid, pissy art project – these people had automatic weapons and corrupt policemen on their team, for fuck's sake. Rosh was hiding his feelings better, but I was guessing he was probably on the same side of the fence.

I didn't know what to think. While we'd been speaking, the guy cleaning the flagstones had worked his way up to the top end of the alley, but I could still hear the steady *swish*. The rhythm had remained steady and every time he moved the brush it felt like it was wiping thoughts from my head. Slow hypnosis. I couldn't get a handle on what I felt, beyond a general sense of foreboding and the memory of everything that Sean and I had talked about as we watched the city tense and untense, like something awful was breathing beneath the pavements. With that as a backdrop, Jamie's story didn't seem quite so strange. There was a dark thread running through the coincidences of the past few days, finishing up here in a knot my mind couldn't see well enough to untie.

Once again, I told myself: *keep it together*.

'So,' Rosh said. 'You did graffiti. Keleigh did these photographs. What did Alison do?'

'Murder,' Jamie said, and then gestured at Lucy's pack of cigarettes. 'Can I have one of those?'

She shrugged. 'Knock yourself out.'

He took one and lit it without saying thank you. After breathing out the first mouthful of smoke, he said:

'Her art was based around murder. When she first started, it was violent crime in general. But I guess there are only so many hours in the day.'

Rosh looked to me for support, but I was having trouble thinking straight. Lucy clearly wasn't going to help, so he went on by himself.

'So what about murder? What does that mean – what did she do?'

'She went to murder sites.' Jamie took another drag on the cigarette and then gestured with it. 'A bit morbid, I guess, but that was her thing. She was edgy like that. Or she liked people to think that she was, anyway. She'd light candles and take photographs, make sketches. Things like that. She was sort of seeing this guy who was working on computer stuff with her. He was helping her create something she could display.'

I realised that I needed to get back into this conversation, and it seemed a nice, easy question to begin with:

'What was his name?'

'Rob Hedge,' Jamie said. 'Something stupid like that, anyway.'

'He's at the university?'

'Yeah. He's doing a PhD. Computer Studies, or maybe IT. I don't know. Something computery.'

'Okay,' I said. So here was yet another candidate for the mysterious boyfriend. 'So what happened? Alison went to these sites. Did something happen to her at one?'

'No. She was usually really careful. She took her boyfriend everywhere when she was working.'

'And this was Hedge?' Lucy said, stubbing out her cigarette. 'Or perhaps Harris? You? Was it me?'

Jamie glared at her.

'Ignore her,' I said quickly, and then did so myself as I saw her glare at me in return. 'So what about this boyfriend?'

'This was a more regular guy,' he said. 'The thing you have to understand about Alison is that she saw a lot of people and didn't really have any hang-ups about sex. She just did what she wanted. She liked it but didn't think that much of it, you know. She was like that with Hedge, definitely. But this guy was more of a boyfriend.'

'A nice guy?' I said.

Jamie shook his head.

'He was a dirty, fucking criminal.'

'Right.'

'Pretty much, anyway. She just picked him up one night at some club in Wasp. I guess he was edgy too—'

But I interrupted him:

'Spooks?'

Rosh and Lucy looked at me a little strangely, and I didn't blame them. Here was a solid lead – a boyfriend with criminal connections – and I was chasing up meaningless coincidences. But nevertheless, I needed to know.

'Was it Spooks?' I said.

'I've no idea.' Jamie was frowning too. 'I wasn't out that night.'

'You say he was a criminal?' Rosh took back control before I could open my mouth again. 'What was he into?'

'Nothing too heavy, I don't think,' Jamie said. 'He wasn't like the Godfather, or anything. And he didn't seem particularly dangerous. I don't know. You got the impression that he knew people. And he'd leave packages at our house every now and then. You know – just for a few days. That kind of shit.'

'And what did you think of this guy? Did you get on with him?'

'No,' Jamie said. 'He was a prick. But what does it matter? Alison liked him. And he was useful to her, so she didn't think about it too much and neither did we. She certainly never felt nervous about anything. She was like that, though. I don't think she ever believed anyone would actually hurt her.'

Lucy said, 'But someone did.'

'Yeah.' That glare again. 'Someone did.'

There was a war about to break, so I interrupted quickly.

'What was his name?'

Jamie looked at me for a moment, and then he said it:

'His name was Carl Halloran.'

He spoke it slowly, and my mind said the surname along with him. I knew that name. We all did. All the coincidences clicked into place in my head, and although I was still too close to see the full picture I knew that everything fit and made sense.

Lucy, suddenly not so indifferent, said, 'Oh fuck.'

Jamie nodded, and then reached out and, without asking, took another cigarette from Lucy's packet.

It's difficult to put faces to names, though. I knew that Halloran had been the last one we'd killed and that it had been a couple of weeks before we'd found Alison's body, but I couldn't picture what he looked like. Not his face, anyway. I did know that it had been Lucy who killed him. Two shots in the back of the head. He hadn't been one of mine.

So that was the first thing Jamie said that knocked my legs out from under me, and a moment later he lit the cigarette and told us the second.

'That was pretty much your friend Sean's reaction, too.'

CHAPTER FOURTEEN

Six months earlier, late afternoon.

In a cramped university bedroom, surrounded by computer equipment, Alison Sheldon was half-lying, half-sitting in Rob Hedge's bed, building a joint.

In life, Alison was beautiful. She had smooth, clean skin; grey eyes that changed colour in different lights – sometimes blue, sometimes green; and honey-coloured, tumble-down hair that was currently in a state of disarray from the sex she'd been enjoying that afternoon. Naked, cross-legged, with the covers resting loosely around her waist, she was quite a sight, and she knew it. Rob, sitting at the end of the bed, didn't know where to look – at her breasts, her face, or whether to watch those nimble fingers. She had a book resting on her lap where the main construction was taking place.

The window was slightly open, and there was a cold breeze drifting lazily in, like steam rising slowly from dry ice. Alison liked it; it had been snowing earlier on and the air smelled crisp. Outside, she could hear the sound of people, and she imagined them huddled and bundled in thick, woolly clothes, breathing out cool smoke that would flicker and swirl in front of their red faces. Winter was good. She associated it with snow sparkling in bright light, with hard blue skies, with the rough texture of scarves and gloves. It was almost a shame to be inside, but at least she'd get out later. It was too bad that Carl was busy tonight. She'd have to remember to call Jamie; she figured he'd come with her if she asked nicely enough.

Now, she lifted the paper carefully to her lips, licked the edge and began rolling something that was close to being the perfect joint.

Rob's flat was cheerfully untidy. Most of the computer crap was on and under the desk opposite the bed, but there were also piles of clothes on the floor, and leftover plates from the pizza he'd cooked them for lunch. The carpet was dark green, but everything above floor level was pale. The walls were beige; the curtains, cream; his bedspread, yellow. She kept telling him that yellow was the most depressing colour to decorate with, but he didn't take much notice. Since he seemed to be quite a miserable guy she'd thought he might be interested, but apparently not.

She finished rolling. It was one of the benefits of seeing Rob that she got to smoke some of the dope she brought for him. The arrangement was a relatively complicated one. They didn't know each other well enough to be friends, exactly. On the surface that's what they were, but it was a pretence: she wouldn't have been here if he didn't help with her artwork. He was a nice enough guy and she liked him, but the world was full of nice guys and he wasn't *that* nice. And without the dope and the sex, he probably wouldn't have been helping her either. And yet they were both fond enough of each other to skirt around these issues.

'Ta da!' She held up the finished joint, turning it around for him to admire.

He smiled at her, kind of sweetly.

'You're so good at that. I wish I could roll as well as you.'

'I'll teach you.'

'You will?'

Alison shrugged. 'Yeah. If you like.'

She thumbed the wheel of her lighter, scraping the flame into life, and then singed the end of the joint, turning it slowly so as to burn it on all sides. The end settled into a dark, smoking bunch, and then she drew on it. It glowed red; crackled a little.

'Where are you going tonight?' he said, watching her.

She took another hit.

'Snail,' she told him. 'I can't remember the address. There's a clipping and some stuff in the envelope.'

'A newspaper clipping?'

'Yeah.' She touched away some ash, rolling the tip of the joint against an old cigarette butt in the dish Rob kept by the bed in lieu of an ashtray. 'It's in the envelope.'

He opened it up to look while she kept smoking. Rob actually didn't smoke that much, so she'd bring him an eighth and they'd smoke a few joints, but she always ended up getting the lion's share of whatever she rolled. God only knew what he did with the rest after she'd gone, but she figured that he sold a little to his friends, smoked a little himself. It didn't really matter.

' "Snail",' he read. 'What a lovely area.'

'Yeah.'

'You going on your own?'

She shook her head. 'Don't worry – I'll ring Jamie. Get him to escort me.'

'Okay.' He read a little more. 'Sharon Cooper?'

'Yeah.'

Alison remembered the article. The girl had got into a row with her boyfriend, which was common enough in that area. Snail was more of a separate shanty town than an actual part of the city and most of the buildings were makeshift – or had started off that way when they were built. The usual rules of planning didn't necessarily apply to parts of Snail: it was all shacks and huts and corrugated roofs, and great iron bins that were set burning in place of proper street-lighting. Half the residents were gypsies; the other half, you couldn't tell. While Bull spread out from the north-east, Snail curled at the south-west corner of the city like a dusty afterthought. It was all poverty. There was a lot to argue about there.

Rob read the article and said: 'Her boyfriend killed her.'

'He was drunk. He punched her and she fell. She hit her head.'

'It was an accident.'

'It's certainly a moral grey area,' she agreed. 'Here.'

She passed him the joint, and he took it a little awkwardly, as though it might break. The first few drags were always painful for him because he wasn't really used to it. Alison watched him, half-amused. What the fuck had Rob done with his teens? He'd been such a good boy, she thought, and deep down he still was. That was why this whole arrangement worked.

He only took a couple more drags, and then he passed it back to her. It was two-thirds down; she'd smoke a bit more and then offer him the end, which he'd turn down because it was too much effort and too hot for him. Now, he lay down on his back with his arm behind his head and his eyes closed, and he said:

'Fucking hell.'

She looked at his naked body. He had a pretty good body.

She said, 'You're stoned?'

'Oh yeah.' He nodded to himself.

She raised an eyebrow and kept smoking the joint,

feeling her body melting away a little. But she didn't stop watching him. His cock looked warm from the sex they'd already had, like he'd scrubbed it for too long in a hot bath.

'You're too easy,' she said.

'Hmmm.' He had his eyes closed. 'That's me.'

Alison finished the joint herself and creased the roach out in the dish.

'Come here, then, easy man.'

She moved down the bed, lifted one leg over him and sat down on his lap, feeling him against her. That got his attention. He opened his eyes and smiled up at her, giving her the same look he always did: a combination of excitement, pleasure and slight fear, this time blurred a little by the fuzzy red warmth of the gear. She liked that look. His cock uncurled slowly underneath her, nudging her, and so she rested her palms on his chest, lifted up a little to allow it space. When it was hard enough, she reached under her and took hold, and then eased back down onto him.

'Oh god,' he said.

He closed his eyes. She smiled, feeling genuine affection for him, and she began to rock back and forth. With one hand, he reached out and touched her hip. The other tentatively cupped her breast. She leaned down harder against him. He needed encouragement. The first time Rob had ever kissed her, he had actually asked her permission. She upped the tempo, rolling her hips against him.

'Come whenever you want to,' she told him, and then closed her eyes as he tensed underneath her.

Twenty minutes later, Alison made the call.

Jamie was having his photograph taken. The curved lens, reflecting tens of circles of light, was close to his right eye; the camera beyond it was black and mottled and still. Keleigh's visible eye was scrunched shut as she centred the lens and prepared to take the photograph. Jamie was anticipating the flash: steeling himself for the burn in his iris. That was when his mobile rang on the other side of the room.

'Fuck.'

Keleigh moved away. Jamie blinked a few times.

'Go on,' she said.

'I'm sorry.'

He stood up, moved over to the table and picked up the phone. The display was flashing, telling him that it was *alison*.

Jamie looked up. Keleigh was pacing on the spot – she'd probably guessed who it was going to be. He looked back at the display and just held the phone, willing this problem to vanish. Alison had mentioned that Halloran couldn't go with her tonight and had told him that she'd phone him later. Not asked him, of course; just said she'd call.

Keleigh stopped pacing and stared at him.

'So, are you going to answer that?'

'Hmm,' he said. 'Not sure.'

Did he really want to speak to Alison right now? If he did then she'd ask him to go with her tonight and he wouldn't be able to say no. She knew that, too. Not so long ago, he wouldn't have hesitated and, even now, his instinct was to press green, say yes, of course. But he'd also slowly figured out that doing nice things for someone wasn't necessarily going to make them like you, especially if they were only asking because they thought you would. So for a few weeks now he'd been torn. Would Alison like him more if he was less available or willing? Very probably not. And did he really care deep down anyway?

He hadn't even answered the phone, and his mind was occupied with her. Filled with the little thrills of anticipation that wafted along like perfume with thoughts of her.

Some time soon, this was going to have to stop.

He pressed red.

'No,' he said. 'Going to leave that one.'

'Was it Alison?'

'Yeah.'

'I wonder what she wanted.'

He nodded, even though Keleigh had managed to sound so utterly couldn't-give-a-fuck that the meaning had doubled back on itself. And she'd been there when Alison and Damian had come round that morning for the art meeting, and so she knew exactly what Alison wanted: an escort. But Keleigh could be strange like that. She was very different to Alison – quieter, more considered, a little more serious and intense – even though the two of them generally got on well. It was the same with all four of them: they were all different, but that helped shape the dynamic and give the group and the project more force. The only area where Keleigh showed any real animosity to Alison was when it came to her treatment of Jamie.

He liked to think he was pretty self-aware, and he knew that he was drawn to Alison for the obvious reasons – her looks and her manner – but also for not-so-obvious reasons that were more about him than her. And it was the latter that found him increasingly interested in Keleigh as well. When she was dismissive of Alison and protective of him, he felt warm inside.

'You gonna ring her back?' she said.

'Not at the moment.'

'Good,' she said. 'You're learning. Assume the pose.'

'Okay. I'll just turn my phone off.'

'Even better.'

Alison would leave a voicemail message, which meant his phone would ring again in a couple of minutes. Jamie held down red, feeling both stupid and vaguely empowered, and after a second his display went blank.

'Right.'

He sat back down on the chair, blinked a couple of times and then stared straight ahead. Keleigh knelt down in front of him. The camera filled his right-hand vision again.

'What colour are you going to do me?' he said.

'Don't know yet. Hold still.'

The camera was digital, and she would manipulate the image afterwards. The resulting printouts, stuck onto walls and walkways, showed irises in shades of yellow as strong as the sun, and greens as vibrant as the grass beneath it.

'Because I'm thinking purple might suit me,' he said.

'I think it would.'

– flash –

Half an hour later, we were making our final preparations.

The reason that Carl Halloran couldn't accompany Alison that evening was that he was booked into a hotel in Mouse, which is as small and incongruous an area as its name would suggest. In the south-west of the city, it's a neither-here-nor-there sort of district: terraces and back-to-backs; a few shops and bars; low-budget hotels. It's a cheap place for tourists, who flock to the city every summer for the annual boxing event and at other times for reasons of their own. On that day, Halloran was holed up in a two-star shit-hole in the north of the district. It had a blue neon sign hanging down outside, running from the third floor to the first, and the rest of it stretched up in a dilapidated six-storey tower drenched in melted snow. We'd been inside already to scope it out. The rooms were nice enough. Thin corridors and lots of stairwells. Easily accessible fire escape. We had our evening pretty much planned out.

Three nights earlier, the post office in Turtle had been robbed: the one that Harris lived almost next door to. It had been owned by a middle-aged couple and they lived above it. Someone had broken in after dark, held them at gunpoint and made off with an unspecified amount of money. Before leaving, he had tied the couple up and shot them. Growing up in the area, I had known them well enough to speak to, and I'd been shocked by the casual and unnecessary brutality of their murder. Nobody had seen anything, but we put out the usual feelers and eventually we got a name back. Carl Halloran. He was a small-time criminal, moving stuff around for people, and the rumour – from a good source – was that he'd run up debts and incurred some penalties. He'd paid those back in the last twenty-four hours, mouthed off a little too much, and now he was lying low.

Not fucking low enough. At eight o'clock that evening, the four of us went in and took him down hard. There was nothing we needed to know and nothing we needed to discuss. The rooms on either side of Halloran had been booked out in false names so as to secure a little privacy, but it really didn't take much time or effort. Lucy put two bullets in the back of his head as he lay whimpering on the floor of the main room. Silenced, of course: two soft whumps, and he was gone. He'd known it had been coming. Sometimes, I think that it's only the tension before death that makes a body look so relaxed and calm afterwards. It's contrast.

We checked out the suite, and we found the black briefcase on Halloran's bed. It was me that carefully lifted the lid and so I saw it first. Inside – piled and tiled neatly – was the money.

My hands hovered there, not quite daring to touch. What we needed to do was this: take the back way out of the hotel, the fire escape, the alleyway behind. A good, sensible plan. So I didn't touch the money – not at first. But I didn't need to count it to know that there was a lot. Far more than Halloran should have had in his possession if any of us had been thinking straight.

There were issues, of course we didn't discuss them. Perhaps we should have left it, but what was the harm? If anybody had known we'd been there, we would have been fucked regardless, so what did the money matter? And, strange as it sounds, we never thought about the possibility that someone might catch us. I closed the briefcase, and Lucy carried it out. We totalled it up later. That night, it transpired, we'd earned just less than fifty grand apiece.

On the surface I was thinking this: *if I'm cautious – if I don't attract too much attention – then that's enough money to keep me and Rachel safe and secure for a long time. Halloran didn't deserve it, and if someone else had taken it then they probably wouldn't have done much good with it either. There were worse people than me who could end up with fifty grand.*

If I needed justification then it was there, and if you asked me at the time that's what I would have told you.

So that's what we did. Halloran was dead. What did the money matter, wherever it had come from? I could tell myself that, but even then things felt different and I knew that something had gone wrong. I'd lost my way.

Halloran wasn't the last man I'd be involved in killing, but he was the last man we'd take out as a group, and by that point it wasn't easy but it wasn't exactly hard either. But because of the money, I went home that night and I felt like a stranger to myself, and I had bad dreams that I couldn't remember.

Sitting with Jamie, that feeling returned to me, and I realised that it hadn't been just a bad dream. Because when you do something wrong – no matter how bad – you can forgive yourself. Even if it's only on the surface. When nobody comes knocking demanding penance from you or pointing fingers, the days pass and you allow yourself to forget. You're only human. You might be afraid that you're tainted, but you don't feel that way all the time, and gradually you get on with your life. I'd woken up from the bad dream and done just that, only now I had the feeling that I'd been kidding myself ever since. The bad dream had still been going on, gathering force, and now Jamie's story was sending me back to sleep and I could feel that dream again, coalescing around me, so much stronger than before. I was afraid. And I was right to be.

'Alison went on her own that night?' I said.
   He shook his head. 'No. Damian went with her.'
   'The other guy in the art group.'
   'Right.'
   'And where's Damian now?'
   'Dead,' Jamie said, not looking up from the table.
   He didn't seem immediately inclined to say anything more, but now Lucy was more interested in having this conversation. After all, she'd been the one to pull the trigger on Halloran. She leaned forward.
   'What happened to them?'
   'The next day. They didn't show up.'

'Show up for what?'

'A meeting. The four of us had already met that day, but we were going to meet again the next evening. Harris was going to be there.'

Rosh and I glanced at each other, but Harris's name had lost a little of its power. Nothing would change the fact that he'd turned Sean in and that he was very probably going to die for that, but everything seemed different now. I couldn't stop thinking about the briefcase and the money. The rest of Jamie's story had a terrible inevitability to it.

Lucy said, 'And so they didn't show for the meeting?'

'No. It was me and Kel and Harris, round at mine. We waited for the others but they never came. Someone else did instead.'

'Someone else who?'

He shook his head.

'I don't know who they were, or where they came from. They came out of the walls.'

'What the fuck is that supposed to mean?' Lucy asked.

Jamie looked up at her and he spoke slowly.

'It means that the flat was locked and bolted,' he said, 'and there was nobody in there but us. But then suddenly, these guys were all around us. There was no way they could have got in.'

'Right,' Lucy said. 'And what did they look like?'

'I can't remember.' He looked back down at the table and shrugged to himself. 'There were five of them. Big guys. Black suits. Guns. That's all.'

'That's *all*?'

'I was scared,' he said. 'Is that all right?'

'That's fine,' I told him. 'Lucy—'

But it clearly wasn't fine with her. She stood up in

disgust and walked off down the alleyway, rubbing her face. Jamie glared after her, and I didn't blame him. She was tired, fucked off and probably very scared – but we all were, and what we needed to do right now was keep calm and take things slowly. That was what I kept telling myself anyway, as I remembered walking out of a hotel six months ago with a briefcase full of someone else's money.

Rosh said, 'Ignore her. She didn't get much sleep.'

'Yeah,' Jamie said. 'Right.'

'Seriously, forget about her. What did these guys say they wanted?'

'They searched the flat. Pulled out all the drawers – went through everything. They said they were looking for something that had been left with us, but they didn't say what.'

I glanced at Rosh again, but this time he didn't acknowledge it. He was playing it cooler than me and – even though we knew the answer – he asked Jamie the obvious question anyway.

'They find it, whatever it was?'

Jamie shook his head.

'And what do you think they were looking for?'

'I don't know,' he said. 'Something to do with Carl, I guess. But we didn't have it.'

'Okay. So then what happened?'

But my mind wasn't on what happened after the men finished searching; I was putting together what had already taken place. We'd killed Halloran and taken his money, and if we'd wondered at the time why he'd had so much in his possession then we knew now. The men had come to pick it up, found him dead and the money gone, and so worked their way through his acquaintances. First, his girlfriend. And when she'd been unable to help, they'd moved on to her friends instead. I figured that by then they weren't holding out much hope: just dotting the 'i's and crossing the 't's. Jamie was lucky to be alive.

'They told us to keep our mouths shut,' he said. 'They said we wouldn't be seeing our friends again, but that we shouldn't report it to anyone. And they warned us that they'd be watching. If anyone got in contact with us, they said they'd know about it and they'd kill us.'

'And then they left?'

'They didn't really leave.' Jamie shook his head. 'It was like when they arrived. There was just a point when they weren't there anymore.'

I looked at Rosh and this time he looked back. Invisible henchmen, apparently, on top of everything else. But it was far more likely that Jamie had simply blanked out a lot of what had happened to him. Unlike Lucy, I thought that was fine.

'Would you look at some pictures?' I suggested. I was willing to bet that if we could find a picture of the police officer we'd just killed, Michael Kemp, then Jamie would mark him out as being one of the disappearing men.

But he shook his head.

'I'm kind of planning for this to be our last conversation.'

'Well, I'm curious,' Rosh said. 'If all this is true, why are you even talking to us now? And why the Missing Persons Report in the first place? That must have been kind of dangerous.'

'That wasn't us,' Jamie said. 'That was the computer guy. Rob Hedge. When people started asking questions, we just covered it up as best we could.'

'You lied?'

From the tone of his voice, I got the impression that

Rosh was about to go and join Lucy. In a way, I couldn't blame him: the opportunity had been there for Jamie or Keleigh to tell this story almost six months ago, and if they had then maybe Sean would still be alive. But at the same time, they were just kids.

'I was scared,' Jamie repeated. 'Not just for me, but for Keleigh. So, yeah. I lied. I'm telling the truth now, though.'

'And our friend, Sean?' I said.

'I didn't lie to him either. Can I have another cigarette?'

'You'll have to go ask her.' I nodded down the alleyway to where Lucy was leaning against the wall. She was busy smoking and pretending that the three of us didn't exist. Jamie looked back at me, deciding to pass.

'He turned up a week ago. I don't know how he found us, but he wasn't like the others. He wouldn't take no for an answer, and he knew a lot of it anyway. So we ended up telling him everything.'

'Where did you meet him?'

'Public places, but always secret. If you see what I mean. He wouldn't give us any contact for him. Said it wasn't safe.'

'Okay,' I said. 'When was the last time you saw him?'

'A few nights ago,' Jamie told us. 'He left me an envelope. Said he was going to meet someone, and that if we didn't hear back from him the next day I should deliver it to an address in Horse.'

'Did he say who he was going to meet?' I said, although the email in Harris's flat had told us everything we needed to know about that.

'No,' Jamie said. 'But the next day he didn't get in touch, so I delivered the letter.'

'Have you seen the men who broke into your flat at all?' Rosh said.

Jamie shook his head.

'And I don't want to. Ever since your friend turned up, Keleigh and I have been moving around, staying away from our usual places.'

'That's probably a good idea,' I said.

For the moment, I didn't know what other advice to give him. In effect, we'd found Keleigh, and now we needed to get our hands on Harris. He'd be able to tell us whether we'd killed all the men and, if not, who the remaining ones were and where we could find them. That was how it would end.

Jamie had been quiet for a second, but now he said:

'I guess I see why you were asking about Harris. You think he told these people about your friend, right?'

I wasn't quite sure how much to tell him, and I was glad when Rosh took over. He'd clearly made a silent decision to be as honest as possible.

'Yes,' he said. 'We think that Harris got scared and turned our friend in to save himself. And it's likely he's after Keleigh now, too. Whoever these guys are, they're using him to cover their tracks and clean up.'

'Fuck.'

Jamie shook his head. He looked sad and disappointed as much as anything else.

Rosh seemed to be about to say something else, but then his mobile started ringing.

'Shit,' he said, standing up. 'One minute.'

He wandered off down the alleyway, over to where Lucy was waiting.

'We're going to protect you,' I told Jamie. Bullshit, of course, but I was responsible for what had happened to them and I wanted to say something. 'Nothing's going to happen to you or Keleigh.'

Jamie smiled at that, and there was something in his expression that I couldn't quite read. It wasn't as simple as disbelief or thinking I was naïve, but there were elements of those things in there. Perhaps something a little like pity, as well.

'I'm going to get some cigarettes,' he said. 'There's a machine inside.'

'Okay.'

He stood up and went back in the pub. I sat for a moment, trying to absorb everything I'd been told. Understanding the situation – as uncertain as it remained – should have brought some degree of comfort along with it. At least now we knew *why*. But there was no comfort; I might as well have been a kid alone in bed at midnight. Something was turning on itself within my mind, whining and growling, hidden only slightly behind a thin screen of skin. For no obvious reason, I was scared. I looked down at my hands and they were trembling.

'We've got Harris,' Rosh said, slipping his phone back into his pocket and snapping up my attention. He'd brought Lucy back over with him.

'Where?' I said.

'Officers found his car earlier on this morning, with him in it. Their initial professional opinion is that he's not alive anymore.'

'Shit.'

Rosh nodded. 'Shit indeed.'

Then, he frowned. 'Where's the kid gone?'

I gestured at the pub. 'Cigarettes.'

There was a brief pause.

'Shit,' I said again.

Whatever I was feeling, I needed to listen to what

my head was telling me and get a fucking grip on it. Guilt, fear – these things could be dealt with later, when thinking about them too much wasn't going to fuck things up. We went back inside Whitelocks to check, but there was no point. While I'd been sitting there feeling frightened, Jamie had disappeared.

CHAPTER FIFTEEN

Unlike me, Lucy and Rosh still had jobs to go to. Following a little manipulation within the department, it turned out that Rosh's assignment would involve checking out Harris and his car, while Lucy would head off to the lab to work the evidence, and – if she had a chance – do some research on Damian, the fourth member of the art group. I was at more of a loose end. Since I had no gainful employment of any kind, we decided that I should go to visit Rob Hedge and see how much of Jamie's story he was able to confirm.

I'd hoped that some time apart from Rosh and Lucy would clear my head a little, but within a few minutes of being dropped off at the edge of the campus I was even worse. More than ever before, the ground felt as though a heart was beating underneath it. The great, slow thuds of it sounded like a clock ticking. The buildings, tall and hard, were like the petals of some dark, malevolent flower: closing slowly around me and beginning to block out the sky. As I walked along I realised that, for no reason I could pin down, the fear I'd experienced at Whitelocks was beginning to turn into panic.

It was only mid-morning, but already hot and bright. The campus was heavy with people. That, the temperature and my mood was making everything hard to take, so I found a seat on a bench next to a girl eating pastry out of a paper bag, and for a second I just sat there, breathing slowly and watching everyone.

Sometimes it seems like there are too many people in the world. Certainly in our city anyway. For all I knew or – if I was honest – cared, the people around me could have been a record that was being played over and over again. It was difficult to imagine so many lives having substance. People like to think they're all connected and part of society, but they're not. In reality, you have a small group of friends and acquaintances, and that's all the city will ever be for you. Everybody else is a mystery – just window-dressing and background colour. As I sat there, people were smiling, laughing, touching each other on the arm. Walking. Hitching up bags. Pointing at things in shop windows. There was just so much *life* going on and it seemed impossible that everybody moving around me had any back story: that they weren't just extras in a crowd scene or swirls painted on the scenery to stop me feeling lonely.

The girl beside me stood and screwed up her paper bag. She was pretty, I thought. She had a nice, neat hairstyle. Her clothes were intricate and detailed. She must be real. But then she was gone before I knew it: disappearing off into the faded smear of this busy world, dropping the bag into a bin. At that moment, I had never felt more abstracted from everything. The people around me were just dabs on a painting that I was sitting too far away to touch.

After a few minutes, Lucy phoned me.

'Okay,' she said. 'I've got Hedge's address. You got a pen?'

'No, of course I haven't. Just tell me and I'll remember it.'

'Thirty-three, Oxley,' she said. 'That's student flats, right?'

'Right. Look.' I took a deep breath. 'I'm sorry about last night.'

'Forget about it,' she said.

'No, seriously.'

'Seriously forget about it if you like.' She sighed. 'I've got to go. Take care and keep in touch.'

'Right,' I said. 'Okay. Good luck.'

'You too.'

So that was what we were reduced to for the moment. It wasn't just me, of course. She had a lot to think about, and one of the things she would be doing back at the department was investigating Carl Halloran – who he was, and where we'd received the tip-off that had marked him for the post-office murders. The money we'd taken clearly hadn't come from there, and whatever Halloran had been doing in that hotel room, it wasn't lying low. A lot of people had died because of what the four of us did that night. We all had a lot to think about.

Later.

I got up, slipped my phone into my pocket and headed off towards the district's centre.

It turned out that Oxley was quite a nice block: newly built, with flats stacked on top of one another and linked by plush, fresh corridors that were all window down one side. It had the community feel of a tower block without any of the usual graffiti, odour or threats of violence. The front door was made of glass and almost impenetrably solid, but somebody had thoughtfully lodged it open with a lump of rock culled from the kerb outside, and so I was free to make my way up to the third floor, squinting against the amplified heat as I went. Then I found Hedge's door and knocked. After a minute or two, I knocked again a little harder. Did none of these bastard students have any manners?

When Hedge eventually opened the door, leaning against the frame, it was clear from both his manner and attire that I'd got him out of bed. He was wearing an old blue dressing-gown, tied loosely at the middle and gaping slightly to reveal a white T-shirt and pyjama bottoms. His hair was short, black and messy, and he was rubbing his pillowy face in an attempt to massage some life into it. He didn't look pleased.

'What?'

'Robert Hedge?'

I showed my badge, and he smartened up instantly. Just like last night – you wave a badge around and it separates the tough guys from the fakers like a fucking knife.

I put it away and said:

'Detective Weaver. I'd like to talk to you about your relationship with Alison Sheldon.'

'Yeah,' he said, and then glanced behind him. 'Um, yeah.'

'Can I come in?' I asked, wondering if he was concerned about any company he might have, or whether it was just drugs.

'Yeah,' he said.

Again, that glance over his shoulder. This was the second time in as many days. Did people think we had nothing better to do with our time?

'It's okay,' I said. 'Unless you've got a dead guy stashed in there, I'm not going to be bothered.'

'Right, okay.' Even now, he sounded doubtful, and I hoped he didn't actually have a dead guy stashed in his room. After a second, he held the door open wide. 'Um, come in.'

'Thanks,' I said. Then: 'Wow.'

Aside from the debris, it was just a standard student flat: one room, with a single bed on the right-hand side and a wardrobe and desk on the left. There was a window in between with a small set of drawers underneath, all of it made out of the same pale-brown wood. Behind me – next to the entrance – a door doubled back slightly into an ensuite shower room comprised entirely of white tiles and bright light, scored by the insular hum of air-conditioning. None of this was the reason for my wow.

'This place must be fun to insure,' I said.

Underneath and on top of the long built-in desk, Hedge had as much computer equipment as I'd ever seen inside a single room in my life. There were at least three separate hard-drive stacks, and all of them looked as though he'd constructed them himself. They were bustling with wires at the back and sides, linking them to different monitors that were in various stages of disarray and destruction. There were keyboards and mice, and the desk surface was a spaghetti mess of cables. Below it, there were more amplifiers, speakers, media players and adaptors than you could shake a health and safety certificate at. Little red power lights were dotted throughout the shadows behind it all, staring out like rats' eyes.

It was the kind of thoroughly undisciplined mess that only a real expert could have switched on and made work. As an amateur, I was quietly impressed.

Hedge said, 'Fortunately, my department pays the electricity bills.'

'Oh yeah? No wonder taxes are up.'

Amongst the mess of components on the desk was a small ashtray filled with the ends of roll-ups. Cannabis debris was resting on an A4 sheet on the bedside table.

Hedge noticed me looking and was about to come up with some excuse that would just have annoyed me.

'I don't care about any of that,' I said. 'You're a student. It's practically compulsory.'

I didn't care, of course, but it was useful. If Hedge wasn't as forthcoming as I wanted him to be then it was a subject we might well return to.

'Can I get you a drink?'

'No, I'm okay,' I said. 'I'm here because I think that one of my colleagues came to see you some time last week? A detective named Sean Barnes?'

It was a guess, but it turned out to be a good one.

'Oh – yeah.'

Encouraged, I tried another. 'He wanted to speak to you about Alison Sheldon.'

'Sure.'

'Well, basically I want to go over the same ground,' I said, making it sound casual – just a formality, really. 'You know? Just cover all the bases.'

He nodded quickly. 'Okay.'

'Can we sit down?'

'Yeah. Um, sorry.' He cleared an old pile of computer magazines off the chair by the desk. 'Here.'

I took the chair and he sat down on the bed opposite me.

'So,' I said, preparing to watch his reaction. 'Alison. Have you seen or heard from her recently?'

He shook his head.

'No. Not in months.'

Just an honest answer, I thought. He seemed eager to help; not at all surprised by the question. If Hedge knew for sure that Alison was dead, he was hiding it well.

'So – not since before you reported her missing?'

'No. It was . . . let me think. I don't know. Maybe a week before that?'

I said, 'Okay. It's just that I want to get a general idea of what you and Alison were about. You were helping her with a computer project – is that right?'

'Right. Yeah.' Hedge scratched through his sleepy hair and frowned. He looked a little confused, but that was okay.

'What were you working on?' I asked.

'Well, it was something to do with her art,' he said. 'She explained it once, but I didn't really take it in. I just did the programming, you know?'

He gave me a nervous smile, and I returned it.

'Were you . . . you know. Going out with her?'

'Oh no,' he said, a little too quickly. 'I mean, we were sort of seeing each other, but it was never anything as official as that. She was just a nice girl, you know. It was just a bit of fun. No big thing.'

'Okay,' I said. 'What did the computer project involve?'

'Oh, that was kind of strange. She had this map of the city, right? And I was helping her animate it.'

'Animate it?'

'Yeah. I just put together this program that did it. I'll show you if you want.'

'You still have it?'

'Yeah.' Hedge frowned again. 'I mean, I showed Detective Barnes when he talked to me.'

'Okay,' I said. 'That would be good.'

Hedge stood up and sort of waved at the equipment behind me, and I cleared out of his way. One of the computers was already turned on, and he sat down in front of it, shifted the mouse to clear the screensaver and then started to scan through a couple of directories.

'Just easier to show you,' he said. 'You know.'

'That's fine.'

'Here.'

I leaned on the desk so as to see the screen more clearly. For a second it was totally black, and then a series of bright white lines blinked into view. There was an outline that I realised corresponded with the city's outside walls, and then more lines dividing the interior into rough districts. I wasn't a cartographer, but it looked to be a pretty good likeness. At the bottom of the screen was a series of makeshift buttons that I figured Hedge had designed himself.

'This is obviously quite basic.' He sounded apologetic. 'You can see the city, but there's no detail. We were going to work on it more – map some texture and colour to it. But the measurements are all right. I took it off maps, and everything.'

'It looks good,' I said.

'Thanks.'

On the way here, the nervous sensation had faded into the background a little. I hadn't noticed it happening, but it must have done because I noticed it again now: rolling back into me like a wave of nausea.

'And what Alison was doing was getting me to plot points on it,' Hedge said. 'They represent places where people have died. Bit morbid.'

'Okay.' I was half-listening, but also trying to force the sick feeling to the back of my head.

'And the program does a few things,' Hedge said.

He clicked one of the buttons. A small red circle appeared towards the top right-hand side of the city. I stared at it. Somewhere in Bull.

'You can cycle through them one by one.' He clicked the same button again and the first red circle disappeared, replaced immediately by a new one further south, somewhere on the edge of Snail. Another click and the process repeated itself, only the third circle was in the top coil of the Snake district. I wanted to look away but I couldn't.

'And so on.'

Hedge clicked more rapidly and the circles disappeared, reappeared, tracing a path around the city, doubling back and then jerking across to some new place. Each one seemed to set the air ringing a little more intensely. I swallowed and found my mouth was dry.

'She was going to have a few computers going at once as part of her display,' he was saying. 'Don't ask me why. There was going to be one – like this – that people could cycle through themselves. I guess she'd have set up a controller or something. Another like this where it was all cumulative—'

He pressed the button on the bottom right of the screen and all the red circles disappeared. *Stop*, I thought. *Stop it now.* But another click and the first marker appeared again in Bull. Then, as Hedge kept pressing the button, more and more dots appeared. Three, four, five. As though drops of blood were falling onto the city. I closed my eyes for a moment, but that was even worse: it felt like something was watching me.

Hedge cleared all the circles away again to leave a blank map. The mouse pointer moved, hovering over a third set of buttons.

'This was the animation sequence,' he said. 'This was what the other officer was most interested in.'

Hedge started it by clicking on a single button and then leaned back in the chair as we both watched the screen. The first circle appeared, as before, blinking out two seconds later to be replaced by the second, further south. The third circle arrived five seconds later. I didn't know why it was terrible, but it was. I leaned away to rub my face, and saw that my palm had left a misty print on the desk.

Hedge seemed oblivious.

'The time intervals are correct,' he said. 'Two seconds on the screen represents twenty-four hours of city time. So the ratio's right. But she hadn't decided how quick she wanted it to go.'

Fourth circle.

Fifth.

Get it together.

I was scared of a computer now, and that was just stupid. So I forced myself to stare at the screen for a full minute, counting the circles. There were thirty murders in that time. An average of one a day. More circles appeared. And with each one, whether I thought about it or not, the fear was slowly intensifying. The only sound in the room was the hum of Hedge's computer equipment, but it was menacing and dangerous.

What was so wrong with it?

I couldn't imagine – but it was as though I was staring into a face I'd had nightmares about. *We were looking at the city so closely*, Jamie had told us, *and so we really shouldn't have been surprised when it started looking back*. That was what this felt like.

Which was fucking ridiculous.

I blinked and said, 'Make it go faster.'

'Give me a second.'

He tapped a few keys and the map disappeared, replaced by lines of spare, elegant code. Black on white: a story written in strange words that only really meant something to the computer. But even in this – its genetic form – there was something unnerving about the program. It looked wrong. Hedge scrolled down and typed over a few numbers, replacing them with smaller ones.

'Okay. This should be pretty fast,' he said.

And it was. When the map started up again, the points of red were sly: blinking away almost as soon as they became visible. You flicked your gaze to look at them, and they were gone almost as you saw them. It was like trying to concentrate on single spots of light as your vision starred over. I leaned in even closer. My heart felt as though it was throbbing: not beating faster exactly, just trembling under a singing tension that was growing in pitch.

Blink, blink, blink.

So quick that they were barely there at all.

'Too quick,' Hedge said, and I jumped slightly.

Get yourself together, for fuck's sake.

I moved back across the room and looked away – out of the window. It was slightly open. Cool air was drifting lazily in, like steam rising from dry ice, and for a second I thought I could smell fresh cannabis and hear the crunch of boots compacting snow. Then, there was just the midday sun again, and a warm breeze through the slightly open window. No smell apart from old linen. I shook my head.

'That's very interesting,' I said, turning back as Hedge shut down the program.

'Thanks. The other officer thought so too.'

Whatever it was about the map that had affected me and Sean, Hedge seemed immune. He was looking at me curiously.

'Are you okay, Detective?'

'I'm fine.'

I wasn't, but with the program shut down I felt

slightly better. The tension seemed to have relaxed a little anyway.

Hedge returned to the bed, and I took back the seat by the desk.

'So the last time you spoke to Alison,' I said, 'what did you talk about?'

We went over a few of the facts. He told me that Alison had been going to Snail that evening; that she'd called both her boyfriend and Jamie but they hadn't been able to go with her. He'd been busy too, he said, or else he would have gone; and he said it in such a way that it was obvious how guilty he felt. I understood. It was the last conversation he'd had with a girl he'd never see again: the kind of conversation you rewrite over and over in your head. Death is such a momentous severance that it makes us relive those last few moments of contact and search for meaning or blame where there is none. Hedge didn't know that Alison was dead; but at the same time, he must have known. I wanted to explain and tell him that he wasn't responsible – that if anyone was, it was me – but I couldn't. And it wouldn't have done any good if I had.

We talked more, but there wasn't a lot else to learn. Reading between the lines, it seemed that Alison had used sex as a means to get Hedge to help her with the project, but I suppose things are never as simple as that, and he certainly had the impression there was more to it. They'd smoke dope and have a laugh, but she'd never struck him as being particularly happy; and he'd felt, at some level, that they were a lot alike. I felt sad for him.

'Thank you for your help,' I told him as I was leaving.

He said, 'I don't think I've helped much. But no problem.'

Downstairs in the entrance hall, I checked my phone, but there were no messages and nobody had tried to call. I wondered how the others were getting on and considered ringing them, but discounted the idea – they'd be in touch as soon as they knew anything.

I walked outside, heading down the path, and I started to think about Hedge and his feelings of guilt. He didn't even know the truth and he felt responsible, when all he'd done was not be there for her. So what did that make me? This was my fault: because I'd wanted to make some sort of difference; and because I'd wanted that money for me and Rachel.

I paused at that thought. It felt dishonest. At the same time as I didn't want to think about it, I was dimly aware that the reality of what I'd done was far worse. And as I stopped for a second, the feeling became thicker and blacker, and everything around me threatened to cloud over.

So I shook my head and carried on walking.

My guilt wasn't in doubt, I thought, but all I could do now was keep moving and try to make it as right as possible. Responsibility doesn't stop with guilt, after all. Even when you've fucked everything up, you can always make it worse for yourself by turning away.

CHAPTER SIXTEEN

It was dead on twelve when I finally left the main campus, and so the Clock Café was busy: crammed from one bohemian wall to the other with students and smoke. I don't know why I went there. I was just walking along, my mind elsewhere, and suddenly there it was. Does it count as a coincidence if you bring it about yourself? Sean told me once that life is full of coincidences, and that when you start looking for them you find more and more, as though the world is racing to show you something. Perhaps right now the world just wanted me to have coffee. I went inside.

It was the same waiter as when I'd met Rachel there two days ago, and he was similarly tardy in preparing my drink. My attention was drifting, though, and I didn't mind so much. I was happy for him to take his time. When it arrived, delivered with a sprinkling of disdain and a sachet of utter indifference, I paid the man and took the cup carefully over to the only free table, at the back of the café.

I sipped it slowly, staring out past all the people at the bright light of the front windows. The crawling feeling that the computer program had given me was slowly returning. I decided that constant sips of coffee and not thinking too much would help keep me occupied. But my mind kept returning to it anyway. What had I seen on that screen that had unnerved me so much? It was just a map of the city, but it had felt like I was staring at something awful and alive. Even thinking about it now was uncomfortable.

I glanced around the café. There were a lot of people here, with a great deal of conversation going on between them. The intimacy and involvement of it gave an impression of bustle and, even though nobody seemed to be paying me any attention, for some reason I felt like the centre of it. Outside the window, bunches of students were walking past. Groups of people pulsing along. None of them even looked inside.

The coffee was already half finished. I stopped sipping and started nursing it instead, warming my hands around the cup and staring at the cracked formica of the table.

After a moment or two, something caught my attention and I looked up. At the next table, a woman was talking to the man opposite her, and she was crying desperately.

'I just want you to love me,' she said. 'And I don't understand why you don't.'

I glanced away quickly and picked up my coffee again. My hands were shaking a little. When I looked back at the couple, they were both smiling and she was holding his hands in hers. I shook my head.

It seemed that Rachel had been lurking at the back of my mind ever since we'd met here two days ago, because now shy impressions of her came out of the shadows, stepping tentatively into my open thoughts. What on earth had happened to me? All around me, there were couples smiling. I'd had that with Rachel – had it in spades – and I'd given up on the relationship because I'd had ideas of something better. Those ideas seemed mysterious now. I tried to resurrect whatever it was I'd felt.

Over the past few months, whenever I'd thought of

Lucy I'd pictured her with Rich, and it had been the worst image in the world. I'd curled up; cried. It had hollowed me out. But I dug around in those thoughts now, trying to make them hurt, and they were only tender, not painful. It seemed impossible to remember a time when they'd been anything more. Surely, it had only been days ago? And yet I pressed hard, and the feelings weren't there. The nerves had gone dead.

I could remember sitting in my flat and crying when she decided to be with Rich, but the memory was featureless and arid: black and white and lacking sound. All those text messages I'd sent, followed by the stretches of time when she'd never reply – I had those in my head now, and they felt empty. Just husks of recollection with nothing inside them. No panic, no pain. Nothing.

What had I done?

That question crept quietly into my head and everything went still for a second.

And then thoughts of Rachel returned, and these were entirely different. When I dug into these, my fingers went all the way. I sipped my coffee and her life came to me – not in a flash or a series of images, but as impressions that I couldn't put into words. I thought of her loving me so much and being so happy; of her being prepared to do anything for me. Leaving herself totally open and not even being afraid that I'd hurt her. And then the bewilderment – the deep, stupid wound I'd made in her. The gathering of herself afterwards. Trying to hold herself together and find some sensation inside her other than pain.

Those emotions – all at once; a rich, awful palette – beating out of my memory of her in a rainbow of fever. In that moment, I realised how much I loved her and how much I'd hurt her; and I closed my eyes.

My mobile started ringing.

I picked it up, thinking it would be either Rosh or Lucy, but when I looked at the display it showed *rachel*.

I held the phone in my hand for a second, just staring at it. The coffee shop around me receded slightly. Although I could tell that people were stopping their conversations and beginning to look at me, they had all faded into the background, out of importance.

The mobile kept ringing.

rachel

Finally, I pressed green and held the phone to my ear.

'Hello.'

'Martin?'

'Yeah.' The guy on the next table was still looking at me. I glared at him and he looked away very quickly. I said, 'I'm here.'

'You were trying to get hold of me? I had missed calls.'

I tried to place the expression in her voice, but I couldn't pin it down. It was too ... normal, I realised. Since the split, I'd become used to deciphering a whole range of her emotions – from anger, hatred and pain to resilience and pride – but right now she sounded like she had before I'd left. Except not quite.

'Yeah,' I said. 'I was worried about you. I wanted to talk to you and make sure you were all right.'

There was silence for a second, and then when she spoke she sounded indignant and annoyed.

'Of course I'm all right.'

'I didn't mean it like that,' I said quickly. 'I was just worried about you.'

'Why – because I wasn't answering my phone?' She

laughed. 'I don't have to answer my phone when you ring if I don't want to.'

'I know you don't.'

'I think you gave up that right, didn't you?'

'What right?'

'Fucking hell, never mind.' She seemed to gather herself a little: to pull the persona back together. 'So is that all you wanted?'

So, I thought, was that all I wanted – to check that she was okay? No, I decided, not really. But I needed to think more carefully about it. She'd had enough of my bullshit and whatever I said at this point was only going to be more of the same.

Fondly, I thought out of nowhere, *I think of you*.

'There's more I want to say,' I said. 'But not right now.'

She gave me a small, sarcastic laugh. 'Very cryptic.'

'Yeah,' I said, frowning. 'Yeah. Look – this is going to sound shit, but it might be an idea to get out of the house for a few days.'

She paused, and then sounded indignant again.

'Well – what's that supposed to mean? Why should I get out of the house?'

'There's been some trouble,' I said, knowing how bad this was sounding. 'And it might be safer for you not to be at home right now. That's all I'm saying. This isn't about us.'

'Well, I'm not at home right now,' she said, matter of factly.

'Right. Where are you?'

'With a friend,' she said. And then: 'A guy.'

A guy.

Not the first, I reminded myself quickly. Over the last couple of months there'd been a few times when Rachel had gone on dates with men, and generally she'd told me in advance, hoping for some kind of reaction. In that, she'd always been let down; I'd felt very little. In fact, I'd told her that it was good, and that I hoped she found someone who could make her happy. It had always seemed to me as though I meant it – and it had probably pissed her off no end.

Now, I did my best to remember how that ambivalence had felt, but I couldn't replicate it. Inside, I was panicked, churning.

'Oh,' I said. 'Right. Okay.'

'Just some guy,' she said. 'I met him last night.'

'Right.'

'Yeah. I went out to a club.'

'Right,' I said again. 'What's his name?'

It seemed like a natural question.

'His name's Sean,' Rachel said.

I picked up my coffee and drained the rest of it in one. I was shaking. He was called Sean, this guy. Of course he was called Sean. That just seemed right.

She said, 'Not your Sean, obviously.'

'No,' I said. 'I'd imagine not.'

'So I've not been home,' she concluded, and I could hear it in her voice that she was hammering the truth home in the hope I might feel it. For the first time, I did. But I surprised myself when something entirely unconnected burst from the back of my mind, and I blurted out:

'What was it called?'

Another brief pause, and then she sounded confused.

'What was what called?'

'The club,' I said, feeling impatient. 'Where you met this guy.'

'Oh. It was Spooks, or something. On the edge of Wasp. You know it?'

'Yeah, I know it.'

Another coincidence. It felt ridiculous, but I'd known what she was going to tell me before she'd said it – Spooks, that shitty club I'd been drinking in the other night, while Jamie had been delivering Sean's envelope to me. Full of rough men and women on the pull. Rachel had gone there too. Coincidence. And now she was telling me while I was sitting in the café we'd been in two days earlier. I'd just been walking past and wandered in. Does it count as a coincidence if you bring it about yourself?

Rachel said, 'Why do you want to know?'

'I was just curious. It's nothing.'

'Oh right. Well—'

'Where are you now?'

'I'm not sure,' she said. 'Somewhere in Turtle, I think.'

'You *think*?'

Jesus. This was *Rachel* I was speaking to. Before I'd messed up, she'd been *my* Rachel, and now here she was, going back to a guy's house when she didn't know who he was. She didn't even know where she was, for fuck's sake.

'It's none of your business anymore,' she said.

'You should just . . . I don't know. You should be more careful.'

She repeated herself in a slow, cold voice:

'It's none of your business anymore, Martin.'

'Look,' I said. 'Just . . . be careful. Okay?'

'I'm always careful. *Really* careful.'

'No, seriously. There are things—'

'So anyway – have you arranged to move the rest of your things?'

I paused.

'No. Not yet.'

Burn it all, I'd thought, but I didn't think anything

now. At the moment, all my stuff occupied a place in my head that didn't have any windows.

'Why not?' she said.

'I looked into it,' I said. 'It's just – it's been at the back of my mind.'

'Move it to the front. And then move the rest of your shit out of my house.'

'Rachel—'

'Goodbye, Martin.'

The phone buzzed in my ear. I pulled it away and looked at it for a moment, as though staring stupidly might magically re-establish a connection.

call complete: 02:41.

I panicked and thought: *fuck self-respect.* Speed-dial button 1 – I pressed it and put the phone back to my ear. Maybe it would make it worse, but there were things I could say regardless, and they'd start with *sorry.* But the phone rang a few times and then buzzed again. I listened as the pre-recorded message kicked in. Sorry, but the phone you are trying to contact appears to be off-line.

Shit.

Without warning, all of that coffee tried to force its way up my throat, and I had to swallow to fight it down. I put the phone on the table and rested my head on my hand. Closed my eyes. Ran my fingers back and forth through my hair a little, massaging my scalp. The air was ringing with the same tension as before.

I'm going insane.

And then I thought: *send her a text message.*

'Sir?'

I stopped, and looked up. It was the guy from behind the counter.

'We're very full. Are you going to order another drink?'

I glanced around and saw that a few of the people nearby were watching me cautiously. When I looked up, they looked away. Had I been talking to myself? Maybe so – the waiter's body language told me that he was ready to deal with me if I caused any trouble. For a second, I hated him so badly that I could barely contain it, and it half occurred to me to pull out my gun and show the other customers what causing a fucking scene would really be like.

'If you're not going to order—'

'Save it.' I stood up. 'I was just leaving.'

He took my empty cup and shadowed me to the door, increasing my desire to shoot him somewhere immensely painful, but my legs were shaky and when I got outside I was grateful for the fresh air.

Clear your head, I thought, but I couldn't. A hurricane might, but not today's slight, warm breeze, not when my head was so brimful of buzzing rubbish. With Rachel. Sean. What we'd done to Halloran. All the coincidences that were maybe just that but seemed like they weren't. I started walking, and with every step it felt more and more as though everything in the world was going to reach out and strike me.

I walked for a while, heading in the vague direction of my flat. It might not be safe and so I had no real inclination to go there, but walking had always had a calming effect on me. As I approached the border, a little south of my makeshift home, I was beginning to feel better. Then, my phone rang again, and I stopped by some railings to answer it.

rosh

'Yeah?' I said.

'Martin?' Rosh sounded concerned. 'Where are you?'

'I'm not sure.' *Turtle somewhere.* 'I'm in Horse. Edge of Horse, I think. Why?'

'Is everything okay there?'

'Yeah. Yeah, it's fine.'

'How did it go?'

'What?'

'Hedge,' he said. 'How did it go with Hedge?'

'Oh – right.'

So I told him about my visit to Oxley, although in hindsight there wasn't much to say. Out in the fresh air, the computer program seemed irrelevant. I mentioned it briefly and Rosh didn't seem overly interested.

'Well, he confirmed parts of Jamie's story, anyway,' I said.

'Okay.'

'How was Harris?'

'Not okay.'

Rosh went through the details. A couple of kids had found Harris's car earlier that morning, idling at the edge of some wasteland in Snail. There was a tube leading from the exhaust pipe to the front window. The kids – being kids – had peered in and had run and told their parents, and officers arrived at the scene a few minutes later. Harris himself was already very dead – slumped in the driver's seat, supported by a now quite redundant seatbelt – and apparently had been for some time. It was estimated that he'd died in the early hours of the morning. The obvious assumption was suicide, but Rosh wasn't convinced and neither was I.

'He had some abrasions to the head,' Rosh said. 'We won't know more until the forensics come back, but I have a weird feeling they won't tell us much.'

'Who's working them?' I asked. Lucy worked most of the murder scenes, but obviously she'd been otherwise engaged this morning.

'Jackman did the scene,' Rosh said. 'But she's okay. It's not that I think anyone'll tamper with the evidence. It's that these people are too good.'

'And what do we think more generally?' I said. 'They knock Harris out, stand around the car and wait for him to die?'

'It's possible, but who knows? Maybe he really did kill himself.'

I knew which scenario my money was on – and if someone had topped Harris then it meant that Kemp and his men weren't the end of it. There were still others out there for us to worry about. Not only that – we'd just lost someone who could have provided us with a lot of very helpful information. Now, we had nothing.

Reading my silence, Rosh said, 'It's depressing, isn't it?'

'For him, too, I guess.'

'I find myself slightly unable to care about that.'

'Yeah – me too.'

Murder is murder, but Harris had given up any right to our concern when he'd turned Sean in. The most that could be said now was this – if we were lucky then the forensics would tell us something and we might be able to take care of the people who'd killed him. Beyond that, his luck was out. We had enough people to worry about.

'What about Lucy?' I said. 'Where's she at?'

'Working in the lab. She's not had chance to do all that much, but she did have time to pull Halloran's file.'

'And?'

'And nothing. Same as we knew. Minor stuff for major people.'

There was a real question hanging over Halloran.

'What about the source?'

'Sean took the tip-off,' Rosh said. 'It was one of his regular guys. You remember Toby Yeung?'

'Yeah, yeah.'

Toby was a street kid who did a little small-time drugs-running here and there. He was just a gopher, basically: he had a bit of a mouth on him but no real malice, and that meant he got to know people and what they were up to. His information had always been reliable in the past. If he said that Halloran had done the post office then I'd have trusted him to be on the level. It just depended on how he'd found out in the first place and why he'd passed it on.

Rosh said, 'You probably don't know this, but Toby's no longer with us.'

'Shit.'

'He got pulled out of the canal in Fish three months ago. Beaten to death.'

'Well, this fucking stinks, Rosh.'

'You should have been there.'

'Very funny,' I said. 'You know what I mean.'

'I do know what you mean,' he said. 'But Toby was in that kind of business. It doesn't necessarily prove anything.'

He was being optimistic and we both knew it.

'Rosh,' I said. 'We've been set up here. Think about it.'

There was a brief, not-very-Rosh-like pause, and then he said:

'I see where you're coming from – Toby passes it on and then he gets rubbed to keep him quiet. But I can't imagine who or why, or how it fits with what's happened since.'

'I don't know who or why,' I admitted. 'But I can see how it fits. Someone got us to kill Halloran and take the money, and then someone else came looking for it. Kemp and his guys.'

'Somebody who was concerned about our bank balances?' Rosh said. 'Why would anyone want us to take the money? Why not just kill Halloran and take it themselves?'

'Okay,' I said. 'That part doesn't fit.'

Rosh sounded tired. 'I need to think about it some more.'

'But if that's true then we might have killed an innocent man, Rosh.'

'He wasn't innocent, Martin. Halloran did those murders. But even if he didn't, he wasn't innocent.'

'No,' I said. 'Right.'

I thought Rosh sounded even less sure than me – but then he'd been doing this longer than I had. He had a bigger list to reassess and to worry about, and a lot more invested in what we'd done being the right thing.

He took advantage of my pause and said:

'Lucy also looked at the other kid Jamie mentioned. Damian.'

'And?'

'Again – nothing we wouldn't expect. Record of birth, a few employment hits in the usual sorts of places. No sheet for anything and no Missing Persons Report. He definitely exists, but the only way we'll find out if he's still walking around is by talking to the university. Or every single one of his friends.'

'Fantastic. No matching bodies?'

'Not so far, no.'

But then, the city had lots of dark corners where people could disappear.

I said, 'So what's next?'

'Well, I'm going to be stuck here for a while,' Rosh said. 'And then back at the department writing up and making calls. Lucy's busy as well, so you're on your own for a few hours. We'll regroup after work.'

'I don't know where to go,' I said.

'Well, I don't know what else you can look into out there,' Rosh said. 'There are things to follow up here, but not really anything you can do. Just think about what we know. And be careful. You don't sound right, Martin.'

'I'm just tired.'

'You get hold of Rachel?'

I paused. Once again, I was surprised by how easily Rosh could nail a problem on the head and hammer it through to the feet.

'Yeah,' I said. 'I've just spoken to her.'

'Good. That means she's okay. Where's she at?'

'I don't know,' I said. 'With friends. Not sure who. She didn't say.'

'Okay.' He thought about it and then said, 'Well, we can talk about that later maybe. I'll be in touch as soon as I can, but keep me tabbed on what you're doing.'

'I will.'

I hung up, and then just leaned against the railing. After a moment, I slipped my phone back into my jacket pocket and stared ahead. The road in front of me was full of cars. On the other side, there were a few shops: a video store, a couple of takeaways. Behind them, the spiked, black tip of a church, and then the looming half-threat of a council block. I looked up at the sky instead.

There are things to follow up here, but not really anything you can do.

All these people driving past, a fair few others walking – all of them full of purpose. I was struck by the same feeling I'd had earlier, except that now they didn't seem like background people – men and women with no real lives. Instead, I experienced something like envy. Once, I'd been a lot of things, and because they'd not seemed right I'd removed myself from all of them in search of something better. Now, it didn't feel like I was anything, and it had taken a letter from a dead man to bring that into focus.

I frowned.

Sean.

My first instinct when I'd received the letter had been to try to find him, but I couldn't because I didn't know where to look. His phone records were dead and his house had been taken over by a new tenant; I didn't even know where to begin. But the fact remained that he'd been doing *something* in the time since he vanished. It was obvious, but I hadn't thought about it in precisely those terms until now. People take up space. He had *been* somewhere.

Not wanting to scare the thought away, I just carried on looking at the sky, watching a single cloud that was drifting lazily overhead. There was something in my mind that I needed to see. It was like when your fingers are reaching for something under a settee and they brush it: you pause, and then begin to move more delicately so as not to lose it.

Sean had arranged for Jamie to deliver the envelope, but what had the contents amounted to? A photocopy and a printout. It had been enough to set me on the way, but that was all; I was certain that after five months of investigation, however fragmented and disillusioned, he'd uncovered more than that. Originally, I'd assumed that he'd sent so little as insurance – as a way for me to follow his trail only if necessary. But now a more likely possibility occurred to me. Perhaps he hadn't known who to trust or to what extent people were being watched. He hadn't given too much to Jamie in case Jamie got picked up and whatever he'd discovered ended up destroyed. In fact, the students didn't even have a contact address for Sean. But the fact returned to me again: he *had* stayed somewhere. If I could find out where, I was certain there would be more information for me. Information that he'd kept safe, but would surely have given me the means to find.

I watched the cloud, stark white against the pale blue of the sky, and thought about everything that had happened.

It all came down to this: we had to work on the assumption that Kemp and his team were looking out for the money. But their resources were limited. They couldn't have been watching *everyone* for six whole months. Alison's parents, with their apparent indifference, seemed to be the least likely people she would have confided in, and so I figured that Kemp or someone might have spoken to them and discounted them. Would the men have wasted any more time on Alison's parents, when they clearly had no relationship with their daughter at all? I didn't think so.

But they were the link that Sean had started me with.

I thought back through the conversation I'd had with Mr Sheldon and after a moment it came to me. *He asked us to get in touch if we heard from her.* How?

My phone had never felt so loved. I scanned through my old dialled numbers, one by one, until I found it: the area code for Bracken. That was the number. I pressed green, held the phone to my ear and waited for the tone to kick in.

After a moment: 'Hello?'

'Hello, Mr Sheldon,' I said. 'It's Detective Weaver here. We spoke the other day about your daughter. You remember?'

'I remember.' If anything, he sounded even more uninterested than before. 'So, what else can I do for you?'

'My colleague,' I said. 'You mentioned he asked you to get in touch if you heard anything from Alison.'

'That's right.'

I was thinking that Sean had perhaps come to the same conclusion as I had about Alison's parents. Nobody would be paying them any attention. Apart from me.

I said, 'Can I ask what details he gave you, please?'

'Oh, I think I threw those away.'

I closed my eyes and did a quick calculation. How long would it take to drive to the other side of the country, shoot somebody, and then drive back? Too long.

'It's important, Mr Sheldon.'

'I think they were on a post-it by the phone. Hang on.'

I heard Sheldon put the phone down on the table, and then the sound of him shuffling through papers, punctuated by occasional sighs and heavy breathing. He picked up the phone.

'I have them here.'

The concern you have for your daughter is an example to us all, I thought.

'Thanks for looking them out,' I said. 'Did he leave an address or anything?'

CHAPTER SEVENTEEN

I knew the guy on the steps was going to talk to me. Even though the streets were crowded, I was still far enough between groups of people to be singled out for attention. Of course, he called out to the two groups as well – it was the nature of the competition round here. These guys called out to anyone and everyone. It was good business sense. Call out to a hundred; lure in maybe ten.

'Hey there, young sir,' he said. 'Looking for company?'

There was always a strange formality to these exchanges. Most of the canvas-men for the brothels and strip clubs in western Wasp were foreigners: immigrants of uncertain origin who spoke perfect and well-mannered English but didn't waste words or strive for friendly conversation. They came over as eager, but polite and respectful.

I stopped. He was a standard example of the kind: blue jeans; white T-shirt; thin, black leather jacket; hair, dark and cropped short. He was sucking on a weedy roll-up and not paying too much attention to the people he was talking to. But when he noticed that I'd actually stopped, he went into the next stage of his banter.

'Hey, young sir, we've got everything inside here. We got the best girls, girls that will love you. We got shows. We got private.'

I looked up and saw the girls that would – I was sure – love me. They were hanging out on the balconies overhead, dressed only in underwear, smoking, waving down at passers-by. Ostensibly, the building was a theatre. It would have the standard three live shows a day, with more personal attention given to patrons upstairs if the money was right; and the price would be cheap enough to be tempting. There was a blacked-out box office at the top of the steps, and this man out front was acting like some kind of spider: reeling in the men and women who passed.

'I'm okay, thanks,' I said.

He nodded deferentially and I started walking again. There were literally hundreds of these theatres inter-mingled with the bars and nightclubs, and yet the competition was placid and easy-going – perhaps because the same few people owned most of them, and so it didn't really matter who went where as long as everyone went somewhere. And everyone did – why else would they be here?

This was the western wing of Wasp. Further east, moving out towards the edge of the city, the establish-ments, architecture and people are far less accommo-dating. The whole district is basically two rough circles, joined at the centre by a thin channel.

The western wing is a sleazy but accepted public attraction. People come to party, buoyed by its twenty-four-hour bars and clubs and constant access to everything you could ever want. There is more neon lighting here than free wall space, and more music than conversation, with a different disco tune thudding out of each bar you walk past. Even in the daytime, the streets and paths are teeming. There are platoons of young men, knocking back shots and staggering from one bar to the next. Couples strolling, sometimes nervously approaching vendors, psyching each other up to go inside. Suits out for quick sandwich lunches, leaning against the yellow and black railings and soaking up the sexual bohemia.

Despite this, the area is surprisingly safe, with relatively little real trouble – beyond the occasional idiot shooting into the sky to break up a fight, anyway. As police, we'd get a few drunk and disorderlies, sometimes a fight or two, but this isn't Horse or Lion and everyone knows it. Wasp is pure hedonism cast in architecture, yet people know they have to behave themselves round here. You get the impression that you are walking around in a theme park designed to look dangerous while being safe underneath, but you're always aware that the reverse is true. So you come to have a great time – to go wild – but you do so within limits that go beyond any hold the law might have. If you set up metal detectors to check for guns on the main roads in then the clientele would probably halve. This all stems from the eastern wing, where you find the people who own and run Wasp. In fact, these people run a great deal of the city.

The tram had dropped me off on the edge of the western wing and I had to walk to get to eastern Wasp. There are no trams to that part of the district because there is a tacit understanding that nobody who needs to use public transport would ever want to go there.

It took me half an hour, during which time you could visibly track the degeneration of the neighbourhood. Despite being off-centre, Wasp is one of the oldest districts, always in existence on the periphery as the city grew stronger to the west, slowly expanding to encompass it. The district had been ramshackle – more wood than stone, and more cobbled paths and dirt trails than actual roads – and many parts of the eastern side hadn't changed that much in the intervening years. Some of it had been modernised, but certainly not in what you'd think of as modern times. I guessed that the people who operated there preferred it that way.

Thirty minutes later, I was there – Parker Street. It was slightly wider than the average road in Wasp, but far more dilapidated and abandoned. The left-hand side was mainly boarded-up shops. There was a liquor store of some kind that looked open behind the yellow and black swirls on the windows, but everything else was shuttered and dead-looking. There were old tenements along the right, but sections of the brickwork had been smashed out of them at random, as though two people had dared each other to knock more and more out without the entire building falling down. The only glass remaining in most of the windows was so grimy that it obscured even the dark inside, and all of the doorways I could see were boarded over with timber.

It wasn't much further north of here before you edged into the industrial alleys of southern Bull, and it showed. The low and broken buildings were nearly identical, and there was the same sense of structural loss – of architecture that had actually died rather than been abandoned. Except it was worse here. Where the streets of Bull had died of old age and heartbreak, here you wanted to open an inquest and have somebody arrested.

I walked down the street. Number twenty-seven was on the corner of an alleyway about halfway along on the right, and it didn't look promising. Once upon a time it had been some kind of bed and breakfast, but now it was just four old stone walls, with nothing but silence and rot emanating from inside. The front door and downstairs windows had been filled in entirely with breeze blocks and concrete; and all but one of the second-floor windows were barricaded with wood. I wasn't about to start scaling the front in broad daylight, though. My first impression was that there was no way in.

I looked across the road. The hotel was opposite an establishment called the CandiBar, and I gave it a quick glance to see whether it was still open or not. There were grey-green shutters down across the main window, with another set over what was presumably the door. The windows above ground level were dirty and impenetrable but seemed intact. Security cameras watched the pavement from two storeys up, where the building finished and the dismal, smoke-filled sky began.

I dawdled for a moment, figuring I'd wasted my time. But I was here now, and so I decided I'd wander down the alleyway and see if there was a side entrance, or maybe some back way in.

Two steps into the alley, I drew my gun and stood very still.

The feeling had intensified: the singing sensation in my chest. Too high-pitched to be anything with a name, but if you lowered the frequency I thought it might be fear. Lower still, terror. Right now, it was just an awful unease caused by something I was feeling rather than seeing or hearing.

I scanned the alleyway. It was only narrow, and there didn't seem to be anything in it except old bins and old bags. No movement. No sound. I glanced behind me at the street, but it was still deserted. Even so, the unease remained, and I was far enough off the map not just to tell myself to hold it together. After a moment, I started walking again, cautiously keeping my gun in my hand.

It was ridiculous – but because of that feeling I now had no doubt at all that this was the right building.

The side of number twenty-seven continued, unbroken, for about fifteen, twenty metres, and then the building stopped and a wooden fence took its place. It seemed that the hotel had a back garden. I pulled the uprights one by one and was unsurprised when four in the middle swung in slightly. I knelt down, my jeans creasing tightly. The nails had been removed from the bottom. Four of them lay, bent and rusted, at the base of the fence.

So this was it: Sean's front door.

I pushed the planks. They pivoted slightly, creating just enough space for me to squeeze through. Okay. The wood pressed at me, hard and sharp, and I had to put my palm down into the wet grass on the other side to help pull myself through. It came away dirty as I stood up. The fence cracked back into place behind.

I wiped my hand on my jeans and looked around.

At one point this had clearly been the hotel's back garden. There were old patio stones beneath the overgrown grass, but they were cracked and buckled out of place now. The sodden remains of a few benches and seats rested closer to the building. Litter had drifted in and stayed, fading over time. The air was moist and damp, as though it was a misty morning and the ground had recently been dug over. There were fences on all sides and they gave the garden a feeling of seclusion – no windows overlooked it, beyond the shattered, hooded holes in the back wall of the hotel itself. I turned my attention to that.

Round here, I noticed, the wall wasn't completely sealed up. At ground level, the windows had been boarded over, but someone had recently pulled away the planks across one. I walked over. The unease hadn't left me, and my free hand was shaking a little as I rested it on the dirt-streaked windowsill and peered inside. All I could tell was that it was very dark.

I listened for movement but the building was silent, and so I stood there for a moment, allowing my eyes to become accustomed to the interior. Gradually, I began to pick out the shadowy details of the room. There was no carpet, just stone and broken glass, and the walls were bare. Still some furniture, but right now they were just odd shapes in the dark.

No guts no glory.

I put away the gun and clambered inside, which was far more difficult than it looked. A few awkward contortions later, my feet crunched down on the floor and I felt the itch of dust in my nostrils. Immediately, I drew the gun again.

Okay, Sean, I thought. *Let's see what you've made of the place.*

There was glass everywhere underfoot, and most of the remaining furniture was skeletal, with scraps of fabric hanging off the frames like old skin. Cabinets and cupboards had been reduced to broken boxes. I worked around it all carefully. This first room had obviously been a dining area, and there was an adjoining kitchen that was similarly stripped and bare. The cooker and fridge and most of the units had been pulled out like teeth. A hallway beyond was empty, ending in a small reception area by the front door. There was a desk running down one wall, with a few faded leaflets still resting on it, covered in dust. Untouched for a long time.

Stairs doubled back on the main hallway and led to the second floor. I stood at the bottom for a moment, staring up. It looked slightly lighter up there – probably because the windows weren't so secure, but it made me nervous all the same. The building could almost be tenanted.

Well, it actually could be, I thought.

Obviously, Sean wasn't here anymore, but someone else might have got in. A homeless guy, maybe; or kids with nowhere fun to go.

I took the stairs quickly but carefully – with visions of broken legs replacing those of masked men and baseball bats. But the steps were sturdier than the damp had led me to expect, and I made it onto the tattered landing without injuring myself. Again, there were no carpets, just dusty old floorboards. And little wallpaper up here either, just pale plaster, chalky-green and wet. A quick glance showed what seemed to be six bedrooms. Only two of them were still in possession of their doors, while the others were wide open and strewn with rubble. A single small bathroom at the far end of the corridor spoke tellingly of how cheap this place must have been in life.

I worked through the bedrooms quickly, starting at the back. They were all empty – even the furnishings were gone – but it was obvious from patterns in the dust on the floor that somebody had been here recently. Each vacant room made me more nervous. But then, as I approached the fourth one, I felt sure I had found Sean's makeshift home.

It was one of the closed bedrooms towards the front of the hotel, but unlike the other this had received special attention. There was a steel strip running halfway across the door at waist height, joining another curl of metal on the frame, and the two were secured by a padlock. It looked like a recent addition, and would probably have been enough to deter a casual intruder from investigating any further. But not me. I took a deep breath and kicked the door hard: stamping at the side near the handle. The door was flung inwards, swinging wildly on old hinges. The padlock and pieces of metal remained intact, but a good section of the doorframe they'd been attached to was torn out with the force.

Straight away, I knew this was the place.

There was a mattress in one corner that looked as though it had been slept on recently, with books and papers strewn around it. It was like he'd been prepping for an exam and then fallen asleep, woken up late and had to run. A torch was resting in the centre, bulky as a brick. When I saw it, I realised why he'd picked this room as his home: no window. From the outside, nobody would have been able to see the torchlight shining through gaps in the stones or beams.

The floorboards creaked beneath my feet as I walked over and picked up the torch: a big, rubber block with padded circular buttons on the neck. I pressed one and a beam of light cut across the room onto the bed. The knotted sheets glowed white.

I swept the beam around. The rest of the room – that corner aside – seemed bare and unused, but then the light flashed across a suitcase by the remains of a fire, and I moved it back and held it there for a moment.

Not a suitcase, I realised, but a rifle case. It was red, about a metre long, and I recognised it: Sean had brought it to the range a couple of times and even let me fire it. As things designed for killing people go, it was a beautiful piece of machinery: a present from his father that he'd cared for over the years. The fact that it had been abandoned in this dirty old building brought it home to me again that he was gone.

I walked over and sat down on the edge of the bed, and then picked up a few sheets of paper at random and started to look through them.

There were a lot of photographs. Some of them had been clipped out of magazines, newspapers and journals, and then stuck to sheets of paper; others were original and loose. As I flipped through it all, there didn't seem to be any obvious connections, but gradually a pattern of some kind began to emerge. Most of the pictures were crowd scenes, often with some insignificant object or person at the front, but I began to realise that what was interesting Sean was the background. Away from the focus, the shots became hazy and often indistinct, but the black circles he'd made in biro made it easy enough to spot recurring figures. He'd highlighted the same blurry faces, and they were usually lingering at the backs of crowds as someone more important smiled for the camera in the foreground.

So who were they? The pictures were too out of focus to see much detail, apart from the fact that all of the men looked old. One of them, he'd marked with a red cross beside a letter 'E'; another, with a 'K'. I stared at each photograph in turn and then placed them back on the floor.

One particular photograph caught my eye. Sean had clearly found this one in a book and then enlarged it on a computer, printing out progressive zooms. The initial black and white photograph showed an old boxing match from the city's annual competition: two fighters in the ring at the centre, thousands of people crowding the main square. The lack of colour robbed the scene of its heat and noise, and the stillness – as with all such photographs – froze the banners and the waves, the streamers thrown into the air. The fighters looked poised, a little apart from each other, both caught in the act of throwing a punch. But Sean hadn't been interested in them. Instead, he'd enlarged a portion of one building on the opposite side of the square: zooming in past the lower balconies and windows that were crammed with people, and focusing on a single balcony three floors up. It, too, was full, but here the people seemed to be sitting quietly and neatly, and they were dressed to the nines, as though they were watching an opera in the rich box at the theatre.

The angle was slightly awkward, and this close up most of the detail was lost, but it seemed both possible and likely that the five men I could see, before a pillar obscured the rest of the group, were the same men who appeared, individually, in the other photographs.

Who had Sean been researching? I wondered.

The photographs he had taken himself raised further questions. A number of them had been shot from a window in one of the front bedrooms of this hotel: they showed the bar opposite. Five of them depicted groups of people either arriving or leaving. The times of day varied, as did the people, but a few of the faces persisted. One of them was an old man wrapped in the cocoon of a black coat, and he always came flanked by three men who were large and ugly enough to scare away bullets. In fact, their blank faces looked kind of resigned to that task. A couple of other men cropped up in more than one photo, as well, and I got the impression they were business people of some kind. But the old man himself was obviously the focus of it all. I compared the clearest photograph I had of him with the enhanced shot of the balcony, and there he was. It wouldn't hold up in a court of law, but the similarity would do for me. I checked through the other pictures and found the one marked with an 'E'. That one was even less distinct, but again, I would have put money on it being the same man.

I left these photographs to one side.

A lot of the rest of the papers were photocopies and printouts, and there was also a book filled with idle scribblings. Sean had written pages and pages of mad, scrawling notes, most of which were hard to make out. Some words were circled and linked – he had tied 'arterial' to 'streets' more than once – and although much of the text was difficult to read, the little I did manage to scan through was reminiscent of the conversations we'd often had, only far more extreme. I could only make out odd words and phrases. The city was alive, he was saying. The city was a living, breathing creature. On one page, he was rambling about cancers and tumours, and it took a minute for me to realise that he was writing about Rosh and Lucy and us. In some places, paragraphs had been scribbled out in fury; in others, Sean had torn out whole sections. It didn't make it any easier to follow.

There were occasional illustrations, as well. He'd drawn maps that didn't make any sense to me: a diagram of a circle with parallel lines inside it that looked like it should mean something and didn't. I put it to one side. There was too much to take in – mad, drifting thoughts that had clearly occurred to him a little too quickly for him to write down clearly. The writing and drawings showed fragments of ideas, but each one seemed to shift to something new before it was finished, and the links in between were all missing. It was delirious.

I started leafing through a few of the books that were piled up at the head of the bed.

The subject matter was varied, and not all of it seemed to have much to do with anything. It was possible that he'd been reading up on the philosophy of language for personal amusement, but scanning a few pages convinced me that he must have been exceedingly bored if he had been. There were a few religious books. A handful of old novels. But what caught my eye most was a thick volume entitled *City Legends: East and West*. Sean had clearly consulted this a great deal, as there were bits of sticky paper emerging at various points throughout. I flicked through.

The book listed local and regional myths about cities around the world, some traditional and familiar – Sean had left a marker on the chapter devoted to Rome and its wolf children – whereas others were strange and new. Some of them were exotic places I'd never even heard of. There seemed to be no rhyme or reason to the handful that Sean had chosen to label.

Except for one. Close to the middle, I found an entry for our city. Beneath the title, it listed the author as Dr Mark Harris.

I stared at that for a moment, wondering what to think about it. Jamie said that Harris had been helping them with their project, and it was, after all, his area of expertise. And yet there was something about seeing his name in print that made me want to throw the book to one side and get out of there as fast as I could.

But I didn't. The article was only a page and a half long. I noticed that Sean had torn away the bottom of the first side for some reason – perhaps he'd taken it with him for reference.

I leaned forward on the mattress, shining the torch carefully onto the open book. Suddenly, I experienced another lurch of nausea, and I looked around quickly for my gun. There – it was on the bed beside me. Within easy reach.

But that didn't make me feel any better. It was as though a ghost had just walked into the room and was now standing there, staring at me with wide eyes. The ringing of silence in my ears was bouncing off the walls, intensifying and becoming louder: building to a pitch that would cause my nerves to snap.

Calm down.

And after a moment of breathing slowly, I turned my attention to the book and began to read of our history.

It is not my purpose in this article to draw out the similarities between the myth of the eight brothers and comparable stories in other civilisations and cultures. Suffice to say that there are several key elements that recur; and it may be argued (see Williams, 96; Deacon, 98) that these, along with the timeless and obvious symbolic nature of the story (see Duncan, 91), are enough to qualify the tale purely as a 'myth'. However, it has a number of qualities that support its classification as a 'legend', most notably the general presentation of the story as historical (albeit timeless) fact and the lack of a purely religious element. See the section marked 'further reading' for links to relevant articles.

The basic tenets of the myth are as follows.

At an unspecified time, there were eight brothers living on a very large estate. Their names were Eli, Karna, Gideon, Napier, Voldun, Sanzer, Harven and Rho. In general readings of the tale, they are presented as self-sufficient, beyond the small number of servants that each brother employed; and the estate is reckoned to have contained everything needed for the family to survive: running water; woodland teeming with animals and plants; fields that could be farmed; vast natural resources; etc. They lived in happiness for some time, and certain specific comparisons may be made to Eden and other allegorical paradises. Additionally, the introduction of an 'outside' element that unbalances the harmony and leads ultimately to destruction is a common theme in this literature (Smart, 82). In this case, it occurred when the eight brothers decided it was time to venture into the outside world and find a wife, each riding in a different direction of the compass. It may be argued (see Roseneil, 71) that linking the arrival of women onto the estate with its downfall adds a historically revealing subtext to the myth; but this is refuted by a careful reading of certain sources. When all of the brothers returned with their new wives and families two years later, they each also brought specialist knowledge and experience back with them. From this point, each brother took on a symbolic role, and it is their subsequent interaction that caused the estate to dissolve.

In most versions of the myth, Gideon is seen as having spent time with traders in the west, returning with elaborate plans to export the brothers' bountiful natural resources and produce in exchange for worldly wealth. Napier learned from the scientists of the day, and began automating the farms: constructing a waterwheel and experimenting with steam machinery. Voldun brought back musical instruments from the south. Sanzer had acquired a thirst for knowledge and debate, and took on the role of teacher to the estate's growing number of children. Eli, who had spent time in the rigid cities of the north, took control of security for the community; while Harven, who had studied medicine and chemistry, looked after their health.

Thus we can see that each of these six brothers embodies an important element of a successful society. (Respectively: finance; power and technology; the arts; education; law and order; and medicine). For some time, the estate continued to thrive, with its population growing around this central disciplined core.

Of the other two brothers, Rho brought back no particular skills or trade, and is seen as representing (variously) life, death, religion, fate and chance. However, all sources agree that the blame for the eventual dissolution of the estate lay with Karna, who had spent time in the ports and harbours of the west, 'consorting with thieves, pirates and blackhearts' (see Williams, 96); and over time, it became apparent that he had returned to his family bearing many undesirable traits. Karna would come to symbolise crime and anarchy. Over a long period, he worked secretly in opposition to his brothers, undermining Gideon's dealings with outside traders while making his own business arrangements with less savoury clients. Eventually, his actions would destroy the founding family.

Then there was a break in the text where Sean had ripped away the bottom of the page. It continued at the top of the other side:

In modern times, the brothers are seen as patron figureheads controlling the various aspects of life in the city as listed above. An alleged representation of Eli can be seen on the crest of the Gaunes Knight at the law courts in the district of Owl; and the city's main hospital is colloquially referred to by locals as 'Harven's'. (A likeness of him is also rumoured to be included in the building's famous hanging tapestry.) Other examples abound (see further reading) but the most obvious is the partitioned nature of the city, which is divided into sixteen districts. Once a year, a competition is held wherein eight districts compete in a city-sponsored event, and this author would suggest that the sport and the legend share similar origins.

By the time I finished reading, my hands were literally shaking. I had no idea why – I actually looked down and stared at them, willing them to stop. What was wrong with me? It was just a book, and yet I felt like I was going to be sick. The feeling was far worse now than it had been all day – even in Hedge's flat when I'd been looking at the computer program.

The image of the city map flashed into my mind; the room started whirling around me. I closed my eyes, resting my head on my knees.

Stop, I thought. *Please stop.*

'Feeling ill?'

I opened my eyes and jumped up off the mattress, picking up the gun and bringing it to bear on an empty room. Flicked it this way and that. The torch fell on its side, spilling light across the floor.

Somebody laughed. My aim shifted round to a blank wall.

'Who's that?' I said, stepping back onto the mattress and leaning against the corner of the room. Even though it was dark, I could see everywhere. There was nobody here.

Out in the corridor? I moved my aim to the doorway.

The voice had sounded closer than that, though – it had been right in my ear. Deep, male and amused.

Whoever it was laughed again and repeated my words back to me:

'*Who's that?*'

241

My aim flicked to the opposite side of the room. Nobody there.

They came out of the walls.

At the time, I'd laughed off what Jamie had said. Now, my skin started crawling. I took a better grip of the gun.

'*Who's that?*'

Closer now, as though the person was sidling across the room towards me. Winding like a snake.

'*Who's that?*'

And then I saw him, out of the corner of my eye, creeping slowly along the wall to the right of me. I turned quickly, almost fired – but there was nobody there. Then I saw him again, on the other side of me. Impossible. And as I flipped my aim round that way he was gone again.

'*Who is that?*'

This time, the voice came from right in front of me.

And there he was. I had time for my eyes to blink a photograph of him, for my free hand to move up in self-defence, and then everything went black.

CHAPTER EIGHTEEN

I dreamed about Sean. To begin with, my mind was simply filling in the gaps of the past few months, and I saw images of him contacting Jamie and Keleigh; of him sitting in his room, reading by torchlight. Taking photographs. Shadowing people on the streets.

Each image flashed up, leaving a mark on my thoughts that slowly faded back to nothing.

Here he was, answering the phone.

Flash; fade; gone.

And then, he was dying. Illuminated cuts of the beating, strobe lit into slow, staccato motion as blows landed. The memories flashed into still life, and then sank back into black mist. Sean on the floor, the bats raining down on him. His body losing cohesion as bones shattered, flesh bruised, joints dislocated. The twitches as, despite everything, the ebbing currents of life continued to spark in him, growing fainter. His lights going out.

'Wake him up.'

His past: about to become my present and future. Inside, I was panicking. There was something pitch black and furious in my mind, pounding the inside of a dark box that was hidden too well to see. As I surfaced and heard the words again, I knew that I was going to lose it badly if I wasn't careful. Now, I really did need to keep it together.

'Wake him up.'

I said, 'I *am* awake.'

'Open your eyes, then.'

I did as I was told, blinking against the sudden light and then looking around cautiously. I was sitting in a comfortable chair, made of black leather that looked and felt as tight as swollen skin. It was a little too close to the floor: my feet stretched out over pale, clean floorboards that had been polished to minimalist perfection.

Where was I?

Probably the bar across the street – maybe a back room.

Take in as much as you can.

For what it would be worth, I did. The room was very spare – most of the furnishings were black or white, complementing the light-brown flooring, and it all looked expensive and well-coordinated. A very old and thin man was sitting opposite me, in the centre of a leather sofa that matched my own chair. Between us, there was a coffee table made of glass. I recognised the man: he was one of the men from Sean's photographs, the one marked by a 'K', only he was dressed more casually now, wearing old, black suit trousers and a white shirt with the sleeves rolled up. It was like he'd been designed to match the décor.

He was leaning forward with his elbows resting on his knees, smoking a cigarette and staring at me a little curiously, as though he'd caught something by accident and wasn't quite sure what it was. Two of his bodyguards were loitering in the background, and they both seemed entirely indifferent and non-threatened by me. It was almost insulting, although I supposed in the circumstances they were probably right.

'Nice to meet you,' I said.

He didn't say anything, but kept staring at me and

smoking his cigarette thoughtfully. I couldn't keep his gaze, so I looked over to my right at a fish tank on the other side of the room. It was large and seemed to be filled mainly with pale green, glowing bubbles.

No windows in here, I noticed.

Was it still daylight? I had no idea what time it was, and very little sense of how long I'd been unconscious. It didn't *feel* long. I wondered whether I still had my phone. I was willing to bet they had taken my gun. But I wasn't about to check my clothes for either of them.

After a moment, I looked back at the man and he spoke in an old, weary voice.

'You're feeling better now, I take it?'

The question caught me off guard. My head hurt, my pride hurt, and I was pretty sure that I was going to die. But since this man was either past, present or likely future cause of all of those things, I couldn't imagine why he might care.

'Not great, no,' I said. 'Thanks for the concern though.'

'Oh – top marks.' He leaned over and tapped his cigarette into an ashtray on the coffee table. 'I'm always pleased when people in *real* trouble can still manage sarcasm and humour. It has a certain existential honesty to it. I'm not likely to ever be in such trouble as you are, Detective Weaver, but I can only dream of handling it so well if I were.'

'I'm not a detective anymore,' I said.

'Well, no.' He conceded it with a slight incline of his head. 'That's certainly true. The reason I asked is because people generally do feel better when they find us. We're a relief. Do you still feel nauseous, for example?'

I felt it stir as he said that – that lurching, panicked

feeling I'd had nearly all day – and found myself swallowing it down.

You're not going to be sick.

And as I fought it back, I saw that he was smiling at me. Like he could tell.

'I don't know what you mean,' I said, but my mouth was too dry and it was obvious I was lying.

He tapped the cigarette again. When he raised it back to his lips and inhaled, there was something slow and dainty about the manoeuvre.

'You were looking for us,' he said.

There didn't seem to be any point in denying it.

I said, 'I'm looking for the people who killed my friend.'

'No – not just that. You've been searching for longer than that. All of you, but you and your friend especially.'

'You've been following us?' I said, not understanding what he meant.

'No. I don't need to follow people.'

'What's that supposed to mean?'

He smiled a little absently. 'I've not followed you because I haven't needed to. But I've seen you watching the city lights. I've sat behind you in bars and listened to you talking. You and that other policeman were always looking for us. It's just that neither of you realised it. And why would you?'

'I've not been looking for you,' I said. 'I don't even know who you are.'

He smiled again, and then took a long drag on the cigarette and held it in for a while, thinking things through. One of his bodyguards started slowly circling the room, moving out of sight behind me. I heard his feet tapping on the wood, and then nothing. He had stopped behind me. My neck started tingling and I wanted to lean forwards. Instead, I did my best to keep still.

'I don't even know who you are,' I said again.

The old man breathed out, and the smoke filled the air between us.

'Do you remember a man named Timothy Hartley?' he asked.

Hartley. Yes, I remembered. He'd been the first man I'd gone along with Rosh, Lucy and Sean to kill – the man who'd taken that little girl and who had then, in his turn, been taken by us. I remembered him and what had happened to him. When Sean had found her safe, Lucy had shot Timothy Hartley in the head. At the time, I'd been shocked, but then my feelings had lessened. He'd been a small, insignificant man who'd hurt a lot of people and with hindsight it didn't seem like his death had reduced anything in the slightest. In fact, the world felt fuller without him.

'Name doesn't ring a bell,' I said.

'You don't remember killing him?' The old man looked mildly surprised. 'I would have thought it would stick in the mind, something like that. It certainly stuck in mine, as he was working for me at the time.'

'Oh right?' I said, glancing at the bodyguard behind him. 'Do you employ a lot of paedophiles and rapists?'

The old man laughed, dismissing it with a wave of his hand.

'Well, they're everywhere these days. Don't you read the papers?'

'I just think you can generally tell a lot about a man by the company he keeps.'

'Perhaps,' the old man said, considering the point for as long as it took to breathe out a mouthful of smoke.

'But Hartley was a hard worker, no matter what else he was.'

'And what sort of work did he do for you?'

'He moved money, people. Other things on occasion. Hartley had a small workshop, you might remember, and we used his accounts a few times. Nothing too important, but serious enough for me to take an interest when he died. You weren't as hard to pick out as you might imagine, and it didn't take long to work out what you were doing. You and your little vigilante friends.'

'Oh yeah?' I was angry despite myself. The girl we rescued the night Hartley died had been okay, but only because of us. 'And what were we doing?'

'Well – killing people.' He looked a little confused that he had to explain it to me at all. 'Killing people you didn't like.'

'Bad people,' I said. 'Who deserved it.'

'No. People you didn't like.' He carried on without giving me time to reply. 'And that's fine. We all do it. I was mostly just relieved to find out that my brother wasn't involved. We have an agreement to leave each other alone, and I thought he might have been going against it. But it only took a few phonecalls to discover that you were doing this entirely on your own. He never had a clue.'

'Your brother?'

'Eli.' He inhaled and then breathed out slowly, allowing the name to hang in the air for a moment. Then, he said: 'Eli powers law and order in the city.'

'Eli,' I repeated. 'Right.'

'You've never met him, don't worry. Not yet.'

'Okay.'

The legend of the brothers who'd founded the city came back to me. I remembered the photographs that

Sean had marked: one with an 'E'; another – this man – with a 'K'.

I said, 'So that would make you ... Karna?'

'That's right.' He stubbed out the cigarette. 'Top marks.'

And despite everything, I laughed.

Karna – or whoever the fuck he really was – kept smiling to himself as he reached for a pack of cigarettes on the table and shook one free.

I could feel his bodyguard standing close behind me but I nodded at the pack anyway.

'I guess that ghosts don't have to worry about their health?'

'Good guess.' The old man lit the cigarette with a match and then waved the match out with a hand that was almost too quick to see. 'Now, let me guess something. You've been feeling sick recently. Very sick. And now, as I said before, you feel much better.'

He was right – I didn't feel great, but I certainly did feel better. When I'd been in Hedge's flat, watching the computer program, I hadn't been entirely confident of keeping myself upright. Now, although I still felt strange, I figured that standing up would have been fine, assuming anyone here would have let me.

'That happens.' Karna pointed the glowing end of the cigarette at me. 'When you begin, you're not equipped to deal with us, and that sickness is what you feel as you grow closer. You start seeing coincidences for what they are. It's us. We bring about those coincidences.'

'Is that right?'

But I'd stopped smiling now, and I felt uncomfortable again; my bravado seemed false even to me. Coincidences. Sickness. I wondered if someone might have slipped me something to create those kinds of feelings and thoughts. It seemed unlikely, but I couldn't be sure. Perhaps.

'We're at the heart of this city,' Karna said, 'and when people are drawn to us they spiral down into that heart. Like dirty water sucked down a sink.'

He made a circling motion with his cigarette hand.

'When you spiral, things start repeating. You see? Maybe you don't recognise it at the time, but that's all it is.'

'Maybe I just had a dodgy burger,' I said.

Without warning, I felt a pressure on the back of my neck that made me wince. Karna shot a glance over my head. A second later, the pain vanished.

'Your friend believed in us,' he said. 'You've seen his library.'

I rubbed the back of my neck.

'And you killed him because of it.'

Karna shook his head. 'I didn't kill your friend. Not directly anyway.'

'Bullshit.'

He leaned back and the leather creaked behind him.

'Your friend lived across the road for a while. He was watching us, I think, but I never had the pleasure of meeting him directly. It was amusing to see him hiding away, coming to the same conclusions as you have. He acknowledged it more quickly than you, but I suppose he was a little more unhinged and didn't have quite so many barriers remaining. On the surface, he was obsessed by that irrelevant dead girl. But really, deep down, he was just drawn to us. He could smell my brother all over her.'

'You killed him,' I said again.

He shook his head more slowly than before.

'No. I understand why you might think that, but in fact I haven't killed anyone recently.'

'Are you going to kill me?' I said.

He paused, considering this. I couldn't see or hear his bodyguard behind me, but I felt slight pressure again. I got the impression the man knew that if there was going to be killing done then he'd be the one for the job, and that he was running the various possibilities through his head right now.

'I haven't decided yet,' Karna said finally.

Perhaps I should have been relieved, but I wasn't.

'Why am I here then?'

He ignored the question. 'I've actually been following your careers with interest. Tell me, *Mister* Weaver – why did you go around killing people?'

He looked at me with genuine curiosity. Despite myself, I felt small and stupid.

'They were men who were above the law,' I said.

He frowned. 'Above the law?'

Even to me, it seemed inadequate. I didn't know why I felt the need to justify myself to this man, who I had no doubt was a criminal and a killer of a much higher magnitude than me. But I did.

'They were men we couldn't put away,' I told him. 'They could either buy their way out, or have it bought for them.'

'That's very interesting,' Karna said. He sounded like he meant it. 'So, it implies there's something *other* than the law that you presume you know best?'

He appeared to think about this for a second, while I said nothing, and then he waved his hand and dismissed his own thoughts.

'You're right on a practical level, though – they could buy themselves out. And sometimes it was me that did the buying. After all, I power crime here in the city.'

'Right.'

'And as I bought these men out, I watched with a certain amount of amusement as you then took them away from me. To begin with, anyway. After a while, it became annoying. But I tolerated you, because I knew that you would be useful to me at some point.'

'Useful,' I said.

'Not a word that you associate with yourself very often.'

'What did you want us to do?' I said, although I was remembering what Rosh had told me about Toby Yeung's body being dragged out of the canal, and I thought I knew what Karna was going to tell me.

He leaned forwards again to tap away more ash.

'You see, just like I can buy people out I can also buy them in. Carl Halloran, for example.' He made it sound like he was plucking a name from thin air. 'Very minor league. Hardly ever hurt a fly. But to a small extent he was in my way, and so I bought him in. A few words in the right ears, and then he was in your way too. And then he was dead.'

'Yeah.' I felt that lurch of inevitability. Whatever else might be bullshit here, I knew that this much was true. 'We killed Carl Halloran. Because you wanted us to, right?'

He nodded.

'I set him up, yes. Well, one of my employees, but it amounts to the same thing. Terrible thing, that post-office murder, and I can assure you that it was nothing to do with me. Opportune, though. I sent the fake information to your friend through one of your usual channels. And you went and killed Halloran for me. It was all very successful.'

He wasn't an innocent man, I reminded myself. Except that I had no idea now what he was. All of the emotions inside me had been so stamped down and muddled up that the only thing I could think of was one single question:

'Why?'

And Karna just shrugged.

'Perhaps boredom?' he said. 'But also, Halloran worked for my brother, Eli.'

'Eli. Who powers law and order, right?'

'That's right, yes. But underneath it all we're quite similar. He understands about balance, and he's a practical man. He doesn't always run things the way someone as idealistic as you might want, but we exist in a kind of uneasy harmony, and our methods aren't all that different. Halloran was doing some work for him – moving money, basically. This and that, here and there. He didn't know it, but that's what he did. And I suppose I had him killed just to annoy my brother.'

'Right.'

'And perhaps to take care of you, as well, but that wasn't so important. You were running around, messing things up for me in minor ways. Eli wasn't letting you get away with it, exactly, but I was still annoyed at him for not running a tighter ship.'

'Right,' I said again. 'So this is some kind of family feud, or something?'

Karna shook his head and smiled.

'Nothing as grand as that. My brother and I need each other; and we both know it. But we don't invent our natures and we can't help what we're driven to do. So we dig at each other a bit, here and there, and we always have. We can't hurt each other directly, but little punches behind the ears that don't leave any bruises – they're fine. You know what brothers are like. Cat and dog sometimes.'

'Okay.'

I didn't know what else to say. He was telling me

that he was basically some kind of ghost, and that he'd made us kill someone just to piss off his brother. What was I supposed to do with that? Laugh at it under more normal circumstances, but it didn't feel at all funny right now. And it was bullshit, of course, but I couldn't work out *why* he was feeding it to me. What was the point? And yet it couldn't be true.

In the absence of reasonable alternatives, I resolved to nod politely until I found out whether I was going to die or not, and then worry about things afterwards.

Karna leaned back and smiled to himself.

'So that was that,' he said. 'A minor annoyance for him in exchange for what I'd felt, and that's where it would have ended. I just didn't plan on you taking his money.'

All that money.

At the time, I'd taken it to secure Rachel and me a safer future. But when I'd walked out of Hedge's flat earlier that day, I knew there was more to it than that. And now it's time to be honest.

I had always liked to think I was a nice guy, but I knew deep down that I wasn't. I can just do a good impression, that's all. On the surface, I care about other people and try to think about what's best for them. I'm kind and generous. I'm even gentle, on the numerous occasions when I'm not shooting at people. But if you step beyond all that – pull it to one side and look behind it – then you can see it for what it is. Everyone's driven to do what's best for them, and it's just a happy coincidence that a lot of what I do comes from wanting people to like me. The moment my interests change, I drop the nice-guy act and behave as rat-like and shitty as everyone else.

That night, as we took the money and left Halloran

dead in his hotel room, I really was thinking to myself: *if I'm cautious – if I don't attract too much attention – then that's enough money to keep me and Rachel safe and secure for a long time.*

That was the justification I genuinely used. But people invent all kinds of good reasons for the bad things they do. They lie to themselves about their motivations because they have to, and sometimes they don't even know they're doing it. Nobody's a bad guy. There are stupid things we're driven to do simply because it's in our nature, and when those things threaten the image we have of ourselves we just switch bulbs and shine a different coloured light on events. Keep switching. Eventually, you'll find a shade you can live with.

I'd been sleeping with Lucy for a while by then, and regardless of how we really felt about each other I'd found myself falling out of love with Rachel as a result. Seeing Lucy had opened a valve in my ankle, and all of the love and happiness I'd felt for Rachel was slowly leaking out. By the time the four of us were leaving the hotel with that money, I was empty.

Below the surface, that was on my mind. I didn't want to be with Rachel anymore, but I knew that I couldn't just leave. I had no money: nowhere to go; no real savings. There was more to it than that, of course – there was the hurt and upset I was going to cause. The emotional trauma for both of us. But the money was a real, practical barrier, and that night I knew that the barrier was gone. I didn't let myself think about it in any great detail: I recognised it and immediately put it out of my thoughts and concentrated on nicer ones. But it's not like you can properly take back a realisation. It sat at the back of my mind and I worked on it subconsciously. On the surface, I could convince myself that I was still a good man, but deep down I was building my exit strategy from that moment on. Like everybody else, I'm good at turning a blind eye to myself.

Now, looking back, I could see that there was a terrible sense of justice to everything that had happened. If you take someone's money then there's always a chance you can pay it back and make amends, but because I'd left Rachel that wasn't even an option. I didn't have the money; I'd invested it in the end of my relationship. It was threaded into the rented walls and floor of my flat, and running through the plugs and cables. Some of it I'd drunk; some I'd eaten. It had been spent on countless things that in my own stupid way I'd thought might make me happy. Things that – right now – I'd have given up in a second.

I'm stupid, but even I'm not *that* stupid.

'What money?' I said.

Karna smiled, as though he'd expected this and would have been disappointed with anything else. But I figured he couldn't know for sure that we'd taken the money – and it was very possible that it had been his all along, and this elaborate load of shit he'd been feeding me was just a way to get me to admit I'd stolen it. If that was true, I was going to end up like Sean whatever I said, but there was no point in worrying. All I could do was deny it, wait and see.

Karna took a drag on his cigarette and said:

'The money that the four of you took, obviously. And it's okay that you took it. I hadn't known it would still be there, but actually it couldn't have worked out better. You didn't just inconvenience my brother. You really, really annoyed him.'

I shook my head.

'I don't know anything about any money.'

But I wasn't even convincing myself, let alone Karna.

'Well – someone took it.' He tapped away some ash and looked decidedly unconcerned by it all. 'Halloran had it, and then he didn't. Some of my brother's people turned up to collect it, and apparently it wasn't there. So *someone* took it. They started looking for it that night. With Halloran's girlfriend.'

I closed my eyes, seeing the coincidences. Alison's death had been a bad one, but the city was full of those, and only now did I realise how fitting and logical it was that it had been *this* investigation that had consumed Sean: the murder that everything else revolved around. We'd been drawn in, not realising that our own actions had created the drag. There were coincidences here, but they felt more like patterns. There was a mad kind of sense to it all.

With my eyes still closed, I said:

'So you're telling me that the police killed her?'

'No,' Karna said. 'My brother powers law and order, and that's not the same thing. But most of the police come under him.'

I opened my eyes and watched Karna stubbing out his cigarette.

He said, 'It has a terrible inevitability to it, doesn't it?'

'Your brother killed her?'

'Yes. He killed your friend too. And he tried to kill the three of you last night, but he obviously underestimated you. He won't make the same mistake again.'

'Right.'

I rubbed my eyebrow. What was Karna's motivation for telling me all of this? If it was his money we'd taken, then he knew enough just to kill me and have done with it. He could find Rosh and Lucy. What was

257

the point in having a fucking conversation with me at all?

'Why are you telling me all this?' I said.

'Why? Like I said – boredom. Amusement.'

'Boredom and amusement?'

He shrugged to himself.

'I can't act directly to harm my brother. But it pleases me to stir things up and make it difficult for him. And this really couldn't have ended up any better, could it?'

'Right,' I said. 'Of course.'

Karna smiled.

'I know you don't believe me,' he said, 'but that doesn't really matter. It's going to be interesting to see what you do next. You and your friends.'

'And what will your brother do next?' I said.

'He's tried to take you once and he failed.' Karna was lighting another cigarette. 'But he'll try again very soon, and the next time he'll succeed.'

'Can I kill him?' I said.

'Could you kill me?' he replied, waving out the match.

'Yes.'

'If you got the chance, you could kill either of us.' He nodded. 'But you'll never get near enough. And Eli will be quick and ruthless now that he knows who you are. He will do everything he can to undermine the three of you, to break you apart. He'll go after those you love, as well – assuming you have any. Eventually, he'll have wiped away all traces of you entirely. He will clean away everyone who's out of place. You, your friends and family, those students – he'll remove all of you.'

For the first time in a few minutes, I was aware again

of the bodyguard standing directly behind me. Something in the atmosphere had changed.

'That's reassuring,' I said, wanting to turn around, but finding that something was stopping me. I tried, but I couldn't even move. After a moment, I realised that Karna was staring straight at me, slightly differently from before. This time, he wasn't blinking.

'That's what you're up against,' he said. 'And now, it's time for you to leave and take your chances.'

I tried to move again, beginning to panic. I was stuck. How was it fucking possible that he was doing this?

'Oh,' he said, noticing my predicament. 'Don't get up.'

And with that, Karna nodded at the bodyguard behind me. Before I could react in any way, everything went black for the second time that afternoon.

'Young sir?'

It was very dark. A man had his hand on my right shoulder, shaking me, and his fingers were pressing into me too hard for comfort. I jerked angrily awake, grabbed his wrist with my left hand and twisted it, standing, coming around with my right to lock his elbow and put him down. Ready to scream at him. He cried out in alarm and tried to cower away, but he wasn't going anywhere.

Hang on, I told myself. Not letting go, but looking around.

I was in a room filled with four or five rows of wooden pews, all facing the far end of the room, where there was a small stage, spot-lit from above. Two naked people were having sex on it. The man was middle-aged and fat; she was middle-aged and plump; and they were both paused in mid-coitus and staring in my direction with annoyed expressions. They obviously felt that they'd suffered enough indignity today without having to put up with my shit too. All the other patrons – and the theatre was nearly full – were watching me cautiously.

The man I was holding was the canvas-man who'd spoken to me earlier that afternoon in western Wasp, and he was struggling against me now without making much ground.

'Young sir, please,' he said, finally giving up. 'You were asleep. Your phone was ringing. You were disturbing the performers.'

I shook my head, aware for the first time that my phone actually was ringing. It was audible even over the hymn music that was accompanying the sex show. How embarrassing.

'I'm sorry.' I let go of the man and headed quickly to the back of the room, fighting my mobile out of my pocket the whole way.

They didn't take my phone, then.

I didn't recognise the number that was flashing up, but pressed green anyway, moving down the dingy stairs at the back of the theatre and out into the light.

'Hello?'

'Martin?'

It was Rachel, but at the same time it wasn't. Her voice sounded strange and dulled.

'Yes,' I said. 'What's wrong?'

'Martin, I really need you to help me.' She swallowed, and I leaned against a black and yellow railing, my heart sinking. Her voice was flat, but there were little oscillations in it that I thought I recognised – peaks of fear. She said, 'I think I've just been raped. I'm not sure, but … I think that's what's happened.'

260

'Okay, Rachel,' I said, trying to sound calm, reassuring. My free hand was clenched so tight that the knuckles looked ready to burst. 'Where are you now?'

'This house,' she said.

'Our old house?'

'No. Some other house. This ... this ... guy's house.'

He'll go after those you love, as well – assuming you have any.

'Is he still there?' And when she didn't answer I said it again more urgently. 'Rachel – is he still there with you?'

'Yes,' she said. 'He's right here. He's watching me.'

The hairs on my neck stood on end. She started crying.

'Rachel,' I said. The district around me had faded away to white. 'Please try to keep calm. You're going to be okay.'

But the sobbing had moved away now and I knew she couldn't hear me. There was empty silence for a second, and then a sense of purpose gathered at the other end of the phone. The buzz on the line was quiet and forceful.

'Hello?' I said.

Nothing. But someone was there.

I waited, moving away from the railing and reaching inside my jacket. The gun was still there. I took it out and checked the clip. A few people who had been walking near me veered suddenly away. Fine; the clip was full. I clicked it back and replaced the gun in its holster.

'I know you're –' I started to say.

'Seventy-eight,' a voice interrupted. It was a male voice. Gritty but young. And angry, too, as though whoever it belonged to was reading information off a sheet for the fifth time and losing his patience. 'Fisher Lane. Turtle.'

In the background, for just a second, I could still hear Rachel crying.

And then the line went dead.

CHAPTER NINETEEN

The address was too far away to make on foot, and public transport was out of the question, so I stole a car. I found a relatively old one parked out of the way and on its own, smashed the passenger window with a brick, cracked the steering column, and in less than a minute I was on my way. A few people saw, and then wisely elected to ignore me. I felt bad, even if I didn't have a choice. Here I was again, though: breaking the law to serve a higher moral cause. But stealing a car felt quite minor in comparison to most of the shit I'd done.

The car hurtled out of Wasp. Two minutes later I was on the motorway, with a breeze whipping in through the broken window. A couple of crunching gear shifts, and I was heading south. Turtle was directly below Wasp, but it was a large district and the Fishers were right at the bottom. I put my foot down.

I had the wheel in one hand; phone flipping open in the other.

I hit Rosh's speed dial number, held the mobile to my ear and waited. But not for long – it was engaged, and the nasal beeps sounded even more smug and annoying than usual. I swore, cancelled and tried Lucy instead.

It rang out; not even an answerphone. Where the fuck were they both?

I tossed the phone onto the passenger seat, swearing loudly. Call the normal police? Not a good idea. If

Karna had been telling the truth then Eli ran law and order and calling the police wasn't going to help; and if he was lying then what was I going to tell them? Just how much of this could I actually explain, and how seriously were they going to take me?

I'd be close soon, anyway, and I'd certainly arrive before anyone else showed up, especially from a random, unsubstantiated call. Even if I did phone it in, I'd be lucky to see the police before nightfall.

Two minutes later and the last exit for Turtle was coming up on the left. I drew my gun, rested it on the seat beside me, and then took the exit a little too fast. The car tyres screeched as I rounded the fat, curling roads leading off into the district's centre.

Rachel.

A flood of images and emotions rushed me, and I did my best to blot them out. Anger was one thing, but I needed to think clearly if I was going to make a difference here.

I thought about the gun instead. I hadn't had the chance to use it when Karna's man had taken me down in the old hotel, and I considered that now. What the fuck had happened? Whenever I'd seen him, it had been out of the corner of my eye; the rest of the time it had been as though he was invisible. Had he moved that quickly, or was there some other explanation? Karna's story aside, I believed my own memory. It had happened, and if I was going to meet more people like his bodyguard then I needed to figure out how to deal with them.

Fisher Lane . . .

Here were the Fishers – coming up on the right. Mostly red-brick back-to-backs.

Fisher Road. Fisher Avenue.

Fisher Lane was the last one, separated from its kin

by a small, neat stretch of wasteground. I stopped at the end of the street, picked up the phone and the gun, and then got out and took the corner on foot. There was nobody around, but I kept the gun concealed, holding my hand inside my jacket.

The guy in the hotel. When I was younger, I'd heard these martial arts stories about people who trained so as to move within their opponent's blind spots. A portion of the eye doesn't receive light properly, and if you could throw a punch partially within this then you'd have an advantage. I didn't think Karna's bodyguard had been doing anything remotely like that, but I had no other explanation. It was as though he'd come out of the walls, just as Jamie had said.

I checked the house numbers – early thirties – and I started to run, abandoning any pretence of hiding the gun. My shoes pounded the pavement: past the forties; into the fifties. There was an old couple on the opposite side of the street. I saw them stop and look at me, and then say something to each other.

One thing about Karna's bodyguard was that he had to actually physically hit me. Not a normal punch, I was sure, but he'd had to get close enough to touch me. These people were flesh and blood – even if it was hard to see – and if they could hurt me then I could hurt them right back.

Number sixty-eight. Number seventy.

I scanned the parked cars up ahead. There weren't that many and they all looked empty, but that didn't mean they were necessarily. I slowed down and started walking, gun held out in front slightly. Good two-handed grip.

Seventy-two. Seventy-four.

The way I saw it, the only person in that house who I cared about right now was Rachel. Anybody who moved who wasn't her, I was probably going to shoot. Given what had happened already that afternoon, it seemed a pretty reasonable and sensible course of action.

Seventy-six.

I checked each car as I approached: aiming in, peering from behind the gun. Each one was empty.

And then here was number seventy-eight: semi-detached, on the right-hand side of its pair. Two storeys. All the curtains drawn in the three windows I could see. There was a small, well-tended garden at the front of the house and a driveway to the right, and I moved cautiously but quickly down that, heading for a door halfway along the house. I guessed it would lead into the kitchen. At the far end of the drive there was a red garage, its wide double door topped by small, black windows, and a path led round the back of the house. I dodged under the kitchen window and quickly checked out the back garden. It turned out to be bigger than the front, but equally well-tended. There were flowerbeds around the edges, and it was divided in two by a small strip of soil where someone had been growing vegetables.

In the centre of the nearest section, there was a bright blue paddling pool and a small multicoloured slide. My aim wavered slightly and I thought:

Children.

There were children here. I scrabbled back through my memory of the conversation, trying to recall the address I'd been given. Was I even at the right house? But I remembered it clearly: seventy-eight. This was the right address. So what the fuck was with the slide and the pool? I couldn't go in and just start shooting. My reasonable and sensible course of action suddenly looked a little shaky.

I moved back up the driveway, and stopped by the kitchen door.

Fall back, I told myself. *Call Rosh, Lucy. Call anyone. It's a possible hostage situation and you're on a roll of fucking things up at the moment.*

I picked out my phone and dialled Rosh again, and – this time – it rang out. No answerphone. I pressed myself against the wall and called Lucy. Once again, it rang out.

Fuck.

Call the normal police then, I thought – that was the sensible thing to do now. But at the same time, this was Rachel. And yes, I'd fucked up more than my share recently, but my mistakes had already affected her life. I owed her more – I couldn't just leave her inside and walk away, and let someone else sort out my mess. Especially when everything that had happened to her was solely for my benefit.

I moved to the other side of the kitchen door, turned the handle and pushed it open quietly. Kept out of the way, waited for a second.

Nothing.

I shifted slightly. The door had come to rest against a tall fridge-freezer. That was white and new, and it had lots of children's drawings stuck to it with plastic letter-magnets. The rest of the kitchen looked empty. I listened. No noise at all from inside – nothing to hear.

I edged around, keeping the gun trained on the doorway. The kitchen was lit by a window facing out onto the garden at the back, and I could see most of it. There was nobody in there. Not even any cupboards or spaces large enough to hide someone, unless they were midgets as well as ghosts. Now or never, then. I stepped inside, turning quickly and training my gun on the doorway that led out of the kitchen. There was a

267

hallway beyond – empty; full of misty, still air. But once again, I felt the subtle difference between an empty house and one where somebody was just hiding and holding their breath.

Keep calm. The emotions were rolling inside me – fear, anger – and that was no good. I brought them out now, so that I could see them, handle them and then put them to one side where they couldn't do as much harm, and then I took a better grip on the gun and moved into the hallway.

My aim flicked round, quickly and carefully. There were stairs leading up from the hall, to the left. A half-open door to the right. The stairs looked clear. The door led into a cluttered dining room. I edged in. There was a huge table in the centre, loads of books, glass sliding doors at the far end that led out into the garden. It smelled of paper and clothes. I worked quickly: round the table halfway, aiming the gun at empty spaces; then round the other side. Clear. Nobody hiding.

Okay. Two rooms clear.

Back out into the corridor. There was another door further along to the right, and then the hallway ended at the front door, where angles of afternoon sunlight were streaking in through a semi-circle of coloured glass at the top. I could see motes of dust floating in the air, swimming slowly in invisible currents.

The next room – but as I started to move, the motes swirled suddenly, like a draught of air had blown through the hallway. I glanced to the right, almost without thinking, and out of the corner of my eye I saw a man moving quickly and impossibly down the hall towards me. My glance flicked back and he was gone, but I was already firing: three solid shots at thin air, the bullets swallowed up before they cracked into the front door. The noise was enormous, and the walls vibrated with each quick explosion. I closed my eyes against the muzzle flashes, and opened them to see a man rolling backwards over his shoulder as he was knocked down, finishing hard against the front door.

My ears were ringing and the hallway was thick with the smoke of violence. I kept my aim on the man, moving closer, ready to shoot him if he tried to get up. But I'd caught him in the chest with all three shots, and he wasn't going anywhere. I took him in quickly – a big guy, dressed in a neat, dark suit. Short, black hair.

Something prickled on the back of my neck.

I was turning before I knew it – firing off another shot that blew shards of wood across the hallway. Half the kitchen doorframe disintegrated into misty splinters. Had I seen someone as I whirled around? I glanced to one side, then the other, whipping my head round. Caught sight of him – coming low out of the dining room. Another big guy, heading at me fast in a crouch. But I'd made him – I fired once, twice, the shots going into the floor like hammered nails, spitting up puffs of carpet fabric, and then I fired again and he suddenly appeared, barrelling at me but stumbling, the top of his head gone. He dropped just in front of my feet, and I shot him in the back.

In the silence that followed, I could hear my own breathing. Fast and thin.

And then, upstairs, a woman started crying.

Rachel.

I stepped over the first man I'd killed, uncurling my fingers from around the gun and taking a better grip. I fired off a shot up the stairs; shot once more down the hall behind me. Hit nothing, but at least both ways were clear. I started up the stairs, moving quickly and carefully, ready to fire again at the slightest movement.

But then I heard Rachel start screaming – properly screaming, as though she was being hurt more than she could bear – and I lost all sense of caution. I charged up the stairs and onto the landing.

The screaming was coming from the nearest door on the left, and I went for it, but something grabbed my wrist and wrenched my arm around.

Fuck.

Suddenly there he was, right beside me. I caught a brief glimpse of him – it was like wrestling with a ghost – and then he was there just like anyone would be. Perhaps he needed to concentrate: he was gritting his teeth and pulling my arm down, then pulling it more, until the gun was pointing harmlessly at the carpet. I fired off a shot anyway, panicking, and managed to jerk my arm a little so that the bullet caught him in the foot, punching a hole through it. He cried out and let go and – suddenly released – my hand sprang back up and I pulled the trigger again; but he was already reacting, quick enough to bat my aim to one side so that the shot just took a chunk of powdered brick out of the wall. And he had hold of me again, the sheer weight of him knocking me over onto my back, knocking the gun out of my hand, and knocking half the air out of me. I was frantic – crying out – trying to do him some damage, trying to get a grip on his ear to rip it off, or his eyes, or his throat. Anything. But he was holding me too well. I managed a weak punch to the side of his head – nowhere near hard enough – and then had time to see him raise his head a little before everything in my vision exploded. My arms went limp and weak and the world filled itself with sickening, hollow stars.

Fuck.

My eyes streamed with tears and closed against my

will. All my strength had gone. Someone grabbed my hands and held them down to either side of me, and the rest of the weight lifted off me a little. I knew it was coming even though I couldn't see: two hard blows to the side of the face. Bang, bang. My head went white and fuzzy and loud. I rolled over on to my side, the rest of the fight gone out of me.

Someone kicked me very hard in the stomach, just to be sure.

Everything receded as I tried to breathe, but I was aware of two of them jostling me: pulling me upright and manoeuvring me awkwardly through the nearest door. *It seemed such a waste*, I thought – *I'd been heading there anyway*. I really couldn't breathe and was going to die, and then I could – just about – and the world came slightly back to life around me. I'd failed again. Rachel was still screaming, screaming badly, and at that moment I would have joined her if I could have drawn enough air into me to let anything loose.

Where's the gun? I thought.

Somewhere out in the hall still. Too far away.

The men let go of me and I dropped to the floor, eyes closed, grateful for the comfort of the carpet. Left alone for a moment, down on all fours, I worked very hard on breathing, trying to blot out the noises that Rachel was making. I wanted to cry. They didn't have to hurt her anymore. They'd got me now; they could stop. But they carried on anyway. Apart from her, the room was strangely silent. I concentrated on my lungs, counted quietly to myself, and after thirty seconds my breath had come back to me again. My nose felt enormous and swollen. I didn't want to open my eyes, but I did. The carpet was beige. Rachel had stopped screaming. Now, she was just crying quietly.

'Get him up.'

The two men from the hall – visible now – pulled me roughly to my feet and then moved away. I was surprised I could stand up alone. Rachel was on a bed, naked, curled into a foetal position, facing away from me and shaking slightly. There was a third man standing close to her, dressed in the neat black suit that seemed to be standard uniform for all of these people. Standard haircut too: dark, short, tidy. His face looked a little more worn than the others, though, and his body seemed a little roomier. Like an older man who might have bounced in his prime but now mainly just told other bouncers what to do. I thought back to the photographs Sean had taken, but didn't recognise him from any of them.

He had a long, thin knife, and he was wiping the blade on the pillow, leaving small red streaks on the fabric.

'Martin Weaver,' he said.

It was the man who'd given me the address over the phone.

I tried to speak and was quite surprised when I managed it.

'I'm going to fucking kill all of you.'

If I'd known my voice was going to work then I might have picked something a little more convincing.

He smiled blankly, and then inspected the knife. I guessed it must have been clean enough, because he folded it up and placed it inside his jacket. My eyes flicked from him to Rachel, who was still crying quietly, and then I glanced back to him.

'That's what your friend said when we took him.' The man wasn't smiling anymore. 'And after a while, he stopped saying that. He didn't say much of anything.'

The images of Sean's murder hit me again, but it felt different from when I'd woken up at Karna's. I'd been scared then, but I'd realised after the first few minutes that I wasn't going to be killed. But these men were going to take me away and hurt me and there was nothing I could do to stop them. Worse, they were going to do the same to Rachel.

'What do you want?' I said. 'You want your boss's fucking money back? Because I can get you the fucking money back.'

The blank smile returned.

'Right,' he said. 'You see, you're scared now, aren't you?'

'You want the money back?'

'It's not as easy as that.'

'No,' I said. 'Well, you've got me anyway. Why don't you let my wife go?'

He shook his head.

'That's not going to happen. But you're right – we don't really need her anymore.' He took the knife back out. 'Would you like me to kill her?'

'No,' I said. But then I looked at her, curled up on the bed with streaks of blood on the pillow behind her head, and wondered if that was the right answer.

The man walked over and stopped in front of me.

'She was easy to pick up,' he said. 'And to begin with, she was happy to be with me.'

'What do you want?' I said. 'Because I'm not interested in this shit. If you want to kill me, then just fucking kill me. There's nothing I can tell you. And if you don't want your money, then what's the point in this?'

'Like I said,' he told me, 'it's not going to be that easy.'

And then he reached out slowly, the way you might reach out to touch a lover's face.

Fuck that.

I hit him so quickly that it surprised even me: knocking his hand away with my left, while throwing good and hard with my right. The impact was solid but indistinct – I just felt an explosion in my fist, and then saw him falling backwards onto the bed. The other men were already moving towards me, one to each side, and so I just launched myself, swinging hard and fast at the nearest. This time, I hit nothing. But I felt their strong grip on me, and the room spun around. I saw the man get up from the bed, seriously pissed off now, unfolding the knife, and I struggled as best I could but I was off-balance. The floor suddenly hit me in the shoulder, and a second later everything went black.

When I woke up I thought I could hear sirens. My head was pounding, but I lifted it off the plush bedroom carpet and listened. I *could* hear sirens. Some distance from here, but the sound wasn't fading. In fact, it was growing louder. I looked around, realising that I was lying at the foot of the bed, and that my gun was resting not too far away from my right hand. I seemed to be alone.

Rachel.

I scrambled to my feet, grabbing the gun in the process – an awkward stumble – and then I stepped back in shock as I caught sight of the thing on the bed and everything else – the room, the sirens, the feel of the gun in my hand – went away totally. It was Rachel. She was naked, and so completely still that it was obvious she was dead. Cut so much that I could smell the blood. I put my hand up to my mouth, ready to scream and just *collapse*, but then reality slapped my reeling brain and it steadied itself as I began picking out details. No, it wasn't Rachel. I took a step closer. It wasn't even female.

I listened. The sirens were very near, and I knew that I had to leave. Instead, I took another step forwards. My shins touched the duvet at the base of the bed.

The body had been left curled up on its side, just as I remembered Rachel lying. A lot of the head was gone. It had been blown off over the pillows and headboard, but there was enough left to see that in life this person had worn their hair short. The colour was pale brown. I walked around the bed and touched the shoulder with the back of my hand. It was still warm. The man had been killed recently.

I knelt down and looked at what remained of his face.

Fuck.

I recoiled back, scrambling to my feet and away from the bed.

It was Rich. The house, the kids – they'd brought Rachel to Rich's house, and then they'd killed him. I looked down at the gun in my hand and realised what else had been done here. I was now holding a murder weapon. The police would dig the bullet out of him and it would match my gun. Worse than that. Lucy worked the crime scenes.

The sirens. I realised that the noise wasn't growing anymore – it was right outside the front of the house, not going anywhere. *Go.* I ran out of the bedroom and down the stairs as quickly as possible.

Someone banged on the front door just as I reached it.

'Hello?'

I moved down the hallway towards the kitchen.

There might be two patrol cars, I thought, which meant maybe four officers, but probably not more. At least one of those would be on the driveway heading for the kitchen door. Presumably, it was still open. I had seconds.

Into the dining room. I pushed the door closed gently behind me.

'Police. Hello?'

A voice in the kitchen. It was inquisitive and cautious, just like you'd expect, but there was also an edge to it that I didn't like.

I moved quietly along the side of the room, between the dining table and the nearest wall. There was nowhere to hide, and it would have been stupid to try. There was a dead body upstairs. The police would tear this place apart, top to bottom.

I tried the patio door. It moved a little but then hit the lock, hitched, angled slightly in its groove.

I glanced back at the closed door. The police would be in the hallway now, which meant they would have seen the first bullet hole: the one that had taken a large chunk of the doorframe away.

I turned around, stepped away from the patio doors and – without thinking – fired once into the centre of the glass. There was a huge explosion, mixed with the sound of the glass shattering outwards: blistering the air across the garden; taking shreds and nicks out of the slide.

'Round back,' I heard somebody say. 'Quick.'

I was already clambering through the remains of the patio door, my mind running away from itself in an effort to keep calm and *think* at any cost. Panicking would undo me. Was I prepared, I wondered, to shoot a police officer? Crunches of glass under my feet, a slight stumble, and then I was sprinting down the garden. Would I shoot at a cop in self-defence? I didn't know.

'Stop!'

I heard you, I thought, hitting the shaking fence at the bottom of the garden, scrambling up and over it. *But you won't shoot me in the back when I'm running away.*

I landed on the pavement behind the fence – another of the Fishers, I didn't know which – and immediately ran to my left. Behind me, I heard a series of steady cracks as police bullets tore the fence apart where I'd been standing.

'Fuck.'

I ran.

Now, I thought, *I might be able to shoot one of these guys in self-defence*. They were firing at a man's back as he ran away, through a fence when anyone could have been on the other side. And they had turned up on the scene pretty fucking quickly, as well. But then Eli had done this, after all, and Eli powered law and order. He owned the police.

'Get after him!'

Just keep running, I told myself. *Just stay calm.*

There was a side road off to the right, and I took it, my feet hitting the pavement as hard as they could. But my legs felt weak, both from being unconscious and probably from the adrenaline too. Had the cops made the road in time to see me take the turning? I glanced back and saw that they had: there were two of them, sprinting after me. Much faster than me. As I saw them, one stopped and took aim. He looked cool and together, aiming carefully. *Fuck*. I dodged and ducked, hearing the shot and the noise as it pranged a car to my right, denting it like a sledgehammer would. I crouched down behind the back of the vehicle. The cops were coming closer. Their shoes tapping on the tarmac.

Keep it together.

I got quickly on the ground, as flat to the road as I could, and watched from under the car. There they were: I could see their legs as they approached. I took careful aim at the nearest.

'Come out from there,' one of them called out.

Not *throw out your weapon*, though. I guessed that an unarmed man might make an awkward victim.

I made sure of the aim. Okay.

The first shot took the cop in the ankle. Two shots, three, and then he was firing his own gun into the sky as he went down. I'd already adjusted my aim and squeezed another shot at the second guy's foot, and then another shot, and a third. He went down off to one side and started screaming. I heard and felt a bullet smacking into the car above me, and then a second shattered the windscreen. I aimed back on the first cop, who was on his side now, trying to draw on me. I could see his face: grim and in pain and determined; full of hate. I fired just as his next bullet scraped sparks and dust from the road beside the car. I caught him somewhere in the body, and he doubled up like he'd been punched, rolled this way and that. Let out an agonised screech. But he stopped firing.

Calm for a second, but only in terms of guns and bullets. The other cop was still screaming, calling out for help. In the distance, there were more sirens. Closer to, a car alarm was going off, and I heard a front door slamming shut.

Getting to my feet, it felt like the world was lurching around – like my vision was zooming in even as I staggered backwards. The cop on the road was barely moving now, and there was blood all around him. His hands had printed mad, red birds on the tarmac. The second cop had fallen sideways through a hedge, demolishing half of it, stippling the pavement and grass with blood from the stump at the end of his leg. He was still moving – trying to crawl out of sight.

Everything was in tatters here. Even if I'd had no choice – even if they worked for Eli and had been trying to kill me – what I'd done was shoot policemen in broad daylight, and that meant I was fucked. I couldn't explain this to anyone. Eli had been true to his brother's promise – his crew had made a good start at excising his city's little cancers. Whatever had happened here this afternoon, he couldn't really have lost.

The cop in the garden was crying. With that sound in my ears, I turned around and I ran away from there as fast as I could.

CHAPTER TWENTY

An hour later, I was sitting in a cemetery in Snake, watching the early evening sky beginning to bruise. Night would be here soon. The sky was growing dark, although – as usual – the city gave off a slight yellow sheen at the horizon that made the air everywhere seem jaundiced and unwell. Pretty soon, the night would arrive properly and everything would be black. In the meantime, I sat on a cold bench in a graveyard and watched patches of stars prickle into life overhead.

I was shivering badly. Round here – perhaps more than anywhere – you could sit and catch your death. Right now, it felt like an option.

The breeze rustled the unkempt grass between the headstones, which in this light had become a mouldering shade of grey. When night fell completely it would lose even that. The colours would be washed away from the world; from the grass, the trees, from everything.

Jesus. Snake is depressing at the best of times – even in daylight. Two immense coils of thin streets where nobody wants to live circling graveyards where nobody does. The district is shaped like an 'S', with the city's two main cemeteries resting within the curls. Each of them is a ramshackle place: an unhappy end if ever there was one. But this one is the worst of the two. The plots come cheap here and you get exact value for your money: stones that sit at angles like broken teeth;

grounds that are overgrown and barely tended. You can tell that there used to be religion here at one point, but now it feels cursed and abandoned, as though not enough people have bothered believing and something dark and lazy has seeped in instead. You could splash holy water around and the soil would sizzle.

There is an old church at the centre of the cemetery, slightly above everything else, and it still retains a certain black majesty. It looks as though it might be concentrating hard on something unpleasant. The bricks are thick with soot and the glass in the windows is so stained that you can barely differentiate the colours from the rusted old ribs. Every conceivable entrance was boarded shut years ago. Nobody ever comes here. You die and end up here, and nobody comes.

As it grew dark, it was like sitting inside a tomb with a stone door rolling slowly shut. Night would fall, and it felt like if I didn't get out soon then I'd be trapped here.

But where could I go?

Out of the city? Ultimately, yes – and I supposed the quicker the better. That was what my nerves were telling me, anyway. The police would have my description by now – and they almost certainly had my fingerprints and the bullets from my gun, even if they wouldn't have matched them yet. Eli had clearly thought all this through. Lucy would be in pieces, and pretty soon she would find out that I was responsible. Fifteen years would lose all meaning in one crushing instant; and all those emails would disappear into noughts and ones, fading into black. Perhaps given time she might believe the truth about what had happened, but for now – if she found me – God help me.

On top of that, the regular police tended to take the killing of one of their own quite seriously, and so there would be helicopters, television coverage, roadblocks: everything. They would do their best to make sure I didn't leave the city – certainly not alive – and so in a perfect world I should have been a hundred miles away by now and still accelerating.

Instead, I was sitting here on this fucking bench. Snake borders the western edge of Turtle, but it had been a complicated journey involving lots of back alleys and more than a little awkward climbing. I'd done it quickly – not stopping running until I'd reached here and physically *needed* to – but now that my breath was back it was surely time to steal another car and get the fuck out of the city while I still could.

On the other side of the cemetery, a couple of birds were gathering together for warmth, huddled in the thin, black skeleton of a tree. It was wavering in the breeze, silhouetted against the darkening blue sky. Night time is inexorable: shy at first, but then the world beckons it on and it loses its reticence and charges in. It would be pitch black here soon. Time to leave.

But thoughts of Rachel kept boiling up from inside me, and my mind couldn't keep its feet. The thoughts left patterns in my head: surges of fear and guilt and hate; bubbles of anger and panic. I couldn't just abandon her. But I didn't even know if she was still alive. The men had taken her with them, but only because the set-up demanded it. One body worked better than two to condemn me.

Despite everything, I'd tried to phone Rosh three times. Each time, the phone was dead. I was on my own.

I realised that I had started shivering badly, and I

rubbed my hands together slowly, trying not to cry. I felt scared and powerless, but angry too – I wanted to find these men and kill them. That wouldn't be so hard. If I hadn't been able to hone a certain kind of personal rage then I'd never have been able to shoot a man in the head, or even knock him around his apartment a bit. So I cultivated that rage now, folding and tightening it until the thought of Eli and his men made the air in my head ring like a struck tuning fork. Killing him would be a very easy thing to do.

But then frustration set in, and I stopped rubbing my hands. I'd seen the photographs that Sean had marked, so I knew what Eli looked like. But I didn't know where to find him. And so what was the point in feeling much of anything right now, when there was nobody here to knock around, nobody to shoot in the head? There was just me and those fucking birds.

I looked up and saw that the branches of the tree were bare – even the birds had gone. I didn't blame them. The spreading pools of shadow between the gravestones had met, merged, and now everything looked black and dead. The breeze remained, though, feeling more threatening than before.

This was no place to spend the night doing nothing. Whatever happened next, it was time to go.

I left the cemetery and found the most deserted street I could, and then I stole another car. I was getting good at that – and even better at not caring. Any vestiges of civic morality were rapidly disappearing in the face of an enormous private need. I knocked the car into gear and set off, glancing at my watch. I was surprised – it was only eight o'clock, yet it felt like midnight.

As I turned the corner and headed for the northern edge of Snake, I felt the pull of death from the district behind me, like a black cloud you couldn't see for the night. And when I crossed the border into the edge of Lion, it seemed that the cloud was following me.

Whatever happened next, I needed some money.

There was a cashpoint in Lion that I knew would be safe – or as safe as these things get. The machine would take a photograph of me withdrawing funds, but that was okay: nobody knew about my secret accounts and there would be no alert tags on the numbers. It was fine. I could smile for the camera, happy in the knowledge that nobody would ever scan these particular files for someone of my description.

The streets were busy, which was pretty standard for Lion. It is the city's smallest district – smaller even than Mouse – and it was originally named in honour of the abandoned zoo at its heart. There had been a siege at some ancient point in the city's history, and after too much time had passed the residents had resorted to killing and eating the animals in order to stay alive. For whatever reason – legend says respect, but I imagine that a certain healthy fear came into it as well – the lions were the only creatures not to end up on the menu. Nowadays, it is like a mini-Elephant. The zoo is a concrete park – all fountains and benches – and at lunchtime you would find executives there, reading in quiet repose or talking on their phones. The small number of streets around it are full of expensive, exclusive bars and restaurants packed with people who could afford to eat exotic animals for pleasure rather than out of desperation.

Eight-twenty, and the streets were thriving and lively. I pulled up by the cashpoint and left the engine running.

I had three fake accounts in all. Each of the

individuals in question had been born somewhere different – a long way away from this city – and they had deposited the money in cash at over nine different banks, spreading the payments out over a few weeks. The first man was called Michael Hutchinson. I slipped his card into the machine and tapped in the PIN I'd given him. And then I waited.

The blue screen pulsed slightly.

we are dealing with your request . . .

I glanced around at the well-dressed people passing me, feeling uneasy. There was music from bars; conversations from groups of drinkers. Laughter. It was subdued, civilised debauchery. There was nobody anywhere near me. In fact, nobody was paying me even the slightest attention, beyond the cautious curiosity that a man with an obviously broken nose has to expect.

But something was wrong.

we are dealing with your request . . .

I pressed *cancel*.

The screen stayed the same.

'Shit.'

I pressed the button again and again, tapping it furiously. Nothing happened for a moment, and then the words disappeared. The blue stayed for a moment – blank and featureless, and it seemed as though someone was staring right out through it. Then the bank logo flashed up, followed by a message inviting me to insert my card.

Get out of here.

I moved straight back to the car, glancing left and right. There was a steady stream of traffic, but all of it was ignoring me. A group of people were approaching from further up the street: young, clubby, rich.

Get the fuck out of here.

I got in and drove away, tyres screeching slightly. This was shit. I had two more cards, but I didn't fancy my chances with either of them. It could have been coincidence, but I knew deep down that it wasn't. How had they found me so quickly? How had they found me at all?

Gideon, I thought. Gideon runs finance and business, and traditionally, there was an alignment between Gideon and Eli. As brothers they had been close, and when Karna had made his move in the past it had been against both of them. It made sense that the alignment would stand now, and that if I was up against Eli then I was up against Gideon as well.

It was bullshit, of course – a part of me had been telling myself that ever since I'd found Sean's notes and met Karna. People might be explaining things they had no obvious reason to, and other people might be appearing out of thin air to back them up, but there was a sensible, logical explanation for all of it. Whatever was really going on, there were no brothers and nothing supernatural was happening. It was just a bunch of criminals at war with a bunch of cops, with me and my friends stuck in the middle for being a little bit of both. That was all.

The result was the same, though. I had the small amount of money in my pocket to live on. Eli – or whoever he was – had already taken back the money we'd stolen from him. It brought it home that this was simply about revenge now. Revenge, and surgery.

So where does a cancer like me go, I wondered, when the doctors have seen me and are working to remove me? They wanted me to run, but what if I didn't? Obviously, Eli wasn't intending to kill me just yet: he was going to leave that to my friends and colleagues – a far more elegant way of dealing with us.

If I ran, I had nothing. If I didn't, I had a little time to ask some questions. And who knew – maybe get close enough to Eli to make all that rage I'd felt worthwhile and useful. It wasn't exactly a fantastic set of choices.

Lion rests between Snake and Horse. At the last major turning before the northern border with Horse, I headed east instead, cutting back into Turtle, undecided where I wanted to end up. But I didn't get far. After a minute, the music on the radio faded out, segueing into the station's news update. I listened carefully, expecting the main item to be about me and the shootout earlier in the day. But it wasn't – the newsreader went straight into the build-up to the annual competition the next day. I listened for a while, incredulous. Two cops were injured or dead, another man had been killed, and a neighbourhood was shot to pieces. If anything in the world constituted main-item material, this afternoon must surely be it. If it had been covered up, I didn't know whether to be relieved or even more concerned. How much power did it take to keep something like that off the news?

Perhaps it would be the second item. I listened carefully as the newsreader moved on.

A few seconds later, as the car began to swerve, I gathered myself as best I could, indicated and pulled over onto the hard shoulder. Then, I sat there and listened, feeling an emotion that was too intense and complicated to name, and I started to shake.

Earlier in the evening, on the outskirts of Fish, police had found the mutilated body of a woman in her twenties. It had been dumped on the canal side in plain view, where it was bound to be discovered. She hadn't been identified yet, but I knew that it was Rachel.

I sat there and cried. I wasn't thinking about anything – I just let my body respond however it wanted, and it turned out to be that. So I cried, and only my seatbelt kept me from falling sideways and curling up across the seats. I let this first, uncoordinated burst of anger and grief run its course, and then after a while I pulled myself into enough of a state to start driving again. My hands were trembling as I rejoined the stream of traffic, but I could hold the wheel steady if I concentrated and I thought it would be okay. There wasn't that far to go. And so, a little more slowly than before, but decided now, I took another turning and made my way north.

Wasp at night time was the same as during the day, except busier and – strangely – more beautiful. It was the lights, I thought, as I made my way through the crowds. There were hundreds of lights in hundreds of colours, all reflecting off puddles and windows, off the sheen of rain that had soaked into the yellow flagstones and made them look like bars of gold. The pubs were dark caves that had fires burning at the mouths. In the buildings between them, women were dancing slowly in illuminated shopfronts, lit up in gorgeous red monochrome like pieces of art. Even the porn shops were bright and pink and inviting. The chill air was warmed by the shouts and the music.

'Young lovers. Come inside, young lovers. We have the best shows, we have the best everything. We—'

The barker cut off his speech mid-sentence as he saw me coming, and he looked like he was about to run. But I didn't give him the chance – stepping into his way as the young lovers in question moved on, oblivious.

'Hi there,' I said. 'Remember me?'

The controlled panic on his face suggested that he

did. He started rubbing his wrist slightly as he cast his gaze around for help.

'Young sir.'

I put my hand in my pocket and glared at him. Hopefully the message was clear. I was just as crazy and dangerous as I'd been this afternoon, and now I had a gun as well.

'You do remember me,' I said. 'I can see you're really busy, so this won't take long.'

He gave up looking for assistance. Instead, resigned to the situation, he took a drag on his thin roll-up and said:

'What do you want?'

'You saw me this afternoon.'

'Yes, I remember.'

'You remember me being brought back here.'

He blew out some smoke and looked unhappy. It was clearly an area he didn't much want to comment on. That was too bad. Karna's men had delivered me here, and if he knew them then maybe he knew about Eli too.

'I don't—'

'I'm not asking you.' I gave him a patient smile that wouldn't last. 'I'm telling you. You remember me being brought back. Now, I want to know about the guys who did the bringing. Who they were, and what you know about them – what?'

He was quickly shaking his head.

'I don't know about any guys. You come to the club and you cause trouble. That's all I know.'

'I got brought back here by people. You *do* know.'

'Please move on, young sir.' He sounded frightened, and he was looking around again for assistance. Or maybe to see who might be listening. 'We don't want any more trouble here.'

I thought: *Eli killed Rachel.*

And then in one fluid movement I had him by the throat, slamming him back into the wall with one hand and holding him there.

'Young sir, please!'

The anger was uncontrollable and it was good. Multi-textured, colourful anger: rage and resentment and self-hatred and guilt all thrown in for good measure.

Keeping the gun inside my coat pocket, I pushed the barrel into his gut.

'No "young sir",' I said quietly. 'No fucking "please". You just tell me, or I'll kill you right here.'

I felt the people walking past on the pavement behind us, their steps faltering a little as they debated whether to stop and watch, or maybe even intervene. And I felt them wisely decide to keep moving. Of course they did. Nobody ever intervenes in this city.

'Please.'

'I'll kill you right here, you piece of shit.'

'I can't say about that!'

I jammed the gun into him even harder, and he started to cry.

'That won't work,' I said, and then again: 'I'll kill you right here.'

'You come here on your own.' He was sobbing pitifully, working through his script. 'You come here, you pay, you go in.'

'Don't fucking lie to me.' I wanted to pull the trigger a hundred times, until he was in pieces. 'You tell me what I want to know. Tell me about Karna and Eli.'

He shook his head vigorously, waving away the names like they were curses. He was gabbling as he spoke:

'You come here on your own. You pay, you go in, you here all afternoon.'

'Fuck you.'

'You here all afternoon.'

I pushed myself away from him and let him fall down onto the step.

'Fuck you.'

He just crumpled up, ignoring me and sobbing to himself. It was grimly satisfying, but it didn't help me much. The barker was scared of someone – of Karna and Eli, their whole bastard family – and because of them he'd rather die than talk to me. I wanted to start kicking him but if I did then I knew I wouldn't stop. And I needed to save my anger for the right people.

'Just fuck you,' I said.

And then I turned and headed off – deeper into the red light district, in the direction of Parker Street. Someone round here would give me some answers.

The CandiBar.

The shutters were still down and the place looked dead. It was nine o'clock, so I'd thought it might have opened up by now, but apparently not. Perhaps it was never open, or maybe you just had to catch it right. Not out of the corner of your eye, exactly, but if the path of your life had a comparable angle then perhaps that. When I was a child, I used to imagine that if I wandered the streets of the city at night I might find a new path that wasn't there during the day. With everything that had happened today, that didn't seem so impossible. And if a path, then why not a fucking nightclub? You get older and things change.

I rattled the metal over the front door, hearing the sound reverberate around the empty street. The security cameras were pointing straight at me, but I couldn't tell if they were working or not. Behind me, the window where Sean had taken his photographs was black and hollow: a socket that was missing an eye.

I started banging my fist against the shutter, over and over.

'Come out!'

I kept punching. Somewhere in the distance, a dog started barking in angry reply. Half the district must be hearing me, but I carried on anyway.

'Fucking come out!'

Nothing. I looked up at the cameras and they hadn't moved, but there was something different about them. I wanted to throw a brick and smash them both off the wall.

The alleyway by the side of the old hotel opposite also continued on this side of the street: it ran down the side of the CandiBar. I moved down it quickly, running my hand along the wall. Here was an old window, blocked by vertical bars; here was another shuttered door. And here, finally, was a two-metre wall at the back. There was broken glass embedded in the mortar at the top, but I climbed it anyway, positioning my fingers carefully and trusting to luck a little as I hoisted myself up, positioned my right foot and then heaved myself over, clearing it without cutting myself or tearing anything. I landed hard in the nightclub's back yard.

It was a neat, paved area: mostly empty – just some old bins, two broken-open bags of sand and a bit of rubble. The back of the club had a solid door and a window at ground level. I grabbed a bin lid and threw it. It bounced off the glass.

'*Come out.*'

There were a couple of half-bricks on the ground. I picked one up and threw that instead. This time, the window shattered loudly, and I felt a surge inside me that was like the feeling I had when the barker had been on the ground crying.

I knocked the remaining glass teeth from the frame and then clambered inside. I didn't even bother drawing my gun. There was no point: if Karna's men wanted to take me then they probably would. The end result would be the same. At least I would get to talk to him, and maybe he would tell me what I needed to know.

The window led into an old kitchen, where it was clear from the emptiness and dust that the place hadn't been used in a long time. As I looked around, I experienced a crushing sensation – that of falling away inside myself – and I moved into the dark bar area beyond somehow knowing exactly what I was going to find there.

Nothing.

I flicked a light switch. Not really expecting it to work, but then it did. Suddenly there was bright yellow light everywhere, and I stood in the doorway, surveying the scene. It was a large room with a bar at the far end, backed by a broken mirror and two long empty bottle racks. All the taps had been removed. Between me and the bar was what had once been the dancefloor; now, it looked like a large, dusty rubber mat. There were booths of tables edging the walls, and the décor was dark red leather – all the stools and curved settees were the same, and all the wall hangings too. And all of it was covered in dust and cobwebs.

It had been a long time since anyone had served or bought a drink in the CandiBar; and I couldn't imagine that anyone had *ever* danced. This was the only place I could think of where I might find some answers, and it was dead. If Karna didn't want me to find him then I wasn't going to.

My instinct was to collapse in one of the booths, close my eyes and sleep, but I didn't. There was something else I needed to see, just to be sure. I found the stairs between the main bar area and the kitchen and made my way up to the first floor, which consisted of a shabby main corridor running down the centre of the building and a number of rooms branching off. As I moved from one into the other, there appeared to be no real design to any of it – it was as though someone had built the top floor one room at a time, adding each on as an increasingly awkward afterthought. Most were empty, although I found a cupboard containing some old cleaning equipment, and another room had a locked filing cabinet and a desk in it.

I explored them all, but long before I finished it was obvious that this wasn't where I'd been taken this afternoon; Karna had moved me somewhere else. Sean had taken pictures of him coming here, but there must have been some other explanation. Perhaps he was looking at it as a business opportunity. But as things stood, this place hadn't been open for years.

My anger was unfolding, dissipating, and I began to realise just how tired and fucking *weary* I was. I just wanted to rest.

I walked slowly back downstairs, and then into the main bar area. The sound of my feet echoed slightly on the dirty wooden floor, and it occurred to me without warning that there was something familiar about the place. I couldn't work out what: I'd certainly never been here before. I figured that it must have just reminded me of somewhere else, and shrugged the feeling off. But as I turned out the lights and headed towards the back yard again, it hit me – stopping me in my tracks for a couple of seconds. Not for long, because I wasn't all that surprised; it made the same kind of sense as everything else that had happened. The CandiBar was laid out in exactly the same way as Spooks is.

Back out on the street, a dog was still barking and somewhere – a street or two away – I could hear a car idling along. But as I stood in the centre of the road, wondering what to do, neither of them bothered to make an appearance.

There were things I could follow up, I supposed. There were Jamie and Keleigh, for one thing. Or else I could make another effort to contact Rosh or Lucy and at least say *something* – and I knew that I probably should. Unfortunately, I didn't have the slightest inclination to do any of it. Apart from anything else, I'd barely slept the night before and I was feeling it badly now. But I also felt beyond all that – segregated from everything and everyone, and utterly on my own. Perhaps the lack of sleep was colouring my thoughts or making them misty, because I didn't seem to be able to think of much. What I wanted to do – all things considered – was collapse and maybe die.

And so I decided to do the next best thing: go across the road and break into Sean's hideout again. It would be damp and cold, granted, but at least I would have a roof over my head and a mattress to sleep on. And maybe there was some detail in Sean's research that I'd overlooked: something that might point me towards Eli. I could read through it again, and fall asleep as and when necessary.

There didn't seem to be any better options, so I crossed the street and made my way down to the back yard, and then in through the window. It was so dark that it worried me for a second, but I had a vague memory of the layout and managed to make my way into the hall and up the stairs without tripping and impaling myself on anything. Made it to Sean's room. I found the torch and turned it on, resting it on its side near the wall, so that light splayed upwards, creating the effect of a fireplace, or perhaps an altar; and then I sat down on the mattress and stared into space.

Not into space, actually. After a few moments, I realised I was staring at the rifle case that Sean had left here. After a few moments more, I stood up and went over and opened it. It was all there.

And as I looked down at it, something strange happened: I felt a huge roar inside my head, as though I was remembering the noise of many people shouting at the same time. I shook my head to clear the sound away, and then I closed the case and went back over to sit on the mattress again. I stared across at it for a little while longer. Thoughts I couldn't focus on properly were fluttering in my head, like birds disturbed among the rafters. I shook my head one last time, unsure exactly what I was thinking, and then I looked at the papers on the floor.

On top, nearest to me, was the photograph that Sean had cut out of an old book and had enlarged. I picked it up and ran my fingers over the closest shot. There were the brothers, up on their balcony, watching the boxing that was happening below them.

Of course they were there. They would always be there.

Another flash of a memory I'd never had: an arched window at the far end of a dusty room. Outside, the sky was so bright that the edges of the windowframe seemed to be dissolving into the light. Beyond it was the sandy, fractured tapestry of our city.

I put the photograph down, understanding now where I would be able to find Eli and what it was I was going to do. The ringing in my ears had returned, but I did my best to fight it down and keep it out of my mind. Instead, I picked up one of Sean's notebooks and began to read what he'd written. And this time, I understood.

Imagine you're walking on a long road. You can't see where it leads but you know it must lead somewhere, and to find out where you just have to carry on walking. While you're on this road, you're only ever experiencing a small portion of it at any one time, but you know that it's just a question of dimensions: that every metre of it exists already, and that if you took yourself up into the sky you'd be able to look down and see the whole thing, laid out from one end to the other. You just need to go up a dimension – roughly, from two to three. Well, that's what time is like too. Because you're stuck in it you can only experience it one footstep at a time. But if you could move up another dimension, just as with the road, you'd be able to see every moment laid out in turn.

You can't visualise it properly, but if you could see time from a distance in this way then you'd notice tendrils of life running through it: little glowing ribbons of existence, like swirls in a marble. Every moment of your life would be there for you to see, all lying next to one another. To you right now, everything feels momentary and transient, as though you're travelling through life from one end to the other, but from the outside you'd be able to see that everything was laid out from the beginning. All the points on the road are there already. From a perspective like that, there's no such thing as death. There's only the fact of your life, hanging there – pulsing with everything you've ever done and ever will do.

From within, life can feel arbitrary and pointless: a series of random events that send us into collisions with others. There's no real meaning or explanation to it beyond the fluttering dust of physical laws that waft around us. But who knows? Perhaps from the outside it looks different. You might notice that all these bright strands of life form a pattern – that sections repeat and spiral around their neighbours with more regularity than we can see from within. It's possible that from the outside, despite how it feels to us now, everything is very ordered and beautiful.

CHAPTER TWENTY ONE

I woke up with the memory of crunching glass. My eyes flicked open.

It was still night time and it took me a second to remember where I was. There was something surreal about the room: it was all floorboards and paper and dust, lit from an ungainly angle. Sean's hideout. I'd fallen asleep with the torch still on. It was pointing at the wall beside me, and the light was stretching up the plaster like a candle-flame. It was also doubling back on itself, pooling around the torch and then cascading across the floor and out into the hallway. How fucking stupid was this?

I propped myself up on one arm and listened carefully. No more crunching glass.

Ten seconds passed with no sound whatsoever – just that awful, premonitory ringing – but my heart was beating like I'd woken up drunk, and I kept staring at the doorway.

Another ten, fifteen seconds of nothing. Then, I saw the light start shifting in the hallway. It didn't make sense and then it did. Someone was in here – at the bottom of the stairs – with a torch of their own.

I got to my feet quickly. Where was my gun? I fluffed my hand over the dark mattress a couple of times and found it, just as something creaked downstairs. *Shit*. I picked up the rifle case and – with a rueful glance back at all Sean's papers and books – I made my way out into the hallway as quietly as I could.

Torchlight flickered across the top of the stairs. Then, it disappeared back down and I heard another creak. Someone was making their way slowly up the stairs. More creaks. I backed down the hallway, but I knew that there wasn't going to be time to get into one of the other rooms. I caught quick, bulky movement at the top of the stairs; a silhouette; flashing shadows. I raised my gun just as light dazzled my eyes, but before I pulled the trigger the light passed over me, zig-zagging back and forth over the doorway to Sean's room. I just stood there frozen as the big figure paused at the entrance. He had a torch in one hand and a gun in the other.

Rosh.

I stared at his illuminated profile for a second, but then he stepped forward and moved into the room. Somehow, he hadn't seen me; he'd moved his torch straight over me and not noticed I was there. I was still aiming my gun at the empty hallway. How the hell had he found me here?

Part of me wanted to call out to him, but I didn't. He had his gun drawn and he seemed . . . what? Full of purpose, I realised. The truth was that Rosh didn't draw his gun unless he thought he was going to use it. I'd have drawn mine too, coming into a place like this at night, but as far as Rosh knew I'd shot two cops that afternoon, and probably killed Rich too. I didn't know how much of that Rosh either knew about or believed, but he would certainly be wanting answers from me. And he'd probably be quite careful about his safety while getting them.

I took a tentative step forwards. Despite the earlier fluke, I figured it was going to be impossible to get past the open doorway and down those stairs without him seeing or hearing me. I could hide in one of the other rooms but he was bound to look in them all eventually.

I heard the sound of papers moving, and guessed that he was looking through Sean's collection. The moment he rested his hand on the bed he'd feel that it was warm and he'd know someone was still here.

Sooner or later, this was going to have to be done.

I walked to the doorway and turned to face into the room. Rosh looked up immediately. He was sitting on the edge of the mattress holding the book of myths in his hands, his gun close beside him. The light was turning his oddly-shaped face into something far more monstrous. I raised my own gun slightly. Not pointing at him exactly – just letting him know it was there.

'Martin.'

'Easy,' I said. 'I hate to do this to you, Rosh. I really do. But I need you to move that gun over my way. Pick it up by the barrel.'

He looked at me for a second. Perhaps he was weighing up the likelihood of me shooting him. I really didn't know what would happen if he made a move instead of doing as he was told – maybe I would actually have done it. And that seemed to be the conclusion he came to as well, because a moment later he picked the gun up slowly and then slid it over the floor towards me. It finished at my feet.

'That's cool,' I said. 'Thank you.'

'No, it's not cool,' he said, nodding at my hand. 'It's greedy.'

'Okay.'

I slipped the gun into my pocket. I could still get to mine before he did his, but a token gesture was better than none.

'Happy?'

'A little closer to being cool,' he said. 'Yeah.'

His expression was utterly blank, like someone who was just soaking up his situation and leaving the thinking for later. I looked at him, searching for some sign that he was on my side. It wasn't there, of course, but at least he didn't seem angry. In fact, he looked slightly sad, and that deflated me. It was like my fucking dad was here, disappointed with my behaviour.

He said, 'So. Let's talk.'

'Okay. What I'd really like to know right now is what you're thinking, Rosh. I've had a weird afternoon.'

'I'll bet. What I'm thinking about what?'

'About me, I guess.'

'About you? Okay. I don't *know* what to think at the moment. I want you to tell me everything, and then maybe I'll make my mind up.'

'Everything?'

'Yeah.' He sat forwards a little; but not quite enough to make me nervous. 'I'll start you off. Tell me why I got a call from Rob Hedge's flat earlier on this evening and found his body there waiting for me.'

It took me an entire blank second to realise what he'd just told me.

'They killed Hedge?'

'Someone killed Hedge,' he said. 'Yeah. And a number of independent witnesses gave a pretty good description of you.'

'I was there,' I said. 'But I didn't kill anyone.'

Except that probably wasn't true – I'd killed him just by turning up there. By taking the money in the first place. By carrying on Sean's investigation. All of it. Pick a fucking reason.

'We've got the bullets,' Rosh said. 'They took three

of them out of his head. Are they going to match your gun?'

I shook my head. 'They won't match my gun.'

'Well, I guess we'll find that out. What about the two cops this afternoon, then? We have CCTV footage of you running, and the next bit is out of frame but both of them ended up getting shot. What about those bullets?'

'Those ones will match,' I said. 'But they were trying to kill me, Rosh. It was self-defence. Just like last night.'

'It's different to last night.' Rosh shook his head. 'There's any number of fucking reasons why it's different. Try a practical one: nobody knows about last night. I'm sure you don't need me to tell you this, but there's a lot of people out there just itching to kill you right now.'

'Oh, I can imagine,' I said. 'Are you one of them?'

He gave me that sad look again.

'I'm surprised you even have to ask.'

'It seems a pretty pertinent question,' I said, nudging his gun with my foot.

'Well, you've got one of those too, Martin.'

'That's true. So what do you think? You honestly think I killed Hedge and the others? Rich? You think I killed *Sean*?'

He stared at me. The sadness seemed stronger than before.

'I don't know what to think,' he said.

'You even have to *think*? Jesus Christ, Rosh. Think of what we've done together. You *know* me.'

'Yeah, I know you. And I want to help you. That's why I want to hear your side of things. But if you want to know what I'm half-thinking, it's this. You're scared of something. I think what that kid Jamie told us is probably mostly true, but I'm also thinking that maybe these people got to you after they got to Sean, and that you're running scared, maybe covering something up, getting yourself into a bigger fucking mess with every step. Working for them the way Harris did.'

'That's what they want you to think,' I said. 'They're dividing us up, Rosh. Can't you see that?'

'Martin, I don't know what I'm fucking seeing.'

'Nobody got to me,' I said. 'I'm not covering anything up. The big fucking mess point, though – I'll give you that one.'

'I tried to call you all afternoon,' Rosh said, leaning back a little. 'I got no answer. Tried your flat. You weren't there.'

'I know I wasn't.'

'Then things clicked into place a little. What Jamie had said; what you said. I ended up calling Alison's parents, and that brought me here.' He looked around thoughtfully. 'So – is all this stuff yours or Sean's?'

'It's Sean's,' I said. 'But I've looked through it.'

'It seems pretty crazy, what I've read of it so far.'

I didn't say anything. Pretty crazy was exactly what it was – but then Rosh hadn't been through what I had that afternoon. And what could I tell him to convince him? About Eli and Karna? A day of being knocked unconscious and having henchmen materialise out of thin air can do a lot to alter a guy's outlook, but I doubted that Rosh was going to believe a word of it right now. It was almost as an afterthought that I accepted that I did. It had been dogging me all afternoon, and it had obviously attacked properly when I was asleep and couldn't fight it off. Conviction.

Strangely, I felt a hell of a lot better and calmer for it.

Rosh gestured at Sean's notes. 'So what's all of this about?'

'It's about the people who've done this,' I said. 'I don't know how to explain it or how much of it's true. But we've taken someone's money and really pissed them off, Rosh. And as strange as it seems it's all to do with that shit there.'

'Halloran's money? So tell me about the someone it belonged to.'

'I don't know how to start,' I said. 'But I can tell you that he killed Rachel.'

Rosh looked surprised for a second, and then I saw him begin to understand something. 'Is that why you did it?'

'I'm not doing anything the way you mean it,' I said. 'They took her this afternoon. That's why I went to Rich's house. They made her phone me, and she told me that they'd hurt her. That's why I went there. So that I could ... I was trying to get her back.'

'And what happened?'

'There were too many of them.' I shook my head, feeling utterly crushed. I wanted to say, *they weren't normal*, but I couldn't. 'Just too many. They had Rachel there, and I tried to save her but I got knocked out. When I woke up, they'd taken her and left Rich's body. I didn't kill him; I was just set up. And then they found Rachel dead in Fish this evening.'

Rosh chewed this over for a moment. I just stood there, waiting for him to reply.

'So let's get back to this someone,' he said. 'Who's doing this to us?'

Us.

A small word but a good one, and for a second I found myself taking comfort from it.

'Someone in the police,' I said – and then started to babble as I tried to explain it all at once. 'We got tricked into taking his money when we killed Halloran,

305

and he's been looking for it ever since. Started with Alison and her friends. He blackmailed Harris, and so Harris turned Sean in when he caught up with the kids, and that's when this guy killed Sean and found us.'

'Someone in the police?'

'Sort of,' I said. 'His name's Eli.'

And I'm going to kill him.

Rosh picked up the book again and started leafing through it. Found the page.

'Eli – as in this Eli in here?' he said.

Fuck it.

'Yes.'

'So – some kind of demon, then?' Rosh raised an eyebrow at me. 'Some kind of fucking ghost is doing all this to us? A man who comes out of the walls, right?'

'I've seen men come out of the walls this afternoon.'

'Really? Well I've yet to have that fucking privilege, Martin.'

'I hope you don't have to.' Something else occurred to me, then, and I said, 'How's Lucy doing?'

He closed the book and looked at me with the contempt I no doubt deserved. 'How do you think she's doing? She doesn't know anything anymore, Martin – worse than me. At the moment, I suggest you stay well away from her, because if she sees you right now she's not going to be doing any fucking talking.'

I nodded. 'Where is she?'

'I don't know right now.'

He wasn't even going to trust me with that.

'They're *fucking* with us, Rosh,' I said. 'Please don't buy into it. I know what you're thinking, but I'm being set up. You must realise that.'

'Okay,' he said. 'You want to convince me? Come in with me.'

I actually laughed.

'No.'

He was staring at me. 'I'm fucking serious, Martin. You trust me and maybe I'll trust you.'

For about a second, I considered it. But the man who was behind all this owned the police, and Rosh didn't understand that right now. He might try to keep me safe, but half the police would cheerfully kill me as soon as look at me – even the ones who weren't in Eli's pocket. And there was something else, too. My mind kept returning to what I'd seen in the hallway – Rosh turning up with the gun. There was something I didn't like about the image. And what had he said a moment ago? I tried to call you all afternoon. Got no answer. But I'd been the one ringing him. I didn't have any missed calls.

'I don't think I can do that,' I said, wanting to take a step back and only just stopping myself.

'Why not?' Rosh stood up. 'So, you don't trust me?'

I reached down and picked up his gun – one smooth motion – and if he'd been thinking about crossing the distance between us he certainly didn't do it now. That same disappointed look was on his face, but as I watched it hardened into something more serious.

'What's in the case?' he said.

I looked down at the case to the side of me. Looked back up. Said nothing.

He'd tried to phone me all afternoon, but I'd had no missed calls.

'Talk to me, Martin,' he said. 'Please. Tell me what's really going on.'

'No,' I said. 'Stay where you are. I don't know what to think anymore.'

'Martin—'

'No.' I shook my head, finally taking a step back. I

picked up the rifle case and said, 'I'm gonna leave you your gun. I'm gonna leave it outside in the yard. You wait up here in the meantime and you don't come after me.'

'Don't do this.'

'It's done, Rosh. I'm telling you. Just wait up here.'

He stared at me, and there was something about the look on his face that made me want to die inside.

'I won't come after you,' he said.

'Okay.' I nodded. 'For what it's worth, best of luck.'

'For what it's worth, the same.'

And then I made my way quickly downstairs and out into the night. Rosh was true to his word: he didn't follow me. In fact, as I'd moved away, I saw that he'd stopped watching me altogether. Instead, he was reading.

CHAPTER TWENTY TWO

I spent the night moving from coffee shop to bar to coffee shop, working my way back across the district but not wanting to linger in any one place for too long. The first bar I went, I headed straight to the bathroom and cleaned up a little: washed the blood off my face and gave myself an honest appraisal. My considered opinion was that the swelling had gone down but I was still ugly, which I could live with. From there, I just kept moving. After a while, my small amount of funds was very much depleted, but that wasn't going to make much difference. More importantly, so much coffee on an empty stomach is never a good thing, and – even with my training – by three in the morning I knew I'd be sick if I drank anymore. I wasn't hungry, but I bought a burger wrapped in greasy paper from an all-night van – a little oasis of bright light and steam and sizzle – and then ate it slowly, sat on a bench. The rifle case was resting at my feet. I didn't look at it once, but its presence was heavy. It seemed to have more weight than I did right now.

Wasp was thick with people. The boxing would be starting in about six hours, and a lot of people went out the night before and drank until dawn, moving towards the main square with their heavy eyes and slightly spinning heads. The bars I went in were standing-room only. Groups of men and women were watching the pre-match build-ups – interviews with the fighters and their camps, footage of the various districts' preparations and celebrations, and re-runs of memorable contests from the past. There was an air of expectation out in the streets: more food stands than usual; more noise. It was like being at an open-air festival. Everyone was loosening up a bit.

Eating my burger, I watched the people and envied the sense of freedom and ease on display. A year ago, I arrested a construction worker who'd got into a fight outside his local bar. He'd beaten the other man so badly that he'd died right there on the pavement. Sean and I went to his house, expecting him either to have run or else for us to have real trouble bringing him in, but when we arrived he was sitting on his doorstep waiting for us. He was very sad, but also calm and resigned. In the interview room, we let him light up a cigarette and he told us that he'd spent the night sitting on the bed beside his wife, watching her sleep, and then gone outside to watch the sun rise. He'd never done either of those things before, he said, and he would probably never do them again; for the life of him, he couldn't imagine how he'd been so careless as to let these things go. You never knew what you had until it was gone, and all that. Life speaks louder at death.

At the time, Sean and I had nodded – but basically had our usual lack of sympathy for the killer. We'd seen the victim after all, and we'd seen his family too. But right now, watching a careless world go by, I understood everything much better, and I felt a certain empathy with him. My life was over. Even if I succeeded in killing Eli and survived the next day, it all just boiled down to running now. It was over for me. Like that construction worker, I simply couldn't imagine how it had happened. It really shouldn't have ended up like this.

Right now, I would have given anything to be sitting on the edge of my bed seven months ago, watching my wife sleep and thanking God I hadn't lost it all.

I finished my burger and stood up, screwing the paper into a damp ball. Time to go. At the edges, the sky was beginning to lighten from black to blue, and it would be best to get to the main square before dawn broke. There were routes I could take that more or less avoided the cameras, but even so.

A group of people walked past me, arms around each other. They all seemed to be as drunk as physically possible, and their loud conversation was distracting. My gaze followed them as they headed off. To the main square, no doubt – and by more straightforward roads than me. It was still early, but people often set up vague drunken camps to make sure they had a good view. A balance was required: I needed enough people to be able to move around unnoticed, but before long it would be too busy to move much at all. So I followed the group of people up the street for as long as I could, and then I turned off down the quieter roads where I wouldn't be seen.

The sky was dark blue above me when I arrived, but already the colour of daylight above the roofs of the nearest buildings. I stood on the edge of the main square, looking up at the balconies that stretched around above me. Across the elevated boxing ring and on the other side, they were far enough away to look painted and frozen and still. Crowds of people were milling around. The ones who were here already – a few thousand, at least – sat in dark huddles, dotted across the square. There was still plenty of room to move between them, and so I did – making my way over in the general direction of the old clocktower, which towered a full four storeys above even the tallest of the other buildings. As I went, I took in the murmurs of conversation, and the smell of frying food and steam and alcohol. A few people, in contempt of the event's official regulations, were feeding torn-off strips of card and paper into small bonfires. Most were just sipping from cans. The morning air was cold, but the sheer number of people and sensations gave the square a feeling of warmth.

I walked through this, carrying the rifle in its case at my side, and nobody paid me the slightest attention. There were yellow-vested stewards around, mostly wandering along in pairs, but they didn't seem interested in anyone. A few of them were putting out fires with great bursts of foam from handheld canisters; others were engaging in jovial small-talk with settled groups of revellers. They were no threat. There were police here, as well, but they were few and far between – easily avoided for now. I was nearly at the base of the clocktower before I encountered the first problem.

Four policemen. Three of them were in ordinary uniform, but there was something about them that screamed 'specialist'. They were too straight and serious, for one thing, but they held themselves well – poised and confident. The fourth man was different. He was plain-clothes, overweight and slightly ramshackle, eating a sandwich as he gave them their instructions. I recognised him immediately: Carlton. I'd worked with him a few times, and he was sure to recognise me if he saw me.

About fifty metres away from them, I stopped and sat down between two groups of drinkers. Occasionally, I looked up to check what was happening. From that distance, the conversation was silent, but it was clear that the three men were here to stay. Carlton wasn't. I kept glancing over, seeing his orders delivered in mime. The fourth time I looked up, he wasn't there.

I looked around quickly, trying to locate him, and then saw him: moving through the square, heading almost directly for me. He had his sandwich clenched between his hands and seemed to be concentrating on eating it. I lowered my head, studied the tarmac in front. If he saw me, that was it. I reached inside my jacket, took hold of my gun and counted to ten.

People were wandering past. Someone next to me stood up and staggered behind me, nudging me with his thigh. Neither of us acknowledged the contact, and I just kept staring at the ground. Why hadn't I bought a hat, or something? The rifle case was just there beside me: plain as anything. I might as well have been spot-lit, or marked with a great big fucking neon sign.

I reached ten, and then forced myself to start again. After that, I looked up – just in time to catch a glimpse of Carlton's trench coat as it swished past behind me. For a second, I could hear his slightly laboured breathing. And then he was gone.

I turned my head slowly to follow him away through the crowds. His thick back disappeared off, heading away in the direction I'd originally come in. He hadn't given me so much as a second glance. I looked down and then – after a moment – back towards the clocktower. The three policemen had moved away a little, but they were still near enough to be a real problem. Each of them was scanning the crowds with a look of politeness. Just appraising – no harm meant – but it was scanning nevertheless. I thought that they were probably just checking out the people in general, and not specifically looking for me, but they'd surely notice me eventually. Would they have seen pictures? Even if they hadn't, it felt as though guilt was coming off me like heat, making the air above me waver and shiver.

I watched them for a while, and they stayed exactly where they were. More people were arriving the whole time, drifting in all over the square. The policemen remained at their post, steadily observing them all in a thoroughly professional manner. At least they were ignoring me right now. It was a small consolation.

Somehow, I had to get past them and into the clocktower. I knew *how* to get in. When I'd been a patrolman, one of my regular duties had been to call round and flush out the drunks and the homeless from the ground-floor level. Generally, that meant shining a light around at a lot of squinting faces, agreeing with my partner that it was empty, and then going away again. The front was locked and boarded, but at the rear of the tower there was a smaller building tacked on. You could get into that through a patch of wasteground in a nearby yard, and from there into the abandoned foyer of the tower itself.

The side-road leading to the wasteground was right there – I could see it, almost to the exclusion of everything else. It ran down by the side of the main entrance. Zoom back a little and there were the policemen, standing just to the right of it by the front steps of the clocktower. Not blocking it but, nevertheless, bang in the fucking way.

I looked over at the policemen. They still weren't looking at me, but they must have at least *seen* me by now. If they were specifically after me was there any real percentage gain in hanging around and doing nothing? Specialist guys, all three of them. All armed.

I stood up. Time to get a hot dog.

Confidence is everything in life. You can try it on your

314

friends. Think of the wildest story you can. Go through it a hundred times in your head until you know it off by heart and you're convinced it's real, and then go and tell it to one of your friends – just drop it into conversation, as casually as you can. You can make anyone believe anything, for the simple reason that people usually want to believe you. All you need is someone with no reason *not* to trust you and a good story that you believe in enough to tell straight. Mix them together, and you have truth. For a lot of people, that's all truth really is.

It doesn't have to be your friends; it can be your enemies too. Find a bad neighbourhood and walk through it. If you walk around like you're at home there then you're a lot less likely to be bothered than someone trudging along with their head hung low, waiting to get attacked. Sit on a train through the area. If you look like you're not nervously waiting for the journey to end, you'll see how much easier it is to get where you're going. Subtle lies, told with confidence. It's genetic – predators pick off the weak members of the herd and don't waste their time with the ones that might fight back enough to hurt. Like blind faith, if you project strength then it comes.

So that's what I did. Once I'd decided what I was going to do, I tried not to think too much about it. There was nothing to stop me going down the road the policemen were waiting by – and a few groups of people had done so while I'd been sitting there. There was no reason why I shouldn't be one of them. I kept telling myself that.

I bought a hot dog from the nearest shack. The guy behind the counter was fat, and his bottom lip curled out and wobbled slightly as he stabbed a bread bun onto what looked like a thin, metal dildo. Then, he plucked out a pale, quivering sausage from a heat tank at the front, shook off the water and squashed it into the hole in the bread. A blast of ketchup. He didn't look at me the whole time.

'Thanks,' I said, accepting the food and handing over my money. Two-ninety-nine. I took the change, realising that I now had a single penny to my name. That was okay.

Once I had the hot dog, there were about twenty seconds when I needed not to think. I just started walking: straight across the corner of the square, heading almost directly towards the policemen. The rifle case was in my left hand, furthest away from them, and the hot dog was in a wrapper in my right. One of them glanced up as I got close, but I didn't pay him any attention. I just concentrated on my meal: scrunching up the greasy paper so as to take a bite. It was genuinely foul, and the disgusted expression on my face wasn't hard to fake. I walked into the side road, not even glancing back.

Nothing happened, but I knew it was fine before that. They hadn't been looking out for me at all. Either they were just regular crowd control, or else they were watching out for someone else entirely.

I kept walking for a minute before turning right into a thin alleyway, and then I doubled back on myself to reach the wasteground. It was bordered by a wall, but I was getting used to scaling these – I rested the rifle case on top and then hoisted myself up and over. The wasteground was probably about the size of a small football field, and it was mostly overgrown with dark grass from unpleasant soil. Apart from a haphazard row of large bins abandoned distantly down one side, it was entirely empty. And relatively quiet, too: the clocktower rising up at the far end drowned out a lot of the noise from the square. I walked along by the wall, watching out for movement, but there was nobody to see – just wavering grass. When I reached the far end, I pushed the rusted, old door on one of the buildings. It shrieked slightly, bending rather than opening, but it was enough for me to clamber awkwardly inside.

The building was dead and silent; I moved through the corridors that would take me to the foyer of the clocktower without hearing or seeing a soul. Perhaps they'd swept the place and cleaned everyone out already, because even the entrance hall turned out to be quiet and still. It was about thirty metres from one side to the other, and at one time it had probably been quite something. Now, it was just empty space and piles of shattered timber layered with dust and muck. In one place there were the remains of a fire; a few discarded needles and bottles; spatters of bird shit; old paper. The air was slightly misty and smelled strange, like a dirty bedroom that had been closed up for too long.

Okay.

A half-broken staircase curled upwards in one corner, leading into a ceiling that was mostly gone. The elaborate structures of floors and steps that had once filled the tower and made it famous were mostly either scattered around me or had been removed and taken elsewhere. I could hear birds fluttering overhead.

Even if the foyer had been cleared out – and even if the police came in again every once in a while – I doubted anyone would be checking above the first floor, and certainly not above the second. To go up there, you'd have to be either suicidal or insane.

And with that thought in mind, I walked over and started to climb.

CHAPTER TWENTY THREE

Another roar.

I stood up and went across to the window, stopping slightly back from it so that the barrel of the rifle wouldn't stick out. If anybody in the crowd – police or civilian – was distracted enough to look upwards then it was possible that they might notice; unlikely, but I didn't want to be caught.

That was almost surprising to realise. On my way here, I'd imagined that I wouldn't care too much: that to all intents and purposes this would be it for me – the end – and it wouldn't really matter what happened afterwards. I might get shot or jump; or I might escape. I hadn't really been thinking about anything beyond putting a bullet into Eli. But even if I didn't care on the surface, deep down I still very much wanted to get out of here alive, and my subconscious had been working on the problem.

If my aim was what it used to be then it would be one shot, maybe two. The noise from the crowd would cover that. It was possible that I could be out of here and away before anyone on the ground even realised anything was going on. Certainly the crowd wouldn't know, and it would probably take the police at least a couple of minutes to coordinate themselves. So, if I took the shot and left immediately then maybe I'd be all right. I could dream.

All but one of the eight fighters had arrived now,

and each of the seven already there was with his respective camp. These were situated a short distance away from the ring itself, with one roughly at each corner and the others positioned halfway along the sides. The boxers were warming up: rolling their shoulders into punches; pacing; having their necks massaged by their trainers. They looked focused and thoughtful. There was a great deal of tradition weighing down on them here, and a lot of expectations. I was almost sorry I was going to tarnish their big day.

A final roar.

I lifted the rifle, peered through the scope and tracked the final boxer as he made his way through the crowd. Eight fighters, now. The draw had been done weeks ago, live on television. There would be four bouts; then two; then the final. By the end, it would only be training, fitness and heart that decided the winner. That was in theory, anyway. The event itself might not go the distance, depending on how much disruption I caused.

I moved my aim back across the ring and up slightly, turning my attention across hordes of people and then towards the balcony on the opposite side of the square. It was a few storeys below me and so the angle was oblique, but I could see enough to work with. The ringing in my ears intensified as I saw them. All eight of them. More than eight, in fact. There were several old men, with police officers standing behind them and a few other people sitting amongst them or standing to one side. Some of them were clearly additional body-guards beyond the police presence, but others weren't. Perhaps they were officials or business people, or important council men. Who could tell? I moved the scope over their faces. Most of them weren't paying attention to the square below them; they were talking to one another or staring into space. Drinking champagne, I noticed. It all seemed very fucking genial.

Three in, I found Karna and paused on him. He wasn't talking to anyone; he was one of the few men actually looking down at the boxing ring, and at the moment his expression was blank. As I watched him, he coughed into his fist, and then looked up as a hand reached in from the right, passing him a glass of champagne. He took it and appeared to say thank you, but then his attention returned to the main square.

The roar of the crowd again. This time, it didn't stop. Down below, the first match was about to begin.

I adjusted my aim. The scope moved to the left, scanning over the faces, one by one. Most of them were just fat old men in suits, grown glossy and tight from feeding on the city's rotten scraps, but you could tell the brothers from the rest. They were just as old, but they still looked lean and hungry, as though everyone around them had forgotten how tenuous things could be but they still remembered. I passed over each in turn, moving up to the seats behind and then back to the right. There – Eli. I paused, his head resting between the crosshairs. Wind resistance aside, I could pull the trigger now and put a bullet into his left eye. It would exit somewhere around the back of his neck and remind him that life could be tenuous in exactly the same way power was.

He was on the second row, fourth from the left.

Back to the ring. The first two fighters – representing Snake and Turtle – were at opposite corners, dancing from one heel to the other to keep warm, occasionally swerving a little, lightly punching the air. I could see the slight give in the canvas at their feet and the sheen of the morning sunlight on their gloves. The referee was standing in the centre, hands held neatly behind his back, staring into space and smiling slightly: dealing with the thrill of the occasion by being very calm. Beside him, the MC was speaking into a black microphone, giving the details of the bout and geeing up the crowd. His voice was blaring out of down-turned speakers on two-storey poles. From up here, it was a nasal, unintelligible dirge, but I got the general idea of it from the crowd's reaction. This was going to be the best thing in the world and everybody had better get ready.

I moved the aim of the scope back up to the balcony, searching out Eli again. Adjusted slightly. I wouldn't risk an actual headshot with other people so close to him, but I could see enough of his body to aim for that and feel confident about landing the hit.

There.

And then I did nothing. I just held my aim and stared at Eli. From this far away, my impression was that he didn't look like much – just one old man on a balcony of many – but as I watched I realised it was possible to make out the sort of person that he was. Like his brothers, he radiated a certain kind of power, as though he was a creature of sinew and muscle sitting amongst men made of fat. A predator that was choosing not to kill. And there was a hardness about him too – even more so than his brothers. He was law and order, but not the friendly kind who might have walked in amiable pairs through your neighbourhood when you were a child. Instead, Eli looked like a drill sergeant. He wasn't morality; he was authority. He was the older brother who bullied you into doing what was best without explaining why or even caring what you thought. If I'd ever wondered how a man who controlled law and order could do the things I knew he'd done, the question disappeared completely as I looked at him.

He had simply done what he needed to do in order to keep the city's clockwork ticking. Perhaps it should have been surprising that someone might torture and kill in supposed pursuit of improving the world, but if so then who was I to be surprised?

I allowed that surge of hate and anger to well up inside me. It was almost overwhelming. I let it build until it filled everything, and I saw very clearly that I hated myself as much as him. My mistakes and motives were laid out clearly in front for me to see. This wasn't even a matter of revenge. Rachel and Sean wouldn't have wanted me to take that for them: it wasn't my place anymore. And taking it for myself felt empty and wrong. The guilt was falling correctly now, like coins in a counting machine, and I knew that I wanted this man dead for everything we'd both done.

Down below, I was dimly aware of the boxers approaching the centre of the ring. The referee began his standard speech; the drone through the speakers was indistinct, but I knew what he was saying. *Nice clean fight, break when I tell you.* I centred in the middle of Eli's chest. It wasn't overly windy and it wasn't that far in the grand scheme of things.

Back to your corners and come out fighting.

The noise from the crowd became almost unbearably loud: a terrifying rumble of cheers and shouts, rising up at me like wind. It felt as though the stone floor and walls of the tower were shaking with anger; as though the air was trembling and pounding itself. The bell rang and the fighters came together, both throwing the first punch. I closed my left eye and adjusted ever so slightly to the right. Licked my lips. And then I pulled the trigger.

My aim was slightly off, but it was okay: the bullet hit Eli in the top of his head, knocking it to one side and leaving a puff of blood in the air. He slumped in his seat, all the tension in him suddenly gone, and then his head began to spurt arcs of blood over his neighbour. For a second, he seemed to be the only one who noticed, and for a second he was too shocked to react. The others caught on a moment later. Through the scope, I saw a woman begin silently screaming. The man next to Eli jumped up and pushed himself away, his hands fluttering at the blood. Panic blew itself into life on the balcony.

I put the rifle on the ground and walked quickly but calmly back to the stairwell. Time to get out of here. As I moved into the doorway, something half deafened me and I was knocked backwards and to one side, onto my back, splinters of wood flying around me. Shit. I looked up. Most of the doorframe was gone. Still on my back, I reached into my jacket and struggled to free my gun.

Shit.

'Fucking idiot.'

'I got him. I got him in the head.'

The right-hand side of my face was on fire. I touched it with my free hand as I pulled the gun out.

'*Wait.*'

'I got him.' A figure came through the doorway, moving quickly but suddenly stopping as he saw me on the ground. One of the cops who'd been waiting by the entrance. As he realised that he hadn't got me at all, he raised his gun – but I was quicker. One shot, smacking him in the mouth like a punch, and he spun back and to one side, hitting the wall and collapsing by the side of it.

I struggled to my feet and half-fell against the wall, taking desperate aim at the doorway.

Fuck, fuck, fuck.

They couldn't have got up here so quickly, even if they'd known what had happened. And they couldn't have known that yet. Even Eli barely knew.

'You coming out to watch the boxing, Martin?'

I didn't recognise the voice. The temptation to shout back was strong, but I kept quiet. Glanced around the room. The window was the only other way out, and it was a hell of a fucking jump. I looked up into the rafters. Too high to climb, nowhere to go if I did. Back to the door.

One of them laughed and fired through the doorway: a nothing shot that hit the wall opposite me, knocking out a cloud of old stone. That meant that we were next to each other. If the wall hadn't been between us, he would have been close enough to touch. I knelt down, still drawing on the door and scanned the wall for cracks. The stones were ancient. In some places, the mortar was missing.

'Why don't you come out?' he called.

Here was one: about waist height. I quickly pushed my finger in and the hole felt large. It probably didn't go all the way through, but what was in the way and how strong was it going to be? I looked at the wall across from me. That last bullet had turned a baseball-sized chunk of rock into powder. In the doorway itself, the first bullet had demolished an even larger wedge.

Another call: 'Why are you making our lives so—'

Before I could think about it, I jammed the tip of the barrel into the hole, closed my eyes and fired off three fast shots, twisting my aim slightly. The noise was terrible, but his words cut off and turned into a scream, and so I fired again. The scream stopped. I pulled the gun away from the wall. The air was filled with dust. I coughed and then aimed back at the doorway.

'Just you and me now,' I said.

No reply, but I knew someone was out there. Three in front of the tower; two of them dead. Unless the third guy was waiting downstairs or outside for me, he was there too. And he'd probably be a lot more careful than his friends had been.

'You don't want to talk to me?'

Nothing. He wasn't going to bite.

I moved away from the wall, edging closer to the doorway, keeping a good grip on the gun. The dead man was at my feet now; I couldn't move any closer without edging around him, and that would make me more visible. I could see some of the walkway outside, stretching away to the left, and there was nobody there. If he was to the right – where his friend had been – then it was possible I'd tagged him as well. But I wasn't usually that lucky.

So – nobody in sight on the left-hand side, and I could see a fair way around. If he was that way, he'd have to risk a long shot. More and more, I was thinking he was back to the right, if he was up here at all. If he was sensible, he'd have moved back a little and be crouching down with his gun trained on the doorway. If I came out straight, he'd nail me. And if I didn't, there'd be more people along soon enough.

Okay.

I reached down and got hold of the dead cop underneath the arms. He was face down and not as heavy as I'd expected, but it was still difficult because I had to keep some kind of grip on my gun as well. I pulled back as hard as I could and got him to his knees, and then managed to lift him a little more. His ruined head lolled against me. I braced myself, straining my arms and leaning back slightly, pulling him to his feet. His head slid up my chest to my shoulder.

This was going to be fucking impossible. *Just keep hold*, I thought, edging to the doorway. It was all or nothing, and I was sure I was going to drop him any second. Finding strength from somewhere, I managed to half push and half throw him out onto the walkway, where he fell down instantly, his upper body smashing through the old wooden railings.

At the same time, gunfire erupted from the right as the cop shot at his dead friend. That was all I needed: I reached around the doorframe and fired off one shot, missing, fired another as he brought his aim back around, and this one caught him in the middle of the chest. As he went down, he fired again but it went wild – up into the rafters – and I stepped out and shot him three more times, knocking him back along the ground. He wasn't moving after that. His gun clattered off down into space. A second later, a shot rang out downstairs. Anyone close enough to the front of the clocktower would certainly have heard that.

I looked around, but I couldn't see anyone else, so I took the stairs quickly and carelessly. If they broke or if I fell, then so be it; if I didn't get out of here now, I never would.

It felt strange to be outside again now that it was properly daytime. When I'd gone into the tower, everything had been bathed in dark blue, as though the world was feeling lazy and sleepy and still yawning in its dressing-gown. But now it was awake. The sun was halfway up the sky, there was no cloud cover and – at least down here at ground level – very little breeze.

I squinted slightly as I walked down the side of the wasteground. *It was going to be hot today*, I thought.

The sun would bake the buildings like clay and everybody would look damp and dry at the same time. A good day to get out into the country.

But halfway along the wasteground, I stopped, realising that it wasn't just the light or the heat that I was noticing. The noise from the crowd remained the same – loud, but muffled by the buildings – and yet it seemed more threatening now. In fact, everything I could hear was the same: low and ominous and sad. The air had dropped into a minor key. The ground felt like it was vibrating slightly – everything from the dirt and grass upwards seemed somehow *charged*, and there was current and voltage running through my body. Half my imagination, maybe; but half not as well. The city was like a child, excited on Christmas morning, only the occasion was darker and the emotion far less positive. Something was very wrong.

I started moving again.

In the alleyway, I could see back towards the main square. The ring was elevated slightly above the crowds, but the figures were too far away to make out. The main video screen, which I could see half of from where I was standing, showed that the fight was still going on. The nasal buzz of the bell announced the end of round two, and the boxers separated, breathing heavily, heads bowed. It had been seven minutes since I'd shot Eli, which was too long. Police on the ground would know by now.

'Don't move, Martin.'

I stayed very still and closed my eyes. The voice had come from the other side of the road, and I recognised it.

'Lucy—'

'Shut up.'

I did as I was told.

'Turn around and look at me.'

I did. She was standing in the doorway across the street, pointing a gun at me. I knew her, but at the same time she was like a stranger: same clothes, but they looked caught on her at uncomfortable angles; same face, but harder than I'd ever seen it. I'd never been on the receiving end of this, and now I realised how scared those men we killed must have been when they'd found themselves facing this. A couple of wisps of her blond hair were trembling in the slight breeze.

'Your gun,' she said. 'Put it down.'

But this time, I didn't do as I was told. I just left it hanging down by my side.

'How did you find me?'

'Rosh told me where you'd be,' she said. 'He said you were going to try something like this.'

'So this is official, then?'

'No,' she said. 'And it's not going to be. Put down your gun, Martin.'

I felt a kind of pressure coming from the main square and turned to look that way. The next round had started, but it wasn't just the crowd's reaction I was sensing – it was that feeling of something being wrong, rolling out in a slow wave that would gradually engulf the city. I wondered if Lucy could feel it too. I looked back at her, and I answered her without thought.

'I can't do that,' I said. 'I need it.'

'If you don't put it down, I'll shoot you.'

'Do what you have to do. If I put it down, I'm dead anyway. I'm dead anyway, regardless.'

She stared at me; I stared back. For some reason, I wasn't scared anymore. A few blank seconds passed, and at the end of them I thought she might be going to cry, but she didn't. That generally wasn't the kind of thing that Lucy did. Maybe once I would have got to see that level of vulnerability, but not anymore.

'Why have you done this?' she said.

I nodded towards the clocktower.

'I just killed the man who's been doing this to us,' I said. 'His name was Eli. We took his money and he punished us for it.'

'I don't believe you. Put your gun down.'

'I already said no,' I told her. 'If you want to shoot me, shoot me.'

'I want to know why you've done this.'

'My life is over, Lucy. This man killed people we all loved and he wanted us to kill each other. He killed Rachel. He killed Rich.'

'Don't talk about Rich.'

'I have to go.'

'No,' she said, showing more resolve. 'You're not going anywhere.'

But it was weird, because I knew I was. It was almost as though this had all already happened and I knew that Lucy hadn't ended up killing me. I could still see the hate and anger on her face, but it looked different to before. I was starting to see shades of emotions there, and I wasn't sure how. Something occurred to me, and I felt very calm.

'Before I go,' I said, 'I want you to know that you were right.'

'What?'

'You were right,' I said. 'About me and Rachel. I made a mistake, and I realise that now. You were right. I was never in love with you. I was just getting confused and messing things up. It was my fault. It was nothing to do with you.'

Lucy shook her head.

'You know I didn't kill Rich,' I said. Her face

hardened but I carried on as though I hadn't noticed. 'The truth is that all the way along, I was happy for you. Unhappy for me, but that was my problem. I tried to work out my own solution, and I fucked it up, and hurt people I shouldn't have. I was being stupid. But deep down I knew that you wanted to be with him, and I would never have done anything to harm that, and I would certainly never have hurt him. I cared about you too much.'

She was staring at me, confused but disarmed, not knowing what to say. Despite the situation, I wanted to smile at her. It felt like I'd gone up a level, and it was the weirdest sensation I'd ever experienced: impossible to describe, but I was bypassing her words and appearance and simply understanding what was going on in her head – seeing the emotions there as a rich fabric of colours in my own. I saw the genuine affection she'd had for me. She still had it, but because of how I'd been she'd known that she had to hide it; and it made her very sad to have lost me as a friend. I understood the indecision and guilt she'd suffered; the way she'd nearly chosen me but had decided to do what she thought was right for us both. The hurt and the self-recrimination. I saw the vulnerability she'd offered up, and how rare and special it was for her to do that. And from there, I could read between the lines of every text message she'd sent me since we split up, and I understood that what she'd really been writing all along were messages to convince herself. *You didn't love me, so it's not my fault. I care about you so much, and I can't let myself believe that I've ruined your life.*

The electricity that was buzzing in the city seemed to surge through me for a moment, and I experienced it as a burst of real love for her. It was so different.

Unlike the feelings I'd had for her before, it didn't make me sad.

'I'm going now,' I said. 'For what it's worth, I've taken care of the man who did this to us, and now I'm leaving. Goodbye, Lucy. Take care.'

'No, Martin,' she said. 'Don't move.'

But I did anyway: I just turned and walked off down the road. I wasn't sure what had just happened, but I knew that she wouldn't shoot me, and she didn't. Within a few metres, I felt that force of wrongness coming from the main square again, and I started to run.

CHAPTER TWENTY FOUR

The immorality of stealing cars had disappeared entirely by now. It didn't feel that wrong, and I found myself wondering why more people didn't do it – it was handy and convenient, and you didn't need to remember where you'd parked. Car crime in the city was actually quite low: the council had invested heavily in the transport infrastructure, and you could get pretty much anywhere you wanted to go by tram or bus. It was just unfortunate that public transport wasn't an option for me right now. So I stole a sports car about half a mile from the main square. If you're going to sin, you might as well sin in style.

From there, it was two minutes onto the motorway, and then I would be driving north. The city gates were less than twenty minutes away, and after that I would be heading to wherever. I didn't know where – I hadn't thought that far ahead yet. I flicked on the radio and found a local station that was playing something rocky but subdued, and concentrated on the road ahead. There was nothing I needed to think about.

Except of course there was. The question of what had just happened with Lucy. That had been strange but at least not inexplicable. Far more concerning was the question of why the cops hadn't taken me down until after I'd killed Eli. That seemed pretty important, but the implications were worrying and I didn't want to think about them right then. I figured that was reasonable enough. I was on a break; I'd think about the whole thing when I got back to my desk.

I turned the radio up just as the song finished and the local news came on. It was the same newsreader who'd reported Rachel's body being found yesterday evening, and I felt a little sorry for him: didn't he ever get to go home and sleep? The main item was that the city's annual competition was underway, and that the first fight had been won by a knockout in the third round. Turtle were through. The second fight had begun, and so far the fighters looked to be even on points. There would be regular updates, on the hour, every hour.

Once again, there was no mention of any shooting incident. Either it was too early for it to have reached the news, or else it was being suppressed like the gunfight yesterday. But whatever – at least I hadn't spoiled everyone's day.

I moved into the fast lane, overtaking a campervan who was going too slowly and being annoying. Speeding to add to my list of crimes, but what did it matter? I put my foot down a little harder.

'In other news,' the man on the radio told me, 'police have confirmed that the body of a young woman found yesterday evening is that of twenty-two-year-old student Keleigh Groves.'

I swerved back in – straight across the front of the campervan and then into the slow lane. A chorus of blaring horns followed me across. There was a lay-by coming up: a patch of dusty land in front of an enormous white billboard. I indicated as I turned onto it, the gravel crunching heavily beneath the tyres.

The newsreader had already moved on to the next item.

Not Rachel, I thought. Rachel might still be alive.

And now I'd killed Eli.

I sat very still, holding on to the steering wheel and wanting to react in some way: shaking, screaming, anything. But my body wasn't responding. I tried to think, but that wouldn't work either. Every single thought slipped away when my mind tried to focus on it. They came and went quickly: a flash of the conversation I'd had with Karna; the men who'd taken Rachel and killed Rich; the puff of blood above Eli's head; Rosh, who'd tried to phone me all afternoon and yet I'd had no missed calls.

It's not going to be that easy, the man in Rich's bedroom had told me.

One of Eli's men, I'd assumed, but only because I'd been led to believe that.

Another flash of Karna. He was smiling, and I heard his voice in my head.

I can't act directly to harm my brother.

And then he was gone.

The policemen in the tower – it didn't make any sense that they'd been working for Eli. But it fitted perfectly if they'd been working for Karna instead.

I turned off the radio. The quiet was immediately filled with the noise of cars whining past: an everyday sound that now seemed full of menace. There was an undercurrent too: the same electric throb that I'd felt as I'd left the clocktower. The same ringing, in fact, that I'd been hearing for days. Since I'd killed Eli, it seemed to have buried itself into the world around me and started to make it vibrate.

I was gripping the steering wheel, feeling sick; when the nausea lurched inside me again I jerked my head to the left. I was directly next to the billboard, which was advertising some hair-care product by showing a woman's head against a stark white background. Right in the bottom corner, somebody had graffitied the words FONDLY, I THINK OF YOU in edged, purple letters.

The ringing inside me intensified as I stared.

And then it became real: a tense, physical buzz against my heart. It didn't surprise me and I just accepted it, but it still took me five seconds, maybe more, before I realised what it was. And then I slowly released the steering wheel and took my phone out of my pocket.

Caller unknown.

Well, my phone might not have known but I did.

I pressed green and said:

'Hello, Jamie.'

There was nothing for a second, and then I realised that he was sobbing – trying to talk, but incoherent.

I said, 'Slow down.'

Patience seemed to be one of my few remaining virtues. In fact, I realised that I might well have fucked up so incredibly badly that there wasn't any point in being anything other than calm. I waited while he got himself together.

'Detective Weaver?'

'Yes,' I said.

'They killed her.'

'Yes, I know.'

I wished there was something else I could say to him, but nothing was going to make it any different. When I'd heard the newsreader yesterday, all I'd thought about was Rachel – I hadn't considered that someone else might be dead. Keleigh. I'd never met her or seen a photograph. She'd been so central to this and yet she hadn't even entered my mind. What the fuck had happened to me?

'He killed her.'

'Yes,' I said, searching for something more profound, something that might be comforting. 'I know.'

'I'm so sorry,' Jamie said. 'I'm so sorry.'

'I'm sorry, too.'

'You don't understand.'

He started sobbing again.

'Jamie.' I said it quietly, just staring straight ahead. 'Come on, Jamie.'

'I just love her so much.'

'Jamie. You need to listen to me. She's dead, and I'm sorry about that. You need to – ' I frowned. 'Where are you?'

Immediately: 'I'm not telling you.'

'That's okay.' I shook my head. 'I don't want to know. But wherever you are, what you need to do is get the fuck out of there.'

He sniffed but didn't say anything.

'Okay?' I said. 'You need to get in a car and drive. If you can't do that, then you fucking run. You need to put real distance between you and this city. You need to get out and not come back.'

'He killed her, Detective Weaver.'

'Yes, I know.'

'Your friend – he killed her.'

'Yes,' I said. 'What?'

'Your friend.' I could hear him gulping in air at the other end of the line. 'He told me – he told me if I didn't meet you all and tell you what I said then he was going to kill her. He told me. And I love her. I never told her, but I do.'

'My friend,' I said. 'Jamie. Calm down and tell me.'

'But fuck him! I did what he wanted and he killed her anyway.'

'Jamie!'

My last virtue had gone.

336

'Jamie,' I said again, more softly. 'Who told you to do this? Who killed her?'

'Your friend,' he said. 'Mister Rho.'

I was driving again, heading somewhere I was starting to know far too well, and all the while I was thinking. I swung out into the fast lane, cutting someone up, and my thoughts swerved along with the car. The guy behind beeped and I thought: *I have a fucking gun and you shouldn't do that.*

I was remembering the firing range where I'd go with Sean, competing against him on neighbouring lanes while people slowly gathered around, eventually egging us on. We graduated from there to killing people together, but – although that was where it had begun for me – it hadn't really been Sean that started it off. Rosh was the one who'd got all of us into this in the first place. I'd joined late of course, because Rosh had recruited Lucy first and then she'd recruited Sean. But the extra-curricular killings had all begun with Rosh.

He'd been doing it long before I'd ever met him. Working beyond the straight confines of the law. Fate and death; the wildcard.

The guy behind blared his horn again. I glared into the mirror and saw him mouthing profanities at me.

I looked back at the road.

I was also thinking back to the fire-fight with Kemp and his men. The guy that Rosh had taken down had vanished into thin air. For a while, that had meant nothing. Then, a lot of people started vanishing into thin air. But now it meant something else altogether. The fact was that either Lucy or I had put bullets in every dead body that ended up there that night. As far as I knew for sure, Rosh hadn't killed anyone.

Rosh had tried to phone me all afternoon, but my phone had never rung. And yet, whenever I'd tried to ring him, his phone was off.

The exit was coming up. I moved into the middle lane and then the slow lane, ready to turn. The guy behind me should have been pleased, but instead he followed me across, beeping his horn again. I checked him out in the mirror and didn't see much. He wasn't a cop. He wasn't a criminal. He was just a dick.

I picked my gun off the passenger seat and held it up so he could see it. The horn cut off and his car swerved into the middle lane, dropping back a little. Good for him.

I thought: *Rosh had owned a farmhouse slightly outside the city's walls.* Nobody knew how old it was, only that he'd inherited it from his parents – and them from theirs – and that it was probably very old indeed.

I thought: *Rosh had told Lucy where to find me, because he wanted to force me into killing her.* I didn't understand quite how we'd avoided that, but that had been his intention. Tying up loose ends by wrapping them together.

And I thought: *I should have been heading out of the city, just like I'd planned.* But part of me had known I wouldn't get far. Like I said before, some people are born in the city, live their lives here and never leave – and I knew now that I was going to be one of them. In the sphere that Sean had talked about, my life was already set. It was hanging there, complete, and it wouldn't have mattered whether I sat down in the main square and waited for them to come and get me, or if I put my foot down and drove for the outskirts as fast as I could. It had already either happened or not, and I knew which. I wasn't leaving the city right now.

But within the parameters of its walls, perhaps I had some leeway.

I put the gun down again, indicated left and took the exit to Wasp.

What Jamie had told me, when he finally stopped crying, was this.

There were four of them in the art collective: Keleigh, Alison, Jamie and Damian. Jamie had been born here, brought up by parents who had died a few years before he started his degree, but the other three were foreigners to the city. They had been friends from the start, meeting on day one and hitting it off, and realising very quickly that they had a lot more in common with each other than with the rest of the students on the course. It's so rare to click like that with people that when it does happen you feel lucky and blessed.

The group didn't socialise much. Instead, they began working on projects that excited all of them. They each brought different ideas and approaches – from photography and straight painting to the more conceptual projects that Alison began working on – but an over-arching theme was always in the background, becoming slowly more focused as the months passed. That theme turned out to be the city they'd moved to. In some ways, like Sean and me, they all felt its strangeness, and they'd been fascinated and inspired by it. But unlike us, they hadn't been afraid. I could understand that: when you're young and enthusiastic you often feel that the world is yours – and that it has an in-built safety net to catch you if you fall.

Jamie had spelled out the truth to me in Whitelocks: if you look at our city too long then it turns around and looks back. The four of them did their graffiti and stuck up their photographs of eyes; they made their maps and painted the skylines; and by a series of coincidences that I could understand without seeing, their work all started to coalesce into a single project. It was shaped by a strange serendipity. First, they found Harris, and he taught them the legends behind the city. And then Alison started seeing Halloran, who knew enough from his own background to hint that the legends might have substance. He should have known better, of course, but Alison was the kind of girl you wanted to impress. Jamie said that if you'd killed somebody then you'd tell her, just to make her think you were special. The project evolved, gaining shape and forming a knot in the city's consciousness that would become an irritant. And eventually the city didn't like it anymore and decided to cut that knot out.

Not the city, to be precise – more a couple of its founding members, acting on its behalf. And at this stage it wasn't a matter of cutting. It was a case of manipulating and moving: creating small shifts that would lead the situation to resolve itself. Creating cancers within the cancers, if you like. That was the way the brothers had always worked; if someone wandered off the path then they preferred just to give them a subtle spin on their heels and send them back again; they could never simply kill someone or make them disappear. But in the situation with the students, Karna and Rho – between them representing crime, life, death and fate – had seen the opportunity to do something else beyond merely righting what had gone wrong. They had seen a way to manipulate me to get rid of their brother for them.

Jamie couldn't know this but I saw it all clearly, and I understood it in the same way I'd understood Lucy outside the clocktower.

It started the night that we killed Halloran. The lead for the post-office murders had come from one of Sean's regular informants, but in reality Halloran had nothing to do with that; he was just a minor player who'd happened to be bottom of the list at the wrong time, dating the wrong girl and shooting off his wrong mouth. Rosh set him up with the briefcase of money, and then we turned up, killed him and took that money away. One down; no real effort expended. The money never meant anything one way or another. How could it? A few thousand – the city turned over more than that in a heartbeat. The money was only ever there as a ghost that, months later, they could fool me into thinking their brother was chasing.

But what would happen if Eli really was following that briefcase? He'd move onto the first people who might know where it was: Halloran's girlfriend and the people Halloran had occasionally left packages with. And so the next one they picked off the list was Alison.

Jamie had told me that everybody was drawn to her. She was one of those girls – the kind that radiates power and seems to have been born with the confidence to use it. Alison was a young woman who knew exactly the hold she could have on people: that she could tense and release her grip on you at will. She had an unconscious feeling that the world belonged to her: that she could move through the stalls in its dark markets, picking and choosing from everything there and whirling away into the crowds without being challenged.

She was always the focus of the group, and for a long time Jamie was infatuated with her. He'd never even had a girlfriend, and so he didn't stand a chance. There was no way that anything so obvious and easy would be interesting to her for long. He chased her, and she laughed and ran away – but she never ran far enough in front to leave him behind. That kind of girl, she can do that with everyone. She'll have ten guys after her, and she'll be dodging in between them like a ninja, laughing as they collide. It's not malicious; it's playful and fair and it's the way the world works.

Damian was another. He was interested in her too, but he played it by her rules: basically ambivalent, generally available – but not always. He'd been with a few girls before and so he worked the odds and won a few dividends. He and Alison were together for a while, on and off, but it backfired on him eventually. To the extent that Alison ever had a concrete boyfriend, it ended up being Halloran. Jamie said he thought that Damian was a hell of a lot more bothered by that than he ever let on.

Jamie was bothered too, but he was easily distracted. If Alison was the focus of the group, Keleigh had always stood close by, slightly off centre. She was just as sure of herself, but confidence can manifest itself in different ways: it can turn both inwards and out. When they went clubbing, Alison would be dancing on the podium, lost in herself and utterly uncaring, and Keleigh would be standing at the edge of the floor, sipping a drink and watching, patient and at ease. It's the difference between being comfortable in a crowd and being comfortable in your own skin, and ultimately it was the latter that began to attract Jamie more. It didn't surprise me much that he ended up falling in love with Keleigh instead.

What he'd told us about the night it began – about when he, Keleigh and Harris had been visited by the men who came out of the walls – was basically true, with one important difference. Jamie hadn't explained that Rosh had been one of them.

It had been Rosh who'd done the talking, but he certainly hadn't asked them anything about any money. Instead, he'd told them that Halloran and Alison and Damian were all dead, and that if they didn't do what he wanted then they would be too. What he wanted wasn't going to be difficult; it involved nothing more troubling than keeping their heads down, remaining in the city and perhaps doing him a small favour at some point in the future.

So they stayed in the city out of basic fear. After all, these men had come from thin air and had apparently murdered their friends. Those alone were good tricks; who knew what else they might be able to do? They didn't dare go to the police, and wouldn't have known what to say if they had.

A couple of times, Jamie told me, they decided to run. Each time, they got as far as the city gates, and then something stopped them. They'd hear a ringing in the air, or feel it in their gut, and they'd look around and not *see* anyone exactly – it was more like catching something out of the corner of their eye – but it would be enough to make them turn around and go home again. After a while, they put the memory of what happened away out back, and they got on with their lives as best they could. Not forgetting, exactly, but nobody was coming out of the walls or threatening to kill them and so to some extent they could kid themselves it had been a bad dream that was over now. Gradually, life returned to something approaching normal.

That was until a week ago, when they'd received another visit – and despite what Jamie had told us in Whitelocks, it hadn't been from Sean. All of that had been a lie; they'd never even met him or spoken to him. Instead, it was Rosh and his men who came calling:

pulling them back into that bad dream they thought they'd escaped. It was time for that small favour.

Five months ago, I believed that Sean had become fascinated by the city's black heart and been drawn into searching it out. Now, I understood that simple truth: if you look hard enough, it looks back. I remembered that, after he disappeared, Sean's flat had seemed as though he'd gone out for the night and simply not returned – and that was exactly what had happened. Rosh and Karna had taken him and kept him for all of that time. The padlock on the hotel room hadn't been placed there by Sean to keep his research secure; it had been put there to keep him a prisoner. They'd cuffed him and left him. Some of the papers and writing there had been taken from his flat. Others, he'd scrawled during his imprisonment, as best he could. They'd crossed out what they didn't like and forced him to write certain things they needed – including the note to me – at gunpoint. Finally, after he was dead, they'd added their own information. Photographs and reference books to help me on my way.

It was all about timing. They'd kept Alison's identity a secret just as they'd kept Sean a prisoner, and when the moment was right, they manipulated me with both: revealing enough so that I could follow the trail and, in time, arrive at the conclusion they wanted. After all, there was only one occasion every year when I'd have the chance to do what I'd just done.

So: while I was drinking on my own in Whitelocks and looking at a photograph of an eye that Keleigh had stuck on the wall, Rosh was paying Jamie another visit. This time he took Keleigh away with him. If Jamie didn't do exactly as he was told, she'd be killed. It wouldn't be too difficult.

As ordered, Jamie delivered the envelope, and then

344

later he met the three of us to tell us what had happened, based on the intricate script that had been prepared for him. All the while, Rosh was there, directing the action from both within our group and without. It was just a matter of watching my life unravel and giving it a little nudge here and there when it didn't go quite right.

There were things that Jamie didn't tell me because he couldn't have known, but in my head they came together.

Jamie wasn't aware of the video we had of Harris, but I realised now that it certainly hadn't been used to blackmail him. They didn't need him for anything. Combined with the forwarding of Alison's email to his account and the fake blackmail message, it was simply another set-up to keep me moving – along with a little background detail to sit the rest of their story on. And it neatly tied up another loose end. After all, Harris now appeared to have killed himself. I had no doubt that at some point the video would surface, giving him a credible motive for doing so. There would be no other real questions to answer, and the case would be closed.

Rosh had rung Alison's parents and visited Hedge, posing as Sean. He'd set up the attempt on Lucy's life, but in reality it wouldn't have mattered if she'd lived or died. All that mattered was that Kemp was there and that I saw him. Later, as Karna fed me his bullshit lies, I would remember that Kemp was a cop and it would push me even more towards Eli.

Rosh had helped to set up the flat opposite the CandiBar, priming me with all the background information I needed. Karna had put Eli in the frame. And then –

And then to give me a real incentive, they'd taken my wife away.

They'd killed innocent people and sacrificed men who were close to them, and it meant nothing. I realised now that there wasn't even a real reason for it either – it was all just because Rho, or Rosh, was fate and death, Karna was crime and Eli was law, and that was the way it worked. Karna had told me: *we don't invent our natures.* So it didn't matter that up until now everything had worked, and that Eli's death would break the balance and destroy the city. It was simply in Karna's nature to do this, and in Rho's nature to help him. They were doing what they were born and fated to do.

But they weren't allowed to kill him themselves, and so they'd needed an idiot to do it for them. Everything that had happened had been carefully stage-managed: an elaborate load of bullshit and pain designed for one single purpose – to get me into that clocktower today, putting a bullet in their brother.

And it had worked too – you couldn't accuse them of overestimating my stupidity. Whether or not I survived the men they'd sent to kill me, or what happened in my encounter with Lucy, the end result was more or less the same: my life was ruined and Eli was dead. Whatever loose ends remained would be methodically destroyed. And now, just as in the legend, the city belonged to Karna and Rho.

But of course, Rosh hadn't lied just to me; he'd lied to Jamie as well. Keleigh was dead and probably had been for some time. It wouldn't have mattered what Jamie had done – he could have thrown his drink in Rosh's face in Whitelocks and spat after it and the result would have been the same.

That was the way these matters worked. It was only ever a case of deciding how much you gave up before you died, and because he cared about Keleigh, Jamie had given up pretty much everything. He was due to meet Rosh at eleven o'clock this morning, when he'd been told he could walk away with Keleigh: free to leave the city; their duty done. But someone in Rosh's entourage must have fucked up, because Keleigh was dead and her body had gone public. And so, finally, Jamie had rung me and told me everything. I gave him a piece of advice in return.

Get out of the city.

I didn't think that anybody would stop him. He was one of those loose ends, but perhaps not untidy enough to chase when everyone was so busy. I told him to get in a car – any fucking car – and put his foot down until he was a hundred miles away.

My original plan, in fact.

Now, I had another.

CHAPTER TWENTY FIVE

Wasp in the daytime again. I'd been here far too much recently, but – one way or another – this was going to be my last visit. Perhaps I would never leave. The district didn't seem overly impressed by this, though, and there weren't many people out on the streets to cheer me off. A few couples and singles were walking along casually, but most of the people who were here were ensconced in the dark bars, watching the boxing on television; I'd hear periodic bursts of shouting as I passed them. Most of the sex shops were closed for the day, and there weren't even that many girls dancing in the windows. The competition would go on until nightfall, and then the district would come alive again: rubbing its hands in glee as people arrived either to celebrate or drown their sorrows.

Despite the relative quiet, Wasp was alive: it was ticking and fizzing in small ways, none of which felt good. The air was sparkling, and the menacing pylon hum in the ground was growing stronger. Nobody here seemed aware of it, but I could tell that the city had cracked at the centre; and now those cracks were slowly spreading. Invisible fault lines in the ground were trembling, alive with potential energy that set my lower legs tingling. And my head had started hurting too. The pain was a slowly flashing siren, throbbing away between my eyes.

Because of the pain – but in spite of the fact that

hardly anyone was around – I didn't see Rosh until it was almost too late. He was standing less than ten metres in front of me, staring into a glass window. I stopped, frozen in place, and it took a couple of shocked seconds before I began reaching into my coat for my gun. Then I stopped. It wasn't exactly busy here, but it wasn't exactly deserted either. If I could avoid it, this wasn't the place to do it. I moved quickly to my right, down a set of steps and out of sight inside a heaving bar.

It was as dark and compact as a cave. There was a bright video screen hanging down at the far end showing a close-up of one of the fights, with a smaller screen in the corner displaying a slow-motion repeat. The sound was being blasted out and was coming through as fuzzy and distorted as in the main square. There were too many people crammed in, and I couldn't make it properly inside – couldn't have cleared a way to the bar if I'd been on fire – but that was okay. I waited by the entrance, ignoring the people on either side of me, and after a minute had passed I went back out again, and up onto the street.

Rosh had gone. No doubt he was already heading to the CandiBar in time for his meeting with Jamie. I'd been planning – if you could call it that – to confront him there, but now I decided to catch up and shadow him, and perhaps see if I could take him down somewhere quieter before we got there.

I started off quickly, but as I got to the corner I paused, and then turned to look into the window where he'd been standing. A woman was in there, naked apart from white underwear, and she was writhing slowly in front of billowing red curtains. It was dancing, but it was more like a slow unwinding, up and down, than anything else. I caught her eye, and she smiled coyly, beckoning me in with a hand I hadn't even seen move.

I didn't shake my head; I just stared as Rosh had been doing, wondering what it was about this woman, other than beauty, that had caught his eye. And after a moment I saw it – or thought I did, anyway. It wasn't the woman at all. To her left there was a pale reflection of my face, illuminated by an angle of sunlight. The light was cut off by the edge of the building, so that only half of my face was clearly visible, and my skin looked slack and doughy and lifeless. The eye I could see there was somehow both black and absent at the same time.

I stared at myself for a moment. The reflection was superimposed both in front of and behind the dancing woman, flicking from one to the other, but I was entirely still. And because of that, there was something about me that was utterly hideous.

I wondered what Rosh, with his strange face, would have looked like.

When I pictured him, I felt anger building up in me. That was good and right, but I swallowed it down for now. If I even thought about it too much, I knew that it would release itself and be gone. It felt like a rage that could level half the city. All I would have to do was let it into my head, open my mouth wide and scream, and buildings would fall.

Rosh was getting away from me.

I looked up and managed to give the woman a smile that was even more artificial than the one she'd given me. She was still dancing, but she wasn't beckoning anymore. In fact, she looked a little unsure – and maybe even afraid. That was fair enough.

I headed off, rounding the corner and walking quickly. Within a minute I'd spotted Rosh's large frame wandering along up ahead, and I dropped back a little, allowing him to remain six or seven buildings in front of me. There were still too many people around to confront him. I could wait.

As always when you head east, the people quickly thinned out, and because they had been sparse to begin with, it wasn't long before Rosh and I were pretty much the only people around. That meant I had to drop back a little further and be even more careful. The few people who were here were junkies and wasters, and since I didn't think any of them were likely to call the police I drew my gun and walked along with it held casually down by my side. I could shoot him right here, but I decided to hold on for now. I wanted time with him, so that he could tell me everything in his own words.

As we walked, I realised that he was taking exactly the same route to the CandiBar as I had done. That didn't necessarily mean anything, but for some reason it felt like it should. Coincidence again – or perhaps now I just knew where to look for the patterns. Like Sean said, once you could recognise the shape of them, maybe you saw them everywhere.

Rosh turned right into Parker Street, and I hung back a little and waited, giving him chance to make it far enough along for me to shadow him without being too obvious. I allowed him about thirty seconds. As I stood there, waiting by the stone wall of a boarded-up deli, I listened. I could hear that same dog barking in the distance, and nothing else. It didn't surprise me.

I peered around the corner, and then started walking. Rosh was right up by the CandiBar, but he was still on my side of the road. I found an old doorway and pressed myself into it, leaning out enough to be able to see him, but not so far that I couldn't hide if he happened to look back.

But he didn't. Instead, he turned right and headed down the alleyway at the side of the old hotel.

I made my way up the street, conscious of the weight of the gun in my hand and aware that I was out in the open now. I drew down on the alley, ready to fire. If Rosh stepped back out there would be nowhere to hide; he would see me and I would have to shoot him. I got closer to the hotel, and with every step I expected him to re-appear, but he didn't. And then I moved quickly around the entrance of the alleyway, ready to fire. It was empty.

There was the fence, a little way down. There was something about it that seemed electric and dangerous, as though it had been connected to a powerline some time since my last visit. The hum was everywhere.

I started down the alley, keeping my gun aimed at the fence.

The boards felt warm as I touched them, but it must have been my imagination – from the angle of the buildings, the sun hadn't made it down here for a good few hours. I crouched down and pushed them in very slightly, glancing into the back garden of the hotel. Nobody there, as far as I could see. I pushed them further and then clambered inside, leading with my left arm and aiming almost casually with my right. Still nothing. Then, I was in. I stood up and moved quickly to the back of the building.

The window that led inside seemed especially dirty and black today. Once again, though – no guts no glory. I climbed in as quickly and quietly as I could, but my feet went down on broken glass and I winced at the noise, immediately heard movement. Rosh was coming through the doorway from the kitchen. He saw me and reacted, but I was quicker. I pointed the gun at him: a good two-handed grip.

'Don't,' I said.

He stopped moving, holding his own gun slightly out and away from him, considering his options. He stared at me blankly. I stared back, trying to make it clear how much I hated him.

'Martin—'

'Don't.'

I circled around a little – more glass crunching – keeping my aim on him. Not at his head: at the centre of his body where there was more room for error. I kept moving until I was well out of his reach. Rosh could tell me whether Rachel was still alive, and so I didn't want to encourage him to try anything that would make me shoot him. Not yet. But at the same time, I knew how dangerous he was and I wasn't going to take any chances. If he moved and I didn't like it, I was going to empty the whole fucking clip into him. If he vanished, I'd shoot all the thin air I could until something started bleeding.

'Throw your gun away,' I said.

He shook his head.

'I don't think I can do that.'

'Well, I think you'll manage.'

He looked me over. If last night he'd had any doubt that I'd kill him, I was sure that it was gone now. But if he threw away his gun, he was fucked. For a moment, I saw the struggle playing out on his face, and then his expression went blank.

'Where?'

'To one side. Over in that corner will do.'

He threw the gun to one side.

'Well done.' I circled around slightly, getting a better view of the entire room. There was the kitchen doorway slightly behind Rosh and a doorway over to the left, leading into the rest of the hotel. Apart from the window, those were the only exits, and if I stared at Rosh then I could see both of them out of the corner of my eye.

'Put your hands on top of your head.'

He moved them there slowly and clasped his fingers together without me asking.

'So,' he said. 'What are you going to do now?'

'I want to know where Rachel is.'

'Right. And how are you going to find that out?'

'Maybe I'll just start blowing bits off you until you tell me.'

'You really think I took her?'

'You can cut that shit out,' I said. 'Jamie told me everything.'

Rosh paused for a second, thinking. Then, he nodded to himself.

'What did he tell you?'

'He told me about you.' As the words came out, I felt the anger surfacing. I saw each word as a gunshot to his head. 'That you killed Sean. That you took Alison and Keleigh. That you were blackmailing him into lying about it.'

'That's strange,' Rosh said. 'That's what he told me about you too.'

'You're not going to bullshit me.'

'I'm not trying to. Can't you see what's happening here? You said you were being framed, but it's all of us. We're all being framed.'

'You're not going to bullshit me.'

I thought about Rachel. Concentrated on her face and let the emotions flood into me.

'We've all been turned against each other,' he said.

'By you.'

'No.'

'It all makes sense from where I'm standing,' I said. 'All a trick to get me to kill Eli, just because you couldn't.'

Rosh thought about this. For a second, he didn't look like a man scrabbling for a response so much as one who was putting things together in his head.

'The legend,' he said.

'Yes.'

'And you think that's something to do with me?'

'You know exactly what I think,' I said, 'because you know exactly what you fucking *are*.'

Rosh was quiet again for a second. Then, he said:

'I've been reading up on it. I don't know whether I believe it or not, but let's just go with it. Let's imagine that these people exist.'

'They exist.'

'Well, in that case, I have a question. Why couldn't Karna kill Eli himself?'

'He told me,' I said. 'None of the brothers can act against each other directly. You can plot and scheme, but you had to trick me into doing the actual dirty work for you.'

'I didn't do anything, Martin.'

'You're not going to bullshit me.'

'I'm not trying to.' He unclasped his fingers, but didn't move his hands. 'If these people exist then I have a theory. I think that the reason Karna couldn't kill Eli himself was that it didn't happen that way in the legend.'

I stared at him. 'What the fuck is that supposed to mean?'

'I have something you need to see.'

He started to move his hands away from his head.

'Don't,' I said sharply.

But he didn't stop.

'You know I'm your friend,' he said. 'Trust me. You need to see this.'

He was wrong about that. He was really misjudging me.

'Don't, Rosh.'

And the part of me that wasn't picturing Rachel's face thought:

Please don't.

But he was still moving slowly, reaching into his jacket.

'I need to show you this. Stay calm.'

'Don't.'

'Martin—'

And right then, I had another burst of understanding. I knew for certain that he had a gun in a shoulder-holster beneath his coat. That this was it – the moment when either he died or I did. I had about half a second to make a decision, and without thinking I just opened myself up totally; I let all the hate and anger and fear explode in my head, and I let that make the decision for me. As he started to bring his hand back out of his jacket, I shot him, knocking him backwards. And then – as the hum in the air intensified, and a flood of real understanding washed through me – I closed my eyes and started to cry.

CHAPTER TWENTY SIX

From within, life can feel arbitrary and pointless: just a series of random events that send us into collisions with others, where there's no real meaning or explanation. But from the outside it does look different. You notice that all these bright strands of life form a pattern – that sections repeat and spiral within and around their neighbours with more regularity than you've ever seen before. You look, and you see how the same things have happened throughout time for the same reasons, and that the weave of this forms a meaningful picture. From the outside, despite how it's always felt, everything really is very ordered and beautiful.

I had the oddest sensation, pushing my way out through the fence and walking back towards the main road. I was experiencing something that I hadn't felt properly for the last couple of days: I was completely calm. Almost serene, in fact. I looked up, and the slip of sky above me was pale blue. There was a very slight breeze in the air – cool but not cold – and I realised that it was actually a lovely day. The world might be ending, but that was okay; at this moment, it even felt right. I don't know why, but I had a different perspective on everything now. When you come to believe that you're just a needle in a groove it can be frightening at first; but perhaps once you accept it you can allow yourself to move where you're put and appreciate the music you're making, if only for the fact that you're making music at all.

Perhaps, anyway.

I walked out onto the street, and there they were – three of Karna's men. Each of them was about ten metres away: one was in front of me; one to either side. They all had guns and they were all pointing them at me.

I was still holding mine. Casual as anything, I reached inside my jacket and pulled out a new clip.

'Put your gun down,' the one in front said.

He gestured to the ground with his own.

'I recognise you,' I said, not looking up. I didn't need to; he was the man who'd been standing behind me in Karna's office yesterday.

'Put your fucking gun down,' he said.

Instead, I slotted the clip into the handle. Racked it.

'Last time I'm going to tell you.'

'That's right,' I said.

All of this was inevitable. I understood it without properly understanding, but that was okay. That would come.

He decided enough was enough and pulled the trigger.

Nothing happened.

At that moment, I saw in the man's eyes that he knew it too. His boss had sent him out here to die, and – just like me – he understood that without knowing how.

They all started to move towards me just as I raised my gun and opened fire. They never stood a chance. Two shots forward, knocking the first man back towards the CandiBar. And then I was following those bullets, turning around on my heels and shooting to the right and behind, catching the second man in the leg, hitting the wall behind him, then sending him in a spin as the third shot took him in the shoulder. I was already moving back down the street putting space between myself and the last man. He was coming for me – running to cover the distance between us – but I had time to see the look of grim determination on his face before I shot him right there, knocking him to one side. His gun – unused – went spilling across the street.

The reverberation of the gunfire echoed around. A few seconds later, there were only the screams.

I used to think I was a good man, but that was all gone now. I was only just finding out what I was and what I was capable of. I put an extra bullet into each of Karna's men. As I walked across the street towards the entrance to the CandiBar, the world was silent again. Except for the sound of a dog, barking in the distance.

Before I'd left the hotel, I'd knelt down beside Rosh and picked up the piece of paper that he'd been reaching into his jacket for. It had fallen from his hand.

I'd brushed the dust off and seen enough to know what it was. And then I'd taken it over to the window, where the light was good enough for me to read what it said.

Rosh had obviously found time to visit the library that morning. The piece of paper was Harris's article from the book of city legends – only this one didn't have the section missing. When I'd first seen all those books and papers, I'd thought that Sean had ripped that bit out and taken it with him for some reason. But he'd never gone anywhere by choice, and I should have realised that Karna had removed it, in the same way he'd censored what Sean had written in his notebook. As I read what was there I understood why. Karna had torn that section out so that I wouldn't appreciate what was really going on.

The missing paragraph said this:

> No source indicates the exact nature of Karna's betrayal, but several imply that it involved his impressionable brother Rho, who was tricked into killing Eli so that Karna could take control of the estate. The plan backfired when Rho discovered the subterfuge and in turn murdered Karna for his crimes. When Karna's associates arrived, the remaining members of the family – including Rho – were also killed, and the invaders occupied the land, beginning again.

I folded the page neatly, placing it in my pocket. The discomfort and unease had gone entirely, leaving only a sense that everything – as terrible as it was – was merely appropriate and as it should be. Rosh had been right. I had been tricked into killing Eli because that was the way things had happened before. Karna couldn't kill him, and he couldn't kill me either. He was bound by the ribbons of the legend, and he could only move within patterns that matched those certain, limited swirls he'd etched on the world all those years ago.

The same as me.

> Rho discovered the subterfuge and in turn murdered Karna for his crimes.

I went upstairs and stood at the front window and watched the three men emerge from the entrance to the CandiBar. They stood outside and waited patiently for me. I wasn't surprised or afraid. I wasn't anything. All the anger seemed to have left me now, and in its place was a sense of purpose. I knew exactly what I needed to do. It was just a case of letting the needle run along the groove and play the music: a tune that felt right simply because it had been played and listened to a hundred times before. Everything I'd done and would do was just a repeating motif: a curl of behaviour that matched and complemented the others.

Those men out there weren't going to kill me. It hadn't happened like that before, and it wouldn't happen now.

I made my way back down.

One of the front doors of the CandiBar was open. I squeezed through, walked down a short corridor and then entered the main room at the side of the dark, derelict bar. I stopped. There was a real hum in the air, but as my feet started throbbing against the floorboards I realised that it wasn't in the air at all – it was in me. And when I concentrated on it, I felt it surge up inside my head as a kind of intense, mental orgasm. It was a feeling of coming home and slotting into place, and it was so wonderfully peaceful that I closed my eyes and was rocked back on my heels by the sheer force of it. It was like my mind had wandered into a wind tunnel filled with warm, golden light, and for a moment I could do nothing except bathe in it.

When I opened my eyes again, the world was coming alive. It had started at my feet. The dust on the floor was blowing away, seeming to disappear as it drifted into the air over the dancefloor. The old grey floorboards were cleaning themselves; they were growing varnish in two huge pools spreading out from me, crackling slightly as it went. The red paint on the walls was flickering and becoming more intense. Lights clicked on overhead, one by one by one. The mirror behind the bar began to shine with their reflections as they grew stronger.

The last bulb came on in time for me to see the final whirl of dust vanish into thin air, and then my bar was complete.

'Welcome home,' Karna said.

I looked over to the right. He was sitting in a booth on the far side of the dancefloor, just out of reach of one of the lights. Two of his men had been in seats nearer to me on the left, and now they stood up. They looked slightly nervous, but I wasn't interested in hurting them. I fixed myself on Karna instead. He was sitting next to Rachel, who was staring at, or perhaps through, the table in front of her, and he was holding a gun pointed loosely at her head.

'It's good to be back,' I said.

'And you know everything this time.'

'Yes.'

It was true. In the same way that the bar had come alive around me, knowledge had bloomed inside my head. I wasn't *aware* of knowing anything, but recent events had become like mathematics to me. I couldn't have told you the answers to certain sums, but I knew the principles necessary to work them out, and this was the same. I didn't automatically understand everything that had happened, but when I thought about it the answers were obvious. When I looked at an instant or a fragment in isolation, I found that I could see the entire strand.

The whole time, images were arriving in my head like camera flashes: snapshots of events I shouldn't know about but did.

Rho. I knew that the picture of him in the hotel across the street had been a fake – just a random old man. I saw Karna and his men moving around the room, planting photographs and papers; I saw him tear out the section from the book. He'd given me enough to work with, but not enough to see things as they really were. The photograph of Rho wasn't real, because if it was going to be accurate then it would have to be a picture of me.

And I knew what face would have been there if mine hadn't. The face was young but weathered, and framed by shoulder-length, black hair that hung almost to the tarmac. The eyes were blue. I remembered his eyes, looking at me, giving me that stare that I hadn't understood, in the second or two before he'd been shot in the head by a man wearing sunglasses and a bandanna. Right before my parents had pulled me away and we'd left the service station.

That was the way it worked. None of us was hundreds of years old, and we lived and died more or less like everyone else. It wasn't about people; it was about roles and identities and functions. It was about patterns.

My phone. I knew that if I picked it out of my pocket and opened it up, the SIM card would be different. While I'd been unconscious the first time, Karna had simply taken my mobile, copied the contents of the SIM over to a new card and then changed a few of the numbers. The speed-dials I had for Rosh and Lucy were a digit out and went nowhere. And whenever they'd tried to phone me, they hadn't got through because my number was wrong.

Another flash. Jamie.

I saw him sitting there, holding his face in his hands and crying. He'd wrenched his purple hair back and forth; it was in messy tufts and his scalp was red raw. Pretty much everything he'd told me had been a lie. He'd done it out of fear for Keleigh and a desire to protect her, and then – when Karna had killed her anyway – out of something more selfish. He'd made his last phonecalls to me and Rosh at gunpoint. In the same way, I knew that Harris had been taken from his flat days before Rosh and I had arrived; the man who'd driven away that evening was another of Karna's employees. Harris had been forced to do what he'd done on video, both to lead me on and to implicate and ruin him. The kid had been a runaway that nobody would miss.

As I said, it's only ever a matter of deciding how much you give up before you die; if you hold a gun on a man then he'll cut his own throat just to stop you shooting him. And my brother liked nothing better than letting his problems sort themselves out. That was why he'd turned Rosh and me against each other – it fit better to have me kill him than just to do it himself. Another one down.

What Karna had done was almost unimaginable, but I accepted it. And I didn't feel angry or blame Jamie for lying to me. He had Keleigh to protect, even if he must have known it would be in vain. When he knew that Karna had lied and murdered Keleigh, he still wanted to live, and so he had continued to do as he was told. I knew that Jamie had been killed after making the phonecalls. He was dead, Harris was dead. The kid in the video was dead. Everyone was dead.

Everyone except Rachel, and now I knew why.

I looked at her. She was still staring at the table, leaning forwards slightly. She was dressed and, as far as I could tell, she wasn't tied or bound, but she wasn't making any attempt to fight or escape. In fact, she wasn't attempting to do anything. The look on her face was blank and empty. I thought that she was very probably in shock, if not something far worse.

'If you make any move at all,' Karna said, 'I'll kill her.'

'I know.'

That was the only reason she was still alive: Karna couldn't kill me but he could hurt Rachel. I guessed he was happy for me to fulfil the legend as far as it suited him, but he certainly wasn't going to let me kill him if he could help it.

Now, he leaned forward a little, moving into the light so that it hollowed out his eyes.

'Put your gun down,' he said.

I looked at the gun in my hand – almost surprised to see I was even still holding it. It felt glued there. Something buzzed threateningly in the air and, before I could stop myself, I threw the gun away to one side.

And it jarred inside me as I did it – the exact opposite of the sense of rightness I'd been feeling. The new menace in the air left me in no doubt that I hadn't been meant to do that. The world didn't like it.

Karna noticed it too. He looked around the bar a little, as though there had been a tremor and he was wondering if the walls might crumble. After a moment, he nodded to himself and looked back at me.

'Now put your hands behind you,' he said. 'My employee is going to make you safe.'

One of the men approached me – the man who'd been cutting Rachel when I tried to rescue her yesterday. I looked back at Karna, trying to fight the panic that was rising inside me. Not only did this feel so nauseatingly *wrong*, but it was incredibly stupid as well. Karna was only keeping Rachel alive to make me cooperate. They would cuff me, leave me powerless, and then they would kill her. What I *should* do was pick up the gun and start shooting. He would still kill her – I was sure about that – but it would be right and it would fit, and at least he'd be dead too.

But I gritted my teeth and ignored the feeling. If I could, I owed her something better than that.

It took all my resolve to put my arms behind my back, and I'd never felt the world protest so greatly; I had to close my eyes against the sensation. The cool metal was clasped onto my first wrist. And then, a moment later, onto the other. And then it was done.

When the man stepped away from me, I was shivering with the difficulty of holding still. Breathing hard. But within the deep revulsion, something small and bright felt like it was curling and unfolding. Strange – with my hands locked behind me, I realised that it felt like liberation. I concentrated on it and opened my eyes.

'Why have you done this?' I said.

Karna blinked.

'Why have I done what?'

'All of this.' I nodded with my head. 'You had everything, and you got me to kill your brother anyway. Even when you knew it would all just . . . be ruined.'

He kept looking at me, and it occurred to me that he had absolutely nothing to say in reply. It was a non-question. Why had he done it? Because he was crime and that was what he did. I was sure that he also thought he was clever enough to get away with it. And with Rachel here, he was probably right.

Except I was fate and death. I was the wildcard.

It was something to cling to, anyway.

'I'm not going to end,' Karna said.

The man who'd cuffed me picked up my gun and put it into his jacket. He took another step back. There were probably about three metres between us. The second guy was still over to the left, sitting in the booth. Well out of reach.

I looked back at Karna.

'Are you going to let her go now?'

He smiled.

'It was pretty stupid of you to throw away your gun.'

'Well, I never said I wasn't stupid.'

'That's true.'

I moved my hands a little, testing the limits of the cuffs. There was a maximum of ten centimetres between my wrists. Not ideal.

I said, 'Can you feel the city breaking apart?'

'No.' He shook his head. 'I can feel it straining, but that's not the same thing. The police are on their way. When they arrive, they'll either arrest you or kill you. I won't be here. And – to be frank – I believe I'll be fine.'

I didn't say anything.

'So we have to leave,' he said.

'I understand.'

His gun was still pointing at Rachel's head, and I watched his expression change. It emptied of emotion, and I understood how this old man had been so successful in his role for so long.

It would actually make a great deal of sense for him to take Rachel away with him. They were going to leave me here, and I was very probably going to die. Then, it would all start over again, because that was how this thing went – round and round in circles, with nobody ever really learning from their mistakes. But even so – the clever thing to do would be to hold on to Rachel to make sure I never came after him. He'd taken women as false insurance before, but it might well have worked. And yet he wasn't going to do that.

Karna nodded at the man who'd put the cuffs on. He moved behind me, out of sight.

'Going to knock me out again?' I said.

'In a moment. I just thought you might want to say goodbye first.'

Karna pressed the gun firmly against the side of my wife's head and placed his finger on the trigger. She didn't respond in any way.

'Goodbye,' I said quietly.

Just before Karna pulled the trigger, his arm whipped around. He struggled against thin air for a moment, making a confused noise, and then there was a flash of light and an explosion that shook the air, clouding it with smoke. The bullet tore into a seat near the man on my left, who clenched up and dived for cover. I turned and stamped out at the man behind me. If he hadn't been gaping, not understanding, I might have missed. Instead, I caught him in the hip and sent him sprawling backwards. He hit his head on the bar and rolled onto his side.

Looking around, I saw the other man coming out of the booth, holding his gun. No threat to me. He stopped, unsure of what the fuck was happening or what to do about it. I looked across and saw Karna, arm stretched out over the table, wrist twisted around so that his gun pointed up towards the ceiling. There was a look of extreme panic and pain on his face. Beside him, Rachel wasn't reacting at all – not even a second later when Karna was pulled bodily out of his seat, clean over the table and slammed hard face down on the dancefloor. His arm was straight out to one side, the gun aimed harmlessly in the direction of the kitchen. As I walked towards him, his arm shuddered for a moment, and then for a second more, and then it shattered backwards at a right angle. He screamed.

And let go of the gun, but somehow it didn't fall. Instead, it hovered in the air for a second and then raised itself to shoulder height.

'This is my friend Rosh,' I announced, stepping over Karna and out of the way. 'He works for me now.'

They knew to look for him, but it was too late. The gun swung around in mid air and shots began pounding out. The man from the booth was knocked backwards, tumbling over. I moved to one side as Rosh, becoming visible, aimed at the man I'd kicked. He was back on his feet, holding his head as he ran across the room towards us. He didn't make it. Rosh shot him in the face. He fell down and didn't move again, beyond bleeding copiously onto my dancefloor.

I looked at Rachel. She was still staring at the table, oblivious to everything. Rosh glanced at her, and then back at me.

'You cut that pretty fucking fine,' I said.

'I'm sorry,' he said. 'That whole thing takes a bit of getting used to.'

'Well, you seem to have picked it up okay.'

'Thanks.'

I looked down at Karna. He'd stopped screaming now, but his face was contorted in pain. He seemed to be making an effort to crawl away from us. I don't know where he thought he was going; he looked like an injured bird. I left him to it for the moment.

Rosh rubbed his shoulder with a curious expression on his face and said, 'My arm's stopped hurting.'

Back at the hotel, when he'd pulled his hand out of his coat, I'd shot him in the upper arm. That had knocked him backwards and sent the page from the book fluttering down to the floor, and at that point I'd decided I'd made enough mistakes that day.

Now, I said, 'I'm sorry about that.'

'It's okay.' He looked a bit confused. 'Like I said, the pain's mostly gone.'

'Perk of the new job, I guess.'

We'd briefly negotiated the contract, as much as we had one. I was a strict boss and didn't pay well, but I supposed what we'd sorted out could be viewed as probation. One penny for the first hour, and then we'd see how we were getting on. There'd certainly be a raise, assuming I could find a cash machine that would pay out.

Karna was halfway across the dancefloor now, moving steadily towards the man in the booth who had dropped his gun on the floor by the seat. It wouldn't do him any good against me, of course, but there was Rachel to consider.

I turned back to Rosh and clanked my hands together behind me. 'Could you get the keys for me?'

'Sure.'

He went over and started searching through the dead man's pockets. I walked across to Karna and kicked the gun out of his reach. He collapsed in defeat and rolled onto his back.

'Don't think that would help you too much anyway.'

He didn't say anything – just turned onto his side and ignored me. I figured that was fair enough. He knew this was it.

Rosh brought the keys over and unlocked the cuffs.

'Thanks.'

'No problem.' He held out the gun. 'Here – you'll be wanting this too.'

'Yeah.'

I rubbed my wrists and took the gun from him. Checked the clip. There was one bullet left, just as I'd known there would be. I listened to the feel of the room – the hum of it – and I realised that the nausea was gone. Everything was right and back on track again. For a while there, the world had been worried that I was fucking things up for all of us, but now it seemed to appreciate that it should have had a bit more faith in me. The pattern had been there all along. I was just getting there in my own way.

'This isn't going to be pretty,' I told Rosh. 'I don't want Rachel to see it.'

'I'll take her outside.'

'Okay.'

I knelt down beside Karna and waited while Rosh eased Rachel carefully out of the booth. To begin with, she moved without resisting or helping him in any way at all, but as they went past me I heard him whispering words of gentle encouragement to her. As they reached the front door, she lifted up her arm and put a faltering hand on his shoulder for support. Then, they were gone.

I looked back down at Karna. He'd closed his eyes and was waiting. Again and again, we fuck up. We always think it will work better next time, but it's so difficult not to be bound by the mistakes you've made in the past.

'You know,' I said, looking at the gun, 'I've done this a fair few times now. The first time was Timothy Hartley. It was pretty difficult, but it seemed to get a bit easier after that. I just had to keep reminding myself how bad the people were. And you're the fucking worst of all, aren't you?'

Clockwork ticking around; cogs sliding into place.

'Just do it,' he said.

'I've done this a few times,' I said again, 'but the thing is, it doesn't seem to make anything any better.'

I took a deep breath and snapped one of the

handcuffs onto his good wrist. The buzzing in the air circled a little, unsure of itself, and then it rose up both inside and out, swiftly becoming devastating. I clenched my face against it and rolled Karna over. Got hold of his broken arm; wrenched it around. He started screaming like I'd never heard anyone scream before. But the buzzing was louder – a furious whine that made my hair stand on end, and my arms begin to shake. The walls were trembling. I managed to clip the second cuff onto his wrist, and then clamber to my feet. Everything was shuddering and vibrating, but I think it was mostly just me. My legs would barely carry me as I staggered back across the dancefloor. Karna was still screaming.

'I guess you're under arrest,' I said.

And while I could still walk at all, I turned quickly and ran to the front door, out into the sunlight, and fell.

EPILOGUE

It used to be services here.

We pulled in; Rosh and I got out, leaving Rachel sitting quietly in the back seat. Even now, the car park was large – space for twenty or thirty cars. But the main services at the far end were gone; they were just a part of my memory – replaced some time since by a petrol station, a small series of low office blocks and what looked like a printing company. The crappy little motel was on one side of the road. Everywhere else, there were trees, rustling together gently.

My legs were shaky but I realised with some relief that they were getting better. For a while as Rosh drove, I'd genuinely felt that I wasn't going to make it, even though I didn't really understand what that meant or what would happen to me if I didn't. But as we passed through the city gates, the feeling had started to reverse itself slowly. Now, I was beginning to feel normal again.

I looked around, closed my eyes and breathed in deeply.

There was a gentle breeze but no cloud cover, and I saw that the sun was really punishing the tarmac. That felt right, but a certain level of understanding was leaving me now and I didn't really know what there was to feel right or wrong about. It was a sunny day. Maybe there was no more to it than that.

'You feeling more human?' Rosh said.

'I think so, yeah.'

'Well if you've got any idea who's gonna win the boxing, maybe you could let me know. It's not too late to put a bet on.'

I smiled and opened my eyes.

'Get out of here,' I said.

'You're sure you'll be all right?'

'I'll be fine. Just get her to a hospital.'

He nodded.

'Where will you go?'

'I'll sit for a while,' I said. 'On the kerb, or something. Then, I don't know. Maybe I'll steal a car.'

'Yeah. But where will you go?'

'Away. At least for now.'

I glanced over at Rachel, sitting in the back of the car. She wasn't looking at me, and that was fine; that part of my life was over now. I'd made mistakes and I wished that I hadn't, but it was done. Whatever either of us thought, what we had now wasn't love anymore. She deserved better, but at least now she was safe. That was less than I owed her, but all I had to give.

'Take care, man.'

I looked at Rosh.

'You take care too,' I said.

We hugged, and then he got in the car and drove away: taking the exit that would lead them back to the city. I watched them go. I could see Rachel sitting behind him, indifferent to everything, and I hoped that she was going to be okay. And I thought to myself that maybe one day, if I ever returned to the city, I might find myself walking into the Clock Café and ordering a coffee. It would take too long to arrive, of course, and then I'd go and sit down and drink it quietly. At some point I'd look up and see that she was there as well: sitting at the table next to me, holding another man's hands and looking happy. Or perhaps I'd be on a train: sitting opposite her and watching her sleep, resting her head on someone else's shoulder.

Rachel, I thought. *Whatever happens. Fondly, I think of you.*

When the car had disappeared, I turned around and walked away from the motel, kicking pebbles, until I found the patch of tarmac. Then, I stood and looked at it for a second. And then I looked away. It was just fucking tarmac; nothing special. The breeze picked up a little, but I didn't hear any ringing and didn't feel any special sense of threat. I looked around and there was nobody nearby: just a couple of guys in blue overalls standing far off in the printing yard, smoking and shooting the shit. I don't know what I'd expected. I looked down at the ground for a few seconds more, and then I turned around and walked away.

The nearest major city was twenty kilometres north. I thought that would be a good place to start. There would be cashpoints there, for one thing. Maybe my cards still wouldn't work, but at least I could try, and for some reason I thought that they would. If not then I'd figure something out. I'm a pretty resourceful guy sometimes.

Space for around thirty cars in front of the motel, and all but four were taken: a nice selection to choose from. Did I mention how good I was getting at stealing cars? I chose a convertible so I could put the top down. Less than a minute later, I was on the motorway heading north at a speed that was illegal, exhilarating and entirely right. There was no black cloud behind me. In fact, I couldn't even see the city. It was a beautiful day.